THREE DAYS LATER

From New England big city life to Florida's small town Main Street, for two people, unexpectedly, worlds collide, changing life's direction.

Peter L. Harding

© 2012 Peter L. Harding
All Rights Reserved.

No part of this publication may be reproduced, stored in a retrieval system, or transmitted, in any form or by any means, electronic, mechanical, photocopying, recording, or otherwise, without the written permission of the author.

Author Photograph – Chrystina Lammers – Paparazzi Productions

First published by Dog Ear Publishing
4010 W. 86th Street, Ste H
Indianapolis, IN 46268
www.dogearpublishing.net

ISBN: 978-1-4575-1515-6

This book is printed on acid-free paper.

It should be understood, this novel is a book based on pure fiction. The characters and fictional storyline are based on nothing more than the pure imagination of the Author. Any association to real people, living or dead should be construed as totally coincidental. Historically, name and location of the city depicted is real, as are many commercial buildings and retail enterprises.

Printed in the United States of America

Dedicated to all who are - or have ever been in love
Treasure the time.

For Lynne, my wife...thank you so much,
for so much in my life

For Lisa and David, Justin and Kerry

To Lynn and Mac – Thanks for your unending,
wonderful friendship

To Kathryn McCartney – In times of need,
you were there - thank you

Three Days Later – My tribute to The City of Deland, Florida

Susan
So nice to meet you
I hope you enjoy this story
Kind Regards
Peter
Peter L Harding 2013

ALSO BY PETER L. HARDING

The Sleeping President
'The title gives the impression one will be delving into the life of a President. Not so fast - an adventure filled with politics and intrigue...' - (Central Florida - West Volusia Beacon)

'If you're interested in politics, this is a must read and if you like a love story, it has that too. It will also make you wonder...can it really happen?' – (Amazon.com)

'Once I picked it up and got as far as the second chapter I was hooked.' – (Amazon.com)

Apology Accepted

A Life's Journey (An Autobiography)
(Not For Publication)

PROLOGUE.

From what seems like forever ago now, in recollection of truth, coming to Florida was not planned – it kind of evolved. From San Diego, where we lived, my wife (Lynne) called me in Australia during one of my regular trips back to my homeland, asking - *"How would you like to move to Florida?"* My immediate, rather cavalier response was, *"No worries, given there's no snow there; it'll be fine!"* You see; I hate the cold and with Florida being the 'Sunshine State', the very same promotional catch phrase statement of my former State (Queensland) in Australia – it sounded like a perfect place, to move to. How could it not be? Within days, Lynne flew out to Orlando and commenced to drive around a given radius, searching for a place; she thought; we might like to settle. Ironically, (truthfully), three days later she called me again, (I was still in Australia), to tell me I would really like DeLand, a city she was drawn to instantly; the place she chose. The call was tinged with some of her humor as she added *'Just think, I'll be able to call you: The Man from - DeLand Down Under!"* To this day I remain, to her and many of our friends, exactly that!

That was in 2003, and apart from three devastating hurricanes the following year, (a shocking eye-opener to us both), we still agreed, *'what a great place!'* As you will discover within these pages, so enamored as we became to our adopted hometown; in my literary, fictional story telling, I really wanted DeLand to be my factual setting, a beloved home base to the central characters of my book. Hopefully, in the minds of everyone who call DeLand *'home'*, I have approvingly captured and portrayed, what the city means to an implanted stranger seeing it for the first time. Also, that I've been able to give due recognition to a place and an area, that is both dynamic and rich, as it applies to Central Florida. I trust that, in Deland, I have seen what many a born citizen might simply take for granted, yet, what so many worked and strived so hard to attain and achieve, and what equally, many more will continue to do, in making the city a place to be proud of – and to be from. Historically, culturally and with geographic beauty, believe me; it was a relatively easy task, as a writer, to embrace, and to participate in what is offered, effortlessly? Through its people and environs – *DeLand 'the Athens of Florida'*, in my eyes, takes its rightful place as a wonderful community I feel so very proud to give full recognition to, be a part of, and to promote loudly (both domestically and globally)...come visit us, one and all.

That said...my book; Three Days Later is first and unashamedly, a simple love story in every way. With degrees of a literary license, woven throughout these pages of total fiction, especially the characters, DeLand will, as the featured home location, burst into life, through actual street names and real bona fide everyday places, both historically and in present time. They are all shared under a banner of what I hope might be, to my fellow residents, interpreted as - with *'respect, love and inspiration'*. Within its depths of fictional reach, the story as told and ends, will spawn, no doubt, a question, which only you, the reader, the individual, will be able to answer. I hope it's the one you would want, or choose, to believe in.

CHAPTER

ONE

The bold words on the cover page said it all. Despite knowing it was coming, with never a confirmed date set for delivery; I was still devastated to see it actually staring me in the face, in eye-popping, black and white. Our divorce was now official. *'Decree Absolute'* stung! From signing a legal document, with agreed wording, that our marriage had 'irretrievably broken down', the six weeks and one day of *'Decree Nisi'* seemed to fly by, and given no-one came forward to contest the divorce, but then why would they, unceremoniously; our day of reckoning came and went. The only one affected was me. The process had made its way through the system to reach this day considered - closure. *'It's done. It's over. End of the line'* was all I could think, realizing, finally, effective now, I was no longer married to the woman I once loved with a heart, which for me, had been true? Jessica had been my wife of twelve years. She had been my best friend, my everyday soul mate, partner, in so many wonderful experiences and now, as I placed the envelope and papers down on the kitchen bench, I had no choice but to come to grips with the fact; she was not only physically, but now, also legally gone.

I glanced around the room and for no explainable reason, my eyes transfixed on a framed photo I'd chosen to leave, over the past months, sitting on the mantelpiece above the fireplace. I had to. It was a favorite. And I loved her…then! The photo was Jessica and me, arms around each other, taken in the heart of London, in Trafalgar Square with Nelsons Column, the four lion statues and a few pigeons as the backdrop. My mind immediately went back to the summer of '94, our trip to Europe, when all about us as a couple was still new, when we vowed to love each other always, swearing never to let one single thing in life ever come between us - something did.

Moving slowly from the high back metal bar stool I'd been sitting on, I walked from the kitchen, across the architecturally designed family room, toward the photograph that today, seemed to jump out of its protective covered glass, right at me. Taking the wooden frame in one hand, I threw it, hard, into the soft leather couch, wanting, expecting it, to smash into a million different pieces; forever ending Jessica's infectious smile, but then again, maybe it was painfully obvious I didn't. It landed face down, safely.

'Damn you Jessica!' I cursed, wishing momentarily our lives had never come to this, and those numerous ugly pages back on the kitchen bench.

'Why? Why did we let this happen to us?' I asked of no-one.

Frustrated, I went back to retrieve and glance at the legal documents that would do nothing, except torture me some more, as I absorbed the words again on the first page of probably six. I didn't actually know how many pages made up the end of my life as I now knew it as I'd chosen not to read any further than the covering folded page that seemed to scream at me, only this time, agonizingly, even louder, **'Decree Absolute'**. *It's all over you fool* they were telling me. Sighing heavily, I perched back up on the kitchen stool.

Looking around at absolutely nothing, I told myself, silently, I'd achieved two things in the last minute. Or so I wanted to believe. Taking that photo from a position of prominence and throwing aside the effervescent smiling photo of us both meant, firstly, Jessica couldn't smile back every time I happened to be in the living room of our once loving home, also; that I wouldn't have to be reminded anymore of that happier period in time, or that she was once my wife. In throwing the frame hard, I had hoped it would hurt her feelings, that she'd feel the same pain I was feeling at this very moment, but I supposed, in harsh reality, that was nothing more than wishful thinking…she'd already moved on. I knew it. In my life; she was long gone.

Feeling very much alone, single, free and so many other cliché' driven words that didn't mean a thing, except, I'd be returning to this empty house alone, forever, or until I did something positive about my life, I quickly realized two more things. I could wallow in misery and reach whatever depths I'd choose, or, buckle down and get those descriptive words of law that had driven me crazy long enough, out of my life altogether. *'Decree Absolute'* had beaten me up plenty already.

It was a Friday, almost 12noon, and on the outside, it looked like a beautiful sunny day, although it was still expected to be a little winter chilly with a forecast high of only 53 degrees. Roll on spring was all I could hope for. With a head shake, changing from my self-pity tact, I decided it would be a good idea if I went for a brisk walk, to give myself a chance to ponder what my next move might be, and importantly, grab a snack while I was at it, even a beer maybe. For too long, I hadn't been eating properly as well I knew – not good for any number of reasons, accepting; according to my bathroom scales, I'd already dropped about five pounds. Within equally as many minutes, five, - I was at the front door and gone.

For once, the weather forecasters were actually right. It was colder than I thought, and I thanked myself ten times over that I had put on the extra sweater and worn a jacket. I needed it. I really do hate the cold. Why I headed straight to the nearby park where Jessica and I often strolled together I wasn't quite sure? The winds blew a little fiercer than I'd expected and as they whistled through the still very bare trees, I questioned myself, why I hadn't gone to the Mall instead. At least it would be warmer. In reconciling the decision, I doubted I could think there anyway and after all, to think and clarify my life somewhat was my main intention; at the mall there would have been way too many people.

The park had a more overall serene feel to it, even without the glorious green leaves of summer. Furthermore, it was just as pretty, in a barren sort of way. But pretty wasn't a word I wanted to embrace right now; I wanted barren…I guessed? Pretty tended to remind me of Jessica, barren reminded me of – well, me! Mentally unproductive was certainly how I felt as I followed the curved pathway along, dodging a bicycle rider here and there, or a jogger. In fact, there were more joggers than I would have believed this time of the day, but fitness was an 'in thing', They say physical activity helps un-clutter the brain, clears the head, something I was trying to do, my way, as I wandered along at a snail's pace full of collective thoughts. The advent of spring was one thing; I so wanted the warmth of summer. I'd hate the seasons alone this year - July 4th, my birthday, Thanksgiving, Christmas. I shuddered at the prospect.

~~~~~~~~~~

Jessica Lewis became Jessica Thompson, my wife, on August 8th 1994. Three years younger than me, our romance started with an unbridled frenzy, and I admit; sex played an integral part of why things might have moved faster than either of us might ordinarily have expected. I did, in fact, amaze myself even, considering the cautious way I had conducted myself over the years when it came to matters of the heart and yet, under the oddest of circumstances, now, I actually believed, that I'd finally met that special someone, as I had always hoped I might. What motivated in the first place this, then, totally unknown woman, to walk brazenly up to me, in a book store I just happened to be in, to suggest a novel she thought I might enjoy reading, and that I'd like the characters portrayed in it, had me completely, one-hundred percent baffled? She didn't know me from a melting winter built snowman and yet, seemed to think, suggested; I'd be delightfully entertained by Jeffrey Archer's book Kane and Abel, all without knowing, if I'd even read it or not? I hadn't! I was, however, aware of the author by name.

"Why would I like the written word of Mr. Archer pray tell me?" I somewhat flippantly asked.

If I thought I was being generally clever in my question, as fast as I had uttered the words, the answer that came back was enough to almost make me blush. Maybe I did.

"Because it's an epic, a novel that spans generations, and a favorite of mine as a reader, plus, you have the look of Kane, the main character as I chose to see him, *that's* my real reason in mentioning it. Somehow, I just had to tell you that. I do apologize, but check it out anyway." With a simple smile, even hesitancy, she turned to go.

Stunned, at every word she had so eloquently, bravely spoken, I immediately had to know more.

'Excuse me" I replied, hoping to hold her attention while framing my response.

Slowly, projecting with style and flair her shapely figure, she stopped, turned, to then look directly at me. There was no question, in my mind; pretty yes, extremely so, but also, this was no doubt, a strong and confident woman.

"Thank you, I take what you said as a compliment." I meant every word.

Returning the smile was easy. Looking directly at her, gazing deep into her glistening green eyes as I did, I posed a question.

"Now, given you've said your piece, maybe you'll allow me to say mine, answer you even?"

Motionless, she flicked her eyes and head down together, then, in a cute but tantalizing way, confirmed it by not moving another step, as if to suggest - yes. A challenge maybe, I hoped?

"Actually, I *do* know of Mr. Archer..." I enlightened her "...but I haven't read his Kane and Abel; however, at your suggestion, now I believe I will."

Our eyes remained riveted on each other. She had held the hint of the devilish smirk on her face. It was time for me to get even bolder; to move forward, say what else was on my mind to keep this woman from leaving. I needed to know more.

"Without sounding too forthcoming, having declared that fact, I wonder if I could ask you to help me find it in this rather huge store, and yes; I know it would have to be in the fiction section, assuming Mr. Archer, but to be more...well, perfectly honest; I was hoping..."

For a split second I stalled in what I was about to propose. Quickly grasping my hesitation, she again tipped her head slightly, and with her smirk now broadening, female wherewithal was in full flight. My immediate thought; she was enjoying the interaction, her flirtation, had even expected my reaction. I termed it - *'games people play'*. Continuing, my inner bravado surfaced as I made my blatant offer.

"...I was hoping, *after* we find the book, *together*, I'd like to invite you to join me for a cup of coffee, or, of course, something somewhat stronger if you'd prefer. Maybe then we can sit and talk books, authors, what's happening in the world or anything else that might allow me to share just a little more time with you."

I couldn't believe it! To this still very mysterious woman, in my instant reply that I had been equally cavalier in, as she had to me, I had calculated, rather quickly; time was of the essence. I certainly couldn't just let her walk away. She was extremely attractive, in fact, striking. I had assumed, visually; she was about my age, and I confess, I *had* noticed her fingers were bare, no rings on her left hand and from that deduction, I hoped it meant she was a free agent in life, just as I was. I'd had other romances over the years but, for whatever the reasons; none was ever the one who could tie me down. In truth, I was more obsessed about work, one of my self-admitted flaws, however, my unfailing belief from within was, *if*, or *when*, the right woman came along, somehow I would know it. Was *this* the woman, *and* the moment? Apart from her natural beauty, I loved the shine, the glisten of her long flowing red hair. Yes - I was immediately hooked.

Reflecting our interaction that afternoon long ago, it had been a pure delight sharing our first coffee together, whiling away the hours, chatting, initially about books, and then life itself, the politics of the day, the troubles the world was always facing somewhere, to finally, what movie we agreed to meet again for the next night. Forrest Gump turned out to be a great choice. What a start-up meeting memory, what an impression. Oddly, the many thoughts of my now long gone ex-wife had sent a pleasant shudder through my entire body, which seemed ironic, I thought, given today's mail delivery. It didn't matter; that memory remained a nice one.

Weeks later, our friendship developing, we'd become almost inseparable. The days wouldn't go quickly enough before we could see each other again, until one day, and I hated to think it might have been impulse; when I asked Jessica to marry me, she confessed openly "*…from that very first day I met you Anthony Thompson, in that book store on Lincoln, I knew you were the man for me. You took my breath away. I was right, and I love you, and yes; I will marry you.*"

When we finally tied the knot, in the words of Forest Gump, for us both; *'life was like a box of chocolates,'* sweet, loving and full of fun. Then, I loved her very much.

However, as I clearly confessed to myself; that was then; now, today, she was gone - forever. Memories are all that remain, all we'll both ever have. Hurting somewhat, I doubted I could love like that again, or allow myself to give my heart so readily, only to be vulnerable to having it broken so badly a second time, maybe? Love is kind, love is fine…but only when it works. Whoever said that was absolutely right! It was time to move on.

~~~~~~~~~~

Tired of going nowhere in particular, I headed for a park bench I could see in the distance, to sit in the sun and let its ray's warm me up a little. Thinking, while walking, my mind was swirling almost out of control with memories of a time gone by and yet, strangely; all my thoughts were, for the most part, basically nice ones. So far, for all I had thrashed around in my head, not a single negative memory had tried to storm its way into my brain to dampen the feelings I had for a woman no longer mine. In my own way, I still loved Jessica and guessed, probably always would, even, that she might come back someday. Wham! Instantly, with that belief, that very thought; my positive yet melancholy mood changed, then; here they came –

all the unhappy reflections began rushing in, just itching to take over, - and did so, very successfully. *'I'll be all right'* I told myself, staring into space, looking at nothing.

The saddest recollection of our years together was, to me, that we never had a child, or children. I'd loved to have had a Tony Jr. We had talked about tests, about IVF and all the wonders of modern medicine that might help us gain our own little person, our own little boy, or girl, but none of it went anywhere. Suddenly, it occurred to me; maybe Jessica never wanted children anyway? Frankly, sadly, I didn't really know. I'd never posed the thought to her face to face, one on one. I wondered why? Adoption was ruled out entirely. Jessica wouldn't go there. Did she know something? It didn't matter now anyway. Nothing did – there was no turning back.

Finding a positive side to the thoughts consuming me would be the reality, no matter what adversities we had about not having children, ultimately; it didn't stop us enjoying life, in fact; we had many more freedoms than any of our friends whose houses were full of the patter of little feet. Flip side, they envied us. It begged the question; who were the winners, who were the losers?

To make up for our childless downside to life, as we termed it, periodically we opted to elevate our spirits and go see the world, to travel. Various trips took us to England and parts of Europe, Scandinavia, almost anywhere time permitted, while here in the U.S. we loved California and Colorado. Unquestionably, they were all the fun days, the joyful experiences, and the photos we took by the hundreds, captured forever, the moments so candidly. With some, we created imaginative slide shows, catalogued to people, places and events, and we played them over and over.

Until one day, we stopped. Everything stopped! Not only looking for the next place to satisfy our curiosity, to board a plane and go see, but even sharing the relived moments in colorful print. How odd, I thought, but accepted, as honest as Jessica's athletic reasons sounded, *'I'd like to play more sport'*. Sport had *never* been on our agenda and *never* discussed, but suddenly, it was a new-found diversion, tennis here, golf there? I enjoyed her enthusiasm, recognizing how good physical activities are for the body, and although not motivated to play a sport myself, I supported her, encouraged her, regardless. Was that my first naïve mistake, I wondered?

Slowly, our regular togetherness drifted wider, until one day, lying alone on our bed, Jessica was on the phone, and for no reason I could ever think of, instinct made me stop at the doorway, just short of walking in to join her. It was at that moment; I overheard the one-sided conversation *'…oh Tony wouldn't know. I'll cover those tracks carefully anyway, let's just do it. Book the convention dates. I'll be there under the guise of a tour with the girls, golf or something, and then we'll spend the time doing what we do pretty good already'.* There was a momentary pause. *'Yeah I love you too Rob. See ya soon. Bye!'*

Here I was, in my forties, suddenly realizing, there had been a whole lot more to the last three to six months, or even longer maybe, than I'd had the ability to see, and in many ways, had no reason to. Blind-sided, I was mortified. I wanted to rush into the bedroom and challenge Jessica for what I'd just heard and didn't want to believe. *'Yeah I love you too Rob'* had cut like a knife. I was obviously no longer the love of her life. Immediately, my whole world began to crumble around me. I doubted I could ever be the same again. That phone call, the overheard words, became the beginning of the end. Right there, it seemed; our fate was sealed, that there would be no turning back. If at some time, everybody's somebody's fool, then I'd been hers. I never saw it coming and yet, I loved being in love, and loving another. I never wanted it to ever be any different – I truly believed in love. Today, our years together, our once love for each other; shattered and over.

Through a relatively simple agreed to divorce, finally, those papers to headline 'Decree Absolute' followed. Oddly, they sat on the kitchen bench, and here I was; in a park feeling pretty cold inside, sitting alone on a park bench. Shaking my head, I could only wonder; how I'd get through this stage of finality, how I'd gather up my spirits and forge ahead to what everyone tells me, has declared, wisely, over and over; *'It's only a matter of time. You'll see. It'll be okay.' A new Tony Thompson will emerge. Move on.'* They were easy words to embrace. The advice was time proven and well worn, but when it's you, not the always that *'someone else'*, it all seems different; somehow impossible. And yet, despite what those papers had done as I'd held them in my hand, the despondency they brought and the way I was feeling today; they served as a wake-up call too. I knew the time had arrived for me to take stock and re-evaluate - Me! I told myself, confidently; I would, as of right now.

CHAPTER

TWO

Walking around the house, it struck me. I had too many memories of Jessica still painfully obvious. She'd taken mostly everything she owned some time ago, plus a few she didn't, I felt, but our break-up was amicable enough not to labor over trivial things, material things, that could be easily replaced. Without protest, she claimed also, the stereo system, most of the CD's except the ones she really hated and gladly left behind; Billy Joel, Garth Brooks, and especially Frank Sinatra, plus and a few others. She had insisted on some of the smaller furniture pieces she adored, select kitchen appliances, pictures on the wall she was adamant about, and apart from a few items I actually *did* baulk at, much else really hadn't mattered. Our time together was over!

Today, as I double checked our lives, appropriately, to my way of thinking, I removed the last of two photos of us both from places of prominence, also a large flower pot with its colorful decorative arrangement that still stood in the hallway, two triple candle stick holders with scented candles she had chosen, a framed John Gould lithograph featuring Hummingbirds and finally, a few books she had collected over the years, many with me. Easy enough to do, those few items represented the last of her personal belongings she chose not to claim that last long weekend when she exited our marriage. As of today, when the divorce papers graced my mailbox, Jessica Thompson, legally, no longer existed in my life. Having heard nothing over many months from her, or about her, I could only hope she was happy out in California with the Account Executive, who stole her heart, and broke mine.

Reluctantly, as remnants of her memory continued to fade, I had accepted in hindsight, I must have done something wrong, although I was never one hundred percent sure, then or now, exactly *what*? Pontificating was easy, bottom line was; I took my share of the broken fault line - I failed her; she failed me, but any blame game now was nothing but wasted time and effort. Odd maybe, I didn't fight to hold her. I had loved her too much not to let her go, and to me, bitterness hadn't belonged in the equation. In all honesty, then, I doubted I could have won her back again even if I tried, so what would have been the point? Life is for living and way too short to harbor ill feelings, hatred, evil thoughts. Believing, when love dies, on any side, the only right thing to do is let the other one go quietly. I did! The old referenced adage *'if they come back it was meant to be, etc'* might be well and good, fact is; it's a rarity, in reality.

Reinvigorated, it actually felt good to begin thinking about starting all over again, despite the one lone agreement remaining, still left on the table to close off. We had yet to sell the house and split the dividends equally after paying out the mortgage. For me, that was always going to be the easy bit. If all went to plan, my estimation projected I'd have at least $45K in my pocket, a hefty sum to put down on my next bit of real estate.

Another remaining question though still played heavily on my mind, more-so lately; would I choose to stay in Hartford, or give myself a complete make-over and move cities, even completely out of State? I was a bit tired of selling real estate anyway and a change might do me good, but then again…more thoughts, more decisions. Such was divorce! There was no doubt, in my renewed tangled mind; I was still a little messed up. I'd hated being, what I had considered, for too long, albeit self-proclaimed, *'a loser',* but that was exactly how I felt about myself. Good as I was at work in my chosen career, personally, divorce, whether finalized or working through, can take a little more out of one than they might ever declare, admit; I was in that category. There are always, way too many memories.

Clearly, as I sat in the silence of my own company, it seemed to me the timing was right, in fact, perfect; I really needed a new adventure, maybe a new job. Today was certainly not the first time I had thought about moving, period, somewhere, anywhere, but for what now seems as the longest time, I accepted; I hadn't found the inner courage to actually do it. Something always managed to tell me *'everything will be all right'* yet here I was, again, still mulling over my age-old dreams and wishes of change, even reinventing myself. Two states had figured in my reckoning if I was ever to relocate. It would come down to 'best reason'.

California was one, but when Jessica moved out there, the Golden State faded fast. The City of Angels, San Diego or maybe San Francisco, all places I'd loved to have experienced, lived, were now out, off the list. They were all what I called *'too close for comfort'*. I wanted my ex as far away from me as possible. Florida, the other, ranked high as a top choice too; however, the more I thought about it, even there; the facts were; I'd had my doubts, although they were all mainly and strictly, weather related. My oft asked question always remained; could I stand the prolonged heat of summer? With due considerations to all I was thinking today; the reality of my present conundrum never changed; until I made a firm decision, nothing really mattered. Slowly, with my mind un-cluttering, sitting alone, assessing my life, casting aside hesitation, drawbacks or otherwise, the Sunshine State came to life again, re-entering my thoughts with a vengeance.

The long walk earlier, that hard park bench, the cool air, indeed cold; they had all played their role. It had been worth stepping out, clearing my head, pondering my dreams, ridding myself of yesterdays never to return. Finally, a major mental breakthrough; an idea formulated.

"Hey Jack, I wonder if I could talk to you for a few minutes?" I asked my boss and partner. I had plenty on my fractured mind that needed some expert help, and he was just the man; I felt.

"Sure Tony, what's up? What do you need? I know you've been doing it tough lately, personally that is, but it hasn't stopped your sales. You're gun man number one again this month. You're running hot, topping the sales charts. So tell me, what can I do for you? I'm listening to every word."

Jack Montgomery was the primary shareholder in Hartford Montgomery Realtors, a multi-million dollar operation, specializing in commercial property and upper-level private sales, in not only Hartford, but across Connecticut State with offices in Bridgeport, New Haven and Fairfield. Through Jack's encouragement, some years ago, I'd become a significant shareholder in the Company, a fact; for no reason, we chose to keep silent. I was pleased for the security of the original buy-in bargain, however; I'd also kept my end of the bargain by always being the top sales executive. How, why, asked many? My self-admitted response, I really worked hard at it! I was proud of my standing with Hartford Montgomery and felt I had always put my efforts and money where my mouth was, and yes, self-proclaimed, like it or not, I was a pretty good salesman. I'd honed my craft and knew my business. Being number one felt good too.

Fifteen minutes into our conversation, when Montgomery began to suspect that a key member of his Company had embryo ideas, to maybe grandiose plans in the long run, that he might want to change entirely, everything about his life, he started to visibly show some minor signs of panic. His reaction was expected.

"*Tony, Tony, Tony, hey slow down*, let's think more about this huh? I can't lose you comrade, and you know that. I don't *want* to lose you to be truthful so, let's see what we can do to help you, accommodate you, okay, that shouldn't be too hard?"

"Well old friend..." I told him, admitting my failure "...as I've explained, I'm in a bit of a mess within myself. I need timeout, time to re-evaluate my life, to finally get past the finality of the Jessica thing and figure out what's best for *me*. I'm worn out. I'm mentally weary and...well, my batteries need a boost I think, frankly; *everything* about me needs a boost"

"I know Tony. I know, and I'm here to help, so, to make this easy on both of us, first, let's at least have a favorable playing ground, let's get outa here and grab us a spot of lunch. We'll head on over to that place you like, where you take a lot of clients, what the heck is its name? Its original name was The Green Frog." Jack Montgomery had a real way about him. Very little fazed him, he took everything in stride except on this occasion, what I had delivered today. "Hey, what was I thinking, I meant The Olive Garden, and I won't take no for an answer."

Smiling at his convenient memory loss, playing for time, the popular Italian style restaurant was our destination. And it turned out to be a heck of a lunch! We arrived back at the office about five hours later, by way of the Hartford Central Tavern, and I won't say '*worse for wear*', but over those few extra drinks, we had agreed on a very workable plan, most favorable to me. I was more than happy, as was my incorrigible optimist, friend and partner, Jack Montgomery.

~~~~~~~~~

CHAPTER

THREE

*T*hree days later - I was heading south on I-95 for Florida; I could have flown, but didn't want to. Montgomery had made it all too easy for me. The leisurely drive I could make to the Sunshine State meant a chance to clear my head, take in the sights, linger where I wanted, for as long as I wanted, and get this beat up body of mine back into shape. I'd lost at love maybe, but at least I could be gracious in the loss and pick up some pieces of my life in a way most *'victims'* would die for. I now had the luxury of time, thanks to Jack. I also had the money to not have to worry about a single thing, as long as I didn't blow the full 'gifted bonus' of $10,000.00 in the first week that would force me to turn around and head back to Connecticut with my tail between my legs. A gambler I was not, so nearby Casino's had no chance of stripping my pockets at anytime, although I must confess, I liked a lot of other things that could easily eat away at my pennies, but I had a mission in mind. *Nothing* was going to interrupt or circumvent it. And I sure loved the latest release Ford Mustang V6 with the panoramic glass roof, Sirius Satellite radio, and a dashboard panel that looked like an A380 airplane cockpit placed so daringly at my disposal. How Jack Montgomery did it, or why even, was a total shock, but I didn't say no! He believed in me, cared about me, and made sure every temptation was put in front of me to return from the agreed three-month hiatus and get back to work to help ensure we keep the Company number one for sales in the State; the honor for us, recorded annually in the history books of Real Estate for the past seven years. He gave me much of the credit, and yes; I'd made plenty of money doing it; however, so did he and Hartford-Montgomery.

    Getting out of a cold Connecticut morning, heading south toward New York City was a breeze. The God's were smiling on me as bright winter sunshine, devoid of snow or rain, streamed through the windowed roof keeping me pleasantly warm naturally, no car heater needed. A steady 55mph speed on the Interstate was unusual, and gratifyingly; it was constant; a perfect day for driving. Ten minutes later, it was all too good to be true! The traffic warning systems placed periodically on the overhead information panels started to alert me to a different story ahead. Frankly, what did I expect? I really knew better, and having lived with this chaos most of my life, I'd grin and bear it, with thoughts of better days and times ahead; anyway, I was in no hurry.

    Thinking positive, if there was an upside to the slow traffic, it was called Manhattan. What a visual site, although I was well aware of the *'push and shove'* that existed on the streets below in that concrete jungle. That was never any fun. Living relatively close to it geographically all my life, New York City always held a certain fascination to me, and for just a while, as I planned my 'getaway' from Connecticut and my job, I'd thought about stopping over for a couple of days, but the traffic mess ahead quickly suggested to me, New York could wait for another day, coming home maybe, right now, I just wanted out of here. Soon, the traffic snarls became murder. Slowly, edging ever closer to the George Washington Bridge that would take me over the Hudson River and on to the New Jersey Turnpike and Newark, I was hopeful, from there, I could make some sort of diversion to finally get off the freeways altogether. My well-set plans were to see a little more of the USA on this drive, to avoid totally, bumper-to-bumper traffic on highways and toll booths, along with stop lights, accidents, sirens, road works and the rest of the nightmare on four wheels that plagued the population at large every day. My wishful thinking still turned out to be slow progress. Getting through the city took me closer to an hour and a half, in fact, almost two.

Finally, free at last, I wound the Mustang up to the full speed limit of the road ahead. Now making time that had no deadlines, cruising along, I turned up the music. Sirius was delivering all my favorites – Stones, Elton, Eagles, Springsteen and when one of my all-time favorites hit the speakers, I cranked the sound up even louder to sing along with the trio Barry, Robin and Maurice making it a Bee Gees foursome. My falsetto rendition with the boys on Stayin' Alive never sounded better, although I doubt *they* would have agreed. I had planned in my head to make as close to Washington DC as I could, for it to be my first stop-over, but the traffic through New York had really eaten into my maximum hours per day driving plans...and *that* had kind of annoyed me! I had little choice but to accept what was, all the while telling myself, *'no biggie, don't stress'*. Baltimore won out, as did a quaint little hotel around Inner Harbor.

That night, I went to the movies to kill time. Bad mistake! 'It's Complicated' was billed as a middle-age comedy and looked to be the perfect diversion. A good laugh would be good therapy for my well being. And who could go wrong with Meryl Streep and Alec Baldwin as actors? Without thinking, I had missed the important part about the word - *'comedy'*; It's Complicated was the antics of a 10 year divorced couple, and although I concede, it really was quite funny, there were too many reminders, and too many Tony Thompson moments that thrust my mind immediately back to Jessica. Next time, I thought; I'll pay more attention to the story line advertising, or then again, maybe I'll just give movies away for a while. I needed a clear head...and sunshine. Roll on The South; 'cause I'm a comin' your way!

~~~~~~~~~~

CHAPTER

FOUR

Three days later - I crossed the State line of Georgia into the Sunshine State. Florida was living up to its reputation. It was a glorious day; everywhere I looked, the trees were green, so many of them bursting with small, lush new season leaves. No winter doom and gloom in this part of the country when it came to what Mother Nature does best. A staple visual stamped the landscape; familiar palms were everywhere. Having never been to Florida, first impressions were all I expected. The rest, we'd soon find out.

Getting here, I had traveled many of the back roads down through Virginia and the Carolinas, fascinated by the trail and history of the Civil War that caught my attention, many times forcing me to stop to learn more about this great country, but nothing took my breath away as much as Savannah. It was there, I decided, I could have halted my journey all together and never leave. I was enthralled. Gone with the Wind was alive and well in a modern way, and as a Realtor, a good one at that, I would *loved* to have sold these southern properties, the plantation style housing with stunning landscaping, the white fencing, the lattice work and the strikingly beautiful, antebellum homes with equally striking individual architecture so renowned in the southern states. In fact, I thought I wanted one, even considered investing in one momentarily, however; I knew my limitations, and remembered my mission.

Reluctantly, I bade Savannah farewell with a promise to return on my way back north, silently thinking, if this delightful city captures my heart again, Jack Montgomery might be forced to open a subsidiary office of our Connecticut base, then send me there to head it up. I'd be just the man and who knows, feeling as I did, I might be lucky enough to find a cute Southern Belle?

Jacksonville, Daytona Beach, Fort Lauderdale, Miami or Key West, the brochures all touted many wonderful reasons to *'come and stay'*. I sat in my beach side motel, pouring over many of them, looking forward to seeing what really caught my attention. They all did! Carefully stowed under the back seat of the Mustang had been my Wi-Fi laptop; reluctantly, I retrieved it for no other reason than to check out Florida's hotspots – habit I guessed. The Internet endorsed the brochures, except with much greater ease; I could flip through so much more by way of photos, facts and figures of the places, the cost, plus points of interest and a host of other *'mind mashing'* reasons to find a comfortable base to suit my needs. While I had no real intention of spending any time on the Internet, especially not wanting emails, a point I had made when alerting most of my contacts back in Hartford of my travel plans, I had warned them, I would delete any I saw, ditto with cell phone voice messages. I would of course take a call from Jack Montgomery; his call could carry a potential 'crisis'. Other than him, my Mother and Father had died long ago; I had no children and sadly, as if I needed reminding; I no longer had a wife. What else could there be for wired technology contact? I was well conditioned mentally. I'd covered all my bases and didn't want to be harassed by anyone.

As I weighed up all the cross check contingencies, a thought crossed my mind. If I had really wanted to disappear, be non-contactable, incommunicado, out of touch, to have gone into geographic remote control mode - period; from a distance point of view,

Three Days Later

I should have gone to Australia. That would have, almost, totally sealed my fate in communication. I had to smile. Hey - what if I'd spent these planned three months in Australia, could Jack Montgomery have opened a branch office there? Would I have stumbled across an Aussie *'sheila'* there? Aaah…to dream! Using techno analogy; I had a head, mind and body, that, like a computer, when it's cluttered with memory, it needs a disk cleanup, maybe total defragmentation. I closed the lid on my laptop and set myself back on course to do just that; defrag!

~~~~~~~~~~

As a location, initially, Daytona Beach won out, for a start anyway I believed. There was so much to do, and I could flit across the State to the Gulf of Mexico's locations anytime, Sarasota, Tampa, even further south to Miami, wherever, but do it all from a base location. Daytona, adjacent to immediate access to Interstate 95, was one of those very central Florida, highly publicized recommended destinations, especially *'spring-break'*. But I was well past that category of visitor clientele.

The Sun King Lodge, as it turned out, was a magnificent first choice too. Touted as *'a place where you are always welcome'*, I was certainly made exactly that! My room overlooked the next familiar billing of these parts, *'The World's Most Famous Beach'* and I couldn't argue with that either. As far as I could see, it was sand, sand and more sand, with an ocean that looked more inviting every time I gazed down from my balcony. I thought of Savannah. No…they are two totally different places, but I began to wonder *'…is everywhere I go, away from Connecticut, going to fuzz up my head as a place I would like to live, to be, to move to?'* I hoped not. I went down to the lobby.

"Hey Gareth, what's the story about all those cars out on the beach? It's a great idea and I'd heard about that as a Daytona thing, but there are a lot more of them than I thought there might be. Is it dangerous at all, and how in the 'you know what' do they ever police it?"

Gareth Harrison owned the Lodge and could always be found somewhere in the immediate vicinity, from the front desk, to the swimming pool or manicured gardens, even the parking area. Renowned, as I was told, to know almost anything, anyone ever wanted to know about Daytona Beach, he wasted no time filling me in on the beach history and its attraction of cars.

"It goes back to the turn of the early 19th century..." he began to enlighten me, and seemingly, by his tone, quite serious, "...cars initially raced out there as a sport. Heck, even that famous Englishman Sir Malcolm Campbell, although not a Sir at the time, *he* hit the beach here, and if you can believe it, clocked well over 200 mph, right out there on the hard sand, incredible!" Sounding almost excited, he took a gasp of breath before adding "That said, let me warn you, it's a very strict 10mph today, certainly not like those early racing days when they'd do over fifty, although that did start the motor sport as we know it these days with NASCAR and, old friend, if you like motor racing, you're gonna have to go to the Daytona Speedway, it's quite stunning, they have a great museum there too..." With a smile on his face, he paused for a moment, again, gulping for breath before continuing, ever the local promoter of all things Daytona Beach. "...but to answer your real question though, it's not really a problem with cars on the beach. A mishap happens here and there, and they threaten to stop it all together, but this is Daytona, the lifeguards and the rest of the authorities, they all do a great job making sure the people are safe. It's a good thing all around, I'd believe, not that I'd take that car of yours out there. Man, that's some vehicle."

I didn't have the heart now tell him the Mustang wasn't really mine. There was no point and anyway – it suited my image of how I was feeling – brand new!

"Well, I've got plenty of time" I told him. "I'll be around for however long it takes me to get bored, if that's at all possible, but I'll check it out. Meanwhile, I think I'll just hang out for now, read a book, walk the beach, take a dip in your pool if it's warm enough, however, I've gotta say, these winter to spring temperatures are amazing with these low eighties seemingly every day. Is this for real, or are they more like Florida's fluctuating aberrations, made to impress?"

"*This is Florida* Mr. Thompson." he started to say before I almost rudely interjected.

'Please, call me Tony. We're all friends around here' I threw in all over him.

"Okay…well, Tony…" he grinned, using my name "…except for hurricanes, that fortunately we haven't had the past couple of years, and don't want, but yeah, we have really *nice* winters. That's what visitors like you come down here for, although you don't seem to be a 'snowbird', or are you?" he asked as if double checking. "Most of the real snowbirds either have trailer-mobile homes, temporary modular or manufacture homes or their own regular places even."

"No I'm not actually…" I confirmed, as if there was a need to "…although I'm aware of that kind of lifestyle I'd have to confess, however, now I really get it. I can see exactly *why* northerners like me if you will, just *why* they come to Florida for four or five months over the winter. Escaping the brutal snow and winds and cold we have every year, *who* wouldn't, but in fairness, you get used to our New England style of living. In reality, that's who we are in the end, and it can be fun too, believe me, but nope, not me, not this time, I'm down here for my *own* escape, which is nothing more than timing really so, I hope you can put up with me for a little while?"

"Stay as long as you like Tony. We can work out a deal, a rate. That's never a problem, and especially in the economic climate we live in these days. Business is precious, harder to come by, and that goes for everyone. We're not immune to what's happening all over the country, *and* we rely on a transient market, so no problem at all. I'll always work with you."

"Don't get me started about the economic times…' I felt I had to add to offer in reply, certainly not wanting an extended conversation about it, probably anymore than he did, '… 'cause that's a sensitive topic for me. I'm in Real Estate in Connecticut, and we've seen tougher than usual times lately and believe me, I could tell you a million heartbreak stories for sure, but enough of that for today, I'm on vacation, not business sooo… let the good times start right now huh?"

It was time to go and I knew I'd see him every day, probably.

"I'm with you my friend. Call on me anytime, I'm always around somewhere, enjoy the Lodge too. If you need any pointers, any help, any recommendations, again, shout okay?"

Planning nothing by design, from the Sun King, I edged the Mustang out on to the open Highway A-1A, content to become simply, the consummate happy tourist. I decided, first, to cruise the coastal beach line, down to Ponce Inlet where, intrigued, I stopped for a while at a wonderful old Lighthouse that caught my attention, to study its history. Named for Juan Ponce DeLeon, an explorer from the 15th century who discovered the region, the lighthouse was built in 1887. Standing 175ft tall, the views were truly magnificent, and it had weathered the elements well, just as it was intended to do of course. Delighted, I considered my visit there an excellent start on my road to relaxation; I was feeling good and for the time spent, simple as it was, I had enjoyed the experience…lesson too!

From the Inlet, I doubled back on my tracks, crossed the bridge to the old downtown area of Daytona and began the second sojourn of my wanderlust trip to nowhere in particular; wandering the wide variety of shops open; especially, the antique stores. Pleasurable as it was, I couldn't help but to be disheartened by the many vacant store fronts, and there could only be the one same answer as to why; the slowing economy that was not getting any better. It was sad. Too many people, clear across the USA were hurting, and surprisingly, to me, even in the spectacular region of the world's most famous beach and yet, the street, the locale, the visuals were all marvelous. I willed it all to *'return to normal'*…sooner than later.

I opted to grab a quick coffee in a quaint little shop that literally enticed me in, through the marvelous array of cakes and pastries in their display window. The clever arrangement and planned ability to make one feel a little peckish at the same time, certainly worked on me. Nonchalantly standing, waiting for my coffee to be brewed, for no reason other than to pass the time, I picked up a brochure that had caught my eye on the well-stocked tourist rack. *'Cruise the Bahamas - Quick Choices For Your Busy Schedule'.* The last time I had taken a cruise was to Alaska, but that was back some seven years ago.

Jessica loved me then I annoyingly thought, while still managing to take the happiness of the memory to a belief that, maybe, a cruise was a great idea for me, now! I'd always wanted to go on another cruise, even harbored plans once, long ago, of someday spending time, hopping from island to island in the Caribbean. By a quirk of fate, I guessed, and for whatever benefit I could gain from it, maybe this was my very chance to fulfill that harbored plan. Jessica or no Jessica, this was my time. I began to feel an excitement build. I pocketed the brochure, in fact, two of them.

Later, I knew; I'd have to break my rules, again, and fire up the laptop to see what I came up with. What better place than Florida to start I thought; the home of every conceivable cruise available, to the very area that once had my attention. The rush of adrenalin kept pumping through my body. I almost couldn't wait to get back to the Sun King Lodge and set my plans in motion.

My whims swiftly changed. Passing up cakes and pastries, a feeling of more fulfilling nourishment got the better of me, now that I had a mission, a purpose, and a meal of substance would sustain me better to get me through the next few hours, on into the evening.

Choosing the Starlite, a 50's Diner complete with a jukebox, framed photos of Elvis Presley, James Dean and Marilyn Monroe over the walls, along with old vinyl 45rpm records and colorful LP sleeves, plus a host of music movie posters, it was reminiscent delight to take in the atmosphere, all, while still being able to select from a simple menu that had a wide variety of food capable of filling any empty stomach. Enjoying the ambience, this was a place I liked.

Forty-five minutes later, after listening to Buddy Holly, The Beatles, Chuck Berry, CCR and many other great old 'Rockers' of the fifties and sixties, all while savoring my double-cheeseburger, flavored fries and malted milk shake, I had to concede, what a memory. It was a *feel-good* although I did think; maybe I was showing my age too? It didn't matter. Good rock music was good rock music, always would be when you put it up against some of the stuff today I couldn't begin to understand, especially hip-hop or rap and more.

Yep, I'd gladly show my age I decided with Summertime Blues fading in the background as I walked out of the diner, smugly approaching my Mustang, a right up to date chromed symbol of my youth.

Finally, I made it back to my adobe, ready to settle in for a session of serious surfing, but not on the always inviting Daytona Beach – this time; I'd be surfing the Information Super Highway, the Internet. My mind was a buzz, swirling; I was feeling exceptionally high, alive, more alive than usual, or of late anyway. I opened the windows of my unit; a breezy cool rush of air filled the room. The sound of the waves crashing below reminded me, I was where I wanted to be at this particular time in my life; at the beach, with a spectacular view, clear out to where the ocean seemed to simply disappear, similarly as I wanted my past life to. And as I pondered a future, with the slowly darkening skies beginning to fall beyond the horizon, tomorrow, I knew, when I gazed out at exactly the same view, it would be to a brand-new horizon, one bursting with brilliant sunshine, with even clearer skies and brighter new visions to light the way. That would be me, in precisely the place I'd want to be – wherever the unknown, the new day, the adrenalin of a clear head and mind, would choose to lead me, take me. I was so ready for adventure, a new and different direction.

I pushed down on the power button of my Toshiba laptop. The screen before me flickered to become a bright blue green, aaah…Windows 7. I smiled. It seemed but moments ago I'd just been picturing the same bright welcoming colors for the skies above and the water below, and had both, blending right into each other; a great mind - mine, and technology were already thinking alike. Fate and team work, hard at play. Seconds later, the website of Caribbean Cruises burst into life. What I immediately saw almost made me utter an expletive I was not accustomed to expressing, in public or alone. My goodness I thought, mouthing out loud, '…*these cruise ships are mighty big*'.

CHAPTER

FIVE

Three days later - I was standing on the deck of one of the largest cruise ships I had ever physically seen. I had learned there were bigger ones operating out of Miami, but that didn't dull the fact, this one, named the 'Calypso Caribbean', had my full attention; it was monstrous. How I would *ever* find my way around it? With all it had to offer in amenities, activities and entertainment, it was almost beyond imagination. Accepting, without reservation, it would be a pleasurable task to take on as a challenge, I decided right there and then to meet it. Sailing the high seas to the sunny Caribbean was about to be my new experience.

My ocean view stateroom was on the right side on a higher deck, in nautical terms, starboard. Close by. there were any number of restaurants, a theater for both live shows and movies, and one place I again vowed to stay away from was the seemingly always, very full, Monte Carlo 7 Casino. I'd already walked around the ship, probably twice, and if I'd been measuring distance, which I hadn't done, I figured, at the very least it would be probably a couple of miles all up.

One fast thing I *had* learned about big ships and cruising, there was a never ending, change of scenery. From coffee parlors to retail shops, spas and hair dressing salons, a library-book store, a fitness center, a jogging track, even mini-golf and a golf simulator, recreational climbing stations, at least two public swimming pools, plus a wave rider for any would be surfers, to an amusement arcade and a variety of entertainment venues, even nightclubs. I began to wonder, who could frequent, or take advantage of so much in whatever varying lengths of time to complete a cruise, then disembark, and lay claim they had seen it all? The facilities were endless; I had trouble keeping track of them all. I guessed I wouldn't try. Regardless, I had a very colorful and very descriptive map in hand. I'd find what I wanted, when I wanted it - whatever that might be? I'd *make* it work.

Five hours out to sea from Port Canaveral, I was leaning on the ship's side rail, content, for just a while, to simply watch whatever world was out there go drifting lazily by. I was miles away in thought. The white foam churning up the Atlantic Ocean behind the ship was quite mesmerizing and had, what might have appeared, my absolute and full attention. Minutes later, I guessed, snapping out of the visual trance, I turned to see who might be around, out on deck. Oddly, I instantly realized, it had been eerily quiet of human beings, no shouting, laughing or other playful noises that might have been more expected.

Anticipating a few people to be gathered by now, lazing on the deck at the very least, instead, to my total amazement, but absolute delight, there was only one person in sight, a lone rather beautiful woman at that. Dressed in a pretty white and purple flower print top, fitted to perfection, showing off the incredible shape of her body, she also wore snug fitting blue jeans and to finish off the coordinated ensemble, a pair of casual smart gold color sandals with straps tied up around the ankle. *Wow*! Judging by her momentary stance, my immediate assumption was, she was probably a fitness fanatic who couldn't wait to get her daily routine planned, or, out of the way. *Wrong!*

"Oh hi…" I offered, the first words to jump into my head, lame as they were, "…you look to me like you're going to get the serious part of your cruise out of the way before settling into the relax mode everyone seems to think is supposed to happen instantly when stepping on board these huge hunks of metal..." I also lamely posed, with absolutely no idea of what I was really trying to say, except to be sociable and make light conversation.

She responded with a soft acknowledging, but throw away laugh.

I felt the need to keep talking, "...but whatever..." I added, looking for, hoping for, a response, anything, "... and if you are, it's really working. You look remarkably good."

I immediately wished I hadn't said a word at all. *Nothing* about what I had just blurted out sounded right. In fact, I felt quite awkward, thinking, how I could *ever* have uttered *'you look remarkably good?'* I could have dived overboard right there and then.

"No, no, no..." she responded, in what I could only accept as, under the circumstances, as polite, but at least with a friendly tone, "...I was actually trying to get a feel for what's on board, of where everything is, and just how it all functions, but I'm afraid it's beyond me. It's quite overwhelming, probably more than I ever expected. I'm even beginning to think, maybe, I should have taken a different trip, or at the very least, chosen a much less daunting cruise first."

Great minds think alike. Earlier, I had actually thought the very same thing. At least we had an inner equal footing in how we felt.

"Hear, hear..." I wholeheartedly agreed, sharing the belief honestly. "...I was doing likewise, but too late now huh? However, you really do have to wonder, *why* do these cruise ships have to be so *big*? I mean, every year it seems the ships just get bigger and bigger? When or where does it all end? Next thing you know, there will be floating mini-cities if there aren't already, and it's quite staggering."

It was all mindless small talk I knew it, but I had a burning desire to keep a dialog between us going somehow.

"There already are I believe." She returned, and with that remark, at least kept me alive in conversation, even bailing me out but then, to my absolute delight, she had more to say.

"Maybe not in the USA, but in some country, if not more than one even, they actually *do* have ships that do nothing else but cruise the world. Some people, they say, buy permanent staterooms, equivalent to probably an apartment, and cruising becomes their way of life. They pay a nominal fee after purchasing it as bona-fide real estate, and then just travel the world. It's not something *I could do* but..." she said, trailing off on the thought, casting the subject off as mere idle chit-chat between us. But she sure had said plenty. Her voice, I could listen to her forever. My turn!

"Me neither, but you know, I've always liked the idea of a sea cruise, especially the Caribbean, which is why I came, and *you?*"

Changing the subject a little, I had to throw in another question. From where I stood and at who I was looking, I seriously did not want her to leave.

"Same, although this is my maiden voyage, dare I admit it. And what about you, have you been on a cruise before if you don't mind me asking"

Mind, I thought. Honesty, I had always believed, was the best policy, and with that thought process, her question from a question, here it came, my chance to find out just *who* this beautiful woman was. If she had a husband on board, then my chances would end before they even started. Equally, if there was a boyfriend, it would still be the end, but if like me, she was just taking a break, a vacation, or...heck, it didn't matter, I simply had to find out, and fast, before she wandered off, never to be seen or found again on such a monstrosity of organized heavy metal that had the staggering ability to stay afloat in water. A wonderment in itself, just as this woman standing before me was right now.

"Yes I have, although with this one, to the Caribbean, I could say I came on board just for the thrill of it, or tell you I was with a bunch of guys and we decided it was a good idea at the time, or some such thing, but to be honest; it's none of the above. I'm actually clearing my head, thinking about making a change in my life, turning a corner from an accident I didn't know at the time was waiting to happen, but when it did I, I er...," pausing, stumbling almost, I now wished I hadn't said what I had begun to stupidly confess, before clumsily adding, in trying to correct myself, "...you know; I have absolutely *no idea* what I'm really trying to say..." I had floundered badly "...as you probably don't either." I expected her truthful reply.

"No, frankly, I don't, but I also didn't mean to pry either so, not a problem. Oh and by the way, don't worry; I can be a little chatterbox sometimes too, but in the end, all harmless stuff really."

Spinning on her heels; my vision splendor motioned to be on her way. There was no question, put simply; I'd messed up our verbal interaction big-time!

"Er, excuse me..." I offered, a little lost for words, almost stuttering, "...look; I'm sorry. I, I was a little elusive then, but I really didn't..."

Too late! She didn't wait to hear the rest of my response, excuses even, ending our chance meeting as fast as it began.

"Gotta go, maybe I'll see you around."

A few seconds later she'd taken the first turn available to disappear completely out of sight.

'Man, what's wrong with me' I muttered under my breath. 'How stupid was that!' I had to believe I'd lost my touch. Not at trying to be conversational with a beautiful woman I didn't know, but more, in being interestingly conversational at all. Years in the real estate business had certainly taught me the art of casual, nothingness conversation, but I'd just made a first class fool of myself. Was I really trying to tell a stranger, a beautiful woman, I was on some sort of a reject downer from a divorce, over losing a wife who found greater interest in another man? What the hell was it that I even said? I began to think, trying to retrace my words? They didn't, wouldn't come back to me, except something about a corner and an accident that happened. Lord, I needed a refresher course in PR, better still; a charisma by-pass maybe?

Annoyed at myself; I decided to head back to my stateroom. Maybe hide myself away for the rest of the cruise. I never made it. Sidetracked, I chose instead to stop off at one of the nice little bars I'd seen in my travels on my self guided tour earlier and get a drink. I think I needed one. No, I *really* needed one, maybe two! A bar called the Tiki Islands became my safe haven. It had a small Calypso style band playing softer music which, on entering; one could be transported to another place and time; like a desert island. Perfect, just what I needed. I sat down and ordered an ice cold beer. Purely a state of mind, I began to feel immediately better, relaxed. Things had to pick up from here I believed given there is so much to see and do, participate in.

It wouldn't have been thirty minutes later, but who should walk through the Tiki Islands entrance? It was her! Oh dear…I took a deep breath and wondered, hoped, if there was such a thing as a second chance. I prayed there would be. Adjusting her sunglasses to the dimmer light of the bar, I assumed she was either looking for a friend or, hopefully, like me, looking for a quiet place to sit and relax for a while. I really hoped it was not to meet someone? Innocently, as she moved further into the lounge, our eyes met; she offered a smile. With a slight nod of her head, recognizing me, it seemed; she began to saunter my way, right up to where I was sitting in the booth. I stood up, anxious to make amends.

"Hello again…" It was a simple greeting I wanted to believe. I was anxious to extend the moment, "…how really nice to see you, so soon after our first, well my first, clumsy hello. Maybe I can buy you a drink and apologize for making such an absolute spectacle, make that, fool of myself in front of you earlier" I had admitted as a form of apology too. I felt it was justly deserved. All I needed now was a yes.

"A drink, sure, and thank you, but as for making *whatever* of yourself before, I doubt the word fool would be fair. I think we both might have had moments of brain freeze, but in the bigger picture of unprepared moments, to be candid, it's quite unimportant."

The booth I was in, although small, could still comfortably seat four at any point if need be. For two people, it was more than perfect, allowing a more intimate feeling of togetherness. I stood up as she moved to slide in across from me; while at the same time, making eye contact with the waiter who, like a hawk, in noticing added company, had already begun to stroll over to, ostensibly, make sure we were comfortable. The added drink order was taken. *'I'll be right back with your drink'* he said walking away.

"I'm Anthony Thompson, by the way, but I mostly go by Tony, either way; I'll always answer" I said with a grin, hoping this time my light repartee might be enough to get me through. She smiled back. What a gorgeous smile I thought, still taking in her beauty. In the darker light of the bar, her hair that flowed to her shoulders appeared deep brown, heading more toward black, while her face showed just the smallest hint of years that I guessed to be probably thirty plus, but nowhere near forty for sure. In putting out her hand to offer a friendly and warm hand shake, she too introduced herself.

"Chelsea, Chelsea Martin, and odd as it might seem on board this ship, I'm all the way from Florida" she laughed, confirming, admitting maybe; she wasn't far from home.

"Florida…" I echoed, without thinking"…what's so wrong with *that*? I love Florida already, yet I hardly know the place, but anyway, pleased to meet you Chelsea, and by the way; you're quite beautiful, and I love your smile, it's infectious" I could now gladly confirm with a growing confidence.

"Why thank you kind Sir…" she almost sang with the lilt of a southern drawl "…I'm so pleased to make your acquaintance and where would you be from?"

"Hartford, Hartford Connecticut…' I answered "…and as they boldly say in all the brochures and publicity pieces for vacation promotions, *'a place, full of surprises',* and I'd have to concur, there's a lot about Connecticut that will surprise maybe you even, if you ever come and visit us."

Subtle, I realized; a personal invitation already. Not bad! I was back. My real estate small conversation was kicking in.

"Okay, but *what* will really surprise me?" she responded as if seeking a bona-fide answer to my claim while allowing also our conversation to flow.

I'd led with my chin. However, that was fine. This kind of a question was easy. I was born and bred Connecticut; I sold it too! I knew my subject well.

"How about the history for starters, or spectacularly every year, the fall foliage, but here's the big one for you. Seeing as you're from Florida, I'm throwing in our mountains and our rolling hills too, of which I'm led to believe, there are none of in Florida, hills that is, rolling or otherwise." Chelsea laughed. We were connecting.

The next two hours seemed to fly by. Our conversation over four orders of drinks covered a myriad of facts about each other, and what turned out to be the biggest delight of all, for both of us; we were single, free, no significant other partners. I confessed my recent divorce from Jessica and why, echoing my sadness at lost love, something that I believed in, a fact, interestingly, not lost on Chelsea Martin. She expressed; of my feelings and honesty, they were more of a quality, and despite being on the losing end of the relationship and marriage, I was, had been, in her words, an honorable man. If she had intended to make me feel better about myself, she had, rather big-time. It then became her turn!

Chelsea had also been married, but it had been dissolved some five years ago. It was a simple case of the right guy who went wrong, who had different views about life and love than she had, and when he chose hunting, fishing, and any number of things *'with the boys'* over her, it wasn't long before their two worlds drifted apart. He went one way, she another. *'Such is life'* she drawled in her own inimitable style. For an unexplainable reason, and I didn't know why, something told me there was a lot more to her story than she had expressed. There had been hesitancy, and I wondered, if what she had relayed might have been nothing more than an anecdotal story to cover another more real situation. I left it well alone. For now, it was none of my business.

Surprisingly, I'd been wrong about Chelsea's age. I was quite staggered to find she was closer in age to me, and yet; at 42 years, she was more like a woman in her lower thirties. Laughing, again, she thanked me for the compliment, not realizing I was deadly serious, but it didn't matter. She was the best reason yet I could think of in making the decision to take a cruise over to the Bahamas, short as it would be, and as a trial, to see if I might even enjoy sailing the high seas again. A rediscovered experience, I already loved it.

Dinner together that evening in the Fine Line Signature Restaurant was a chance to savor the moment of our chance meeting, and delight just a little more in our lives, such as they had been, and even, with much discretion, some personal hopes and wishes for another day. With shared smiles of reflection, great minds were thinking alike when Chelsea and I both agreed; unaware of our relationship, when we had arrived, the earlier suggestion of our maître d to seat us at a larger table to meet other passengers, was an innocent case of, who could possibly have known - we'd already met other people – Us! With sincere thanks, we declined his most gracious, innocently intended offer.

Too soon, our wonderful evening together, was drawing to a close. Sharing a leisurely stroll along the soft lit walkways around the deck of the ship, complete with imaginative décor meant to impress, it was a beautiful night, one I didn't want to end. I hoped a million quiet times over; Chelsea didn't either? To our mutually shared delight, a full moon shone brightly on the shimmering, glistening water, allowing us to steal a few extra moments to enjoy the visuals of it all before giving in to reality; recognition that our day and night was over.

Before parting, we reconfirmed our next rendezvous, a light lunch having already selected The Sunrise Café, a most highly recommended spot by our friendly waiter. A small hug, a kiss on the cheek, and a hand that squeezed mine ever so gently as we said good-night, told me, my chance meeting of a truly delightful lady was hopefully meant to be. I'd had a wonderful day. Before closing her stateroom door slowly behind her, she peeked around to give me one last smile. Then I heard the click! With a sigh and a smile, I wandered back to my own room, poured myself a JD and sat on the side of the bed.

Three days remained on this mini-cruise. Three days left to learn more about Chelsea Martin. Like a schoolboy, I couldn't wait. I gulped my drink. As fast as my head hit the soft pillow, visions of Chelsea flooded my mind. Sleep came easy.

When Chelsea Martin had closed her door, she stood, for the longest time, with her hand still on the handle, her back leaning against it. She breathed a deep sigh before moving into her room. The drapes were still wide open; there was nothing but darkness through the window. She walked forward to stare outside, blankly, into the night. Turning, the soft light of her state-room gave her a peaceful feeling – this night too had been a most enjoyable one, unexpected. She turned toward the bed. Pulling back the sheets, it looked incredibly inviting, but, she thought...? Lying alone, choosing for no reason to sleep naked tonight, she draped the crisp, cool sheet over her body. In the darkness, she let her mind wander to places she had not been in a very long time. The imagined setting was beautiful, the feeling, wonderful. In the depths of her mind, a mind full of thoughts so long denied, he was standing there. Her breathing lifted, but why? He came closer. A hand touched her body...whose? Thoughts in her mind overtook her, engulfed her, tortured her, and finally, satisfied her. And soon...Chelsea drifted away...into another world!

~~~~~~~~~~

Did I really sleep through until just after nine o'clock before stirring to face another day? Where *am* I exactly and *what* in the devil is *that*...? Through blurry eyes, I saw a black coffee pot on a side ledge table, above it, on the wall, a picture of three orchids, all different colors, in a large white frame. Not my normal sight when I wake up. I shook my head into the pillow. My eyes shifted over to the clock on the bedside table under a small lamp. It read 9.17. I lifted my head again from the pillow, even the bed was facing the wrong way from my normal direction. *What was I thinking?* I'd lost every sense of my whereabouts, momentarily forgetting, I was on a cruise, on a ship, and a helluva big one at that - of course!

Slowly, I re-found myself. Forget Connecticut, the drive to Florida, Daytona Beach or any place else – *I'm on a cruise ship!* I took a deep breath gathering my thoughts, and as I did, I gathered the most beautiful one of all. Chelsea, Chelsea Martin. '*Whoa*' I remembered. We have a lunch date. I breathed an instant sigh of relief as that was still three plus hours away yet.

Pushing my face back into the pillow, I allowed my mind to return to The Tiki Islands Bar to see again the most gorgeous woman to grace its entrance, Chelsea's arrival, and then thinking, to my absolute amazement; she didn't know I was already there. An irony, or expectation, or was it *meant* to be? Maybe she *did* know I was there? Care factor – zero! The rest of the night, I remembered, had been totally and absolutely, pure magic. Lonely, yes - I had been, often, since Jessica had left me, but right now, *any* thoughts of ever missing her were light years away. After what seems so long, in every way, at last, fate - a new angel had entered my life. I couldn't wait for 12.30 to arrive. I closed my eyes, searching for the visual memory of Chelsea's face again. She appeared before me as if a miracle had been performed. Not wanting to lose the image, for just a moment I too, drifted into another world! Two world's were colliding and yet – in distance – worlds' apart. Could they come together?

~~~~~~~~~~

Three days later - if it had been possible to fall in love in such short a time, then the possible happened. I'd fallen in love with Chelsea Martin, head over heels. And Chelsea fell in love with me. Was it the ship maybe, or Nassau and The Islands of the Bahamas? Was it the dolphins, the shipwrecks, or the coral reefs we could only see from above in our glass bottom boat as we glided over the crystal clear Caribbean waters? Was it the 18th century Queen's Staircase where we stood halfway up the 65 limestone steps to have photos taken, the forts maybe, or the caves, or that great little sea-food restaurant on Rawson Square we didn't want to leave?

Exploring Nassau together during our all too short stay had left us breathless, wanting more, but as they say, when all the stars are lined up, and heaven appears to be in one's midst, the reminder so evident in everyday life re-emerges; time waits for no-one - the moment of reckoning always arrives.

When the inevitable happened, re-board the ship for the homeward journey and Florida, two hearts couldn't have been sadder. Heaven was closing its doors on a chapter in life, now written. Cruise ships don't wait and time was certainly not waiting, especially not even for Anthony Thompson or Chelsea Martin.

~~~~~~~~~~

CHAPTER SIX

Our last night on board The Calypso Caribbean came harder than either of us expected. Where could we both possibly go from here? Connecticut and Florida might be some, one thousand miles apart, but the hearts that beat inside us both, sitting back in The Tiki Bar, were as close as two people could be, knowing, when tomorrow came, we'd have to part. Could we simply go our separate ways? Could we pretend the last three days didn't happen? My feelings were real; I opened up my heart. The words came easy.

"My dear sweet Chelsea, what have you done to me? I can't bear the thought of us going back to our normal lives, separately, alone. What are we going to do?"

Unashamedly, I'd meant every word I'd spoken, hoping at the same time, that maybe Chelsea had the same thoughts, same feeling, and the same inner dilemma as me. She eased my mind.

"We knew it would probably to come to this Tony but…" she momentarily hesitated, before drawing a deep breath."…I don't really know, yet, however, I do have…" Her apparent look of forlorn probably matched mine. My emotions ran ahead of her completing her sentence.

"God, can you believe this? Look at us." I seemed to blurt out. "We're not exactly kids and yet we have a problem expected more of twenty-something's. On one hand, it's great, while on the other...*damn!*" My mind was racing; I had to think of something. There had to be an answer. Across the table, Chelsea moved in her seat, about to pick up where she had left of seconds ago. Taking my hands in hers, she looked directly into my eyes.

"You know, here's a thought..."

The cruise we were both sharing might be ending, but it still left Chelsea with five days of her vacation break, leaving open the chance, that I took immediately as *'opportunity'*, for us to make some additional short term plans together. She lived a mere 25 miles or so from Daytona Beach, she informed me, where I had planned to ensconce myself anyway, so what better place to head for and make the most of our time left. My hopes had lifted greatly.

"Twenty-five miles from Daytona, is that all?" I asked, genuinely surprised.

"Yep, in a wonderful little city called DeLand. I'm guessing I'll no doubt show it to you somewhere along the way, but for now, being close enough to Daytona, no problem at all. We can make it work."

"Brilliant, absolutely brilliant!" I declared, thrilled at her logic and suggestion of the moment.

"I'd hoped for that reaction..." she quickly threw back. "...honestly, I'd have been a little saddened, embarrassed too, if you had found a way to tell me that we both had to come to grips with reality, that our time was over. You've no idea how much better I feel already, thank you."

As if needing something to do, Chelsea picked up her gin and tonic, took a long slow sip before carefully placing it back down. Her comment had been fair, and frankly, could have worked both ways. I understood her small doubt and knew instantly that I needed to reassure her.

"Chelsea, I could *never* have done that. I've had a *marvelous* time and believe me; you're a whole lotta fun to be with and be around.

My God, if I was to be so bold, again, you're so damned beautiful to me, how could I *ever* let you out of my sight *now*? I really *want* to see more of you; I *want* to be with you. As of this moment, I can't think of how I'd spend any time ahead, alone, knowing you're out there. I need you to be with me, somewhere, anywhere, *it's what I want!*"

"Thank you Tony, that's a nice thing to say, but do you mean it, because…?"

To think she had to double check. I stopped her, again, mid sentence.

"*Mean it!* Let me tell you my dear sweet lady, if I wasn't *such* a gentleman, I'd take you in my arms this very moment and never let you go. Heaven knows; I could ravish you with a passion I might not know exists within me or you either, so there! Take that as a fair warning."

"Why I declare Mr. Thompson, you're making me blush" she replied in a southern drawl that could have been straight from the mouth of Scarlett O'Hara. About to continue, she hesitated.

"But what Ms Martin, but what, pray tell me?" I queried in my best Rhett Butler accent "…because I really do give a…ah well, you know." I was immediately intrigued.

"You know…' she started "…maybe I shouldn't be saying this at all, but…," Dipping her head slightly to look directly at me, Chelsea began to confess, in a softer voice, "…it's been so long since I er, that I, er well…" She hesitated again.

She raised both her eye-brows as if to emphasize shyness, doubt maybe, about the subject matter? I had an inkling of where she was going with her thoughts, and just as I was about to allay her fears to make it easier on her, she continued, this time somewhat more unabashed, becoming more confident, indeed, straight to the point.

"Oh to heck with it, I'll just say it. To tell you the truth, I haven't been with a man in such a long time, and to be perfectly honest, right now, I'm a little scared, maybe more than a little, I mean, I'm 42 years of age already and the time gone since I…" her words momentarily stumbled and again, she faltered finding the right ones.

Quickly recognizing it would be unfair not to let her express what she was feeling about such a delicate subject, I chose to remain silent. I had to let her say her piece, to say nothing of the devil in me that had surfaced too. With degrees of obvious difficulty, she continued the sensitive topic already started, probably wishing she had never gone there in the first place but, too late!

"...well, since I actually made love with a man, and I admit it. I'm truly scared about it all. I want to, and I've actually thought about it... thought about it with you even but, well, oh Tony, I've said enough, I'm sure you know what I mean. Gosh, this is so hard, believe me."

As if it was a safety latch, a prop, she again picked up her drink to take, this time, a much larger than normal gulp. I shared the moment, imitating her actions, buying an extra moment of silence.

I was truly moved. Facts were; it had been a long time for me too. Maybe not as long as Chelsea I guessed, but a long time, nevertheless. I'd had a few chances along the way, but thoughts of Jessica always stood in the way, and why; I never knew. *She* had been unfaithful to me; she had left me and yet; I had harbored for too long, deep thoughts for her. Whatever chances with other women who had come my way, somehow, I always found a way to back out, not really caring either; sex was just that, to me, purely physical! I always wanted more than simple, gratuitous sex when it came to being with a woman, and in time, I believed, hoped, I would find love again. I just never knew where or when, until now, when suddenly I'm where I really wanted to be. Chelsea had been honest about what little of her past we'd shared, her relationships, her broken marriage too, yet here she was, sitting in a bar, on a cruise ship, pouring her most personal thoughts out to me when it came to the most enjoyable, and frightening part of all in a relationship. How unique I thought, how incredibly brave? This was all quite new, to me.

I cast my mind back over the past three days, thinking; I should maybe pinch myself. Suddenly, I find myself sitting in front of a most beautiful, make that stunning lady, someone who has truly left an indelible mark on me, and yet, like teenagers of a bygone era, we both have the same problem. And it came down to sex, or maybe I should have labeled it, intimacy! Could it be that The Calypso Caribbean has done its job? All that it is ever expected to do? That it had brought new life, adventure, happiness, even found new loves for lost loves? I thought so. I also thought seriously about how to frame my answer, my reaction to her. In the end it was easy really; it came down to one word - honesty.

"You know; I understand Chelsea, and we'll do only what we think is right, whenever it's right. There's no urgency between us about that subject. It'll find its own way, one way or another, and that seems fair to me. Have I thought about it – yes? Let's just take one day at a time though; we owe that to ourselves equally."

There was no question, Chelsea needed reassuring and in being honest with me and my conscience, I knew, whatever we felt for each other, really would find its own way. Would I like to make love to her, tonight, this last night of our cruise…of course? However, love between us, simple sex, it could wait. I wanted Chelsea to be happy, above everything else, but also to be very sure of not only her and her feelings, but of me too. I shared what I thought could be a workable plan for us both.

"Well Chelsea, with my rather nice little hotel back in Daytona Beach, at our disposal, parting tomorrow won't be something we now have to think about, and given as you live as close in, what was that city again…?" she reminded me it was called DeLand. "…yeah, Deland, we'll be able to make some better plans from there. You've obviously got a car back at Port Canaveral, and I do too so, maybe; from Daytona, we'll see where life takes us. We can make it all work I'm sure, and do it all on very neutral ground. You'll always be close to home if you have a need to go there, that's okay and a given so, agreed?"

Without a moment's hesitation, Chelsea nodded her head in approval. And as for the smile that came with the nod, I felt ten feet tall. If she felt relieved, I was equally so.

"Great, now, let's get you to your stateroom little lady, the figuring of it all comes later huh?"

Strolling hand in hand, for the last time, under that same Atlantic moon, happy as two people could be, we tried to count some stars in a group in the heavens above; we even saw one shooting star dart across the sky, upon which, in mutual agreement, we each made our silent secret wishes. Slowly wandering, meandering, hither, thither and yon, it would be half an hour before we reached Chelsea's stateroom, to stand outside the door, just as we had done every night since the day we met. The light hug, her gentle kiss on the cheek that very first night, had now progressed to a hug that told its own story. Tonight though, especially, I never wanted to let her go, just as Chelsea's actions indicated to me, her feelings were exactly the same. I drew back to gaze directly at her most beautiful face, cupping my hands under and around her chin as I did, before kissing her soft lips. Our kiss was gentle; the flaring passion was real. Unexpectedly, she pulled away from me, stepping to one side as she did, at the same time, reaching for the door handle quickly opening it. A soft light in the room glowed behind her. Chelsea reached down to take my hand and with a gentle tug, silently invited me to enter. As the door closed behind us, she latched the lock before turning to fall into my outstretched open arms. The intensity of our embrace was mind shattering, the kiss that followed as our lips found each other, was raw passion, while our hands gently, but excitedly, explored each other's body as if to be sure we were both real. Soon…we were one. Everything was new again, as if for the first time. And it was!

~~~~~~~~~~

Three days later - metaphorically speaking, we came up for air. Admitting it, Chelsea Martin was a self-proclaimed new woman who delighted in knowing, by my similar admittance, she had transformed Anthony 'Tony' Thompson into a brand-new man. The Sun King Lodge had been a safe haven to the newest of lovers who could be found every afternoon, walking the warm winter days of Daytona Beach, wondering where life had been and where it was heading.

'I think I love you' she sang as a melody line on seeing the same words someone before us had written, with a shell, in the hardened wet sand. Seconds later, a larger incoming wave washed the words

away. *'Oh no'* she wailed trying to kick the water away. Cute, I thought.

"I've heard that song before Miss Martin, but I've forgotten by whom, not that it matters..." I sang the same line back to her *'... 'cause I think I love you too...'* it was a bad rendition, but had the desired effect. We laughed like two kids.

"What an enjoyable day, but they're all slipping away too fast" were words I didn't want to hear.

Chelsea was melancholy happy; I was deliriously happy. We fell in the soft sand together. I kissed her; she kissed me. Love was in the air, on the beach, in the water – everywhere!

Daytona had been the most perfect place for me to get my batteries recharged, as I'd told Jack Montgomery, I needed to, never dreaming they were charging rapidly for reasons I had never expected, and I certainly wasn't about to call him, to tell him; I was running way ahead of schedule. He'd want me back in Connecticut, and in a million years, I wouldn't be leaving Florida any time soon. Actually, I thought; I might never leave at all, and who knows; I could be opening up his new office in DeLand, not that I knew what this place called DeLand had to offer, but that didn't matter – yet! At this moment in time, it held the key to everything I thought desirable in the world right now, and that, was one hell of a start.

"I'm staying Chelsea.." I told her. '...in case you might not have worked that out yet. I'm staying, at least until we know more about you and me, whatever that might turn out to be. I'm only a couple or three weeks into my three months out, and I have plenty of time to roll with the flow, and that flow my dear lady, is you. Tomorrow, when you have to head back to DeLand, I'm coming too. You can show me your town, your pride and joy, and *then* we'll see what we're up against. Does that work for you?" I asked. Thrilled, she smiled, nodding an anxious yes.

That night, together, in each other's arm, an inner peace seemed to overcome us both. Reflecting the virtual half way point in years, of both our lives, we marveled at finding each other, as if by some huge default. Who could ever have imagined, how two people

Three Days Later

would seek a small refuge in their lives, for no reason, other than to find an inner peace, and yet, impulsive as both our separate decisions were, flee to the safety of what we felt was right, a good idea, onto a cruise ship to sail the ocean blue, thereby, allowing ourselves time to …think! We sure had a lot of thinking to do. But it was a nice problem.

~~~~~~~~~~

"Hey Tony, you've been a little scarce these past days, whatch'a been doin'?"

Lodge owner, Gareth Harrison had called out to me to make his presence felt as he saw me wandering through the foyer entrance. I spun around to greet the ever smiling host standing behind the front counter, always ready to fraternize with any and all who wandered through the reception area, many looking for things to see and do, places to go, or as was often the case, just to listen to his many anecdotal stories of Florida, or Daytona, and he had plenty of them!

"So you missed me already huh?" I asked, jokingly, wondering if he'd seen the most attractive lady in the whole wide world spending time at his resort.

By choice, I'd sauntered over to the desk to speak more one on one with the congenial owner. He really did have a nice demeanor about him, always hospitable, something that would be a 'must' in his line of business. He handed me a complimentary copy of the News Journal suggesting I might like to catch up on some local news and events, especially one coming up this weekend, at the Shell, over by the Daytona Pier; he alerted me. Many a free concert was staged at the popular venue, and 'it *was a nice place to kill time*' he threw in with a smile. Before I knew it, the commercial side of everything he did in life surfaced.

"I don't know whether you've been over to the NASCAR complex on International Speedway Boulevard yet, or if you're going to, but I should tell you, if want to book ahead for the 500, remember, I can set up the tickets and the best of accommodations of course."

What a salesman I thought, always thinking ahead. He could match me in real estate selling anytime I believed and then see what the records Hartford Montgomery would write at year's end. But then again, this hotelier was one successful businessman already, with a, geographically, choice piece of real estate, all his very own to boot - and on the beach!

"I might just take you up on that Gareth. It's a great thought, but I'll see how the next few weeks go first I think. I've got a lot happening. Right now I'm just having a good time so, we'll see. Life's good and I'm a happy man. Can't ask for more than that huh?"

"Anytime Tony, anytime, I'm here for you, just shout!"

I guessed he knew about Chelsea, that someone was here with me, but as any fine host would do, he left the subject alone. He'd seen plenty in his time; I was sure, when it came to matters of the heart. From the young to the old, and the many in between, life was meant to be fun, to be enjoyed, and Gareth Harrison had made a career out of making sure everyone who visited his establishment, had a stay and time to remember. No-one could fault the amenities, service and position of his beloved Sun King Lodge.

"Thanks Gareth. By the way, nice touch."

I was acknowledging his respecting privacy - this time, mine. While I was at it, I also extended my stay at his establishment, paying in advance to the end of the month, still with options.

After a leisurely breakfast around the pool, Chelsea and I headed back to the room to change, collect her bags that had already been packed, ready to make the quick trip over to Deland to get her settled back in. She had work to do tomorrow.

Kicking off the short shorts she was wearing, and then stripping off her Florida Gators T-Shirt top for a quick shower before we set out became her first mistake. It was a delightful mistake to make. The sight of her, almost naked, except for a flimsy, blue, virtual see through thong, took my breath away. I was immediately drawn to her, and boy, she knew it! Totally unintentional as her actions had been, she smiled her cheeky devilish grin, realizing what she had brought out in me...again! The devil in us both took over. *Game if you are'*, became the only words spoken before we locked together in an embrace, and sure to delay our intended departure for DeLand. Could I ever get enough of this woman who could draw me to her like a powerful magnet? I doubted it. And for the next hour, we made a diversionary trip, but this one was to a place called heaven. As if ritual now, we never wanted it to end. However, heaven knows when the seeds of love have been sown, when life on earth has to be re-visited. Gloriously satisfied from the journey, it was just after midday before we were on the road to yet another world I was yet to see for the first time, Chelsea Martin's real world, where she spent her time and made her life.

    The sign post read – Deland 23 miles. Turning off International Speedway from Daytona, we headed north on 17-92, Woodland Blvd, for about a mile before the sign pointing west read Glenwood. My Mustang followed Chelsea's Ford Explorer onto picturesque Glenwood Road, following it through to an old cemetery, then over what they labeled 'the truck route' and past what might be a handy little tavern on the corner, a fire station, a church, before continuing through on the extended most delightful tree-lined street with many equally delightful houses, some large, some smaller, all bursting with flowers in the gardens, shrubs, trees, foliage. One thing I did notice, even the street names had a quaint individuality to the area – Emerald Forest, Meadowview, Glenwood Plantation, Briar Patch, Azalea. Someone, I believed, had had a rather vivid imagination to come up with so many descriptive names; regardless, they all suited.

    Enjoying the drive, moments later, with indicators flicking, we turned into a short, extended fern lined dirt track driveway that came out at a low set, green and brown painted ranch-style home, draped by huge majestic oaks. I swung my Mustang on to the red azalea adorned half-circular drive, parking out from the front door with its large friendly *'Welcome'* sign clearly visible.

    "Very nice…" became my immediate reaction and spoken with complete honesty while getting out of the car. Casually looking all around me I added "…you have a wonderful setting, and so far back off the road. I doubt you'd hear any noise from passing traffic out there."

"Nope, none at all" she replied making an offer at the same time. "Now, would you like a tour of the outside first or shall we head straight inside, although you must be famished, maybe we should have lunch instead."

"Whatever you say dear girl, whatever you say. I'm at your beck and call."

"Now *that* Mr. Thompson…' she lilted "…could be very dangerous but…" She never finished.

The house was a proverbial show piece. Working in real estate, I had seen many a home, from two-storey big, to town house small, brick to wood, clean to dirty and many differences in between. Chelsea Martin was obviously a woman who liked nice things, liked a house to be neat and tidy, and probably, quite fastidious when it came to décor and accessories. Her home would present well to prospective buyers. My thoughts snapped back to where they should be - her house was not for sale!

Over a ham salad croissant and a beer, in a capsule sort of way, I was brought up to speed about DeLand. As I listened, it occurred to me, we hadn't talked much about where either of us lived, Connecticut for me, Florida for Chelsea, although we had considered miles, the distance that separated us, that might come between us in a relationship. Cold hard facts now seemed somewhat more appropriate, real…our cruise had ended, real life continued.

DeLand, she enlightened me, was originally called Persimmon Hollow when the founder arrived however, through the incredible tenacity, work and community spirit of the early settlers, today it could boast some 30,000 in population. Important to the city was the world-class university, founded as a school house academy in 1883. It would later be re-named Stetson University under the auspices of a major contributing trustee, the hat magnate John B. Stetson, a dear friend of the city's founder, Henry Addison DeLand, who had talked him into coming down from Philadelphia in 1888. Small, historical and friendly was the way Chelsea described her hometown, and yes again, she was an original, born and bred here, a Bulldogs supporter…and very proud of it.

Lunch over, '…*so show me around*' I encouraged her - time to see this DeLand.

She was right! The drive into the small city downtown area was a pure delight. Entering through the wonderful tree lined (Woodland) Boulevard, through the most picturesque setting of the Stetson University grounds; Emily Hall was quite the masterpiece. Next came Flagler (a tribute to the railroad magnate), then Allen Hall, also Elizabeth Hall, named after the wife of John B. Stetson. Chelsea enjoyed pointing out to me, her attentive New England visitor that The Elizabeth Hall architecture was designed after many rather majestic buildings of Stetson's hometown of Philadelphia, including the cupola atop, modeled from the one on Independence Hall. He had wanted a reminder of his northern home, living, as he did through ill-health, every winter in DeLand, continuing to do so until his death in 1906. Unquestionably, the building was quite different to most of the others. Regardless, all were individually unique. Driving on, past the Stover Theatre beyond the Museum of Florida Arts, who could have asked for more? Even Deland Hall, a wood frame Second Empire style building with a bell tower, the original little school house built in 1884, the oldest building in Florida in continuous use for higher education, was still standing - a resplendent tribute to history. Many students filled the magnificent grounds, their books clutched tightly; natural Florida flora and fauna of many varieties graced the campus area, complimenting an absolute 'feeling of the South'. I had no doubt I would be back to learn more about the Stetson University history and to enjoy its surrounds.

Entering downtown DeLand, the shopping area, on the immediate other side of Stetson, Chelsea took the first available parking spot which, ironically, to me, was on the corner of the aptly named New York Avenue. It crossed Woodland and was deemed, from Deland's embryo of settlement (Persimmon Hollow) of the land bought to develop, the absolute '*centre of the city*'. Through the beautiful water-fall walkway of Chess Park in the Courthouse Plaza, we strolled through to nearby Indiana Street, and my guide, Ms. Chelsea Martin, couldn't have been more proud, particularly when she led me onward, well planned, to some stunning, mostly very large murals that abounded on so many of the downtown buildings. They told her story visually.

From the city namesake Henry A. DeLand himself, elderly handsome with his thick long gray beard and huge mustache, to the Riverboat Landing for new settlers, then, the Old Spanish Sugar Mill, also DeLand at the Turn of the Century, then came a cute one titled Old Style Bicycling the Boulevard, to finally on this part of our walk, a riverboat and Victorian style dressed travelers titled Pioneers at the Parceland - the carefully depicted paintings seemed never ending. I quickly began to learn much about Chelsea's hometown in a very unique and different way as she informed me, the huge stylized paintings would always remain, *'a work in progress'*.

The historic district of the downtown area of DeLand was quite a treat for a Northerner like me. I was used to seeing British heritage in street make-up as a background, and British architecture in buildings, very typical of our region, rightfully dubbed New England. In too many ways, it was exactly that and for the area, most appropriate. DeLand, meanwhile, offered a view visually much more Florida, southern in Americana, yet different enough again, not to emulate Virginia or the Carolina's, or other well known cities and places I'd taken great delight in seeing for the first time while venturing deeper into the Southern States.

Leisurely, we walked the Boulevard where many unique, small traditional stores abounded. Astoundingly, no franchise or name chain outlets were to be seen. It was wonderful! Grrs & Purrs for all things dogs and cats, Wolfe's for sculpture, gifts and pottery, dolls of every kind, from large to small, modern to vintage at the well stocked self-titled Dolls of DeLand, Mr. Bills or Cook's Kitchen for snacks, or maybe Dick & Jane's. Sweet Things had chocolate strawberries and other delights. Studio 308 was a home for budding local artists. Somewhere In Time specialty consignment, Anita's Home Décor, The Quilt Shop, Lace & Accessories, Treasures of the World with gifts from many countries, a Western Clothing store, also, a delightful book store called The Muse. Everything in this town was at one's fingertips, all in a setting both picturesque, entertaining and wonderfully fulfilling, for a shopper. To my inquisitive mind, there was no doubt about it; DeLand had captured a slice of American lifestyle and living that I loved. Add many delightful restaurants to the array of specialty shops that, in a million years, the conglomerates of the day, catering to mass consumers, could never capture or even re-capture, I was wandering through and around, a not only historic but an extremely unique and pretty city.

A couple of places I wanted to spend a little extra time browsing were the Antique stores, filled to the brim with a bye-gone era of products under the banner, *'everything old is new again'*. That could have been my first mistake; as fast as I had acknowledged my love of *'the old'* when it came to *'things'*, Chelsea took me by the hand saying nothing more than *'...you enjoy nostalgia and the like, things tied to yesterdays, there's one place you'll have to see.'* Loving music as I did, I thought it was going to be a place called Groovy Records I saw coming up ahead, but when we walked right by, two doors onward into Carassells on the Boulevard, my jaw about dropped. From comics to sports memorabilia, books, toy cars and die-cast figures, pop culture, postcards and posters, board games and so much more, all I could say was *'another day sweetheart. I need at least a couple of hours here, or more.'* The owner, I believed, dressed in a vintage car print shirt and very proud of his mass array of everything collectible and imaginable, was noticeably disappointed, but I assured him, *'you have my attention Sir, and like you know who, I'll be back!'*

Slowly, fascinated, I had seen and learned, through my most congenial and proud tour guide, what became my delightful entrée into Main Street America, southern style, a vivid reminder of so many vanishing aspects of the USA I recognized, yet felt, rightfully, should be preserved for future generations to share. The swift moving age of technology, selfish corporations and big business is slowly killing the small towns, changing the very face of a great and proud country, and for all the reasons proffered by Chelsea of her beloved Deland, in her adamant pontificating way, she gained no opposition from me.

This city, with elevated designer pavement sidewalks, large colorful potted plants, old-style street lamps and trees galore, was a picture-postcard example for old town America, an example to protect, to never be lost to the monopolies of multi-national business and chain stores. Call it the Mom and Pop store generation; too many were disappearing from the landscape. I was very impressed. As qualified by Chelsea, the promotionally, what must be, very active Deland Main Street Association, had every reason to be proud of their united efforts.

My tour over, I wondered if she had appeased me, of sorts, by taking me to the Boston Coffee House, just off the Boulevard, for a light snack and a latte', given it was visually eloquent, ala old-style New England, complete with an outside, chalk written board, highlighting the faire to be enjoyed. Acknowledging her choice, it had the desired effect, evidenced by my empty plate and a big smile that I knew pleased her.

Completely relaxed, our welcomed break together seriously over, it was time to call it a day and head out. For me, that should have meant to Daytona Beach and the Lodge. It wasn't about to be. Chelsea had other ideas. She wanted me to share the night with her, in her home, in the sanctity and peaceful serenity of her most idyllic setting…and how could I say no? This lady had already stolen my heart; I was clearly heading into unknown territory and deeper unchartered waters, and both were capable of bringing huge changes in my life. Being showered with so much love and caring, I was beginning to think that Jack Montgomery, and the State of Connecticut, might never see this born and bred northerner again. Unashamedly, I already had serious thoughts about defecting across state lines, and on this occasion, with all that was at stake, in what I'd shared, the South might finally win! I further began to think; I didn't know what to think at all, because Chelsea Martin had messed up my mind completely. I didn't want to leave her side. Her suggestion became a no contest. We headed back to Glenwood.

Comfortably ensconced, she poured me a spicy Captain Morgan over ice with a very small dash of cola at her well decorated built in bar. Different, I thought, while gracing a comfortable bar stool, drink in hand, glancing at the many delightfully framed feminine posters; mostly fashion styled that decorated the wall. Looking through to the long living room, separated by very tasteful French doors that were wide open, it too was decorated beautifully. I couldn't wait to see the pictures that hung resplendent, or the many photos neatly displayed on the end tables that matched the glass top coffee table, adorned with two large coffee table hard cover books. I immediately wondered what they might be. Pictures, posters, books, they could all tell you something about a person, their likes and interests? And the leather couches looked most inviting; everything was telling me, Chelsea Martin had immaculate taste, in fact, the couches, right down to the deep green color, looked eerily similar to mine back in Connecticut. Unknown great minds had thought alike. I snapped back to the moment.

My snatched eye-flitting visual tour of the room over, we opted to chat, instead of retreating to the nearby family room, known in Florida, for some unexplainable reason, as *'the Great Room'* where the huge Panasonic 50" plasma hi-def television was installed. Somehow, TV was not conducive to our first night in her home and would have been quite counterproductive of our desire, to just *'sit and talk awhile'*, her words, and I had no problem with that. I wanted to know more about the woman who had so far, since we met, not missed a single beat in making herself, not only alluring, but intriguing, and quite fascinating to a man, who sought nothing more than simplicity in life, a little lovin', and above all else, honesty, especially in longer term commitments. I'd already had a bad one! That, in itself, was hard enough. As for a relationship, where two people could share a common bond, I was already beginning to feel one with Chelsea, as I believed, fervently hoped, she was too, however, unquestionably, there was still so much we didn't know about each other. In conversation, the evening would become an extension of mind over, certainly a lot of small talk... and certainly – passion! There could be no better setting for what turned out to be a very interesting night.

CHAPTER

SEVEN

Three days later - I phoned the Sun King Lodge in Daytona Beach to tell Gareth Harrison; I was not lost, that I was still in the land of the living, assuring him; I would be continuing my stay at the resort and *'not to worry.'* He was grateful for the call, and yes – he had been concerned, but not overly, he added with a laugh in his voice, after all, as a guest, I was more than paid up; he reminded me.

"Something's got your attention..." he proposed, "...and I can only assume, maybe, that it might have a little something to do with that absolutely gorgeous lady I saw you with here at the Lodge last time. Am I close, or has Florida's brilliant weather kept you traveling around the State?" He'd broken his own rule; curiosity had gotten the better of him, but I didn't mind.

"You're right, on both counts actually. Chelsea is her name, the one you saw me with and well, yes, she's won my heart for sure, but truthfully, so has the never ending sunshine. I can't lose really can I Gareth?"

"I doubt it, but don't worry; your room is safe, just keep me posted, I'm here to help no matter what you might need, okay? Call anytime."

Three Days Later

If there was one thing I liked about my commercial landlord host, it was his everyday relaxed attitude that exuded attention to detail, care of the customer, and a genuine warmth that had to get him plenty of repeat business, or at least I'd like to believe so. He was definitely consistent.

After my discovery tour of DeLand, Chelsea had urged me to stay with her; especially given she had to head back to work after what was termed, nicely, a mind altering and even life-changing experience for us both – the cruise. She had framed her thoughts in such a way I just couldn't say no when she posed the idea that was gratifying, but more, a really wonderful feeling to hear *'…it'd be marvelous to have you home when I come back from work. It'd make me feel special, cared about, even if only for a day or so, and truthfully, I like the general thought of it all too.'*

In many ways, it was a very bold statement for her to make, one I gladly accepted, all the while inwardly knowing, I too, more than just cared for her, and I would have moved heaven and earth to make her feel special, loved. And in being totally honest with myself, I certainly *did* want to spend more time with her. Fact was, the way I was feeling about now; I didn't want to leave her, leave DeLand or for that matter, Florida, at all, *if ever!*

Oddly, accepting once what might have been the inevitable, and was prepared for it, I had never dismissed one very logical thought; that when the cruise and Chelsea's few vacation days were over, I'd have to face stark reality and head back to the world and mission I had created for myself in my quest for some sanity in my life; a clearing of the head and the re-charging of my batteries. It was, after all, my original plan and yet, right now it all seemed so very unimportant.

When Chelsea suggested *'hanging out at home a little longer'*, her words, it was a very easy yes. I loved the idea, the challenge for us as two people, to find out if the timing was right in my own personal psyche of it being an accepted, natural thing to do. I'd concluded a yes, yes and yes to pretty much every conceivable reason I gave myself *not* to head back to Daytona Beach. Furthermore, without question, for me, Chelsea's home was a very inviting place to gain some easy lay back downtime after our somewhat hectic few days - despite my empathy for her given, *'duty called'*. That was a most unfortunate downside, but in her profession, Doctor's, had huge demands made on them – every day.

Seven o'clock came way too early. When the piano of Frank Mills burst into life playing Music Box Dancer from somewhere in the room, initially, it mildly startled me. It was certainly a different way to be woken up versus an annoying series of beeps or the traditional ringing of an alarm. Chelsea leaned over, tapped the small white digital box on the dresser to stop the music, and then, gently flipped herself over to look directly at me. Eyes half open, my head was still down low in the soft pillow. I couldn't resist looking up at her. She smiled, lovingly. She was to me, also, early morning beautiful.

"Good morning Mr. Thompson. I trust you slept well last night?"
You just had to love her.
"Are you kidding?" I jokingly replied "After last night, I think we might have to swear a truce and regain some energy. You are wearing me out Miss Martin, literally, wearing me out, but don't get me wrong; I love it. Oh, and to answer your question, yes, I slept like a log."

She leaned forward to kiss my cheek. Everything I had just said became totally irrelevant. I reached for her, wanting her to lie close beside me for those few extra minutes before her new workday really began.

Showing no resistance, she snuggled into me, under the blankets, pressing her soft, warm, naked body gently into mine. Instinctively, she knew I wanted her. Moving slowly, with ease, she raised herself to lay her body over the full length of mine, her arms wrapped around me. We lay there, in silence, almost still. Shared temptation began to take over. With just the slightest of movements, effortlessly, as if it were meant to be, we were one. Our arms held each other even tighter. For the next few moments, we lay together, almost still - slight movement, then still again. Chelsea snuggled deeper into me, nestling my head with hers. It was a beautiful, tender moment;

two people joined together, then, expectedly, to coin the phrase; the earth moved uncontrollably, followed with a heavy sigh, and a shudder, that made my whole body tremble. There were no choices. It was all true. I'd been a victim, under the spell of a goddess; I was captivated, consumed, satisfied to surrender, without the hint of a fight.

Chelsea Martin had a charm I could not resist. With her body entwined with mine, I heard the words I was enraptured to hear, but mildly, still, scared to believe, given I was of the same mind. *'I love you Tony, every day you make me fall deeper in love with you'.* Under the blankets, in the soft warm bed, we didn't want to part, leave. We lay in each other's arms for what seemed the longest time. Without hesitation, my heart was telling me it was all right, *'I love you too Chelsea. You've changed my life. You've changed me, and where we go from here, I still don't know, but nothing will ever stop me from telling you, that I love you too'.* Soon, sadly, morning, our day, began anew.

~~~~~~~~~~

Chelsea, I had learned, over our many long verbal 'get to know each other' conversations, a Doctor, participated in a three-way partnership practice locally on Stone Street with two other doctors under the shingled banner 'Darin, Martin & Barnhill'. It was a busy office, almost too busy, as they had elected to include patients under both the State Medicaid and Medicare programs, something many of their fellow doctors were unwilling to do, because they could make more money catering exclusively for patients with private insurance.

It was interesting to hear her explanation of why their practice did what they did. By including both programs, they could help many more people, and especially, many who would be denied even a basic consultation, based on nothing more than money. She was appalled at the belief; money, and money alone was a huge driving, motivating factor for too many of her chosen profession. Noble and necessary as the profession is, joining it wasn't always for the betterment of people, society, or to help eradicate life-threatening diseases or illnesses. Facts are; it was a job, a highly skilled job, and therefore, the perfect way to accumulate personal wealth. There was also a certain elite image that went along with being a doctor, and most knew it, dwelled on it, and many took advantage of it. Chelsea and her partners were quite the opposite.

Over many occasions of being able to simply sit and talk, she had pontificated at length; her different slant on wanting to be a doctor, her philosophy being quite simple; to be a responsible care giver and to benefit humanity at large. She constantly gave of her time and service to help others less fortunate, or disadvantaged, with the more recent example being her biggest yet; six days in Haiti after a devastating earthquake that took the lives of thousands and left many more homeless, without food, water or shelter. The tiny nation's biggest problem was the threat of disease, the need for medicines, the children, the elderly – help was needed, especially from doctors. Chelsea had heard the call, and as her heart had told her, heeded the call - she replied.

As for family, her Father had died in Vietnam while she was still a child. Her Mother, Rose, devastated as she recalled, then, witnessing her many year's heartbreak, sadness, never chose to remarry. *'She couldn't get over Frankie'* Chelsea shared, referring to her Father. *'Mother loved him too much'.* Raised an only child, mother and daughter would remain forever close. Still, today, Rose lived not far from her over on what Chelsea simply called 'Hidden Hollow'. I assumed it to be a street nearby. *'You'll meet her'* she added softly, with reverence. There was an obvious very strong love between the two.

~~~~~~~~~~

Reading the locally delivered DeLand Beacon newspaper, learning the entire goings-on in around the city, and neighboring towns, including Volusia County, the well scripted pages were an eye-opener to this Main Street USA town I was beginning to absolutely enjoy, more and more every day. I was certainly looking forward to more personal interactions with the locals. Accepting that premise, gaining local knowledge was one thing; too much idle time was another.

With Chelsea away at work, I had no trouble amusing myself. From watching a DVD or reading Jeffrey Archer's Paths of Glory, my choice of book had me silently wondering if it was a hangover from my days of Jessica, who I recalled, had introduced me to the writer years ago. I hoped not! Another diversion, considered odd for me I well knew, sometimes I'd even take a little nap, tired maybe from doing virtually nothing, especially given my normal lifestyle of work back in Connecticut. Nothing mattered though; I was on vacation, thoroughly enjoying my relaxed downtime.

A more active and delightful chore I was able to physically undertake, much to the delight of Chelsea, was some easy needed work in her once, obviously, very nicely landscaped yard, now though, just slightly overgrown in places. The end result was gratifying, much more so when Chelsea gushed verbally of the visuals, she wholeheartedly approved of. That was a personal feel-good to me and I always welcomed a *'feel-good'* moment. They did the soul wonders.

Then, a new revelation! After her work one evening, while sitting and chatting over a drink, I was not sure if Chelsea remembered exactly what she had told me on board our Caribbean Sunshine cruise. Relaying a somewhat added to, a different story of sorts, she expressed a lot more of the intimate details about her former husband that were certainly contrary to his simply preferring hunting, fishing, and being more with the boys. Confessing, with more clarity, his background in itself was most enlightening; her now long gone ex, Robert Martin, was born and bred in Nacogdoches in the Lone Star State and after graduating from the University of Texas in Dallas, from experience gained, he finally landed a position in DeLand, at Stetson University. It was here they had met and married. Her embellishment in greater depth revealed, specializing to a Master of Arts in Political Science; he was a well respected academic of many years, but a scandal, they both could have done without, would force his move, not only from the area, but from Florida altogether. He went on to re-settle in Tulsa, Oklahoma, but not before their divorce that had very quickly followed. Chelsea qualified; she had not seen or heard of him since. For reasons known only to her, and I never asked for specifics; she chose to leave the finite details of the scandal that rocked the town alone, suggesting rather simply *'it was a sad demise of a good man but, in life, there are consequences. Everyone paid a price on that one'.* I got the drift, and while intrigued, again, decided to remain silent, conceding to myself only; while I'd like to know what really happened, right now, it wasn't important. Regardless, it had been quite a revelation already, and undoubtedly; *that* break-up had real substance.

Meanwhile, as the days ticked by, I became more fascinated at what was probably fast looming, someday, to be my new hometown. Anxious to learn all I could, back in the historic downtown area, I took many photos of the painted walls I had loved seeing previously with Chelsea, only this time; I was partaking in an official DeLand Historic Mural Walk tour. Included, as part of it, were many of the buildings so wonderfully preserved?

First, majestic and stately, the magnificent Volusia County Court House, across from which was the seemingly abandoned County jail with its eerie looking elevated exposed exercise yard. Next came the stunningly beautiful, now fully reconstructed, Athens Theatre that dated back to 1922, its stage have graced the talents of a bye-gone era; Eddie Cantor, Sophie Tucker, Fannie Bryce and even the silent movies screen legend, western megastar Tom Mix and his horse Tony. Today, the Athens is as popular as it was I was told and judging by the shows coming up, I knew it would be long before Chelsea and I ventured there to enjoy the experience.

Back out on the Boulevard viewing some stylish lattice work on the 1910 DeLand Opera House that reeked of southern charm, and for some 60 years now, still housed Hunters Restaurant; everything around me portrayed the obvious; DeLand was a spectacular, well presented and protected town. One sight that brought a tinge of a lost yesterday to my mind came when passing a once familiar red and white striped barber's pole of Freddie's Old School Barbershop, another relic of a visual past and fitting for an historic downtown tour. I hadn't seen one in years.

Most thoughtful, rarely seen in any community, were the many public seats readily available allowing one to simply sit and watch the world go by. I graced one more than once, thinking, the more I see, the more I like what many take for granted. I vowed not to.

The lush green spacious and beautiful setting of the Stetson University grounds had many informative reasons to visit, including the Museum of Florida Art however, none more special than the original old house of the city founder, Henry A. DeLand. Stepping back in time to when, as Chelsea had already shared with me, on his arrival, the area was known as Persimmon Hollow, it was easy to see the vision forward as he set out to make the required homesteaded 160 acres he had bought for a mere $1,000.00 for his (then) "Athens of Florida." As a Yankee from the north, which, for the likes of me (and he) could be endearingly termed, then and still, there was something special about southern hospitality that I could see and feel all around me.

Slightly detoured, I ventured to find the Old DeLand Memorial Hospital. Given Chelsea's profession, I had a need to see it, understand her hometown history. It was a moving tribute; the memorial wall was dedicated to all veterans of all wars of the USA. Of special note was the special plaque honoring Deland's Tuskegee Airman, Charles T. Bailey. I'd seen the powerful, well made movie depicting their valor, and understood their rightful, historic place in history. I was sincerely touched. I was glad I visited the site.

A never tiring sight to behold, I loved the Spanish moss that grew and hung so delicately and intriguingly picturesque from the trees. Beneath them, around them, I could clearly hear the South through the many locals, although in Chelsea, I never heard the heavier southern drawl many inhabitants had, just a delightful ring of pure charm when she spoke, with mere tinges of a southern accent, emphasized particularly when she threw in *'y'all',* and the many other cute phrases used; *'sack'* for a grocery bag, or *'hankerin'* meaning a desire, then, *'fixin' to'* when planning something, *'ornery'* being irritable and *'every-which-a-ways'* meaning...here, or there, or somewhere I guessed? You had to concede to the differences. And yes, it was catching! Sometimes, but only when I was comfortable in doing so, I even mimicked them.

For all my exploring and learning about DeLand, I couldn't wait for Chelsea to come on home. Today, I had so much to share and wanted to ask her. First and foremost though, importantly, one thing I always wanted her to know and to draw comfort from; that at the end of her day, I'd be there, waiting for her. She would always call in advance to tell me she was homeward bound. Standing in the driveway, as I tried to do most days, as her car turned in from the street, down the dirt track to where I longingly waited for her, the smile on her face was worth a million dollars. Thankfully, she too couldn't wait to see me. Bounding out of the car, even leaving the door wide open, she fell straight into my waiting arms. That hug was quite an original homecoming hello. I responded accordingly, returning the love I felt.

"Oh if you only knew how long this day seems to have been and how long I've been waiting to see your face again. God I'm so happy right now..." she confessed. Chelsea held on to me as if I were gold, adding, "...I think I might need a drink!" before slowly, reluctantly, pulling away.

"To be perfectly honest girl, I feel exactly the same way."

A drink, a chat – it was a magic formula. Heading for the bar, she stopped, turned, looked into my face, beamed that smile again, and then hit me with a string of questions, worried I might be getting bored out of my mind.

"So how was your day anyway? What did you do, where did you go, anywhere?"

She was delighted to know I had wasted no time making myself familiar with the city. Glued to my every word, over our quiet *'stiff drink'* in the Florida Room, overlooking the lawns and rose garden, I shared my experiences.

When she was quite sure she had learned everything I had done, every place I had been, and every sight I had seen, right down to *'had I met anyone interesting at all?'* when I finally managed to pose the same question *'...so how was your day'*, she delighted in telling me in one word only *'Boring!'* then, after a pause added, *'...because I knew you were home or out there somewhere, without me'.*

We'd missed each other. My heart melted; what a marvelous way to have expressed her feelings.

'Okay, over to you again" she said, leaning back, now completely relaxed, ready it appeared. "You had something you wanted to ask me. I'm here to listen?"

"Yeah I do Chelsea. It has to do with where we live, and it's been on my mind most of the afternoon and...no, I don't mean Glenwood or this house."

Instantly, I saw the intrigued, almost confused expression on her face, fearing no doubt, a change for us both in plans or direction was about to come. Taking doubt from her mind, I threw water on the fears.

"It's about my travels today and my insatiable appetite of needing to know, after all, Deland and you are both consuming me, but don't get me wrong, I love it, really, I do!"

Daytona was obvious, DeLand, I was embracing daily, rapidly; however, I really knew little about the broader region known as 'The South'. Anxious to learn more, I took the subject up with enthusiasm. Locals today had shared some of their thoughts with me, I wanted the real story. Fortunately, it seemed my subject delighted Chelsea. Happy to accommodate, she took a more comfortable position, then, to have me better comprehend it all, she began to explain.

Her opening point; one has to understand as realistic overview, the distinct differences, as to how the South is perceived, and, in reality, its defined geographic region. Distinct for reasons such as; culture and certainly history, but also, she added with conviction; music, literature, art, cuisine, language, customs.

To this boy from the North, the information imparted was intriguing; there seemed so many, so much diversity, and Chelsea had nailed it all down, all in one sentence?

In broad terms and as is generally understood, I soon became aware; the South is made up by as many as sixteen states from as far north as Delaware and Maryland, across to the Virginia's, all the way down to east Texas, clear across to Florida. Meanwhile, the 'Deep South', a very commonly used expression and recognition, comprises primarily Alabama, Mississippi, Georgia and South Carolina, taking in parts of Arkansas, Tennessee and Northern Florida from the Panhandle to the northern section, including Jacksonville and Tallahassee.

DeLand, Chelsea chose to add, is probably a slight stretch, maybe a little too far down the state to be included, not that it deterred her southern pride and claims. However, as she explained succinctly, it didn't stop there.

Next came; The Old South, The Upper South, The Gulf South, Southern Appalachia and Dixie until finally, and I can't say I was shocked at the geographic lesson I had just been given; I was more confusingly mystified, while at the same time, somewhat lost too.

Frankly, learning all I had in school about American history, or particularly, the Civil War as it related to the subject we were discussing, the South had never taken a special hold on me any more than the Lewis and Clarke Expedition, the California Gold Rush, The Alamo, the Louisiana Purchase or many other major events that shaped our country. Important yes; but they were but incidents of history. My sudden realization was; I had obviously not given much thought about history in general at all, or to the many differences and contrasts that went on to grow our Nation - period! Now, though, this very day, when I started to look at making a home here, in what I believed was very much a part of the South, deep or otherwise, everything took on a different perspective.

Chelsea had been quite the teacher, a missed vocation I momentarily thought, but regardless; as of this moment, I had a greater respect for the region, especially Florida, but specifically, the area I was in, Volusia County, and the people, many who gave so much to make the South a most unique part of the United States.

Our discussion over, my tutor lightened the moment; a social event awaited our presence.

Three Days Later

Not that I was a culinary expert, but I knew my way around a kitchen. However, good as my original intentions were, tonight we had decided, well me anyway, was not going to be the night I'd make my often promised specialty dish, homemade spaghetti full of herbs and garlic. We'd already established we both liked pasta, but another time maybe. We'd dine out, *'my treat'* I told Chelsea. She made a quick phone call, after confirming it was all right, then shared that she wanted me to meet a couple of her dear friends, neighbors. I had no problem with that, in fact, welcomed the chance. I wanted to know more of Chelsea's life and friends.

'I'll pick you up' she told them before pressing the screen on her Droid to shut down her cell phone. Minutes later we were gone. Neighbors or not, we needed transport.

Turning into Ben Franklin Drive, Meghan and Mark were waiting for pick up, having re-sealed their home cooked meatloaf meal already prepared before the invite. Ever the best of company in Chelsea's life, they loved dining out, so it was an easy call for them to put their dinner into the freezer for another day. However, they made it quite clear as they joined us; first, we have to meet the dogs, their playful babies. Little Rosie and Maddie, ever faithful, had followed them to the door and were now anxious to clamber all over these new-found people standing in their midst. I could see why they adored them both, excited and friendly as they were, running around our legs, jumping up as if to say hello. And of course, they loved to be patted.

With the welcome doggie visit over, Rosie and Maddie back inside, Meghan wasted no time declaring, she and Mark were famished. *'Let's get there'* she threw out as a cheerful order. Easy to figure, they were already layback 'fun folk', a Chelsea-ism! Minutes later again, our pre-dinner drinks served; we ordered Italian from the small but rather varied menu at Luigi's at Brandywine; a favorite of everyone's in the group. This being my first for Luigi's, I vowed to reserve judgment. It would turn out; they were absolutely right.

~~~~~~~~~~

Jack Montgomery called – again! He had left at least seven voice-mail messages, either on my private cell phone, or, at The Lodge. I was not in the habit of turning on my cell, and in fact, lately, had hardly checked it at all. I'd been adamantly clear at the outset; I didn't want to hear from anyone. Jack meanwhile, on one of his messages, had called it *'ridiculous, overkill'* to not at least double check him out, *'just in case'*, adding that I was being overly sensitive to life, whatever that meant? Out of the everyday loop, on hearing what sounded like urgency in his voice, I knew I had to call.

With Chelsea at work at her practice, I had headed over to Daytona to check on my room, ready to consider my next move, option? Decision time was looming; I knew it. The Sun King Lodge or…graciously, relayed with much love in her voice, Chelsea shared; she was more than happy for me to spend what time I needed, as a base, with her in Glenwood, rather than pay for a hotel. On one hand, it was what I wanted, while on the other…? I'd lose my freedom, a small downside given the way I felt about her, and yes; it was a very tempting offer. Realistically, unquestionably, with time spent, I was being drawn to Chelsea more and more. And yet - as much as I had once thought I would drive all over Florida seeing the many wonderful sights as a tourist, clearly, I hadn't left my base at all, and for good reasons. Things had changed, drastically. Now I knew - I was certainly not ready to leave Florida (Daytona) anytime soon and most certainly not ready to leave Chelsea either – yet! Ever?

"Tony…' Montgomery started "…you don't want to hear this, and I don't want to have to tell you, but comrade old pal, I have no damned choice!"

His tone, the urgency, the words, set me back. It didn't sound promising. I braced myself for something he was probably right about - that I wouldn't want to hear it. Then, the bombshell!

"It's Jessica." He said, inflecting her name harshly..

Two words spoken and he was one hundred percent right - I didn't! The last thing I wanted to hear was anything at all about her. She was a long-gone memory. I'm well over her. Unfortunately, he then let loose with the bigger bad news.

Three Days Later

"She's back in town and back here at the office, and I mean, *at the office*. Every damn day Tony and she's almost *demanding* to know where you are, and what you're doing. She wants to talk to you and from what I gather, it's over between her and whoever that other dude was she left with way back then, but I have to tell you old friend, she won't take no for an answer. She's poured her heart out and apparently her heart wants back to you, *with you*, so what now comrade? It's hard to listen to I'll tell ya that!"

Furious, I was about to respond when he started up again, this time, the question posed sounded more like an afterthought, although I might have guessed the subject under the circumstances.

"What *are* you up to anyway, speaking of that, because I haven't heard a word from you along the way, not that it matters that much really but..."

I chose to interrupt him. I'd heard enough. What he'd relayed to me, was already loaded.

"*Jack*, the only thing I can say is, I don't particularly care *what* Jessica wants, *what* she does, *what* she thinks, *what* she feels, or any other *damn* thing else. She left me long ago; it's all over; we're divorced for Christ's sake, and I really couldn't give one royal *you know what* about her, or about *anything* she wants, for that matter, I'm so well done with her. *Please*, tell her that and tell her to take a hike, a *big* one, no deal."

"Say what you will Tony..." my friend threw back at me "...but it's out of my hands, out of my control and hell, what can anyone do but *you* to shut the whole mess down if that's the way you feel, I mean, there was a time when you'd have given the world to be back with her and sure, I know it's over, divorced and all that, but look; she's *not* going away and oh, by the way"... he paused "...frankly; she's still looking pretty dang good I have to admit."

That was something else I didn't want to hear, my mind was closed. I was also sorry I had checked my voice mail and returned Jack Montgomery's call, not that any of this was his fault. Now, I had no choice, but get back to Jessica, thankfully, however, strictly through Jack.

"Tell her I'm not interested Jack, in fact, you can tell her I've found someone new and whatever we had is over, gone, dead and gone. Tell her anything, embellish it, and tell her anyway you want to, but just be sure to tell her, okay?"

The call, the news, everything, had really infuriated me. My partner, nevertheless, agreed to help.

"I was only kidding with that last remark Tony, but be assured; I'll do whatever I can, however, do one thing for me will you, stay in touch, at least in the short term. Whatever's going to happen to will, but you have got to know; she's kind of frantic. I have to assume she fouled up badly with the other guy and has now had a big epiphany about *you*; so, here she is again, *back* on your doorstep. I guess it's just as well you're not here because I'll tell you; the scenario is not all together pretty. That said and agreed though, let me ask, backing up a bit, enlighten me comrade. Are you telling me you've found someone? Have you got something going on you want to share with me man, anything at all?"

I wanted to tell Jack about Chelsea but after listening to what I'd just heard, I felt the timing wasn't right. It could wait. A bigger problem existed.

"No Jack" I lied. "If I did, you'd be the first to know. I'm just enjoying the sights, the sun, the freedom and I needed it, as well you knew, and by the way, thanks; you're a good friend to have. Right now, I'm more than happy to hang out here in Florida. I'll talk to you later, okay?"

I didn't let him answer, hitting the end button to cancel, while uttering a loud profanity, this time by absolute, preferred, choice – anger! Now what, I thought, lazing back on the hotel bed. Even the shimmering water of the ocean couldn't get my attention. I didn't need this hassle, and didn't need Jessica wanting back in my life. She'd made her decisions and made California her life, so what could she *possibly* want from me? If it had all gone wrong for her, after all this time, if the guy she left me for had done to her, what she did to me - it wasn't my concern. My life with her was over. I had loved Jessica; I'd been good to her, but I'd also moved on. Heck - my life was already changing in ways I never thought possible. I was happy again. Heaven forbid, I thought; I have some looming major decisions of my own to make, thankfully though, they were all one-hundred percent nice decisions. Once, I believed, I could have taken Jessica back, and back then, I even wanted to, would have, but now, there was no hope. Jessica, for me, would remain where she once put me, totally out in the cold. My time and that chapter of my life, was closed.

The very thought of all I had just heard had me heading for the small balcony for some fresh air. I actually thought I might gag! How dare Jessica to be so cavalier and expecting. I looked out across the Atlantic; the water was its usual deep green, the skies above, a contrasting, ever faithful, bright blue with only the hint of clouds. It was another perfect Sunshine State day; the Florida sun of a welcomed spring-time beat down on me. It was wonderful. From thoughts of cold, I was warm, deliriously warm; all I could think of was Chelsea. It was a beautiful feeling, to know; I was once again really loved. My inner decision was final. There could never be any turning back.

A return call from Jack Montgomery woke me from the light doze I had been in. How long I had been 'out of it' I had no immediate idea. On listening to him, if he had shocked me the first time, this time, the updated news he relayed was a double shock!

CHAPTER

EIGHT

Gareth Harrison was a little disappointed when I told him I'd be checking out. That business called, that I needed to make an urgent quick trip back to Connecticut. He understood, promising, if all worked out, and I came back; my room would be waiting, that he wouldn't assign it to anyone unless the Lodge filled up, which he highly doubted this time of the year.

"Have a safe trip Tony, call me anytime. We're at your service here, you know that. Either way, stay in touch and come on back now, ya hear?" Southern talk?

"Thanks G…" as I now called him "…appreciate it, and I'm sorry for being a little elusive before in telling you I had to leave, but frankly, it's an ex-wife problem. Just when I thought, my life was getting some even keel balance about it again, a problem, and man, I don't need it, but you do what you've gotta do. I'll be back though and hopefully sooner than later."

"I hear you man…" he said, and I thought, now, mimicking me "… believe me; you're certainly not on your own with that one. I've seen plenty from around here…" briefly explaining, there had been many times when people, single, alone, or couples, had come to the

Sun King to find each other again or, alternately, often, escape someone. '…it can be like a doctor's office' he added innocently.

The word doctor jarred me. I hadn't mentioned a thing yet to Chelsea about Jessica, wondering even, if I should. *What!* I shook my head. *I'm* the one who had talked about honesty in relationships with her, and yet, here; I doubted if I should tell her about the drama back in Hartford at all. My better instincts gave me the answer, the last thing I wanted to do was throw all we had found, with, and in each other, under the proverbial bus.

Shaking hands, bidding G, 'mine host', a fond farewell, instead of heading straight for I-95 North, I slipped the Mustang into gear with the more sensible plan to head back on 92, westbound for Deland. It was a Saturday; Chelsea was off for the weekend. With good intentions, we had originally planned a trip over to Mt. Dora to the popular long weekend Renniger's Antique Fair. I knew I could have waited until Monday to share the bad news with Chelsea, but my nagging pangs of honesty, and guilt, had really gotten the better of me. I decided to air, fully, my Jessica problem with her under my banner of, 'no secrets.'

"You can't be serious…" was her instant response to my delivered Connecticut problem "…*who* does this woman think she is, to just try and burst back into your life like that, it's outrageous. Surely, you have, at the very least, some legal avenues to put in place, to end the stupidity. I mean, isn't *what* she's doing considered trespassing too?"

Her response was nothing more than pure logic and hearing it put that way, absolutely true.

"I know, and you're right Chelsea, but I *have* to fix it and frankly; I can't do it from here, there's no simple way out of it, which means heading back up north but that's no doubt the easy bit as I see it. The fact is, I'm more worried about *you*. You and I, that is, and *that's* the truth."

~~~~~~~~~~

Jessica, not remarrying, and still carrying my name was probably the first shock to me after hearing of her antics from Jack Montgomery. I had fully expected her to have married the man she left me for when they moved to settle out in California, but I guess he had thought differently. I had no idea why they had broken up, but in returning to Hartford now, if it was simply to believe she could pick up where she left off, then she was horribly mistaken. Our divorce, while amicable and easy in its execution, was exactly what it meant – divorced – over, ended, fini, no more. Surely, even she understood *that!* My love for her died forever the day I read the two words, that back then, had haunted me for the longest time - *'Decree Absolute'*. I remembered them only too well.

According to Jack, with the new added information as he understood it, Jessica, seemingly, had other ideas. Unfortunately, compounding the problem, I had also made a rather bad mistake. *Make that huge mistake!* I had never changed the locks on my door and frankly, never really thought much about it…until now. After our divorce, I had elected not to sell the house we owned together, choosing instead, to pay her out in settlement of the property when I decided to keep it. Real estate then, still, now, wasn't exactly buoyant, and I wasn't about to take a loss on any *fire sale* due to a divorce. I understood the business; I chose the easier way in settlement. Jessica had been paid out, in total, for every penny owing, for what was rightfully hers, her share. Our once joint home together, legally, by deed title, became mine.

I was mortified to find out; Jessica had taken up temporary residence in my home and planned on staying there until I returned from wherever she thought I was, in her words, *'so we could sit and talk'*. She was desperate to see me, and according to Jack Montgomery, had absolutely *no* intentions of going anywhere, at least until that happened. He was as stunned as me but didn't quite know which way to turn.

"I can't believe you never changed those locks Tony?"

Me neither, I sadly realized.

"I can tell you this though…" he continued, "…she is most adamant about talking to you, clearly implying, if you're not with anyone, which I must admit I did elude to, then she was going to wait. She asked me where you were, intimating correctly, that I'd probably know, or would certainly have a good idea as to just where, but believe me comrade; I told her nothing, absolutely nothing. She said *'well, I'll wait'* adding *'I have nothing else to do'*. That was it. I have to say though, the lock thing threw me. However, to think, even after all this time, she *still* had keys Tony. Incredible, I can't believe it, or you." His sarcasm registered.

"What did you tell her about trespassing, the police, or breaking in? Did any of that come up in conversation?" I asked, shaking my head in disbelief at the absolute bizarre situation I faced.

"Yep, and all she said was, *'whose gonna call the cops Jack, you?'* I was stumped!"

"Yeah I understand Jack. It's not exactly your problem and sure; I have a case if I want to call the Hartford Police, but how in the hell can I really do that, I mean, I was married to her for 12 years, what kind of a crap thing would that be to do, but then again…hell, *what am I gonna do?*" I questioned, not expecting a real answer from my friend who had been kind enough to take care of the place while I was away which, under normal circumstances was a breeze. Now, with all I had learned, I was more than aware; I had a problem, and a big one, one I'd have to sort out quietly, unless I elected to go the other way, probably the right way, and be mercenary about it? I was in a momentary silent quandary when Jack made a simple suggestion.

"Tony, why don't I just straight out call the cops and have her evicted; *hell,* charged even if you want to. I can fix it faster that way, although it could get a bit ugly of course, but whatever you think, just tell let me know, gimme your thoughts, and whatever they are – consider it done! I'll have no problem with it."

My head was spinning as I pondered his, probably, most logical suggestion. Seconds later, I proceeded to impart the dumbest decision I might ever make.

"Here's all I can really think Jack, the only thing I can logically do. I don't *want* to, but I guess I'll come on back and sort it all out myself, in person; however, you've got to let me go again. We did have an agreement about my time away from the office, and I still want that. Is that okay?" I proposed, expecting an immediate affirmative reply.

"Sure it is, that's okay I guess, but something tells me Tony, there's a lot *more* I should know? It's just a feeling, so over to you, is there something you haven't fully come clean about yet?"

I had the chance. It was more than a fair question and Jack Montgomery certainly deserved an answer.

"I'll tell you more when I see you Jack, but yeah, there is, and I'll explain later, bear with me huh. I'll see you in a couple of days or so. For now, let's leave it at that. I'll call ya!"

~~~~~~~~~~

Cautiously, I had told Chelsea all I knew, explaining myself and the circumstances of all that had transpired, as best I thought I could. She looked confused as well as, a first for me, and us - slightly aggravated. I tried to defuse it somewhat, admitting there were choices to solve it.

"I figure that's about all I can do Chelsea, either *that*, or call the cops and have them fix it by remote control from here. It's very much a kind of a catch twenty-two, but as you can see, I've got to do *something*. The whole thing is obviously, maybe absurdly, but unquestionably, a rather big mess all up, and I hate the thought of it, what's happened?"

After a lingering moment of silence, Chelsea responded. In doing so, she proceeded to say everything I really didn't want to hear.

"Well Tony, I'm really not sure what to say. The reality of the situation is, *she,* somehow I can't seem to endearingly say her name, *she,* has virtually burgled into your home, keys or no keys as they do not rightfully belong to her, but she certainly has no rights to just enter your home, which could effectively be *anyone's* home. The situation would be the same. This woman does *not* belong there; she's trespassing, which is the important secondary factor if you took away the burglary aspect. Facts are; you simply can't just wander into someone's home, so called know them or not, and take up residence. I mean, who is kidding who here? It's a form of unlawful squatting, but the short, realistic answer from your point of view, to me is, *yes,* in a stand-alone situation, call the police and have something done,

Three Days Later

which you'd do whether you're down here in Florida or not, because, frankly, you could have been anywhere. Now, on the other hand, maybe you could instruct your caretaker, in this case, your friend Jack Montgomery, to get the police over and between them, make an agreed 'good faith' civilized plea to cease and desist, leave immediately, or face charges, whatever they figure them out to be. You've given Montgomery the lawful guardian right, the keys and custody of your property, and heaven forbid; you're both realtors anyway, so you must have *some* ideas between you. It's logic to me. There, you asked me, I've told you."

"Silly question I'm sure, but here goes anyway. I don't suppose you could get any time off to come to Connecticut with me huh?" I asked, hoping Chelsea might, and also, that I might have posed the very question she actually wanted me to ask of her. I was dead wrong! She was adamant.

"*No, I can't* Tony, there's *no* way. Too many people rely on me. I have an awful lot of patients with confirmed appointments. I'd scheduled the time away I wanted before, enjoyed it immensely I must say, even met you, however, to get more time now, the short answer is still no. I can't."

"I didn't think so" my obvious reply. "I just wasn't sure, but the thing is…"

I never got to finish as I started out to tell her, I really understood. Chelsea reacted, talking over me, remaining equally adamant, but this time, much more direct. She was obviously miffed, or could it have been, angry? I was about to find out – diplomatic anger would be the verdict.

"Tony, here's the way I see it. You and I have something special. I love you and have told you I love you. I do. I truly want to be a part of your life, to share my life with you, and work out what's good for you and me, Connecticut or not, Florida or not, whatever. We have some issues of our own and fortunately, until this moment, I thought they were all wonderful issues, one's I wanted to sit down and see through, but now, your *ex-wife* comes into play, and you buckle, *buckle!* What does that tell me? How do you think I feel? This is cut and dried; I'd believe Tony, but ask *yourself* that question.

Is it? Is it cut and dried? Did that divorce end it between you both, or is there a little extra something that burns away inside you that still spells Jessica? Lord help me, I don't even know the woman, haven't even seen a picture of her, but *one* upset, *one* manageable drama, and you're all over the place with it. Is *that* what I'm to expect maybe? Is *that* the way we'll handle our situations for a future, if there was ever going to be one? I have only one thing to say about it all. *Deal with it!* Make a decision, and act it out, one way or another. Solve it from here, or choose to run back to Hartford. Run back and take care of Jessica, run back and change your door locks, run back and do whatever, but remember, I am *not* at all happy about this, and I'm sorry.

And yes, in case you are now wondering what that does to us, believe me Tony, I have *no* idea? I can only tell you, I've loved our time together, short as it has been, and I fell in love with you, but love is only as good as it's shared, and how, but right now, with you, love's just a pain in the heart. I am *not* a twenty, even thirty something; I'll move on. I'll be a 'get over it' kind of person. I'm someone who enjoys life and company and believe me; I have loved what we found together. You won my heart Tony, and you won my love, but now it's up to you. Embrace it, nurture it, enjoy it, or throw it away, but remember, people are not disposable objects or items, and I am certainly *not* going to leave myself open and vulnerable, in a position to be treated that way, to be disposable goods. If you go to Connecticut, take my love with you, because I am not sure, it will still be here if and when you ever choose to come back. And I'm sorry. You asked my opinion – you got it!"

Without so much as looking at me, she turned and walked away.

I had a self-inflicted; huge conundrum on my hands, and solving it wasn't going to come easy. However, it should have been. Chelsea had retreated immediately to her bedroom, the very place we had shared so much love we had found in each other. It would be a hard room to go back to and tell her what I was going to do, how I was going to handle my dilemma. Sitting in the single couch seat I had originally chosen in the family room of her home to broach the subject in the first place, the fact was, for some still unexplainable reason, I still wasn't even sure exactly *what* that decision even was?

The house was deathly silent. I doubted now I could even approach Chelsea and suggest that I sit on it, that we spend our Mt Dora weekend as planned anyway, at least through until Monday. I quickly accepted; any lack of decision would be a red rag to a bull. I erred on the side of caution.

Before another step was taken in the idyllic setting I had really begun to enjoy, with a rapidly spinning mind going every which way but the right way, I was more of the opinion, in fact, quite sure, if I did approach her, Chelsea would want to know *exactly* where she stood with me, what course of action I was planning to take, and maybe force me to make a decision, one way or another; stay, or leave, win or lose, make it or break it! Calling me out would have been fair, because as of this very moment in the relationship, she did not realistically know anymore, where she fitted in, if at all?

Deciding on Connecticut meant we were probably over, that our short love affair had run its course, while staying in Florida would give us a real chance to go on, to make decisions for us as two people and not for 'spent' partners from another life. I wondered for a moment how I would feel, how I would react, if the shoe were on the other foot. It wasn't! The problem could only be solved by me. It was an onerous task, decision. The heart is such a fragile thing as well I had already learned. I was emotionally spent. I hated where I was, my position.

With a huge sigh, I stood up to face the next few minutes, to see where our lives might go and what directions they would take. It was totally, one-hundred percent up to me. I had created the problem; it was up to me to fix it, to choose wisely? Staring blankly through the window at the picturesque garden, with flowers in full bloom, color everywhere, all I saw really was darkness, emptiness. My heart was breaking inside. My nerves were shattered, my thoughts…lost! Turn and go back to my past, or stay and protect my future. Bridges? How could I *ever* have put myself in this position I wondered?

If I had owed Chelsea one thing, it would have been respect, and unquestionably, a whole lot more. She had come into my life at a low point, at a time I was searching for something, a new direction, a new place to be, even the new person I wanted to be. She found me, she had lifted me up to heights I thought I might never reach again - so why did I make the choice I did? I knew of, and could find no fathomable logic at all. And if I really thought about it, as I should have, immediately, what could Jessica possibly bring back to my life? *Why* would I head in her direction? Just to see her again, to change the locks, have an argument as I was sure we would, to verbally set her straight maybe and then tell her to get out of my life, a second time? Was that what I had in mind? Even if I did all that, then what, for me; simply pick up where I left off?

In all honesty, I had no idea, not the slightest idea! It was all I could do to wonder, what had I already done to Chelsea and me, questioning over and over, *why, why and why*? She, of all people, on God's green earth, had not deserved my irresponsibly delivered heartbreak. Yes, I was deserved of the crown I was wearing; I was king of the fools – I knew it.

I-95 North, even at 70mph, was very lonesome drive, I couldn't believe my decision, my actions, the reason of how or why I had even reached the one I finally did! It was totally foolish, probably one of the most foolish things I had ever done in my entire life so far.

I owed Jessica nothing; I owed Chelsea – everything. Tears welled in my eyes; the road ahead became mistier by the minute.

~~~~~~~~~~

CHAPTER

NINE

Earlier, from Jacksonville, where I pulled in, I'd placed a call to Jack Montgomery to tell him my story, what I had done. My heart was heavy, I was desperate to talk to someone; he was the only man I could trust. I know I poured my heart out to him, and he listened, as any faithful friend would. He was thrilled to hear about Chelsea, but was quite clear also; I may have burned the best bridge I'd ever built behind me. As a pick me up, it was encouraging to hear the sincerity and warmth in his voice, urging me not to despair, to let him take care of my business in Hartford, while imploring to me at the same time, almost in the same breath, to head straight back to DeLand, as fast as I legally could, and try to do a whole lot of fence mending, that is, he threw in, *'if it was not too late already'*. I prayed to God it wasn't!

Reassuring me, in a most confident way, he was in no doubt he could resolve the situation with Jessica without revealing where I was, he added, that if necessary, he would call in his old school buddy, a Sergeant with the Hartford Police Department. He emphasized, his law enforcement friend could be relied on to be tactful, and would make the departure of Jessica as easy as possible on her. There was an added caveat; failure to comply would bring a stern warning of ramifications through either continued presence, or repeat actions, and either could result in dire consequences. Everything Jack Montgomery said, sounded good to me, the almost perfect plan. He would urge Jessica to go back to California or weigh up the legal meaning of *'harassment'* if that's what it came down to. He accepted, albeit reluctantly, my repeated, explicit instructions; I really didn't want charges pressed against her, just a warning and timely advice. I owed her nothing, yet felt sympathetic, hoping it would be helpful. Ending the conversation, a huge weight was lifted from my shoulders.

Now mid to late afternoon with the sun still high, I was only an estimated 90 plus miles from Chelsea. Full of remorse, well counseled, I'd long made up my mind to turn back, to see if I still had, maybe, a second chance? Reinvigorated at the very thought, and the Mustang fueled; I made the easy cut across back to the Interstate. I was thankful I could get on a freeway that would make the next hour or so fly by. My real problem though; would Chelsea even see me? I had to try, and much as I'd been a fool, I tried to tell myself, only a four-hour fool so far. I did the speed limit, not wanting any more delays on my quest for redemption.

~~~~~~~~~~

On the outskirts of Daytona, a mere thirty-five miles from Glenwood, with Chelsea on my mind, my cell phone rang. Why, I'll never know, but I really hoped it was her, that she felt the same as me, and wanted to tell me we had both been a little too hasty in our handling of the Jessica debacle and to please, come on home. And that we should talk. Sadly, I wasn't even close! Wishful thinking over, I glanced at the caller ID before picking up – Jack Montgomery.

"Don't tell me, another problem already?" I asked in a probable, exasperated, but understandable negative tone, after all, it had only been an hour since we chatted and had an agreement.

"No way..." he almost gloatingly told me"...but I wasn't going to just sit on it either. I took this as a life-and-death kinda thing and

Three Days Later

we; *you* that is, needed this behind you so, here's the scoop comrade. Here's what has gone down. It's over." I gulped, hearing the last two words.

When Jack Montgomery had turned up at the door of my home back in Connecticut, Jessica almost did a double back flip. She was shocked to see not only my old friend, someone once near and dear to her, but a police officer too who had accompanied him to arrange the escort of her from my private property. *'I had no choice'* he told her. After two phone attempts and a personal visit, one on one, she had to realize, she was not welcome, and did not have one single right to have entered the house in the first place. All her pleadings to stay, to wait, were irrelevant. Jack Montgomery had been adamantly plain, *'I'm acting per my client's directions,'* he told her – *'But he was my husband for twelve years,'* she begged – all to no avail. The law was the law he told her, repeatedly, but she had ignored the warnings, confidently vowing to stay put until, as Jack relayed to me, *'I did all I could Tony. I met with her, spoke with her, told her it was not going to happen, hence the cops!'*

Montgomery went on to quantify; he had wasted no time springing into action, knowing exactly what he had to do to swiftly bring the Jessica saga to an easy, abrupt end. It turned out; he was more than angry with her, at what she had done to all of us, as friends, over the years. He saw no good in her returning to Hartford, or looking for me. He wasn't going to let her come back, to re-enter my life, or anyone's lives again, and personally; he wanted her long-gone – forever! His revelation about her actually surprised me.

Meanwhile, I was more than just relieved to know she had seen the error of her ways, had said she meant no harm, had understood her actions were certainly illegal and, in handing over the keys, vowed, with Jack's Hartford police sergeant friend as a witness to her words, *'not to be a nuisance any more'*. She had apparently left peacefully, for good this time I was confidently assured.

Jack's added sideline to the story, that he insisted he tell me, was both mildly flattering, yet at the same time, concerning. Before Jessica left the house, while collecting her few personal possessions, on my bathroom mirror she had scrawled, in lipstick, *'I still love you Tony. I'm sorry.'* Montgomery had thought it pathetic but also, quite funny; I took it only as sad, very sad. The woman obviously rued what she had done, to me, just as I rued right now, what I had done, to Chelsea. Did that make us even in matters of the heart? I doubted it.

Fearing rejection, with absolute trepidation, in what I was about to do, I turned the Mustang off Glenwood Road, to edge slowly down the familiar dirt driveway, onto the paved circular loop, stopping at the front door of Chelsea's home. The feeling today was far removed from the very first time I made the same journey, when it was a thrill, our relationship new, with much to look forward to. The sun was just beginning to make its final exit. Its slow sinking deep red rays shone through the trees; it was going to be a most beautiful sunset. I hoped for a similar result.

For a split moment, I collected my thoughts. My heart was pounding. What would be my first words, or would I be ordered from the grounds immediately, just as I had ordered Jessica from my home? What an incredible chain of events playing out in two different cities, separated by 1,000 miles. I took in a deep breath before exhaling deeply. *'Here I go'* I thought while opening the car door, preparing to step out; to face my fate.

With butterflies swarming in the pit of my stomach, and my hands trembling, I felt like the absolute wreck that I must also look. Suddenly, a noise caught my attention. As I turned, looking sideways toward the house, I saw the front door open. It was Chelsea. I was sure I detected the faint, very faint hint of a smile. Or, was it again more wishful thinking.

Wearing a clinging white designer style dress top with a tasteful print of two puppy dogs on the front, it was tucked neatly into her blue jeans. She looked as stunning as the first day I met her, only now, she was even more gorgeous, but for many different reasons. I not only knew her outer beauty, more importantly; I also knew her inner beauty. And I wanted to share it all again, to never let her out of my sight. Realistically, in my stupidity, the best I could hope for was that she still had even the smallest of small sparks for me.

Three Days Later

Our eyes met. Standing, as if frozen, rooted to the ground, leaning for support on the open car door, I managed to say the only words, I knew as the truth, the whole truth and nothing but the truth.

"I'm truly sorry Chelsea, truly sorry. I was a fool; I know it and I apologize."

My legs wouldn't move. I wanted to rush straight to her, take her in my arms and never let her go, but I couldn't. My feet wouldn't budge. All I could do was look at her, and wait. The next, mere few seconds, seemed like an eternity. Chelsea's eyes had never blinked; she seemed to stare straight at me. Then, softly, she spoke the words I longed to hear.

"Come here Tony, come here and hold me. I missed you so much, and let me say also, I was a fool too. We were *both* wrong, *both* of us. We *really* were."

My heart skipped a beat, or was it three? With the deepest of sighs, my frozen body freed; I literally bounded from the car, straight into her now outstretched arms, to embrace her as if I had just returned from a year and the ugly war in Afghanistan. It had been only five hours and yet; it was like I had not seen the greatest love of my life since…forever.

Was I the happiest man in DeLand right now? Could any single soul claim the right to have topped my return as I hugged the woman I had almost let slip away from me? Chelsea was like gold…precious, precious, gold and I could not have felt more relieved, just to see her again, for her to welcome me back home, back to her arms, back into her heart. And as we kissed, the tremble through my body overtook me. Right where I stood, my legs felt like they were quivering, like jelly.

"Oh God, Chelsea, we can't let anything like this ever happen again. I love you, and oh, oh, my God, if you only knew, if you only knew how I missed you, even for the few short hours we were apart, I was so, so…"

With love, I was stopped in my tracks.

"And I missed you too Tony. I also thought I'd lost you. It was awful, awful. I'm sorry that…"

It was my turn to interrupt.

"Chelsea, it was *me*. *All me*. I was the fool, an idiot, an out and out dumb-ass and knew it. I just *had* to come back to you. I couldn't lose you now; you're all I want in this world, and baby; I love you. I so love you."

Words could never explain either of us. We were like love smitten teenagers, both wanting to accept the blame for what could have been so simple, as obvious as any normal, rationalized people would have known. But something had gotten in our way.

"Let's get beyond it Tony, it's over." Chelsea was still holding tightly on to me.

For the second time in an hour, there were those two words again. Stunned, for no reason, the words *'it's over'*, for a split second, almost made me gulp with fright. 'It's over' had not meant the two of us; it was the silly event we had just been through. As fast as the moment of terror ran through my mind, it was, thankfully, gone again.

"Chelsea, don't say that. You scared me. We can't *ever* say *'it's over'* again." She knew instantly what I meant, even what I might have felt.

Laughing, we let each other go then, together, hand in hand, chose to walk around the gardens and lawns, stopping momentarily at the waterfall to watch the clear falling water tumble over the picturesque, decorated, fiberglass mountain, into the pond, where the many colorful goldfish loved to swim. If they were in their water heaven; I too was in heaven, my heaven, it was Glenwood - revisited.

We sat on the small white metal chairs, watching and waiting, until the sun completely disappeared. And yes, it was the most beautiful of sunsets, seemingly, timed to perfection, allowing us to drink in its beauty, its serenity, its colorful glow, the same glow that had returned to our relationship, our almost lost love. As it did, and as darkness slowly began to take over, the soft green overhead spotlights came on, automatically timed to shed a different glow on the now more manicured garden settings. Looking at the freshly planted flowers, I was pleased to have left my small mark that brightened the surroundings where we sat. I wanted so many more sunset moments like this one with Chelsea. Re-invigorated, I was once again, a happy man.

"There's something I have to tell you Chelsea" I told her cautiously, not wanting to alarm her, the last thing I'd ever want to do right now.

"*Oh no*, is it…" I stopped her immediately. I guess I had alarmed her. A small, worried frown furrowed her brow as she looked directly at me.

"Hey, it's all *good*. No problems, but it does have to do, obviously, about you and me."

Relieved, "All right Mr. Thompson, in your words of course, pray, tell me."

I suggested, rather boldly I thought, that we move inside first, out of the slightly chilling air, where I would then enlighten her to all I had to share. I couldn't help myself in a return visit for another hug as we stood up; it was enthusiastically returned.

Wandering back through the Florida room, into the bar area, Chelsea couldn't resist a quick quip in her *'welcome home',* with both arms stretched out emphasizing the room, the house. It was a wonderful feeling to know our indifferences were being so easily put behind us. As the perpetrator of all that had happened, I was not only relieved, but more than grateful for where we stood with each other at this moment. Chelsea, meanwhile, had been, thankfully for me, certainly forgiving, but in the bigger picture, it didn't really matter as together; we helped each other over the difficult patch that should never have presented itself in the first place. I pledged openly to be more careful, not to be so sensitive about issues that should have been easily resolved, irrelevant, that instead had become potentially destructive to our very well being, our love for each other.

From our self-inflicted sadness swiftly becoming a thing of the past, to our now renewed joy, blossoming, not that Chelsea asked, over drinks, I chose to relay in detail, the events of what had happened, and of how Jack Montgomery had handled, what I called, my Connecticut concerns. *'Aptly put'* she acknowledged, now listening intently.

Finally, with all bridges of the episode crossed, as best I could tell my story, in closing, I declared my epiphany of enlightenment, but very specifically, confirmation of Jessica, and how she was out of my life, never to be mentioned again - period. The only response from Chelsea was short, sweet and simple. A kiss, a smile and a repeat of two words I loved hearing again – *'Welcome home'*. I knew one thing; I never wanted to hurt, or be scared like that again, ever, in my life. That night, to say we loved each other with a passion, was an understatement.

~~~~~~~~~~

Renningers Antique Fair in Mt. Dora was a wonderful way to spend our Sunday. Picking up where we had left off, dismissing totally, everything that had transpired yesterday, as if the day never happened, under brilliant warm sunshine; we strolled the fair. The many shops and ground stalls were all filled with not only marvelous antiques, but so much more. It was collectors' dreams come true and certainly lived up to the claim of *'something for everyone'*. To have chosen the Sunday labeled, *'an extravaganza'*, where up to a thousand or more dealers converge on the outdoor setting under what was billed as, *'Nature's Own Great Blue Canopy'*, was nothing short of a coincidence, but it ended up being quite the thrill.

Chelsea loved searching through the sterling silver and pottery, while I scoured through the many record collections and CD's, looking for a rare item, an old favorite song, as well as books and magazines. Together, enthralled, we spent the best part of almost five hours rummaging, and yet, at the end of the day, totaling up our big day out; we'd spent a grand total of only $155.00. It was well spent, according to us.

She chose a turn of the century boxed set of cutlery, and a vintage vase designed to hold just one flower that I thought was cute, but wondered, how just one flower could make a design, a setting? I accepted it as male thing, while Chelsea shook her head muttering *'Men! Why is it, with some things, you never understand?'* At least she said it with a smile.

I walked away with two biographical books and five old 12" vinyl long play records that to me meant, both excellent reading, and excellent listening. My choice find of the day though was an old

Beatles LP titled 'Yesterday, Today, Tomorrow' that I knew had a far greater value than the incredibly low $30.00, I paid, given it was the much sought after, valuable, 'Butcher Cover' release of the 1966 album. A music lover, a collector, would automatically know it; however, the vendor I dealt with obviously had no idea what he was in possession of, and anxious to make sales on the day, was happy to take my money, gladly offered. I was of the opinion; I could probably have bought it for even less if I'd haggled, but I wasn't about to take any chances, there were too many shoppers around me. Excitedly showing it to Chelsea, she had no idea what I was talking about, music was a not a driving force in her life. All I could say was, *'wait until I land this one on eBay, then you'll get it, and sweetheart, when I sell it, I have something very special in mind I'll use the proceeds for'*. It was a light-hearted promise, but I really did have something special in mind. Oblivious to any of what I said meant, she still offered a smiley-face look at the remark. It became another one of those *'feel good'* moments, to me.

It was time to leave. Our Sunday outing was a win, win day, and the best part, Chelsea and I couldn't have been happier, with still, much to talk about and look forward to in each other.

And Sunday evening, inadvertently, became another small, but typical pleasure as it turned out. Opting for an early dinner, we couldn't have chosen better, or Chelsea couldn't have, electing to head to Brian's Bar-B-Q out on the Truck Route. What a great call! Typically country in decor, right down to John Wayne, his cowboy contemporaries and a host of memorable old photographs from the movies including Gone With The Wind, Rhett Butler, Scarlett (there was southern thang again). Of particular note also were the many displayed awards for fine food over the years. I feasted on chicken, beans, slaw, and a couple of ice-cold beers, all the time wondering, *'how many more great secrets can this town called DeLand have?*' Happily, our lives were back in sync; love was again, in the air.

Topping off our night out, when we settled in for an evening of easy view television, unknowingly, both of us, in our previous unknown lives, loved to watch the reality show The Amazing Race and lo and behold, there it was. Coincidentally in tune with each other, a chardonnay in hand; escapism for a night of TV was a given. When I suggested maybe we could apply to become team contestants on an upcoming series, Chelsea's instant retort was, *'are you kidding?'* I wasn't. However, it was obvious; it would not become a high priority on either of our future agendas. Still, I thought; I'd love to have the chance to participate someday. I'd work on her about that.

Tomorrow, and as always, I hated the thought; Chelsea had to return to work. *'It's my duty, and it should never be shirked'* she told me, adding, with a slight degree of pressure at the same time, in the same breath, that I concede, give up on the hotel in Daytona and come stay with her, in her home. I didn't have the heart to tell her that I already had. It wasn't important! *'...I can't let you out of my sight, lose you again, can I?'* she added as a loving footnote.

Two minds in tandem, I felt exactly the same way, and I could think of no better demand, well, offer really. I *wanted* to be with Chelsea.

~~~~~~~~~~

CHAPTER

TEN

Jack Montgomery was pleased to hear me confirm that I was about to head back to Connecticut. In fact, he was relieved beyond outright admission, simply qualifying, there was a lot to be done, that a fair amount of work was now back-logged, and to have me in the office again would take a lot of pressure off a few people, particularly him. I took his *'It'll be nice to have you back speech'* as a good thing, but also, maybe, a bad thing. Given all I had shared with him about Chelsea, things in my life were changing rapidly; a pre-warning phone call wasn't the time though, it could wait. A face to face, heart to heart, was the way to handle him, that, I knew, only too well.

~~~~~~~~~

Thankful, in timing, with less than a week for me left in Florida, I was still around for a major event that would have killed me to ever miss. Chelsea's birthday would be an occasion to remember. Although she hated the thought of yet another year being tacked on to her already unwelcome forties, 43 still sounded like a pretty good number to me. There wasn't a soul that didn't believe she looked more mid-thirties - any number! Vivacious, and outgoing, her natural beauty, infectious smile, her youthful, smooth skin, envied by many, suggested a look of, ala, well...movie star? Her slim, extremely well proportioned figure fitted her persona, that of a woman who really took care of herself. Unquestionably, her charming personality captured most people the moment they met her, a fact endorsed by her few close friends that obviously adored her. Today, they rallied to the occasion.

Gathered together, many of those friends made up the most perfect crowd to celebrate a birthday, and as the night wore on, I was so proud she had chosen me to be 'the man in her life'. Equally proud, she made sure everyone knew it too.

Unexpectedly, at a moment of idle mingling, Meghan, number one favorite neighbor and host with husband Mark, of Chelsea's birthday event, in a form of equal jest I was sure, aided also by an extra drink or two she had partaken, brashly, slipped a simple question to me '*...so when are you going to make an honest woman of Chelsea. She's a beautiful lady and she loves you, but then again, you probably know that already. You'd have to.*'

To say it threw me off a little would have to have been an understatement, but at the same time, I wasn't about to take umbrage at her directness. I actually didn't mind. I had certainly thought of that very point many times, strictly to myself, but it did momentarily make me wonder too; had Chelsea and Meghan covered this subject in private time, alone, along the way? I'd never know and generally speaking, what was the difference anyway, reality of the moment was - it really wasn't important? Her question, unbeknown to her, was right on the money.

"I think you're being a little mischievous here Meghan, aren't you, suggesting what I think you are..." were the only words I could find as a reply, not wanting to answer the question anyway, flippantly adding, "...but ain't she just so cute?" We both grinned, accepting; it was a nice try.

Ironically, fortunately, Chelsea's eye caught mine, just as I said it. Lifting her glass, with a returned smile, she mouthed clearly, making sure I couldn't miss the message, '*I love you*'. I returned the same compliment, looking forward to when the celebrations were over, to when it was only the two of us again. Yep! I was a long way gone, well smitten I'd say, over Ms. Chelsea Martin. Meghan had caught our *'across the room'* interaction.

"But aren't you heading back to Connecticut shortly?" she questioned as if looking for time-table confirmation of my soon intended departure.

"Sadly, yes, but you know I'll be back as soon as I can. Can't stay away too long can I?"

"*No*" I was swiftly, firmly reminded, but could that have been a subtle message too? The tone of her reply, the way it was snapped back, I kind of took it that way.

"Unfortunately Meghan, I haven't got a choice. Chelsea and I, our meeting was so fast, and *wow,* so much has to be thought about, my head's fairly spinning I must confess, but hey, enough of that. I'll be up there and back again as fast as you can say, whatever it is they say, when they say that, okay? That's a promise."

Confused, she nodded an obvious yes. Taking advantage of the moment, continuing our idle, small talk, the timing was perfect to ask for a little, what I felt was, inside information, advice, on a thought I'd had and wondered about, looking for support at the same time.

"Can I ask you a question Meghan, between you and me only of course?"

Glancing quickly at me while twisting her mouth downward suggesting visually as an expression an unsure yes, or a definite no, it didn't matter; I was in more than friendly company and it wasn't as if my question was of world shattering importance in the bigger scheme of things.

"Go ahead, no guarantees of course" she answered, obvious protectiveness in her voice.

I would have called it an overreaction, not quite what I wanted to hear, but I proceeded to ask my question anyway. At least we were communicating, socially.

"Do you know enough that, if I asked Chelsea, do you think she'd come back with me to Hartford for the drive, and maybe spend a few days to see more of my neck of the woods? Or do you think she's way too tied down at the practice? It's just a thought for now, and I'd understand a no but…" That was it! Slightly waffling I'd conversationally said enough.

Meghan hesitated a second or two, seemingly considering the question momentarily before offering, not only her reply, but at the same time, a suggestion.

"I shouldn't say this really, but here's what *might* work."

She had my full attention. I was very anxious to know or find a simple way for Chelsea to come with me to Connecticut.

"I actually think she really might. I do know she *wants* to go there, *wants* to see your side of life, she has said that; however, she wasn't going to broach the subject too quickly, and *that*, I know. Now, in answering you, here's the all important *but*…"

Oh no, the dreaded but! Nevertheless, I couldn't wait to hear *'the but'* explanation anyway.

She continued. "… but, the sooner you ask her, the better the chance for a yes, for her to clear her patient schedule. I *will* share *this* with you; she *has* drawn back on her commitments to her appointments anyway, and I'd suggest there was a reason for that so, for what it's worth, short answer, pose the question asap. I think she might. You've got her heart you know Tony, and from me to you, *don't break it,* or you'll have *me* to answer to. Do you hear me?"

The message had been loud and clear and naively, in my response to her, I added my confession.

"I won't. I came close to breaking it once and *that* was enough." I'd blurted out, not thinking.

"*What!*" she exclaimed. "You came close *what*? Tell me more."

Meghan obviously didn't know. Woops, I thought, suddenly accepting way too much, way too quickly in a friendship. Thinking rather rapidly on my feet, I made light of it, understanding immediately, thankfully; Chelsea had not shared a word at all of our Connecticut concerns, our little mishap of love. It had been a between her and me thing, exclusively.

"Oh, it was nothing really." I told her, about to flirt with the truth, floundering in my reply.

Three Days Later

"It's just that we had joked how people, us, others, many are so flippant about love these days, younger people we were talking about mainly, before wondering, could they accept as readily that older folks hearts break just as big as theirs, so the point was, we chatted all about broken hearts one time, believing; we'd never break ours, each other's that is. We won't of course."

It was flimsy as an explanation, but I tried. Painfully obvious, yet thankfully accepting it, Meghan, I was sure, couldn't quite grasp my feeble attempt at my protective, self-imposed cover up, and I could certainly understand why. I had rambled, saying absolutely nothing of substance, but then, if confusion reigned for her, my mass of words amounting to zero as an explanation had worked. Fortunately, we moved on. She left it alone. I picked up where we left off.

"I'll do it..." I told her "...I'll ask her tonight. We still have a week, *just* that is, but enough time maybe, at least I hope. And thanks Meghan, you're the best."

"What are you two scheming?" Chelsea asked as she sidled up alongside me, having sauntered across from the other side of the patio, her mother right behind her. "Is there something I should know?" Lightly laughing, we fobbed off the question, declaring not a word.

"Of course not sweetheart, why would we hide anything from you, or Rose?" as I called her Mother. They looked at each other, and then Chelsea looked back to me.

"Hey, hey... Mr. Thompson. You've got that boyishly devil look on your face. We think you and Meghan are cooking something up, huh Meghan, right?" She was still looking for an answer.

Meghan tossed her head to one side, nonchalantly, as if to say *'see all, hear all, say nothing'* like the three little monkeys. It turned into a light-hearted moment that allowed Chelsea to again thank her friend for being so hospitable, for showering her with a most wonderful birthday gathering, and arranging for many of their select friends to join in on the event, fortuitously, to meet me at the same time. She was one hundred percent right; it truly had been a very entertaining evening. To me though, apart from being enjoyable, it was also obvious, there was a real camaraderie between a few of the neighbors of the area, and tonight; I'd met most of them, all with their open invitation, of not to stay away too long, some with the familiar southern ring, *'adios'* and *'y'all come back now'*.

The event over, it was time to head home. Hours earlier, in the broad daylight while coming to the party, we had taken the short cut to Meghan and Mark's house from Chelsea's – their homes being so close; they had cleared a walkway, through the ferns and foliage of the unfenced area of the properties. Simple and ingenious as the idea was, the stepping stone pathway was also lined with solar night lights; perfect to make it an easy walk through home at night. Now, with only a half moon shining above, following the clearly lit solar path back to Chelsea's home, I paused for a moment to steal a kiss, in advance. She didn't complain, returning the feeling with just enough frivolity, and tenderness, that led me to believe, her birthday, our night, was not over yet. It wasn't - but only after Mama Rose was safely home on Hidden Hollow.

With Chelsea back at work, I had a couple of missions in mind and plenty of time to activate them. My under worked laptop again became my best friend, with Wi-Fi, my contact to the great outside. By the time she got back home, she found me dozing on the couch in the living room I had at one stage thought looked most inviting. It'd had the desired effect, as it wasn't until I felt her hand on my body that I stirred, to see her captivating smile that was winning my heart more and more every day, if that was at all possible. *'Wake up Mr. Thompson, guess who's home?'* I shook my head before doing what came naturally, reaching up to hold her. Fait accompli. Chelsea fell into my arms, content to lay with me, for just a little while, on the couch. I held her close. She felt so good. It was a glorious feeling to know this delightful lady was mine, to have and hold – and I wanted her with me – forever!

Showered, refreshed, dressed and ready to share a planned evening together, we headed out to the St. John's River Marina just off SR 44. There was a little restaurant that had caught my attention, surfing the Internet, looking for that somewhere extra special to take Chelsea. With time running out and my sojourn to Florida coming to an end, I had to make the most of what was left. Tonight was especially important to me.

I'd found the relatively hidden, Shuttered Firefly, that was anything but shuttered that is, not fireflies! The wood style building, with its huge outdoor patio jutting out over the St. John's, was a diner's delight complete with snug little booths, or open style seating, both available inside and out. Taking my chances, with expectations, I'd booked to be outside, right at the water's edge where I was confidently assured, in probability, but not guaranteed; that we'd catch a show? Thankfully, it wasn't long after we sat down to enjoy a glass of fine chardonnay, the first of the fireflies made their grand appearance. It was electrifying; Chelsea was mesmerized, literally, not so much at the fireflies themselves, although brilliant, but the fact that they seemed to arrive *right on cue*, surprised equally it seemed, that I even knew of such a place.

"How did you ever manage to arrange this concert of Mother Nature, just for me?" she asked.

I was delighted beyond words. She was thoroughly impressed, and it showed.

"It's all for you darling, the setting, the fireflies, the show; it's all for you. This night is *your* night. I want it to be forever special"

"I'm so in awe. It's wonderful, especially this quaint, rather picturesque restaurant that I am almost ashamed to admit; I didn't even know was here, let alone for how long. How in the world did you, a complete stranger to Deland, ever find it?"

"I traveled hither, thither and yon…" I told her "…all over the city, up and down roads, everywhere, until I could find a place that might become exclusively yours and mine, and I don't know why, but this one, The Shuttered Firefly, caught my attention, and believe me; I'm delighted you've never been here, now it can *truly* be yours and mine."

Grinning all the while, but serious, I purposely left out that my fingers did all the walking, trekking frantically over a computer keypad.

The waiter arrived to take our order, informing us it would be about twenty-minutes thereabouts, unless we were in a hurry, if so, he could speed up the service a little. Little would he realize, his offer was in fact, the last thing I wanted? However, the very words he'd chosen slammed home, reminding me that I was certainly on a falling time limit - now, down to just three days. Tonight, I wouldn't think about it. We had all the time in the world. I'd make it memorable. I raised my wine glass to propose a toast.

"To you and me Miss Chelsea Martin."

Our glasses clinked. The tone was crisp. With a sip and a smile, all I could see was beauty in the lady across the table. Chelsea saw fireflies. Surreptitiously, my hand moved to my inside pocket. Delighted, enthralled at the spectacle, when she turned her head back toward me, about to make a comment; my open hand displayed the custom designed diamond ring I'd ordered downtown from Ferrell Jewelers (since 1957), my most cooperative and obliging creator of the strikingly beautiful cluster. As her hand moved immediately to her mouth, simultaneously; she gasped, *'Oh my, oh my'* Chelsea was visibly taken aback, totally surprised, shocked! I was delighted. What I had set out to achieve, she had willingly succumbed to. My next planned five words came easy.

"Will you marry me Chelsea?"

They were the only words I could manage to get out before I heard a tiny squeal as her rush of excitement flowed so naturally.

"Whaaaat! Are you *serious* Tony, are you *truly* serious I mean, you're scaring me, I, I…"

"I could get down on one knee but…" I started to say, pushing my chair from behind me.

"No, no, no I mean, I mean…"

Her hand moved to touch the ring before she quickly clasped my hands in hers holding tightly on to them

"Oh God, how beautiful, how beautiful" she uttered over.

I slipped the ring on her third finger, left hand. It was perfect, made for her, and fortunately, an absolutely perfect fit too. Keeping tradition alive, now moving from my chair opposite, I went down on one knee in front of her, watching her as I did. Her still shocked look said it all.

"I love you Chelsea. I love you dearly. I want you to be my wife, will you…" I started to say, officially.

I didn't have to finish. Her reply was excitedly delivered.

"Yes Tony, yes, yes, yes, I *will* marry you. Thank you, thank you" she spluttered, throwing her arms around my neck. "I love you too Tony, but how did you, how did you *ever* manage to do all this, whatever did you…?"

Timely, I moved back to my seat, as if choreographed. Just as I did, the waiter arrived with our first course, surprised to see Chelsea wiping tears from her eyes before instantly realizing, something big had happened since he was last at the table. Chelsea lifted her hand showing him the diamond ring. The fireflies had momentarily lost their glow; the diamonds had taken over. It didn't matter, as if a programmed part of the joy of the moment; they still lit up the night, glistening in the three-quarter moonlight that shimmered on the river, and again, as if on cue; their mass of flickering light was made more spectacular by the ripples of water from a slow-moving sailboat heading for its mooring. From glancing at the firefly show, I looked Chelsea's way.

"To think…" I couldn't help but share "…to think, how we met, where we started, from a similar ripple on the water, but back then, on a huge cruise ship. And the water, the Atlantic Ocean but still, they were *our* rippling waters, just as these river waters are too. How ironic, how romantic, how beautiful, and I want you to know Chelsea Martin, I'm a fortunate man to have found you. You're my dream that's come true. I love you, and I'll do all I can to make you happy."

Unashamedly, I felt a small tear in the corner of my eye beginning to form, hoping all the while it would stay where it was. It didn't! Chelsea noticed it too. It touched her. Gently wiping the now large about to fall tear away with her napkin, she lingered, resting her hand on my face.

"We've so much to talk about now Tony" she realistically reminded me.

"Tomorrow sweetheart, or tonight, whenever, but I want you in my life, always."

"And I want you Tony. I'm yours, forever. I love you, thank you. You have made me so very happy, and like you, how *glad* I am we found each other on that big ol'ship."

All too soon, the morning sun peeked its head over the horizon to brighten the way for another day. For me, for Chelsea Martin, although I liked the sound of Mrs. Chelsea Thompson better, the start of a brand-new day heralded a much bigger, new beginning. There were also some major challenges to overcome, but we remained undaunted. We vowed we would meet them gladly, together.

CHAPTER

ELEVEN

It had been a long haul and try as I might, to drive straight through, I had no chance. DeLand to Hartford was just a little too far. The last thing I wanted was to be in an accident, out on a freeway. I now had way too much to live for. My decision to break the journey back to Connecticut, I considered, was a wise one. Fayetteville, North Carolina was as good a choice as any. It meant nothing to me except a place to lay my head, ready for the next morning, and an early start to get the trip behind me. 'What a contrast', I thought, compared to my original trip, when my time back then meant nothing - places and sights did. Sadly, Chelsea couldn't juggle schedules enough, and the hardest thing we had to do, after three months of virtual bliss, came in having to say goodbye to each other. The tears that fell were at least happy ones. Accepting the inevitable, the consolation was, the challenges ahead were all good, and it wouldn't be long before we'd see each other again. After '*I love you*', her last words were, '*...you drive safely now, ya hear!*' Her charm was infectious. I knew I still had so much to learn and always would about my Miss Chelsea Martin.

An update phone call to Jack Montgomery as I approached New Jersey, not only made him feel in the loop, but he caringly reminded me; he would leave a key in the mailbox, so I could at least get into my own house. Good point, I knew; I hadn't given that a second thought! With the locks long ago changed, *that* simple fact could have been a fatal error on arrival back in Hartford, now scheduled to be just a bit later than I'd hoped, but, to then not have keys? Midnight had become my new do-able time; however, I was fast realizing, back in the hectic hustle and bustle of where I still officially lived, after DeLand, and Florida, anything could happen. At least my adrenalin was running faster than even just a few hours earlier, keeping me well motivated.

Finally, looming amazingly bright and majestic, once again, the downtown skyline of Manhattan came into full view, and while there would definitely be no stopping, as I'd considered when I was leaving, heading south, those buildings were more than a welcome sight, and just ahead - the border line of Connecticut and beyond that, Hartford and home...but sadly, without the *one* person I dearly wanted by my side. Plus, *'home'* really seemed the wrong connotation now.

I'd called Chelsea during the day; how could I *not*? I missed her terribly, and regardless of how long, or often, we talked; the stark realization was, from here on in; nothing would be as before for me, without her. Realistically too, to walk once again into my own house, it would never look, or could ever be, the same. Everything, to me, would be slotted, *'in the past.'*

The first and probably biggest dilemma I'd begun to formulate in my mind would actually be Jack Montgomery at the Realtors Office. What was I going to say to him, I wondered, as I kept my speed of the Mustang to the designated limit while passing through New York City? Too many thoughts of a work-related nature began badgering their way into my mind as I drove; it wasn't long before it began to get way too cluttered. Hartford, Chelsea, Jack, the office, clients, DeLand, and heaven forbid, even Jessica jumped into the mix helping to mess me up a little more. Why Jessica, I had no idea, believing only, that it had to be because I was nearing my home. She did after all once share my life, but we were long divorced for goodness sake I reasoned, but it didn't stop there. Next loomed the problem she had caused that had almost derailed me with Chelsea. *'Stop!'* I said to myself. Shaking my head vigorously, I quickly rid myself of all negative thoughts, wondering, why, after a most wonderful hiatus, some of those old time bad days had managed to somehow get back into my head. It was too much! I decided to pull off the freeway at the next exit to grab a cup of coffee. I needed a pick me up anyway!

~~~~~~~~~~

My cell phone went off to its familiar opening musical riff of Peter Gunn, the old detective series theme, and for whatever reason; it actually gave me a fright. I had been dead to the world and could have slept another ten hours; I guessed, although highly unlikely. Still slightly shaken at the phone's rude intrusion to my sleep, in a haze, I glanced at the clock on the bedside table. I was horrified; it read 9.32. I wondered who would want me already. I'd told Jack I would be in the office sometime after twelve noon and not to disturb me before then. He hadn't; it was Chelsea, worried that she hadn't heard from me by now. She couldn't hold back any longer making the call, if only just to ease her mind, and to know I was safe.

"Darlin'..." I said, with both surprise and delight, I'm sure, in my voice "...I made it home finally at close to one o'clock, and I must say, literally died. I was beat, and I'm sorry. I wanted to call, let you know I was okay, that I'd made it unscathed, but not at that time." It wasn't an excuse. She more than understood, quickly starting to apologize for waking me.

"No way, I'm glad you called. I mean it's late. I'm shocked, at me that is!"

Chelsea blurted out everything she wanted to say.

"I just wanted you to know how I miss you. Nothing's as it was here anymore. I miss your face in the morning and all the things that, that..." I felt the same. I was glad it was mutual.

"Me too" I claimed back, talking over her. "What a journey and for the whole trip, believe me, all I could think about was you. You have turned my world upside down Chelsea Martin, but don't get me wrong; I love it, and I love you too. I miss you like crazy and hey, now I've got another crazy feeling."

I thought momentarily, a mere split second in time, what I was about to say, deciding to say it anyway. Did it matter…it was true?

"I wish you were here, to jump in my bed. I so wanna hold you, touch you, feel you, see you." I honestly admitted.

"Well I'm working on it." She confirmed. "Working on joining you, and believe me Mr. Thompson, my dear sweet man, right now, if I could, I'd come on down the line, through the atmosphere, however it all works these days, and be there. All I want to be is to be with you too…but I can't, so I'll wait until you come on home again, or I get there of course."

Her words, spoken excitedly, yet truthfully, made me feel like a million dollars. Make that ten million! I was about to answer when her voice echoed down the line again.

"I hate to say it Tony but I've got to go. I'll ring you as soon as I'm home tonight, okay? And good luck with everything up there. I love you and stay safe for me won't you. Love you Tony."

Way too slow off the mark to respond, I was too late. The call was over. And just like that, my Chelsea was gone. Lord knows, how I missed her. Being her own boss, literally, I knew she was trying to reschedule as fast as manageable, but facts are, *that* part of her life, and work, would always be difficult, the sole reason *why* she couldn't come with me initially, however, I never doubted, it wouldn't be too long before she was clear. We'd already agreed, if she could get away, Chelsea would take the easy route and fly direct to Connecticut when she was physically able to. I couldn't ask for more, although, not that I said it, wouldn't even allude to it, her physical absence, in the early initial days of my return to Hartford, would at least leave me that much free-er to consider my next set of moves, and there were plenty of them.

Hard as it was, still a little tired even, I managed to drag myself out of bed to head straight for the bathroom. Walking in, I'd forgotten something? Instant shock! Written in a bright-red lipstick, *'I still love you Tony. I'm sorry'* had remained on my bathroom mirror, Jessica's parting message. I'd seen it last night when I got in, and up until this very moment, had thought no more about it. In the early hours of this morning, after the long drive back, dog tired, I had ripped off my clothes and fallen straight into bed. I'd deal with it in the morning I had told myself, at the time. Nothing, and no-one, except Chelsea, albeit momentarily, had graced my mind last night. However, now, in the cold hard light of a new morning, seeing the words again emblazoned across the mirror, did nothing but infuriate me.

I grabbed the nearest towel, dampened it under the running water from the sink's faucet to begin, angrily, wiping them away, as fast as I could. *'I'm done Jessica',* I told her out loud, to no-one, *'I'm done. Get out of my life, and stay out. I don't need you or any of this, this…'* I was exasperated. It seemed, the more I rubbed the lipstick, the bigger the smear, and soon, bigger the aggravation. I walked into the kitchen, found a bottle of green, friendly, glass cleaner, and began squirting the magic liquid all over the mirror. Less than a minute later, it was clean; no more Jessica, no more reminders, just a very red stained hand towel I'd have to throw away, more than reminiscent, of how I'd been discarded by the perpetrator, the woman who changed my life, unwittingly then, and now, for so much the better.

A warm shower felt good, gentle reminders of more than a few I'd shared with Chelsea lately. A rush of pure delight ran through my body. Thinking positive, I couldn't wait for her call me, to tell me when we would be back together, side by side again, but this time, hopefully, forever the optimist, in Connecticut.

~~~~~~~~~~

"Jack, great to see you after so long, and I gotta say it, you're looking well. Something agreed with you; that's for sure."

Walking back into the relatively plush offices of Hartford Montgomery Realtors, it was like I'd never left. Where had the time gone, and to think, the waters that had flowed under my proverbial bridge? But what a sight, nevertheless; friendly faces, a huge

'Welcome Back Tony' sign draped across the window of my office; I couldn't have been more supported, even a rare hug from Kerry-Ann, my secretary. However, the welcome back and good feelings didn't last but a few minutes.

Staff hello's over, Jack was straight down to business, having made it quite clear, there were a number of pressing issues that needed swift follow through, along with numerous -clients waiting to hear from me. Unfortunately, none of my mild, early concerns about aggression and attitude seemed to resonate with him, there was business to be conducted, and he wanted it done – now! Little did he know it, but his seemingly, brash, heavy-handed approach and tone toward me, coupled with an almost demanding way of re-establishing me back into the landscape of what he saw as crucial, became extremely counter-productive. Being away was one thing; however, I am, after all, a shareholder, a key partner in the company, his well understood 2 I/C. It seemed like all of that had, for now, conveniently escaped him. Start the way you plan to finish being a motto I had no trouble living by; it had served me well throughout my working life. The way he was talking, had made me feel, caused me to think, maybe I'd throw my personal hand grenade early.

"Jack, hold it just a minute. Slow down; let me say something will you?" I asked firmly, with civility. He wasn't listening.

"Why Tony? We've got a mountain load going on in here or haven't you noticed?"

"*Notice!*" I threw back angrily. "I haven't had a chance to notice *anything*. You haven't slowed down, or stopped talking, since I walked in the building, and that was almost half an hour ago, *damn it!*"

"Well comrade, I had to get you up to speed didn't I, and now we've simply got to move, okay?" he suggested, stone faced, still, without any sensitivity.

"No, it's *not* OK, *not for one minute*. Look at yourself Jack. Listen to yourself; you are like a man possessed. What the hell is your problem?"

"*Problem, possessed, yes!* Do you want us to lose all we've got, worked for Tony…" he retorted, his voice raised with a slightly angrier tone than I had displayed "… real estate is suffering; people are suffering, and in case you hadn't noticed, foreclosures are on the rise big time, and I mean, *big time*. You've been out of the loop for a while; maybe too long, but as fast as I can make it clear to you, right now, we have some pretty important decisions to make. Sales are down; inquiries are down, and there's a price at the end of the day if we don't harness what we have and find a direction, *that's* where you come in as I see it. Does any of that make sense to you? C'mon man!"

He paused momentarily, moving his head in an every which way direction as if looking for something, maybe time. I gave him a moment. He obviously hadn't finished yet.

"Look around you Tony; I've never seen things so bad. Is *that* a good start to where I'm coming from, as a problem, or what bothers me right now, *is it?*" he seemed to now want to challenge.

I was taken aback at his barrage of probable facts as they stood, but in putting it the way he had, sure wasn't making it easy to immerse myself back into any sort of routine, the way it was before I left. I leaned back in my chair. Some of the rapid-fire information, the basic everyday news facts, I was conscious of, but not to the extent of how it was beginning to affect us personally, our Company, our core business. Jack Montgomery had every right to be concerned, and every right to be glad I was back, sitting in my office, where at least he could share the load. Reality was; that's the way it had been over the years, and while the good times made it all too easy to maybe float along, the bad times, or certainly the now worsening times, evident all around us, *that* had become another story, it was new to us a company.

Miffed as I personally was, and felt I might have an absolute right to, based on his upfront raised voice barrage presentation; I quickly grasped reality, guessing I'd better back off a little. I'd been gone three months; Jack had been my solid back-stop, my friend, even bailed me out with Jessica. I knew instantly; I had to readjust *my* attitude, that I was the one actually wrong. Immediately accepting that as a fact, I was pretty glad, too, that I hadn't added to his woes and hit him with some of my own personal news first, fast concluding, *my* situation was secondary, certainly not as important. I'd find the right time later. What *was* more important, I knew, was that I jump back into the fray and help my friend, my partner, and put my pedal to the metal and help keep our once more than buoyant business afloat.

"You win Jack and frankly; you're *right*. Man you are so *right* and I'm sorry. I get it – now! That said, let's get down to business, fill me in, what are the numbers, where are the problems, who do we have to meet with, what's our inventory like, how are we sourcing properties, are we losing money yet, or is it just potential for what we know, but if so, how much?" I had a ton of questions.

The smile, now beaming across Jack Montgomery's face, said it all. He'd been shielding me and shielding me well, but he was worried too. And rightly so.

"Now I can say it like I mean it" he chimed in by way of reply. "Welcome back Tony. Good to see you, and the personal stuff, and I know you've got some…" he acknowledged, intuitively "…we can cover that later, okay? I'm not *all* grouch you know" he said with a grin while standing up, extending his hand to shake mine, alerting me, he'd be back shortly.

He turned and walked out of my office. His actions left me with one question of my own – where would I start?

I looked at the white graph board on the wall. The green checked sales indicators, all heading down, told me only one thing; dollar volume and units. The red numbers at the top of the board were equally concerning. All I could do was shake my head, wondering, for a moment, what my immediate move should be. I decided, initially, to call Chelsea and share the bad news, at least she would brighten my so far, very badly started, down day.

What I had hoped for was not playing out; a clearer direction, one of survival, was playing out in front of me. I realized, the first course of action was to keep the company moving forward. It certainly had to take precedence over my personal life. I owed Jack Montgomery, indeed myself, *that!*

Accepting the premise, I wondered how Chelsea might take the news, my call. Cancel her planned visit maybe? On the other side of the coin, if she did come to Hartford, *when* would I get the real time to be with her, as I would surely need and want to? Spending the last three months away from our business, returning to see and hear all I had, and fast, I was under no illusion, the Company was now beginning to suffer. The overall situation also told me, a small conundrum, maybe a large one, was looming. An uncomfortable feeling from within joined it.

Accepting my quandary, dilemma, with a sigh, I picked up my cell phone preparing to press the name – Chelsea Martin. Hesitating, for just a moment, my mind swirling, I reminisced.

~~~~~~~~~~

Having to return to Connecticut and honor my commitment, to get back to work, Chelsea and I had needed to talk. And talk we surely did, about a couple of topics that would need resolve. Being two responsible people, with past lives and a career, there were matters to deal with we both knew were going to infringe on the obvious. To be in love, wanting to marry, and share our lives and a future together was one thing, facts of life were another!

We welcomed taking on board what many people find difficult to do, believing, it *'kills the romance, cheapens the love'*. We chose not to see it that way, and so, the sensitive subjects of a pre-nuptial agreement, and a living will, had both found a place on our conversational table. Quickly finalized, mutually accepted, our pre-nup would be in force for five years, with agreements; in a marriage failure, either side walks only with what they brought to the union.

Meanwhile, the living will made provisions for, through death by accident, or from any life-threatening sickness that ended life, any surviving partner of the marriage would assume executive control of the other's portfolio, in its entirety. It was simple, amicable, and shared with love, along with a genuine belief; we'd both live until…well, accepting these days it was quite possible; we chose 100 years old! If *that* calling wasn't a reason enough for a toast to each other's good health and togetherness, then nothing would ever be. We sealed it with a small kiss and a big *'I love you'*, the balance of whatever else we might dream up was held over for another day.

On a roll, our other concerns, easy as they may have appeared to talk about, had more to do with, what happens to me and my business, plus, setting an actual date for our wedding. Unbeknown to Chelsea, for me, neither was ever going to be a difficult decision. As a Doctor, she had her many patients longer term well-being and busy general practice to consider, also, the incredible work she did as a public service in her community. Truthfully, I could not compare our professions, no matter how good I thought I was, or how successful I might want to claim to be. I had no trouble accepting, someday; soon maybe, I might not only have to re-establish and re-locate myself, but also, even, re-invent myself too, which was unquestionably, the easier direction for us both. We broached the subject with care, realistic goals prevailed.

Without reservation, or hesitation, much to Chelsea's delight, I committed myself to geographic change, to move from Hartford to DeLand. I did it with confidence and love. In not wanting to sound too cavalier, with complete honesty, I'd always seen that as *'a relatively easy decision'*. I truly liked DeLand, indeed, Florida. In accepting, Chelsea could not have been more gracious, or thankful, that we had found what seemed to be, easy common ground, dreading as she had, initially, to where it all could have led us both, concerned especially for me.

With our location settled, our pre-nup and wills out of the way, our final agreement for the immediate future became; I would put my property up, short term, as a rental in Connecticut, and that the Sunshine State would become my future home. All that remained was our date to say 'I do'.

Proposing my first well intended thought, Chelsea was immediately ecstatic. *'I could never have dreamed such an idea and one so simple, but I so like it'*. We toasted ourselves again, over another, *'I love you'*. Slotting the third Thursday in November was perfect, and to be able to give thanks for finding each other, finding love, and finding such comfort in one another, to plan and prepare for our future, Thanksgiving Day this year couldn't have been more suited. We had, to all intents and purposes, the whole of the coming summer to fully prepare, including, settling my business affairs with Jack Montgomery.

Three Days Later

Deliriously happy, it seemed appropriate; I posed *another* desire that had always and long been on my mind. For Chelsea though, with never a previous or second thought of the subject, if it did nothing else, it took her by complete surprise. In fact, the whole idea threw her entirely off balance; she was caught well off-guard.

"In prefacing what I'm about to say with, for me, the answer is already yes, but my dear sweet Chelsea, have you ever thought you'd like to have a baby?"

Her head immediately went back, in tandem with her jaw that seemed to drop, stunned at the very thought! Recovering just as fast, smiling, she answered without a moment's hesitation.

"Unequivocally *yes!* Yes, I would *love* to have a baby, *your* baby, I've always *wanted* a baby, and if we can, *please yes*, let's have a baby."

What could I say, except, that was easy?

As if for a celebration of a well-planned future, that evening we took the short drive from Glenwood to a quaint, almost primitive, ramshackle, rustic looking place I'd been told about, one Chelsea had never been to, and again, couldn't say why except quip, '*You're beginning to make me feel like I've lived a sheltered restaurant life in DeLand*'. It didn't matter in the bigger picture. I loved finding new places to share with Chelsea. It gave us a sense of new beginnings on both sides.

Our chosen place, to casually dine out, was called the Shady Oak Restaurant. Some called it a tavern, others, a fish camp, more; a great place to go. Any of the descriptions would have been apt, because it turned out to be, to this Northerner, all of the above, and maybe even a couple more.

Built right at the St. John's River edge, across from Pier 41, this place had a charm all of its own. Shady Oak style, it was a pure delight to simply sit and watch the boats sail the river, churning up the waterway, although you couldn't help but empathize, when the nearby clearly in view draw-bridge went up to allow the taller craft, the yachts, the houseboats, and larger vessels all to sail through, and everything else came to a standstill. At the same time, of course, one could also sympathize for the backup of roadway traffic that inevitably followed. The lines were, for the best part, relatively short, and if that was country living, to a guy from the city from upstate Connecticut, you had to smile. Those drivers, trapped for no more than a few minutes or more, in an idyllic setting I'd suggest, would have hated the alternative, as I knew it, lived it. That said and accepted, for us, the viewing public down at the Shady Oak, with a cold drink in our hand; all of that visual entertainment was absolutely free!

From chicken wings to catfish, and other choices in between, even alligator at times we were told, tonight, this unique *'very local'* spot attracted quite a crowd, and as we soon discovered, also many *'out of towners',* snowbirds too. We enjoyed their company. Easy to please, Chelsea and I settled on wings with a chilled chardonnay. We made the most of not only of our very delightful evening out, in a very convivial atmosphere, but also, our rapidly dwindling time left together.

By midnight, in each other's arms, we relished the thought; we had so much to look forward to. Love filled our happy Glenwood home. Brightened by just the hint of light from the moon high above, its glow filled the open draped bedroom window. The tall oak trees gently swayed in the night breeze, we could even hear the wind whispering through the rustling leaves. We wondered, in fact, decided it was, indeed, the sound of nature's melody of love to us? We believed it so.

~~~~~~~~~~

There was no question, Chelsea, DeLand, Florida, sunshine, memories – my mind was full. I doubted I could ever be the same again. Life was surely changing, had changed. From 1,000 miles away, alone, in the real estate offices of Hartford Montgomery, looking down at my cell phone screen again, this time I moved forward, pressing down on the name – Chelsea Martin. It began to ring immediately. It was not a call I wanted make.

~~~~~~~~~~

CHAPTER

TWELVE

*U*nderstand darling I do, believe me, I understand but…" I had always hated the sound of the word *'but'* however, I was not about to interrupt. Chelsea's logic had been too often proven right, and anyway; I needed her support, to say nothing of input. I was all ears! "…it makes no sense for me to leave DeLand to come and visit, only to be somewhat stranded up in Hartford, because that's what would happen, I know it. I so desperately want to see you, and be with you; however, in your words, *'there is so much to do'* and it seems to me; you should *throw* yourself into the problem and settle them as you and this Jack Montgomery now find the local situation to be, *then*, maybe, *together*, well…put it this way; two heads are always better than one, especially level heads in times of added stress, and you guys have plenty of it right now as I'm hearing it. Remember, you have the whole summer ahead of you as well, so maybe, over *that* period, all the right directions can be found, and after that, that's when we can then pick up where we left off. Consider this Tony, if need be, the wedding can wait…"

"*No, no, no, the wedding can't wait*" I implored emphatically "…our plans are our plans. Our life is much more important than making sales or doing deals, heaven help me, I do believe that much.

Putting it as blunt as I can, *no,* I *can't* and don't *want* to hear anything about changing our wedding plans Chelsea."

"But Tony, listen to me. This is *not* about summer, sales or deals. It's about survival, about loyalty, about friendship, about partners, big or small. *That's* the bigger picture. You *can't* just walk out on a man, a company, and believe it's not relevant. It *is*, unquestionably. I would be *mortified* if what you contemplate, if in fact I hear you right, if *my* partners, *my* fellow partners had an agenda and turned their backs on *me*, fully expecting me to continue, alone, as if nothing happened. *That's* what you're saying I believe and Tony, I simply *can't* let you do that."

Instantly, I heard the message, the logic, and above all, cold hard facts of life, the truth. Chelsea was right! Heart over mind wasn't going to fly, and rather quickly I surmised; I had probably been a little irrational in being somewhat heartless to just go ahead and believe I could let Jack Montgomery face the future alone, while I walked away without what might be determined as, 'not a care'. I *did* care! If there was one word that resonated heavily to me, it was *'loyalty'*, and here I was, giving the appearance of being *very* disloyal. If the tables were turned as Chelsea had clearly alluded to with her medical practice, what then? The forward vision I needed to embrace had suddenly become much clearer; level-headed Chelsea clearer.

"God Chelsea, where would I be without you? You are *so* right, and yes; I've been a little selfish, not for the *sake* of being selfish, but more to do with how much I so want for us to be together. In my absolute blindness, I've missed a couple of very key points, and now I feel bad about it. Thank you sweetheart, thank you for being so open, emphatic, so observant, and yes, *honest* with me, but it'll still begs the question; if I stay longer, it's still going to be a case of, what then, what now, at some stage? I'm actually a little more worried about what happens to *us, you and me*, over that period because I can't see us fixing our internal company problems, and find new business opportunities, *that* quick? This downturn, this housing slump if you will, could last a couple of years maybe or certainly longer than we might know, or anticipate, and that prognostication is according to many analysts, experts. You *do* realize, if *that* happens, we'll have to resort to some up and down traveling to keep us together, and that'll get to be kinda hard, hard on *both* of us, for sure."

Maybe I should have known better. What followed immediately was more Chelsea logic.

"Tony, haven't you heard the phrase; love conquers all? *That's* what we have, *that's* what we'll do; conquer the short-term problems as they arise, okay? Love always finds a way."

From a female point of view, she was right. Male logic always seems to differ. Mine sure had!

"How do you contemplate our wedding plans, our Thanksgiving date…" I started to ask.

Chelsea didn't wait for a proposed long-winded series of questions, an analytical look at the future, or reasons why, or why not. She jumped in, right over me.

"I don't see a problem with *any* of that." She quickly offered in reply, as if she had framed a stand-by plan already, or at least anticipated me. "Our wedding is the easy bit; that's simply a date and we'll keep it. As for the place, we know where that is, and when it comes to the people we'll invite, we pretty much know who they'll be, so Tony, for now; we can leave all of that part of the equation of the future fully intact and let it ride. *That*, my dear sweet man, is not a problem. *Now*, in tackling the harder part, our goal number one is, as I see it, *you* need to throw yourself into your local situation in Hartford, find the solutions with Mr. Montgomery and work them. Then, coming out the other side, given you get it right, what you'll need is to make sure you have a satisfactory follow through plan, one that *you're* personally comfortable with, in the knowledge that, it can be one hundred percent, fully functional. If the stars all line up, I don't see any real difficulty in making the rest of our…make that, *all of our plans* work. To be honest, or maybe practical, it's a time and motion thing, as I see it."

"Meaning *what* exactly?" I interrupted, a little confused at the mountain of words spoken.

If the truth was known, I was probably also a little miffed, make that, angered, at the simplicity of what she said, even the way she said it, however, I bit my tongue and listened. Chelsea was too often, mostly right, especially when taking practical, many simple situations, into account. Maybe it was the Doctor in her – always dealing with problems, and I knew first hand, everyday; she faced many of them, serious or frivolous. She continued.

"Meaning, you at least have the complete summer in Hartford to get everything done, or as much as is realistically possible, and who knows, it may not even take that long, no-one really knows right now. Regardless, what I am saying is, we can still keep our wedding date as Thanksgiving, we'll eke out a quick three or four days for a mini honeymoon somewhere, after which, assuming all the positives for the road ahead are intact; you might be at a point of only tying up loose ends anyway. We don't know that far out. The main thing is Tony; from your side, you have to completely see through, that the Company you plan on leaving in time, still functions, and that nothing you, or *we* do, infringes on Mr. Montgomery, or disadvantages him in any way, or at the least, too much. And that he still has a viable, operating company. Everything *can* and *will* work out, I'm sure. We have to be positive; it's all we've got."

My head spinning, I had to agree. It all seemed to make sense and was articulated to perfection.

"No wonder I love you Mrs. 'future' Thompson. Your suggestion and thoughts are nothing short of brilliant and I feel better already. Thank you as always; you're a gem, *my precious little gem!*"

I had to hand it to her; the most beautiful, perceptive, level-headed Doctor Chelsea Martin was a whole lot smarter than Real Estate, 'whatever', Mr. Anthony Thompson. Put so succinctly, everything she had verbalized, equated to a very workable, feasible plan, one that allowed us to get on with our lives. No wonder I missed her and our everyday interactions, conversation. Many times, often, I was in awe of her. She was an inspiration and yes, quite the intellect. Since leaving her in Florida, not a second had gone by that Chelsea hadn't been on my mind. I couldn't wait to see her again. Then, remembering her words about *'shirking duty',* or *'responsibilities',* I knew I had a job to do, and I'd better get on with it. Sitting around, moping, worrying about tomorrow and the like, wasn't going to get what I really wanted in life, done! It was time to knuckle down.

With our mutual personal solution at least in verbal place, I planned immediately to sit down with Jack Montgomery, preferably over a lunch, and lay out my thoughts and future plans that sadly, ultimately, sooner or later, was no longer going to include me in the Company we had built together from virtually, the floor up. I accepted; he probably wouldn't take kindly to anything I had to say, however, for the long term, I had no choice. In life, we all have to make decisions, oddly though, mine had been made for me sometime back with an ex-wife's departure, not by calculated design, but more from fate and kindness. My new life was already so much richer, happier and settled, and we had plans. There was something about 'the second go-round'.

The only thing dogging my thoughts, and messing up my mind a little, was the fact I had not yet had a real chance, since arriving home to Hartford, to openly, and honestly, completely fill Jack Montgomery in on all that had actually happened *to* me, and *for* me, in Florida. I doubted it couldn't wait any longer. I had a window of about six months, maximum, and thank heaven, with Chelsea's blessing. My only hope was that I could cut the odds, work hard and long with Jack to maintain our so far good fortune with the company, allowing me, then, to return to Florida, Deland and Chelsea, where together; we could make a real life for us both, even with children. It was a wonderful feeling, a reason and quite the challenge. Chelsea's timely words, just spoken – *'love conquers all'*, spurred me on. I was about to become a real estate 'dragon' slayer!

~~~~~~~~~~

The warmer winds of the approaching summer, that we longed for in the North, blew in gently, giving Jack Montgomery and I a different feeling to what we hoped would be, a harder but buoyant season. By contrast of concern, Florida's forecast, that I now paid close attention to, was vastly different to Connecticut; the biggest fear to me being the always well publicized hurricane season - June to November. I'd never paid any mind to it before, seeing it only ever as, *'that's Florida for you'*, but now, it was a situation of a new kind. The love of my life lived there; I wanted no harm to come to her. I was not immune, nor had been the rest of the country, to the well remembered, almost freak season of 2004, when hurricanes Charley, Francis and Jeannie, slammed into the State, all within about nine weeks, only to then have a fourth one, Ivan, come in right behind them. All four devastated many parts of the Sunshine State. The words that came to mind were; death, damage, destruction and heartache. I not only shuddered at the thought, but immediately, belatedly, wondered, how did Chelsea fare through that period? I had to remember to ask her.

Casting hurricane thoughts aside, I was fast concluding, deep down; Hartford could never be the same place again. Summer might be arriving, but my heart was not where it normally would have been, and work hard as I would, nothing was ever going to make me feel better until I could be with Chelsea again. Thank God for cell phones, IM's, web cams, Facetime or Skype, they would all become our saving grace in being able to see and talk to each other, as often as we wanted, and as the moments fit our far away schedules. The thought reminded me to get a new whizz-bang, updated, unlimited data iPhone; updated tools of technology that spelt, togetherness.

Scheming, searching, scheduling, I elected to throw myself into work, hoping, between Jack Montgomery and myself, that we'd hold our targets and achieve the results we were looking for, despite knowing they'd come harder than ever before. Record low mortgage rates were one thing; however, readily available finance from banks and lending agencies was another, and good credit scores were huge determining factors with finance, making borrowing much more difficult, a fact that aggravated too many people trying to keep pace with the changing economic conditions. Too quickly, it seemed doom and gloom was everywhere. Bank bailouts, politician promises, rising unemployment and more, were all downward spiraling measures ready to take a serious commercial bite, especially in my industry, and specifically with foreclosures that were on the rise.

Three Days Later

It was getting harder to cast aside negative business thoughts given all that was spewed daily on mainstream media and cable television, but in having to, it was imperative one concentrated specifically on where *any* of the plus factors were. Personally, I so wanted out of Connecticut. And *that* became my driving force to succeed. Finally, a small, simple plan, in a bigger picture emerged, to enhance our efforts, as well as provide me with a perfect platform of change – major personal change. I confidently submitted the idea.

"It seems to me Jack, that our hands are more than a little tied in correcting our course of this downturn in activity, so, as long as we don't overly embrace the words 'bigger and better', the one major tool available to us, and of course, our competitors' as well, is the Internet."

It was a relatively simple suggestion; one I tabled over a chosen cup of iced java given the first near 80 degree day was forecast, the heat coming much earlier than normal in the season ahead.

"I don't think *anyone* can sell much of *anything*, until, or unless, people are really *motivated*. We need; I believe, to fire up more Internet action to keep ourselves out there, in a way that makes it easy, and I mean like *real* easy, for the shrinking number of prospective clients who still choose, or have to be, in the market, itching to find just the right property and quickly. So I'm thinking, maybe we should do all of our listed properties as a *'highlight offer'*, and by that I mean, one that's emblazoned large on the screen, one not to be missed, then add to it; a reduced agency percentage commission, or even a flat-rate realtor cost, where we save the buyers, *or the sellers*, precious, outgoing, not wanting to part with, money. Not a penny more and not a penny less, just a flat, determined, across the board cost that can be budgeted, clearly known, up front. As well we know; closing costs can be a killer!"

"Well I'll be damned. I think you might be back. You're actually thinking again. That's great Tony, maybe we should have thought along these lines ages ago." Jack Montgomery conceded. It was time to add the rest of my thoughts.

"While we're at it Jack, we also need to boost our virtual tours, expand the basics of the service, consider a form of 3-D, plus, add more photos, and not just ones of a little bathroom, toilet, or empty bedrooms with a window; they are all mindless, not impactive. In expanding that theory, we need to include more of the property outside, the yard, the trees, foliage, or whatever else we can find to liven up a property listing, to make it more desirable. During the seasons, we need glowing, colorful pictures of what the house or property looks like when the yard, the gardens, the trees are all in full bloom, not bare, barren or the emptiness of winter as is too often seen.

Next, we need to turn each property into looking like a mini movie. It'll help the buyers and sellers, who, as we like to say, can view it all from the comfort of home, so when they make the physical trip that we know has to follow anyway, it'll seem like they've already been there. There's no doubt, we'll stand out and to be honest; it's all fairly simple to pull off when you think about it. And last but not least, let's have a 'limo pick you up' service available, and hey, we could even throw in a free Dish Service TV package for one year that we'll fund as a bonus" The last two ideas I had enthusiastically added as an immediate, after thought.

Jack Montgomery sat for a moment moving only his head, first side to side, then up and down. Maybe it was too much to absorb in one hit? His look, his silence for that few seconds, gave nothing away. Then, shifting in his chair, looking directly at me, the hint of a small grin formed.

"I have to say it Tony…" he began, after listening to my non-stop onslaught of suggestions "…to be honest, they are all excellent ideas my man. Where in the *hell* did it all this come from?"

My proposal had struck the right chord. Frankly, any idea that made life easy when it came to selling, especially real estate would have been a good idea. Summer was the period we knew, traditionally, that could be embraced with confidence, readily accepting; we made most of our sales and our bottom-line results primarily April through October. It seemed to me, no matter what the economic challenges were ahead, the Internet was going to play a much bigger role in selling virtually *anything*, and that we either embraced it on a grander scale, or wither somewhat on the vine of business. Online selling and marketing were booming, and it was a simple case of 'use it or lose!'

Three Days Later

Acknowledging I had proffered the idea; I was more than gratified, that over the years, I'd had the common sense to hone my skills and knowledge, had taken courses, sought out the experts, and skilled myself to become more than computer-savvy literate, with a receptive understanding of the power of the Information Super Highway, the Internet. I was ready to jump in, boots and all, to achieve our next, fast agreed, sales expansion. I also had another thought; an ulterior motive even, and wasted no time posing it. The timing seemed perfect. I was on a roll, and my partner seemed impressed.

"Jack, let me put something else to you."

Deep furrows formed on his forehead as his eye-brows shot upward, suggesting *'what now?'* Since returning, our many conversations so far had been simple enough with no, generally speaking, disagreements; maybe my latest idea might fly too. I had to ask.

"You know, apart from basic *'in the field'* selling, which I love and will continue to do, of course, I also pretty much, single handed, manage our website, do most of the web page designing, make the changes, handle maintenance and the rest of whatever is needed for the company, and I do it all, right here, in house, on site. Respectfully comrade…"

I had chosen to use Jack's term of endearment, and as much as I had always hated his use of it while never knowing *why* he even did, when I said *'comrade'*, it wasn't lost on him. The grin on his face said all I needed to know – he agreed; my personal specialty was exactly what I was looking for. Acknowledgement accepted, I had to remember to drop comrade it as fast as I'd picked up on it. As a word, it was never going to make into my dictionary as vocabulary and could certainly never be my way of acknowledging a friend. But Jack was different?

Continuing, "…consider this as an extension of that activity and accept, that I can actually do all of that work, *anywhere?* I don't have to sit at a given desk, be here in my office, or operate from this building to do any of the Internet things we've spoken of. Fact of the matter is, when it comes to the Internet, I could be anywhere in the world, except of course, for the immediate on-location shots."

This time, when I saw the look on Jack's face move from general concentration to a faint grin, I knew instinctively he had caught on to *exactly* where I was going with the conversation. Having sat back and quietly listened to my business thoughts and ideas, now, he couldn't wait to hear the rest. I took the opportunity to cover, down to every last detail; much more of all that went on in Florida during my vacation hiatus.

As if mesmerized, Jack Montgomery never interrupted once. In fact, probably fifteen minutes later, when he felt that I had really finished…and I had, all he could do was look at me in what I'd call a vacant stare. Finally, even with an element of surprise, he stood up, motioning to shake my hand.

'Well, well, well Mr. Anthony 'Tony' Thompson. You are one *helluva* dark horse. What can I say? I'd never have believed it unless I had heard it straight from your mouth, what with marriage and all. Who'd have thought, but *damn*, I love it. How can I fight *that*? You've actually floored me. I get where you're coming from."

Hand shake over, he sat back down and again simply looked at me. Silence prevailed. I thought it best to stall a moment. Stunned at his earlier actions, his basic acceptance, waiting, clumsily I shifted in my chair, wondering where it might all go from here. Then, just like that, as if he had gathered his thoughts, he continued.

"Okay, so, let's see how we can embrace it all because somehow, frankly; I don't see that I have much of a choice. If you can't beat 'em, join 'em they say so, let's see how best we can put all we need to together and accommodate you old friend. I'm sure we'll find a way."

This time, it was my turn to smile. I'd used his word *'comrade'* in my conversation, while he used mine, *'old friend'* in his. The endearment tables had been switched, but then, everything about us as a team was being switched as we planned our attack to forge ahead. One thing I had noticed, felt; there was a comfortable feeling about all that had transpired; it was as if we were exploring new territory. I guess we were really!

~~~~~~~~~

Three Days Later

Chelsea was thrilled with the news, that I'd be able to spend many on and off weeks in both Hartford and DeLand. My well-prepared and personal interactive computer program, to be set up between Jack Montgomery and me, that allowed us daily contact anytime we were apart, primarily through webcams and networking links, that also enabled our computers to literally *'talk to each other'*, was listened to and embraced willingly. He had, understandably, asked many questions. It was a very simple approach to what once may have been an insurmountable problem, and any doubts I may have had about getting Montgomery to embrace the concept, turned out to be quite the opposite. In the end, he had no qualms about it, in fact; he was quite excited, especially as it also provided an opportunity for him to learn more about the rapid, ever-changing technology and its capabilities, more than he had ever known, or had ever believed possible. He accepted, graciously; he really needed to *'get on board'*, understand more about computers, thereby compete, and allow himself, personally, to move confidently with the times. Unaware, as he seemed to be, nevertheless, I was not comfortable with his reference or inference when he registered greater awareness of *'needs or ability'* and using the term *'in case of the unforeseen, like, one being hit by a bus!'* I let it slide as a figure of speech.

Agreeing to work on and off from Florida, for me, became an easy solution to both our needs. I also volunteered a reduced remuneration to ease the pain of our, what could be, lesser sales; my act of good faith to be with Chelsea. *'We'll see'*, was all Jack said about the offer. Operating an away from the home office wasn't ever going to be complicated to the Company, it's just that, initially, it was quite different, *'but we'll make it work'*, again, became Jack Montgomery's supportive reaction. A major recognition also surfaced from our agreement; reiteration of the trust, and the strong bond of the friendship we both had in each other. We were a great team, and over the summer, well into the early, leaf changing fall, we planned never to miss a beat in business. We would prosper we believed.

Lying in Chelsea's arms one night, just before drifting off to sleep, I felt her hand touch my arm lightly. I moved to touch hers in return. A sort of love touch we both felt, as if silently, to tell each other, we were close, together. In words barely audible I heard her say, "I love you Tony; I just want you to know that before I leave you in sleep." She gently squeezed my arm adding, "Good night darling." What a beautiful way to end a day, to drift off to sleep.

"Goodnight sweetheart, love you too" I managed to say, sighing lightly.

~~~~~~~~~~

Freedoms in operations meant I could plan my days to whatever made sense to me in both home bases, and I seized every opportunity I could. Two delightful events Chelsea and I could share together for the first time, included the Volusia County Fair that brought with it, not only the traditional fun of fair, the Ferris wheel, the food, the rides and music, but a host of activities that were designed for the whole family. What a treat as we watched the clog dancers, the wood choppers, the talent quest, there were even alligators and snakes. The County Fair was small-town fun and frivolity, second to none, and we loved every moment of it.

Another event suited us both, but this one, this time for a very special reason. Anxious to give each other a memorable gift for our planned, much-anticipated Thanksgiving Day wedding, now almost here, the Annual Deland Fall Festival of the Arts was the perfect venue to find the perfect gift we wanted for each other.

Being one of those small-town Main Street USA activities DeLand was famous for, the closed down Boulevard allowed the many vendors to exhibit their marvelous work including sculptures, paintings, glass, art, photos, wood carvings and ceramics…what an array. We made an afternoon of it; first, listening to the staged music performers, then wandering in and out of the many booths before stopping for a stall cooked bratwurst sausage lunch and a glass of wine, then, back to the booths again. And so the time passed by.

Three Days Later

Later, we agreed to split up, to finalize our personal gift shopping, something we had mutually decided on, but not declared. I racked my brain as to what had caught Chelsea's attention while we had casually wandered around, I was sure she did the same. I had a couple of things in mind, specifically, the booth that had a backdrop sign with the name Lightning Ridge on it and a kangaroo. It had to be Australian, and I was well aware, the best opals in the world come from the Land Down Under so, problem solved, maybe? The owner and I got to talking. Finally, I settled on a magnificent large opal, perfectly cut and shaped to fit into sterling silver, on a chain. The necklace was beautiful, and I was sure Chelsea would just love it.

Half an hour later, back together again, our gifts were wrapped and saved for the following week. The packages held our secrets. A great day, we headed back to Glenwood.

~~~~~~~~~~

November 23rd - it was our Thanksgiving to remember, forever. Our wedding, held in the back yard of Chelsea's, soon to be our lovingly shared 'married' home, was a relatively short ceremony, conducted by a marriage celebrant, preceded by the strains of a most wonderful piece of music from Phantom of the Opera that I had discovered a few years ago. It had left an indelible imprint in my mind. Songsters from England, Sarah Brightman and Cliff Richard sang, All I Ask of You, their words epitomizing everything I felt about Chelsea.

As my best man, Jack Montgomery was magnanimous during the reception, in his responses to my somewhat longer drawn-out speech, of where my life had gone over the past many months. Being equally accommodating to my needs personally, sanctioning all of my carefully explained plans, including our wedding, in delivering his closing, even heartfelt speech, he posed an interesting surprise *'...I could never have stood in your way comrade, my friend. We did it well in Hartford, now, why not DeLand; let's make what we have, work bigger and better, south of the Mason-Dixon line'.* Had I heard him right? Open a bricks and mortar office in Florida, in DeLand? While my head was spinning and I was grinning ear to ear, Chelsea looked at me, whispering softly '...*it was the right thing to do Tony. Friends are so hard to come by, and in your lifetime, you can count real true friends, all on just one hand. Jack's a good man*'. Again, Chelsea, now my wife was right; in Jack Montgomery – I had the best.

The ceremony, the afternoon and evening over, the guests all gone, we were finally alone. In our own moment of peaceful silence, we opened our gifts to each other. With the wrapping peeled away, I thought Chelsea was going to faint as she carefully separated the tissue, to see and hold, her opal necklace. Having never owned one, always wanting one, I had chosen well.

"Whatever made you think of such a wonderful gift?" she asked, not expecting an answer. "I've seen them, marveled at them, but there was never an occasion to own one, and now, *look at this*. It's so *beautiful* and the *colors*..." She looked across at me. I'd chosen well.

With her opal glistening around her neck, seemingly unable to stop touching it, feeling it, making sure it was still there; Chelsea relented long enough to hand me two wrapped packages. She had broken the rule, one gift, but it didn't matter. The DeLand Fall Festival of the Arts had delivered as promised in different, unique.

The 'Forgotten in America' booth I recalled only too well, had been a collection of photographs the extremely gifted and well imagined owner/photographer had chosen to represent, with his fast fading images that once was the USA. Buildings, cars, signs, scenery, streets and more, shot in both black and white, and color, were spectacular. In package number one, Chelsea had chosen for me, knowing my love of all things 'old' or 'antique' that represents *'lost Americana'*, an 8 x 10 framed photo of a somewhat rusted 1948 station-wagon delivery vehicle, standing outside a by-gone era *filling station'* named Clifton's Gas & Corner Store, complete with a tall, red metal gasoline stand, its hand action pump and clearly marked gallons, glass bowl on top. Wow! That was truly a masterpiece in my eyes. I loved it.

Gift number two was era similar; it too, was one-of-a-kind. A virtual unknown process, drawing art by burning method, it was a depiction of a country town Amtrak railway station set into the landscape, again, of a bye gone era, although remarkably, to me, it was clearly reminiscent of Deland's Amtrak station, still very active today – in fact, that it might be the DeLand station was my very first thought. Proud of her selection, Chelsea explained, the artist takes a flat piece of smooth pine wood, then, using a hot metal tool, as if a pencil, burns, stroke by stroke, the picture into the wood – *'true art by burning'*. Both gifts were quite stunning. Chosen with love, we had found for each other, the perfect wedding gift, and an extension of a Thanksgiving to remember.

Three days later, our short honeymoon was over. Having chosen the scenic route, driving to Florida's Panhandle area had been a marvelous trip we both really enjoyed. Singling out the magnificent coastal areas, the inviting beach cottages, and the historic waterfront of Apalachicola and more; it was a place we earmarked, to be sure to come back and visit someday in more depth; a little promise, we made to each other.

With a busy doctor's office in DeLand, many patients who needed continued attention, and a satellite realtor's office, more active probably than many back in Connecticut, the marriage of Mr. Anthony (Tony) Robert Thompson, and now Mrs. Chelsea April Thompson, was brought back to reality as we returned to Glenwood to make a once lonelier, interesting home, into a loving happy home and soon maybe, the sound of little feet. Both Chelsea and I wanted a baby, our ultimate declaration of love for each other that could be fulfilled, despite a sadness of sorts; that we hadn't found each other much earlier in our lives.

~~~~~~~~~~

A personal endorsement of my working relationship and co-operations with Jack Montgomery, and her new-found friendship with him, came direct from Chelsea. In her sincere and very heartfelt phone invitation that he join us for Christmas and New Year, she emphasized how wonderful it might be to celebrate somewhere else for a change, and that he forsake, this year, Hartford's snow and snowmen, slush and sleet and leave it all to his Connecticut connections. He accepted immediately, agreeing with her; that he'd love the sunshine, Spanish moss and Southern hospitality, and that it would do him good to switch States, and pass up for the first time ever, as it would be, he confessed - a white Christmas. Sounding almost serious, he mourned, *'Bing might never forgive me, tradition was tradition'* however…?

A self-confessed bachelor, he had not made any plans, and *'yours was always going to be my best offer'*, he jocularly added with a laugh. Making a point of his bachelorhood left the door wide open for Chelsea to add to the moment as she threw back, although she meant it, deep down, maybe it was time for him to *'get a better life'* adding *'and a woman might be just the answer you know. We're not all scary prospects. You should think about it Jack'*. He promised he would – someday!

Keeping the secret, we'd known somewhat earlier, New Years Eve was the occasion we chose, to finally, share our good news. Chelsea's pregnancy had been confirmed, but announcements were delayed until we were comfortable there wouldn't be any complications. Being a Doctor, she knew the hoops that had to be climbed over, age, specifically, and was cognizant of the need to be totally satisfied the tests were safe and one-hundred percent accurate with absolutely no room for error or setback. She was also aware of the care she would have to take of herself throughout the pregnancy, especially no doubt in the later stages. When the countdown started to herald in the New Year, so did the countdown for Mr. and Mrs. Tony and Chelsea Thompson. After hugs, kisses, shared words and jubilation of friends surrounding us, with a puffed-up chest, I gladly took center stage, quieting the crowd.

"Ladies and gentlemen, friends and neighbors literally, one last thing to say and share before we head into the night, although the party's not over yet, we're not trying to get rid of you…" I very quickly added amidst light laughter "…Chelsea and I just want to add one small thing with y'all, as you say down this way…" The room was now silent, "...come August, thereabouts; we are proud to share with everyone here, the news that our own, very little DeLand-ite will grace our lives and..."

My speech ended right there for me. I couldn't get another word in. The immediate response was beyond expectations. Amidst cheers and hand clapping, more hugs, and words of congratulations that immediately followed, I simply gave up trying to say another word. There was no point; I'd said it all anyway. Music and refreshed drinks were more the order of the evening and moment. Our deliriously happy, next-door neighbor Meghan summed it up to me personally with her warm and loving embrace.

'What a wonderful thing to happen at this time in your life. You are both so right, so good together, as always, and I can only wish you all the love and happiness in the world. You are beautiful people, and it's our blessing and good fortune to be so close to you both..." then, holding her pointed forefinger up at me, smiling of course, added "...*but you make sure Mr. Thompson*, any help you need, *any time*, you *know* that Mark and I are here for you okay. You *will* remember won't you?"

I might have been the relative new kid on the block, but I knew, had seen, was sharing, the friendship that existed between them all. Meghan's request, demand, was a no brainer! I was more than grateful to have been welcomed so kindly into the fold. Florida was already far out surpassing Connecticut. The warmth of the people matched every bit all the Sunshine State stood for, and certainly nicer than the northern chill (of winter) and yes, spending more of my time, now living in small-town America, in contrast to big-city lights - it was all I could ever wish for. Today, tonight, was one of the happiest days of my life. I felt truly blessed - from whence I'd come to where I was – safe in the arms and love of my wife, my dear and most beautiful Chelsea.

CHAPTER

THIRTEEN

Not a beat was missed on two fronts. Chelsea was growing more pregnant every day, proud of her little bump. Glowing with pride, she was a beauty to admire and adore, and I did both. And the small heart that beat inside the body, of what we knew would be our little baby girl, was healthy beyond expectations. We'd already started the name game, but were in no hurry to settle yet. All I was ever anxious about was for Mother and daughter to be well, although I certainly had no fears when it came to medical care and attention, the Doctor's that surrounded Chelsea's very life made sure of that.

~~~~~~~~~~

Business in Connecticut continued not to miss a beat either. With a slightly milder winter than normal so far, brisk activity fielded through the Internet from the Hartford Montgomery website, kept our sales figures ahead of corresponding months to register a sliding upward modest percentage increase in sales. Jack Montgomery said I could stay away forever if the current rate of business inquiry and successful closures kept up, swiftly confirming, he was obviously.

Three Days Later

'just kidding around', which I gathered anyway. Our original agreement was working out somewhat better than expected, and it augured well for the plans we had for later in the year taking the company in bigger and more diverse directions.

Jack's only point made, that bothered me a little, was the expectation of me, maybe, spending extra time in Connecticut in the summer months, especially, even, when the weather changed during spring. With Chelsea pregnant, my feelings about *that* course of action ran quite the opposite in expectation. I reserved my thoughts to a later date sticking, for now, to my already in place, planned visits, as programmed. Chelsea and I had decided and agreed; she would accompany me later in the year, either late spring or early summer, but certainly not until the cold and snow had well disappeared. Regardless, we'd pick the first logical opportunity, knowing, as we dearly wanted; traveling to Hartford would help her understand more of my past life. I took great delight in adding, in jest of course, *'before you stole my heart and changed it completely - for the better.'*

~~~~~~~~~~

The biggest New Year treat afforded me personally came quite unexpectedly. Friends of Meghan and Mark threw out the best offer I'd had since sharing my first Christmas/New Year with Chelsea; a chance, finally, to attend the NASCAR Daytona 500. I couldn't wait. The thrill of watching those cars race and bank on one of the world's most famous tracks at the legendary venue on International Speedway in Daytona Beach was beyond expectations, and to think, no more than 25 miles from our own front door. It was an experience never to be forgotten.

Despite being surrounded by it year after year, not being a race-car fan, it wasn't, never had been, a *'must do'* for Chelsea, whereas for me, since I was a kid, I'd only ever dreamt of it. Why, I don't know, but an unexpected reaction of being there was the cacophony of noise and frankly, I should have known better. Nevertheless, the smell of oil, the speed, the roar of the crowd completely took over.

And so, with the laps complete, and the sight of that checkered flag waving, finally, I could at last claim, *'an experience no longer left to the books and movies – been there, done that!'*

For old times' sake, after the race, I took a little time out to visit my old friend Gareth Harrison at the Sun King Lodge remembering; he was the first one ever to tempt me in attending the Daytona 500. Not surprised at seeing me again, his words, *'you saw the light and moved to Florida';* I might have expected! He hadn't changed. Accepting his kind expressions of happiness for Chelsea and me, true to his style of promoting everything Daytona, in my farewell, he had to throw in the next event, *'...and you gotta witness it!'* he implored. I would; I assured him.

Bike Week immediately followed the Daytona 500. With riders and enthusiasts in the area by the many literal thousands, I wondered if the rest of the country ever really knew what they were missing down south. DeLand spearheaded the ten-day event by closing its streets, and what a sight downtown, bikers flocked by the thousands to park their machines then quickly gave in to either shop, wine and dine, or listen to some great rock and roll bands. It was an absolute eye-opener to this northerner who was only just beginning to fully understand the difference, the beauty, the imagination, of the will of the people of the South to make their part of the country truly a way of life and style, their own, and at the very least, always fun. Florida was winter warm and sunny, alive and well, quite the contrast from digging out from the snow or the cold winds of Connecticut. I really loved not only my life, but all I was learning, experiencing, as it was evolving, indeed believing, the South would always be - constantly rising. And Chelsea was getting bigger too!

~~~~~~~~~

The advents of spring to summer were most wonderful months. The trees, flowers and bushes had all transformed from dull and bare, to full bloom color. Work may have remained very much a part of our regular schedules; however, it, nevertheless, remained my

Three Days Later

always sought *'feel good'* time, of not only the year but also, everyday life for Chelsea and me. Apart from the glorious colors now all around us; love too was in the air - ours.

Finally, the time was also perfect for us to share together; our too long ago wish, for our slow northern trip to Connecticut. Slow only in wanting to enjoy the journey, to see more of the USA, something we were both a little remiss in not having done much of, at least lately. What we had seen was mostly by accident and contained realistically around Florida, closer to home.

Apart from this trip, reality was, with Chelsea well pregnant; we had little choice but to accept, unquestionably; it might be quite a while for any considerations of shared travel, after the baby arrives, the circumstance's dictating, we'd be prone to stay more at home, at least until the baby began walking. Watching others from afar, children changed everyone's lives. We were now so anxious for our turn.

A reflection in conversations about children, and of course love, was certainly something Chelsea and I had shared many times along the way. From her point of view, two things prevailed. Her unexpected divorce had brought to a complete halt any thoughts of children, and as time passed, by her own admittance, she doubted she would, or wanted to, fall in love or even get married again anyway, concerned more that if it failed, she would only put herself through the same misery of a world falling apart. For a while, she declared, she actually had an anti on men, all men! As I listened, I was thankful that I was able to enter her life at a time when, while she might not have been consciously looking, conducive and timely as a cruise might have been, a fact I was sure made all the difference in the end, the much nicer part was; we still managed to find each other anyway. Broken hearts, love and marriage never did any soul any good, we both knew it – agreed. Slowly, together, we'd both changed a lot of late.

For me, on the other hand, I repeated, for a marriage to have lasted as long as mine had to Jessica; it had never ceased to amaze me that she didn't fall pregnant. In the early days it was true, we didn't want children. Years later, casting aside our selfish agenda in favor of travel, mellowing in thought about it, Jessica still did not conceive. If she had planned it that way, I didn't know; always, an admitted shortfall of mine. When we broke up, it was only then I was actually thankful there were no children. However, in openly talking about it with Chelsea, confessing really, I realized the shallowness of my thoughts and reflections. In my life, in truth, I would have loved a child. Thank God I told her, that we met, that our lives have taken the path they have. I was now so looking forward to finally fulfilling a dream, and to be able to share it the way Chelsea and I both could was, somehow; the way God meant it to be. Yes – I began to believe quite deeply in the old adage – *'God works in mysterious ways.'* For us, it appeared to be more than true.

~~~~~~~~~~

"Well, look at you two all matched up," were the first words out of Meghan's mouth

She and Mark joined us just before we were about to head out on our drive to Connecticut. Her reference was to the matched t-shirts we were uniformly wearing, for no other real reason, than staying comfortable for the initial leg of the long journey ahead.

"Is this your way of being true to Florida while you're gone, or is this *your* way Tony to put a big stamp of what we all might construe as being, approval of your new home, city and State?

"All of the above..." I told her emphatically "...and cute huh?"

Having designed the idea, I had ordered the shirts from Special T's downtown, on a whim, a gimmick. When I showed them to Chelsea, she thought they were perfect, proud as always, of course, in anything to do with DeLand. The custom-made shirts were of a license plate design visually, with Deland printed through the middle and the zip code FL 32720 below it. Stenciled on a blue shirt for me, pink for Chelsea, they were simple enough, different and had the desired effect given it registered with Meghan and Mark. They liked 'em! To me, that was endorsement enough. If deep down they were thinking, *'corny'* – then that was okay too!

"Bye you two, have fun. See all you can see, stop often and importantly, drive safe and carefully. Oh, and make sure you stay in touch." She added, not as an afterthought. We assured them we would, on all counts.

Of huge consolation, to me, they were also looking after our home and property. I was anxious for all my newly acquired plants and shrubs not to die while we were gone; they'd need water, fertilizer. Of late, the garden had been a small passion of mine. I wanted all the color I could muster to be in full bloom on our return. Fuss as I might have, in her own inimitable way, Chelsea had told me *have a little faith, your garden will look nice; Meghan and Mark won't let you down*. I knew she was right, but that still didn't stop me issuing my instructions to them. With a slight nudge, coupled with a smile, we were urged to be on our way, with absolute assurances; all will be well.

"I am really looking forward to this trip, this break" Chelsea's confirmed as we were pulling out of our driveway, on to Glenwood Road that would take us directly to State Road 11 and Bunnell, anxious as we were to stay on the back roads before cutting across to Highway 1. Easy to agree with her sentiment, I nodded an approving yes.

"I feel wonderful, so happy, and…you know something Tony, do you realize; this is our first *real* vacation together. We can't count the cruise we were on as we didn't know each other then, or the quickie honeymoon trip, well I don't think we can unless you do."

It was unanimous; both of those times together were different. This trip – we'd make it a *real* vacation.

First stop was St. Augustine. If the explorer, navigator, Columbus discovered America, then *who* discovered this most delightful little town? I soon learned it was the Spanish explorer Ponce DeLeon in 1513, however; it would be another 50 years before it was settled making it the oldest city occupied by Europeans in the United States.

I immediately thought of Ponce Inlet and the lighthouse I'd visited, and started quickly trying to put it all together, in my head.

'Dates aside, Columbus, Ponce Deleon, native Americans, culture, religion, language, buildings and more - wouldn't someone, anyone, feel intimidated 'discovering' an already inhabited land' I suggested, before accepting history is history, no matter how it is written? Too many had a claim on 'discovering America',' I believed.

Wisely, Chelsea dodged the whole issue. It was a conversation she didn't particularly want to enter into…too controversial! She did mumble softly though, *'It does beg the question, why Columbus Day?'* I took that as passive interest without laboring the subject. 'Gotcha', was my only thought.

100 miles from DeLand, a road-trip holiday, history abounding, already my mind was swirling. And our journey only just started. What could be next that we'll discover I soon wondered? Not long after our late lunch, over the border into Georgia, we were heading directly for Savannah, my choice as the first stopover. Silently, for no reason, I couldn't help but remember the last time I had started to make this journey, although it was not a thought, I was going to air – ever! In its own way, it was a *bad* memory, and on this trip, I only wanted good ones. I had to inwardly cringe though. By a close call, the very same woman who occupied my mind last time, who I could have lost along the way, thankfully, happily, was now my wife, pregnant with our child, and sitting right beside me was lovingly sharing my life. And I was at peace with my world at this point and time, so looking forward to many more years ahead with her.

Making good time on our journey, Chelsea began to get tired, Reluctantly she'd tell me so.

"Then we stop darling', can't have the little baby fretting now can we?" I gladly told her.

"I think we did just a little too much walking around that Castillo de San Marcos Fort in St. Augustine, and I'm paying for it, so if you don't mind…" she started to qualify as if it were a burden to our travel plans.

"Mind…' I exclaimed "…I don't mind *anything*. You and the…" I paused. The timing was perfect to cover the topic "…you know Chelsea; we're going to have to settle on the baby's name soon I think. I don't want to keep calling her *'the baby',* do you? What do *you* think? Will we stay with one of the four chosen front-runners for us soon?"

"I do, and actually, truthfully; I'm leaning toward Sarah. I *love* that name" she instantly wanted to claim.

Twenty-five miles outside of Savannah we were settling on our, about eight or nine weeks to go yet, little daughter's name. Fortunately, the conversation helped dispel Chelsea's tiredness; an excellent deflection.

"Okay, but are you *really* sure, *a hundred percent sure?* Once we start calling her by name, even *before* she's born, we can't change mid-stream I'd doubt, so think about it. Rebecca, Austen and Emma, they're all nice as well and are in the mix." Chelsea glanced sideways at me.

"Well…' She hesitated, "…well" she repeated, still obviously in thought. I gathered she was about to get serious. I hoped so because I really wanted us to know her name and start using it in all we loved to discuss about her, especially nearing closer every day to her arrival date.

"…how about Sarah Austen, it's a combination of two of my front-runner favorites of our chosen names so…now it's back to you, your call."

I had no problem with *any* of the names except; I thought, we should have added Chelsea as the baby's middle name, but she would have none of it; she was adamant, *no Chelsea*. I couldn't understand it and wondered why, but in fairness, it didn't matter. We were delighted; Sarah Austen Thompson. It was a good name, a strong name while still being nicely feminine.

For the next thirty-six hours, Savannah, Georgia was our stop. I delighted in showing Chelsea what little I had learned on my many moons ago southern sojourn, which was factually, not a lot but still, most enjoyable and enlightening. Once the Colonial and State Capitol of Georgia, today it was more a seaport. We spent most of our time in the delightful historic district, then, slowly wandered a few of the small inner-city parks before visiting the restored nineteenth-century warehouses on the most elegantly presented Riverfront Plaza. Dinner was typically southern; we chose the simplest of all, fried chicken and corn with homemade biscuits and gravy, and for me, a beer brewed locally. It was a wonderful occasion, a beautiful evening; we couldn't have been happier, and although we'd only just begun, we never wanted our traveling to end. And we still had a long way to go. Chelsea had declared already having never been there; allow three days in New York City. Her wish became my command. With at least eight hundred miles to go before we reached *that* mega metropolis, it was easy to agree. And I wanted to anyway.

"Where are you already?" were the first words to jump out of the phone when I called Jack Montgomery back. Without waiting for a reply, he added, "How long does it take to drive from Deland to Hartford for Christ's sake? What is it, *another* holiday you're taking?"

I wasn't expecting what I called a rant and rave; his hostile tone caught me off guard. Somehow, it seemed eerily déjà vu? I didn't like what I'd just heard coming at me.

No sir..." I replied sarcastically "...it's called taking it easy, looking after the family and nice things like that. Does that ring a bell, does it?" I challenged in reply.

"A bell, no it *doesn't!* It just tells me you don't have any urgency about getting here, not quite what I thought I must say." Sarcasm and contempt of sorts defined his mood and attitude.

What was it about Jack Montgomery sometimes? When you least expected it, he seemed to verbally, conversationally, run hot and cold. But why? I couldn't believe it. For whatever reason, this time, he had adopted an attitude that I could only read as, confrontational; it was very evident. My immediate conclusions were, it was probably because he wasn't getting laid, hated being a loner as he had most of his life or, there was a jealousy about me now, or certainly since I had remarried, something that had escaped him. I was also very aware; it wasn't because he was gay!

"Jack, we'll be there in a few days okay. Live with it. We don't exactly have a problem right now from a company point of view, unless you've created one in the past three days, and assuming you haven't, Chelsea and I arrive, when we arrive. Not a day earlier, not a day later okay, that's when we'll be there and that's it! Now, what else bothers you today?"

Cynical conversation in return, it didn't matter. I'd had enough; I didn't want to talk anymore. Changing instantly, he must have got my message.

"Oh all right" he seemed to lightheartedly, casualy, concede "Just give me a call Tony when you're a day out thereabouts, and I'll confirm the hotel reservations. Sorry about that little outburst. I guess I'm a little frustrated, story of my life these days; anyway, I'll still be glad when you're here though. Call me later huh?"

The phone went dead. Rudeness aside, mellowed a little, Montgomery was gone as fast as he had arrived. That might have been just as well as we were probably both a little agitated I chose to accept, egging each other on maybe.

"What was *that* all about?" Chelsea queried having heard the one-sided interaction.

"Oh nothing, it's just Jack being Jack. We need to find him a woman" I told her. "He's such a grouch lately. I'm sure it has something to do with his lack of attention, and I mean from *women*. He needs to settle down and get a life, or at least have something, or someone to look forward to when the day is done. He's a real, you know what sometimes, but likeable, as well we know."

"He's not gay is he?" Chelsea innocently asked.

Her retort made me openly laugh out loud given I had only seconds ago already dismissed that as an absolute no way, but it was eerily strange she should think it. I made sure she knew he wasn't. However, then again, *could* he have changed, and I didn't know it? If he had, I couldn't pick it either.

Having eaten, we relaxed in the Jacuzzi in our room before retiring to the huge king-size bed that graced the charm of decorative southern décor at the very comfortable, Azanalea Inn. The nicest feeling I could ever experience, when any day was over, was lying together, in the arms of my wife, snuggled close, holding her body to mine. Rubbing my hands softly, gently over the growing bulge of her tummy, was as rewarding as any man could ask. Her womanhood and love were a given…and oh, how I loved this lady, who carried my baby, our newly-named little baby girl, Sarah Austen, who I couldn't wait to see, and hold in my arms someday, soon. Sleep came easy as we anticipated another day of bliss, doing nothing really, and sharing each other.

Next morning over breakfast we'd decided, well me anyway, to head for Norfolk/Virginia Beach, then on to Washington DC, unless something else captured our imagination on our way to and through North Carolina. At this early point in the journey north, we didn't have a care in the world, enjoying only, being together. With our bags packed, relaxed and looking absolutely radiant, Chelsea eased her way into the passenger seat of the Mustang, alongside me. Carefree and full of abandonment, we headed out, welcomed by another day of not only magnificent sunshine, but also a day of leisurely driving, stopping wherever and whenever our little ol' hearts desired.

With Savannah fading in the rear-view mirror, forever changing our inquisitive, impulsive, touristy minds, it didn't take long to realize, that our carefree approach to life and travel was already facing trouble in destinations. Gazing on all the huge billboards, you couldn't help but be bludgeoned over the head with, as they beckoned travelers to make so many choices - Charleston, Myrtle Beach and many other attractions, in between, or beyond.

On one hand, it didn't matter time-wise, while on the other hand, well…I didn't want to think about it. Jack Montgomery had annoyed me; our conversation memory lingered still. We'll go wherever the road takes us, I had now firmly decided, feeling even more wanderlust, freer spirited, the way life should be sometimes. And yet, fast as I got over Jack's verbal nonsense, accepting we would do the journey my way, wherever the wind blows, I couldn't help but conjure up a smile, as it occurred to me; if we continue to have such a casual mood about our unplanned road trip, we could well be two weeks, even three, getting back to Connecticut and Hartford. Now, wouldn't *that* really test the PR skills of Mr. Jack Montgomery? I instinctively knew, as my more sensitive and fair-minded wife suggested to me, *that* wouldn't be wise, and I shouldn't test him. I guessed I wouldn't.

Free as two birds in flight, on back road secondary highways of visual beauty, we cruised silently onward – at peace with all that surrounded us.

CHAPTER

FOURTEEN

The screeching of tires was the last thing Chelsea heard as she lifted her head from the light doze she had been in, only to see a semi-trailer truck that had swerved across the highway, heading straight for us. I had no choice! I had nowhere to go. The truck was too big to avoid, leaving me absolutely no chance for any accurate evasive action that I had calculated immediately as - zero and none! With Chelsea screaming, hitting a highway mileage marker post first, I veered toward the grass-covered decline of what I believed was, probably, nothing more than a ditch. At that point, the car became partially airborne, and at the same time; it began tipping to its side. When we hit the ground, the car flipped over...and over! Beyond that, it was all a complete blank.

On opening my eyes, all I could see was a blur of white. Slowly, lifting and turning my head slightly, left, then right, nothing changed, everything remained a blur, I had no idea where I was. In my mind; I could picture the last image I had physically seen; it was a truck coming straight at me. I well remembered pulling hard on the steering wheel, shouting, but had no idea what I was shouting, or, at that moment, to whom? I moved my head back,

Three Days Later

then to a forward position. The blur of white remained except, this time, much brighter.

"Where am I?" I asked, to no-one.

My body didn't want to move. Then, *a voice?*

"I'm Doctor Justin James Jefferson." I heard "You're in a hospital Mr. Thompson, and let me tell you, you're safe"

"Hospital..." I cried out loudly. "*What* hospital, *where*, *how* long have I been here? What's *wrong*, what's wrong with me?" That *voice* again?

"Three days, you've been here three days" I heard in reply. "You've been in a light coma, but to hear you speak is already a good sign. Don't worry; we'll take care of you."

"Three days, a coma. What happened? Oh, oh...the car. Did you say three days? It can't be, it...I, I can't belie..."

Some things were slowly beginning to come back to me. I felt I was panicking; I knew I was anxious but needed more information from *'the voice'.*

"Take it easy Mr. Thompson, *please*; you need to relax, take it easy. You were in a car accident, but you're safe now. I'll answer all your questions in a moment, first though, now that you're awake, we need to check some vital signs so *please*, keep as still as you can."

I felt a hand touch my shoulder that strengthened as I was forced to lie back in the bed. I was scared. I had no control over me. However, there was comfort in *'the voice'.*

"But I can't seem to see Doctor; all I'm seeing is a blur...although, wait...it's moving; I can see the blur, moving. Is that you? Are you wearing white, dressed in white or something?"

"Yes I am, *but please; I beg of you*, lie still for a moment and concentrate on me. Look directly at *me*, at the white you see and concentrate as if you're staring. Try not to blink your eyes."

I followed the directions I'd, thankfully, heard with clarity. While trying hard not to blink, I saw the blurred outline of a man, ever so slowly, emerge more clearly into view. As each second passed, there he was, *'the voice'*, the Doctor, now leaning closer into me, staring, looked directly into my face, my eyes. As if by magic, the vision kept clearing.

Black hair, darkish skin, a thin moustache, rimmed glasses, a shirt, blue, an open collar, a stethoscope draped around his neck, his buttoned up white jacket. Aaah…with the earlier blur of pure white, coming into focus, I saw *'the voice'*, standing before me.

"I see you Doctor. I see you quite clearly" was the best I could offer, with a degree of excitement; I was sure.

Why it should mean anything I don't know, but I felt the beam of a smile on my face even? I suddenly felt a whole lot better, knowing I was back, in the land of the living.

"Excellent, a very good start" he told me "You're on the mend already, very good."

As the Doctor pulled back from me, his outline began to get blurry again, however, nowhere near as bad this time. He must have anticipated what I was about to say as he immediately assured me *'…if I'm still blurry, that's okay'.*

Lifting my arms from my side, one at a time, bending them up and down while holding my elbow, to have me lift my legs, also one at a time, bending them at the knee, to then poking and prodding somewhat all over my body, my stomach, ribs and upper chest, then feeling around my head and neck, the Doctor finally withdrew, taking two steps back from the bed.

"Amazing, very good, exactly what I wanted to see, *excellent*. Now let's make sure your vision is responding. Can you still see me?" I nodded affirmative. "Clearly, or blurry still?" he questioned.

"Pretty much clearly although there is a little haze there still" I confessed.

Momentarily, disturbing, to me, although my vision was slightly impaired, I could distinctly tell, the doctor was shaking his head.

"I might take a much closer look" he suggested.

Stepping forward to immediately lean right down into my face, again, shining a very bright light straight into my left pupil, then the right, before ending up looking directly into the center of both eyes, what was he looking for I wondered? I had no idea, hoping only he would continue with his positive words, and say something encouraging. I tried not to blink. Finally, he pulled back from me to stand upright.

Three Days Later

"Excellent…" he declared again "…excellent."

I felt better with those words. Maintaining his stance, he immediately began writing notes on a clipboard that he finally placed at the foot of the bed.

Suddenly, without rhyme or reason, I shocked myself. It was as if my mind went into a full remembrance mode. *Why* I hadn't immediately asked about Chelsea, before I allowed anyone to do anything to me, I could not fathom? Clear as clear, I remembered with vivid recall; I was not alone in the car wreck. Was it the three-day coma that deadened my mind, my brain? Was it the blur of life I saw when I came to or…what was it? None of it mattered? Now that I knew *where* I was and *what* had happened, rather loudly, I burst into a series of questions, seeking and needing immediate answers.

"Doctor, doctor…" I called out in almost a panic cry.

Spinning around as if he had an emergency on his hands, looking directly at me, I could see the immediate consternation on his face. Not meaning to, I obviously scared him a little.

"My wife, my wife, Chelsea." I asked, probably a little too loudly. "What happened to my wife, the baby? Oh God, tell me Doctor, please, tell me they are all right. What has…"

"It's all right Mr. Thompson." He said in a soft reassuring voice of authority." Your wife is just fine. She can't wait to see you; she'll be here as fast as we can…"

"Oh God, thank God", I cried "Thank God, but the baby, what about th…"

"Mr. Thompson…" I heard, this time more forcefully in reply, while a nurse pressed her hand lightly on my upper body. "…listen to me, calm down, and listen to me."

Doctor Justin James Jefferson, his badge name tag clearly visible on his white coat, a small point that I had not noticed before, pulled up a chair to sit alongside me, imploring me, in a soft, kind tone, to calm down. *But how could I? Nothing would ever be right again in life without our little Sarah Austen.*

Having to watch the Doctor take a moment selecting the chair, then move toward me to sit down, sent chills through my obviously tired body. Despite his diagnosis, of seemingly all clear, my fact inner reality check was, I ached all over, and to move was difficult, but not knowing about the baby, Chelsea? Each turn, each motion of my arms, my legs, sent a pain right through me. However, that didn't matter for now; all I wanted to know was that our baby was safe, alive. Telling me that Chelsea couldn't wait to see me was comforting, but the doctor had hesitated with news of our baby.

Erring on the side of the best medical advice we knew, Chelsea was estimated at a maximum of twenty-nine or thirty weeks into her pregnancy, a long way off forty. A plus factor would be; Chelsea was an extremely fit woman, had taken care of herself, was healthy, and since her pregnancy, had held to a strict diet and daily routine. Being a Doctor herself, she knew all the exacting needs to be undertaken, especially in being an older woman carrying a child. We were well outside the normal period of gestation that would allow a baby's organs to develop, one of the biggest problems being the lungs. A 'preemie' was always at great risk, despite the many inroads made over many years, and I knew straight away, Chelsea and I were very much on the wrong side of the ledger. The Doctor delivered his answer with care and compassion.

~~~~~~~~~~

Powerless to do anything, my faculties all definitely with me, all I could do was lie in my hospital bed and wait, wait for Chelsea to come and see me. Minutes seemed like…forever. It was gut-wrenching. I was a wreck.

The best and most productive thing I could do, watching the minutes tick by, waiting, looking for Chelsea, was to call Jack Montgomery to give him the bad news of our journey and plight. What should have been a wonderful trip had now turned into a total nightmare? What we were all going to do in the immediate future, I was unsure about, at least until I could talk to Chelsea, who obviously knew much more. There was so much to worry about, to cover, and so much more I needed to know. I needed her desperately – certainly more than as a Doctor.

Three Days Later

"Take all the time you need Tony, work can wait, get better…" was reassuring, but it wouldn't have mattered what Jack Montgomery had said, nothing mattered to me right now. My life was at an all-time low, my body ached, and my heart ached more. I was inwardly, very scared. "…and by the way, my friend, I'm sorry. I'm really sorry I spoke the way I did on that last call, which was unkind. I knew it straight away and heaven forbid, if your accident had turned out differently, how could I have lived with myself? Again, I'm so sorry Tony; I really am and I hope, truly hope you'll forgive me." I clearly heard the hurt in his voice. It seemed everyone was hurting.

"It's okay Jack; it's okay. I knew you didn't mean it but really, having said that, from where I am laying at the moment, the best I can share with you my friend is to just make sure you get your life together in a way you want to and should. Find yourself a good lady, you deserve it. You really do and believe me; I can vouch for it. I mean, look at me, look at me right now Jack. If it wasn't for Chelsea, I can't imagine it. I don't wanna sound like I'm preaching but let me tell you; life's too short, I know it now. Work, money, things, whatever; they aren't worth a fig if you haven't got someone you love, who cares; who enriches your life? Do it Jack. Turn over a leaf is all I can say, but anyway, enough of my philosophical grandstanding and ramblings, my epiphany if you will? I'll see you when I see you, okay. I'd better go now. I'll call ya later again."

I tapped the screen of my cell phone and placed it back on the small table beside me. My body might ache, and my mind might be racing, but I really did feel a tiny bit better having closed the book with Connecticut until I could work out what was going to happen from here on out, for Chelsea and me. And as for the baby, our precious little Sarah Austen?

The room lit up like a Christmas tree, as soon as I saw her face as she turned the corner into my room. Bruised a little, a bandage wrapped around the length of her left leg, Chelsea maneuvered herself into the hospital room, in a wheelchair, as if she'd been practicing all day for her grand entry to greet me.

I hadn't forgotten; it already was three days later for me that I'd been in the hospital, and had not really given one single real thought, what *that* fact alone might have done to Chelsea, how she had endured? She came to my bedside, lifted herself with a little difficulty from the wheelchair, and leaned forward, placing her cupped hands around my face, under my chin, as she did – I flinched!

"I'm sorry darling. I didn't..."

"It's OK" I assured her "I'm just real stiff, and I sort of hurt all over, but I'm okay they tell me, but hey, I still want your kiss."

She lightly pressed her lips on mine. For a split moment, heaven was mine again.

"You are okay I know, have known all along. I've spoken to Doctor Jefferson many times. He's given me all the reports, all the updates"

To my delight, she again softly kissed my lips, and then my forehead before moving back to brush her lips on mine a second time. Seeing Chelsea, feeling her closeness, her hands on me, being able to hold her, albeit gently, was the exact medicine I needed, craved. Already, I was feeling better; from this moment on I could start being the man on the mend I wanted to be, needed to be, and devoid of ailments, aches and worries; Chelsea was my breath of fresh air. She was, had surely become, and would always be, my very life, my reason for living.

"The baby..." I asked her "...Sarah Austen, what's going..."

Chelsea quickly stopped me by placing her index finger on my lips. She sighed heavily before bringing me fully into the picture. Was I really ready for this, I wondered?

"Doctor Jefferson didn't say too much to you about Sarah Austen because he knew I would handle it quite differently to him, and of course; he's right. The hospital has been truly wonderful, and as soon as they knew I was also a doctor, not that they wouldn't for anyone; she qualified diplomatically; they still moved heaven and earth to make sure all of us were as comfortable as could be. The difference is, all and every procedure or diagnosis affecting us as a family was brought to my personal attention. We were fortunate we were wearing seat belts as it turned out otherwise, no-one would

Three Days Later

have survived, but anyway, banged up as we were in that wreck, and are still now, our general diagnosis is good to very good, even excellent, and more-so since you came out of the coma you were in, *that* was the scariest part of all. I was able to see you over those three days, and I did, and my heart ached as you lay there, motionless. I prayed as I watched your instruments and checked your vital signs, my consolation was; they were as stable as you, but..."

God how I hated that word; too many people use it; unwittingly, it has such connotation. However, her utterance of *'but'* forced my reaction. I was still in the dark; I still didn't know about the baby.

"Chelsea, Chelsea..." I interrupted. I couldn't help myself. "...the baby, little Sarah, you haven't *told* me, *please.*"

I braced myself, clearly understanding; Chelsea knew everything. Now I needed her to tell me both the good and the bad.

"She's on life support Tony and its fifty-fifty. That's it! Ultra critical and I...."

"*She's alive, alive*" Little Sarah Austen is *alive*. Is that what you're telling me Chelsea? We have a baby. She's. She's...?

I was momentarily overwhelmed, joyous at the same time. Expecting the worst, I was given the best news a man could ever get. Not only was our baby alive, I was also now - a Father, albeit, one in distress but yes, still a Father.

"Yes, I am telling you that sweetheart, she is alive, however..."

"I don't care about however right now. However, means nothing. It's like...!" The news had excited me. "The main thing is, our little girl, she's *alive*. It's a miracle Chelsea, *isn't it, a miracle?*" I questioned, seriously wanting her to agree with me.

"Yes it is Tony. It *is* a miracle, but you have to know; we need a couple more yet, maybe *more* than a couple miracles" she warned with an obvious despair that added to the cautious sadness in her voice.

"*Oh my God*, I can't believe it. No wonder the Doc wanted *you* to tell me, but still, how great is *that*, and here I was all this time thinking we'd lost her, lost her. I don't know how I could have taken that to be honest."

"We might *still* Tony." Chelsea warned me, speaking in her position as a Doctor, not a Mother. She had to condition me for what could be, even probably will.

My euphoria fell rapidly. Now quieted a little, as I processed her words, all I could think was, how could a tiny baby, not yet fully matured in the womb, then be involved in a car smash the way we all had, be expected to survive? It truly was a miracle. I had to cling to the belief of a miracle, knowing they are scarce. I willed a miracle and with Chelsea's loving care, we'd get one. Clinging to every word, tears rolled down my face as she explained, in medical terms, and stark reality of what we were both facing with tiny Sarah Austen. It could be weeks yet before we know if she might pull through and even then, being positive, she emphasized in clear and concise terms; we will still have to worry about complications. Some may be serious, that could surface later. I took it all in, desperate for every little detail, every problem, big or small, every challenge ahead. I wanted to be prepared and share the burden.

It was a heartbreaker of gargantuan proportions, to me, as a layman of medic speak, to listen to the medical terminology, starting with meningitis, sepsis and pneumonia, moving on to respiratory distress syndrome (RSD), meaning mechanical assistance to help breathing, but x-rays and blood tests would help keep it in check, or apnea, requiring careful monitoring, to include a simple tap on the feet or gentle patting to help correct the problem to get the baby breathing again. Then, there was jaundice, (IVH) intra ventricular hemorrhage, or bleeding in the brain, but *that* she explained was more likely in the first three days or so and had not been a problem so far, suggesting we were probably over that already. Then she added, patent ductus arteriosis (PDA), a worrisome heart problem pertaining to the ductus, which, if it doesn't close properly, can cause failure of the heart.

Having concentrated on every big medical word Chelsea was saying, despite her cognizance of my sensitivity, now, about to share the next set of what seemed like a never-ending list of immediate or probable longer-term problems, I finally had to ask her to stop. I couldn't take it. There were far too many of what were obviously crisis concerns, and my sadder realization quickly became, could she, would little Sarah Austen make it all?

While my *'daddy'* heart was breaking a little inside, Chelsea said yes, preferring not to spell out the historical odds, adding emphatically, she wouldn't let anything go wrong and urged me to also be strong, to pray, to accept the challenge with her. There was no way I wouldn't. I would be with her no matter the odds, or the tumultuous task ahead for all of us, but especially, the baby. *'She'll make it Tony. She will.'* Chelsea assured me, taking my hand in hers.

Weak as I felt in the body, I could only admire my wife's strength, her passion, her dedication to life. The doctor in her immediately propelled me to greater heights, to believe, always believe. Her chosen profession was to *save* lives and today; she had one very special reason to save one very precious life; our little baby, no matter the odds.

Together, today, tomorrow - God and Chelsea were working in tandem. Without hesitation, I too signed on to become the loyal guard and helper, to watch over one of His helpless little children. Little Sarah Austen had to survive.

As if I hadn't heard enough already, but almost not worth the consideration in the broad and bigger picture of our problems, Chelsea explained, from our own personal points of view, we would remain in the hospital, for up to a week at the most, before being released. Lying in a hospital bed, grateful that my life had been spared, to help and be there, for all I had just listened to, *my* plight, *my* very fixable, banged up body, wasn't important at all, in fact, *I* was irrelevant. Within days, I'd be back up, functioning again. I knew it, trusted in the prognosis, believed it. I could only think of Sarah Austen. Our little baby couldn't fend for herself, so who was *I* to utter *one* single word about my situation. I was mighty fine by any stretch of the imagination.

Forgetting, as I had, to ask her where we actually were, when Chelsea finally told me, *'in the Savannah General Hospital'*, the only bright side of my condition, I could raise for the day, was in my collective thoughts, of always wanting to spend more time in the city hospital's namesake. Loving the city and the area, I never dreamt I would get to spend more time here, recuperating from a near-fatal accident. Would I ever get to see Savannah as a tourist, I wondered? And what about all that real estate I fell in love with on my first trip here, my Gone With The Wind memories? A light-hearted moment, it was refreshing to manage that faint smile of well-being and hope before quickly returning to the serious side of just *how* we would proceed with our lives from this point on.

For Chelsea, for me, having each other was undoubtedly our greatest consolation. Together, in prayer, we willed, by His good grace, for our future, that our little baby, our little Sarah Austen, born by cesarean, a 'preemie', that she could, and would, always be with us, protected. Unashamedly, we begged for that miracle – a little baby's life.

CHAPTER

FIFTEEN

Released simultaneously from the hospital, Chelsea and I committed to spending at least another two to three weeks in Savannah, watching, waiting, hoping and praying for baby Sarah Austen to show signs she might make it through to be victorious in the battle for her life. Every day would always be one more day of hope. It was all we had. Chelsea was a rock, and through gracious approvals of the hospital management, they allowed her to participate in the well-being of her baby, becoming a literal *'temporary on-site doctor'* to the Savannah General.

While she was there, in passing time, I did try to rally, see some area sights, and lift my spirits a little until finally, I knew it was pointless. Reality was; I'd been wandering around in no-man's land, aimlessly, desperately, trying to pull myself together, and impeccable as the city was that spoke volumes of century's old history; nothing about it could ever be what I wanted it to. Stunning architecture, horse-drawn carriages, people happy and smiling, enjoying the entire South and what Savannah had to offer; I, remained in a world of emptiness.

Finally, I chose instead, the serenity of the city's natural beauty; the visuals of the Spanish moss picturesque on stately oak trees, the azaleas in the manicured parks, or the many gardens with their blaze of magnificent colorful flowers; all served me well. There was nothing better than to revel in the glory of Mother Nature to whom we owe so much. Alone, I begged that my many prayers, offered, spoken, be answered, that He might take the joys of spring on into summer, and make stronger, the tiny heart beat of our incubated little baby who, someday, I hoped, might also see the beauty surrounding us, the premature place of her birth. Slowly finding my clear, satisfying, inner peace, I implored Chelsea to join me, to share the precious moments. She did, willingly. It soon became our ritual, then salvation as, daily, we prayed together.

Day after day, Sarah Austen hung on to life, bringing us much-needed hope. Touching her tiny hand brought us inspiration. She was truly our gift from God, and it seemed; He was surely watching over her. Other little newborns came and went, a joy in itself, and although seeing the happiness, the total delight on the parent's faces hurt just a little. We could never deny their moment, in the honest belief, soon; it will be our turn.

Day after day, too, Chelsea gave of her services to the hospital. Her returned *'pro-bono'* contribution for the privilege of being able to participate in baby Sarah Austen's care. An irony of her temporary tenure; she was offered a position, anytime she wanted one, and would be welcomed gladly if she ever thought of leaving DeLand to come to Savannah. Chelsea was Floridian; DeLand was her home. Soon, we never stopped believing; it would be Sarah Austen Thompson's home too.

At night, in the comfort of our small, but the most delightful little hotel, overlooking the Savannah River, we held each other as if to breathe life into one another. Clinging to the love we had found, the love we had shared, the love that had given us baby Sarah Austen, we prayed, we cried, sleep never came easy, Cognizant we had a life-or-death mission, we knew, well understood, the need to be strong, to never waiver, and to always believe. And as every day passed, hope would lift a little higher.

Two weeks later, well rested, and feeling as back to normal as I could be in the time frame, I made a quick two-day trip to Connecticut to meet with Jack Montgomery before returning directly to DeLand. To say our neighbors were staggered at what had happened, on hearing my news of the events, now in part behind us, was an understatement. Chagrined a little, understandably so, Meghan was gone the very next day, heading straight for Georgia, which certainly made things a little easier for me, allowing me to re-open the house and start to make some needed preparations for when Chelsea, and if our prayers stay answered, little Sarah Austen.

The better news; within the week, it appeared our prayers, our pleas for mercy, were being heard. Chelsea informed me, with great delight, if Sarah Austen's condition continues to improve, with no set-backs, she would be given approval to have our little daughter air-lifted back to DeLand, within a couple of days, understanding; she would see out the next few weeks of continued observation and care, at the Florida Hospital locally. The important and best part of the news was; she was rapidly gaining ground with all her vital signs remaining one-hundred percent positive. I could have asked for nothing more. What a glorious day!

~~~~~~~~~~

Soon, our every day had a normalcy about it. Now re-settled into a routine again, Chelsea juggled her schedule between the clinic practice and the DeLand Florida Hospital. Three times a day she would visit with Sarah Austen, making sure nothing could go wrong, that her vital signs all stayed intact, that she was well tended to, although, between her, and her many doctor friends and associates, all pulling for the little baby, no-one was *ever* going to let one single thing happen. Everyone confidently believed, one day very soon; our little girl would be taken off life support to start breathing and surviving all by herself. So far, everything was working, running to schedule, totally as planned. Someone was watching over us all.

Within the month, Jack Montgomery flew down to Florida, with, his words, *'a mission in mind'*. He had a simple proposition he wanted to run by me; he needed a decision, and by his actions and conversation - fast!

Accepting the offer to stay with us, I picked him up at the Daytona International Airport and without further ado, headed straight back to Glenwood. Purposely avoiding immediate business chat, making convenient idle conversation instead, he started with the Florida NASCAR Headquarters, given he noticed it as we passed by. Gushing with complimentary words he immediately admitted; he was *'more than impressed'*. On his last trip, for our wedding, he'd flown direct into Orlando and missed it, not realizing it was so close by to where we lived. Acknowledging the huge structure, the venue, on the very aptly named International Speedway, it couldn't really be missed by anyone anyway.

'Gotta go there someday" he remarked straining his head, still looking at the spectator stand.

He'd forgotten, probably conveniently, that I had previously told him I'd enjoyed the experience, however, bragging rights at this moment was irrelevant; I left the subject alone.

His next probable, pre-planned, killing time comment, *'this Florida has really got to you, hasn't it?'* would turn out to be, as I'd learn, pre-amble forethought, an opportunity even. He was right though, Florida and Chelsea had certainly changed my life. It would turn out; his bigger picture was yet to be declared.

~~~~~~~~~

"Let me know if this works for you" was the very frank, opening line, from Jack Montgomery as he began to outline his latest plan. I listened intently, cognizant of the fact; it seemed; Jack had a twofold mission; to allow for my personal situation as it stood with Chelsea and Sarah Austen, which was admirable, in thought only, but importantly, to his regaining control of the company that bore his name, no more partners – Me!

Little did he know; I could have cared less? My priorities in life had changed. Work was nothing more than a means to an end. I worked to live, *not* lived to work, a trait that may well remain the charter of what was about to become my former partner and friend. With a little baby, clinging to life, *that* was a far greater priority, challenge, and I was going to meet both head-on with a wife who loved me, who herself, was doing all she could to make sure the most precious gift in our life, got her chance at it.

I agreed to sign the papers with barely a word of conversation, and absolutely no concerns for lengthy negotiation, or for a better deal, a procedure and action of mine that, as it turned out, more than shocked Jack Montgomery. He'd expected a different response, a far different reaction from me.

"I don't believe it Tony. I expected at least a *little* fight, a little objection" he told me.

"You missed the bigger picture Jack, the picture that spells life, not money. I said that to you from the hospital - remember? What we had, were doing, now, will make no difference to me at all. Sarah Austen does, and I hope maybe, someday; you'll see that too. I've tried to tell you along the way lately, find a good woman Jack, get a real life, it beats money every time. The company is yours but again; go find what's really missing in your life, seriously."

"Well comrade, I guess that's a part of what this was all about, because I heard you. I really did and now; I'm happy to tell you, share with you, that actually I *have* done something about it, my life."

What he told me next actually surprised me, but shouldn't have. I did remember the girl we both once knew by the name of Robin, although her last name escaped me. She was quite the looker too as I recalled, and the fact she had been divorced, had a child now, about nine years old, was not really important to the way Jack relayed his story. Apparently, they had always been in touch, but not for any real reason, and certainly without motive. He added, they'd also saw each other around Hartford here and there, except the last time he saw her; of all places, it was in a supermarket, where he casually asked her, *'what have you been doing lately?'* It turned out to be very little. He then took great delight in being able to confirm to me that his immediate follow-up question; cautiously asked; her response to it was, yes; she *would* like to have dinner with him sometime. Quite a few dinners later, he was delighted to share; they are now seeing each other regularly.

Wow – I was impressed! My friend, Jack Montgomery had definitely changed, for the better.

"I'm beginning to take a really big shine to her Tony" he gingerly admitted. "We get on great; her child is extremely well disciplined, and polite, which is good so now, who knows? Next time we see each other, we might be a real foursome, plus two of course, her child Lisa Melinda, and your miracle baby, Sarah Austen."

"What a beautiful thought Jack, and so eloquently put. Thank you, I appreciate it, and I know Chelsea would love to have heard you say that. However, what a great thought. I too hope, maybe; we can be that foursome, and of course, if there's such a word; we'll really be a six-some."

His last statement, its sentiment, endeared me even more to him as a friend. The cold hard facts of life were; Jack Montgomery had played an important role in my life over the past many years, and we'd been highly successful in our mutual business relationship. Conceding to antagonism between us of late, that he annoyed me a little, in fairness, I admitted, *that* might have been more *me* than him; however, I couldn't forget the comfort and caring, he shared when my marriage failed. Back then, it was Jack who came to the rescue.

Never in a million years would he have known, at the time; his gesture of a sabbatical for me from the company would be the catalyst and the full thrust for all we were sharing today. *How* all our lives had changed; were continually changing. In retrospect, the chain of events, ever developing, had been quite remarkable. And from where we all stand today; as it's turning out; for the good.

Pre-dinner drinks that night at The Elusive Grape set the three of us up for an even bigger, impromptu, unplanned, celebration at Emmy's Time Out Tavern out on Old New York Avenue. The most delightful German style restaurant just oozed with atmosphere, a perfect recommendation from our ever faithful neighbors Meghan and Mark, who belatedly, but always so graciously ready, said 'yes' on invitation and joined us. We all had an awesome night, something very important for Chelsea and me. More Chelsea really who deserved a much-needed break from the past very many days and nights, spearheading all we continued to endure, done, however, with the love of each other and our baby. Could we be happier? It abounded, including the most important fact of all, updated reports were; little Sarah Austen was still continuing to do exceedingly well, beyond expectations.

In the cold light of the next new day, Chelsea took care of her business, and more, while I finalized mine. Jack Montgomery had officially sealed our agreed to deal; he bought me outright. Handing back the pen that bore the Company name, I'd signed the papers while he prepared to hand over the six-figure check that, in securing it, looked mighty fine to me. I'd officially become a free agent.

The one down side, I realized, with circumstances now changed beyond belief, there would be no more once dreamed of, south of the Mason-Dixon Line, Hartford-Montgomery Realty office/branch, however, in accepting it gracefully; to me, it was, would become, unimportant. Our friendship, it would remain intact; Business, we would both go our separate ways. Handshakes over, the rest of the afternoon was ours. Known only to him, Jack had another mission in mind?

"Now, along with showing me exactly what it is that you *really* sold out to me for, maybe we can take time out for a little one on one personal chat too. I'd like that" he suggested, looking for, it seemed, not only to share some easy going convivial time, but also a chance to get personal too, lift some weight of his mind maybe?

He'd sounded serious, as if he wanted to pour his heart out and clear his head about a few things that were on his mind? For a moment, I wondered, could it be about Robin?

We headed straight for the Main Street Grill. It was!

Over lunch, we spent the next two hours sitting and talking. Listening intently, I offered advice only as was appropriate, not wanting to pontificate any personal suggestions as I learned firsthand of his changing situation. Level headed, as well I knew him to be; Jack Montgomery had gained a strong hold on where he wanted to take his life from here. It was most encouraging.

The only reason a continued, or extended long heart to heart chat was shelved that afternoon we spent together, had more to do with one grainy old character we met later in the Old Blind Pig Pub, across from City Hall, where we'd moved on to.

Sitting by himself, a beer in hand, for some inexplicable reason, after a while, he made his move, seemingly wanting to claim us in conversation. *'You don't sound to be from these parts hereabouts'* he drawled as if a question. Quickly learning we were both from 'up north', his terminology, he pontificated a belief that *'you damn Yankees still have a bit to learn about this here country, the South',* he openly declared, not caring if he offended us, or not. He didn't! With little else to do, Jack and I decided to hear him out, accepting he was probably right, especially me. Either way, quickly, we began to enjoy his company.

'We might a lost our battles down here to y'all up there once' he begrudgingly wanted to remind us while, simultaneously, adding any number of southern linked connections he seemed to think justified somehow, the way he thought things would have made things better, and that we Yankees would've had to have embraced! We had to smile. He had a wonderful down home charm about him that was addictive; he talked the talk and rather eloquently in the process although often, neither of us had any idea what he was talking about.'

If we'd had gotcha y'all back then, things would have been different in America', he told Jack and me, exampling, as if deadly serious and without the hint of a smile even, quoting; '*...all those black robed court people wouldn't a been supremely sittin' up in Washington',* adding immediately, *'Graceland for sure would've been The White House',* while tacking on for good measure, *'...and Tallahassee woulda been callin' the shots politically'* - he seemed to love spouting that line being born, what he called himself as, *'a died in the wool cracker'.* We were lost on that one and I knew I'd have to check it later, believing, it had to have a Florida connection? On a verbal roll, he then suggested, still maintaining his stern serious stare '*...and guess whose faces you'd be lookin' at on the folding stuff in your wallet?'* There was no end to his espousing of his pride for the South. "*...and as for campin', huntin' and fishin, we'd teach all a that in schools. Now wouldn't that be sumpin?'* He leaned back on his stool, now grinning.

You had to love the guy, his presentation, his wit, his charm, indeed, his drawled accent, pure southern; he was a modern day Will Rogers! I could have listened to him and his quoted anecdotal little stories for as long he kept them coming. However, considering our time schedule; and boy, how the time had flown; it wasn't long before Jack and I both thought we'd better retreat, and *'get while the getting's good'* as this delightful man, who had not spoken one foul word, or threatened anyone in our midst, might tire of talking to two *'damn Yankees'* as he had called us more than once, and demand that we sign a pledge, to join his democracy of southern pride and humor, or more?

Light-hearted, it really was a rather different way to end our day out together. I couldn't wait to tell Chelsea. I was sure she would find as much humor or fun in it all, just as we had. I wondered much later, what Mark Twain would have thought about such verbal vision splendor, one's way with words or how his beloved tales of the south might have changed for Tom or Huck's adventures. I'll never know. Jack, meanwhile, was mesmerized, in awe of the verbal entertainment, vowing to take a few of the stories back to New England and maybe enlighten a few more folks of the benefits of the South, as he now saw them?

Three days later, sadly, I thought; Jack Montgomery was gone, but not before he declared, with truthful reverence *'I get what you mean about Florida, it's mighty addictive. I've had a great time'*. As he boarded his plane, I trusted, hoped, he'd spoken the truth and not fade forever out of our lives. I'd miss him for sure.

As each day passed, Chelsea grew more confident little Sarah Austen was going to be fine. What longer-term ramification her premature birth was going to have was still undetermined, but the words she used, the interpretation professionally proffered, made me feel so much better. Her guess-timations for discharge were still two more weeks. I couldn't wait.

We agreed; the buy-out by Jack Montgomery was sizeable, and for some very strange reason, even most fortuitous, by sheer default. We seized the moment. In the immediate, I would not seek another avenue in work, and as 'Mr. Mom', would give my full love and attention to Sarah Austen 24/7, allowing Chelsea to reach more semblances in her own partnership Doctor's practice. In a perceived emergency, she would never be more than a maximum of ten minutes plus away. That became our plan; it was put in motion. Happier than I'd ever been, for all the right reasons, our future began to look up.

And the day little Sarah Austen finally came home, as we tucked her into her specially chosen crib, wrapped snuggly in a warm, pink blanket, holding each other's hand, Chelsea and I stood and watched her for the longest time, sleeping, on her own. Each little breath she took was a delight to share, and when she twitched, even the slightest, we had the quietest of laughs and smiles…all of joy, absolute joy. The most precious, most brave little girl in the whole wide world had overcome the first, the biggest, and the longest battle, of what could now be - the first day of the rest of her life. And Mommy and Daddy couldn't have felt more blessed.

In the quiet of the dark night, for what had been far too long, our crisis was fully arrested; Chelsea and I held and loved each other as if it too, was the first time all over again.

"I love you darling. I love you and thank you" I told her. Spooning, I felt myself drifting to sleep.

"I love you too" was Chelsea's ever so soft reply, coupled, as always, with a small squeeze of my hand. I never heard the added, "I truly do."

The night had already claimed me.

CHAPTER

SIXTEEN

At six-months old, Sarah Austen had defied all the odds once rallied against her. Relentlessly vigilant, Chelsea monitored our baby as if she were the guard on the door to the vaults at Fort Knox. More valuable and precious than all the gold the Fort might hold anyway, every test, every x-ray, every diagnosis for her well being, always brought the same set of words in a verdict – *'steady, encouraging, better than expected'* and more. She had her share of *'frights,'* also diaper rash, irregular waking times for feeding, and bouts of crying as any baby might, but one common trait we did seem to avoid; separation anxiety. Daddy was always at her side, anytime of the day, while Mommy kept her close by her, as soon as her day was over. Sarah Austen never had to worry; safety, love, big *'smoochy'* kisses were hers to be felt. Even her waking moments told us she was aware of her surroundings, and every smile she would beam, through wind or otherwise; it would be a smile infectious enough to make us both react similarly, including, laughing outright back at her, our little miracle. What an excuse, but we were always looking for ways to brighten any day in the life of our baby, grateful for all we had been blessed with in her health and well being.

Calculating, from exactly the day she was born most unexpectedly, to this very day, we took Sarah Austen down to the clinic where her Mother had her practice with fellow doctors and partners, Penelope Darin and Warren Barnhill. With parental license, it would be considered a double celebration; eight months of life for our daughter, and the official unveiling of the re-named neon signage at the location entrance to the building.

Unable to have done it sooner due to our extenuating circumstances, Chelsea had been most anxious to drop the name Martin from the outdoor sign until finally, with our life more settled, today turned out to be the day when all would be revealed.

Mingling with the gathered, invited crowd, she was most obvious in her display of affection for me, for her daughter, and the thrill she derived of having us both in the audience to see the Martin name replaced for *Thompson*, our family name, on the newly inscribed, attractively designed sign - 'DARIN, THOMPSON, BARNHILL – THE STONE STREET CLINIC'.

Considered local news, the DeLand Beacon had decided the event was newsworthy, enough, delighting Chelsea, who gladly posed for photographs with her partners and chatting with journalists, for a more detailed in depth story. Only once did she balk at the idea of a photo, not wanting Sarah Austen portrayed at all. *'Another time maybe'* she suggested politely. Her wish was notably respected.

Previously seen only by clinic colleagues, or hospital staff, since being given the 'all clear' for her health and well being, indeed survival, the ceremony actually marked the official 'first time out in public' for her. The ooh's and aah's by the many gathered were sometimes quite hilarious, and of course, to be told she was beautiful made our hearts sing, because she was – to us. The day was a success, which led to out proposed next major event for Sarah Austen; her first birthday. And we hoped, maybe walking by then too.

As the weeks went by, the routines both Chelsea and I kept were basic ones, simple in their execution, and predictable as one day could be to another in the general flow of work and family. By seven-thirty or eight o'clock, Chelsea would be gone to the Clinic;

while I made sure Sarah Austen was bathed, clothed, fed and entertained. It was a thrill beyond description as I watched her every move, every action, whether sitting or swaying in the play swing, trying to make the ball on a string move, picking up a toy and gripping it tight in her little hand wondering where the noise came from as it rattled.

Everything she touched was a challenge, and everything she managed to pick up, or grasp hold of, would always start to find its way into her mouth, or at least she'd try to, but spoilsport Daddy would be there to make sure it never came close. In her high chair, with her little binky placed on the tray, Sarah Austen would pick it up and as if by accident, over the side it would go, onto the floor. I'd hear, *'uh-oh!'* She'd stare into nowhere. Sure enough, I'd pick it up; put it back on the tray, only to hear, again, *'uh-oh'* as over the side it would head, straight to the floor. That little exercise alone would be, to me, the funniest of almost everything and anything she'd get up to. The *'uh-oh's'* were just way too cute!

Rolling over on her tummy and rolling back again was a game, sometimes by design, but mostly, natural, unexpected. I'd never figure it out; it didn't matter. Meanwhile, bath time was a treat, with Sarah Austen loving the lukewarm water, splashing her hands up and down into it, creating havoc to anyone around her – namely me, Daddy. Floating duck toys intrigued her, while any soap in her eyes was a tragedy, and called for crying at the top of her now very proficiently working lungs. All cleaned up; it was back to splashing.

Diaper changes were not my favorite task, but I was well aware; a clean baby is a happy baby. Feeding time was mostly fun, also, many times, very messy! Baby's food all over the mouth and chin, grabbing for the little spoon, all of it became part of a natural progression.

Slowly, as the weeks' seemed to fly by, when Sarah Austen started to crawl with precision, eagle eye would be on the case, traveling right behind her, interrupting many of her planned journeys, knowing she was about to bump her head or crawl into a place she might find she didn't want to be. And while each day moving forward was like a yesterday repeated, there were inherent joys in watching her abilities grow.

Ever blessed, and reminded, that each and every day was one that we came so close to never having at all, no matter the triviality or monotony of it all, soon; I'd have to accept; our baby would be a child; the child would become a little girl, and the little girl; Whoa! I shuddered to think! I vowed to make sure not one single moment was ever lost to a whim of indifference, or indeed deference, when it came to life, our baby's life.

The short video clips taken on my cell phone of her would become Chelsea's entertainment in the afternoon or evening when she'd get home; they all delighted her. Urging me not to erase them, they'd be downloaded to the laptop and coordinated in chronological order by dates; keepsakes for our old age memories.

Important to us both, as new parents, were the needs to keep our very lives active, not to stagnate. While I had the easy, pleasurable job in Sarah Austen, Chelsea had a schedule that was both rewarding and demanding, and too often, I truly felt for her. The joys she showed and shared, watching our baby grow, in part from a distance, also gave her a sometimes *'left out'* feeling. It saddened me to see, although she never once complained.

A small consolation, but huge in our well-being and gladly accepted, at least once a week, Meghan would wander over from next door to look after the baby allowing Chelsea and me to enjoy an evening out. Sometimes we'd go to the Athens Theatre if there was a show we liked and wanted to see, but mostly, we'd go to a restaurant, The Abbey, Oudom Thais, De La Vega, The Brickhouse Grill or Bellini's; they were all very handy downtown establishments we loved to support. Needless to say, the time alone to us was immeasurable.

The past, soon to be one full year, had been both a strain and joy on everyone. Our future from here-on in, looked to be much more of what we chose to think of as normal. We dismissed the times when our patience had worn a little thin, or stress had reared its head, challenging us both. We were human.

For the few times that circumstances might have appeared too hard to bear, or questions were raised; *'should we have relented and let*

Three Days Later

our baby be free, released, from so much suffering'; Chelsea was horrified. Doctor or no doctor, as a Mother, she would move heaven and earth before she ever gave in to such negatives, adamantly confirming *'...and let no-one ever tell me anything different. She will live. Little Sarah Austen will live, as should any child'.*

There were times it had taken its toll on us but as fast as we weathered the minor storms, soon, calmer waters became the welcomed, long-awaited forecast ahead.

By choice, just the two of us, over dinner at The Cress one evening, we toasted ourselves *'to a job well done.'* Strangely, sitting there quietly, reflective, in an almost melancholy mood, Chelsea posed, "On an evening such as this Mr. Thompson; I'm surprised we never chose to go back to The Shuttered Firefly. It's been too long, and I'd like to." I could have kicked myself, wishing I had thought of it earlier. It was where we pledged our love, planned a future, and accepted our love for each other. The Firefly would always be more than just a restaurant – it was special; it was *'our place.'* I made a mental note to myself.

~~~~~~~~~~

It was a beautiful day. Working outside, I had earlier trimmed a few dead branches from the small, fast growing palms, and then pruned back the rose bushes that seemed to bloom endlessly with gorgeous red roses before, finally, re-directing the very colorful, light green potato weed that gave wonderful ground cover when it was positioned to perfection. Standing back, admiring not only the two elegant pink trumpet flowering Tabebuia trees I had just planted, and of course, all of my general handy work so far, suddenly, I felt a little faint. It was an unusual feeling, a form of dizziness, and it wasn't from the heat or blazing sun given the temperature of the day was a very mild, nice, 76 -78 degree; perfect weather.

If being light-headed meant I had probably squatted too long and raised myself up quicker than normal, then instinct told me, all I had to do was either stand still for a moment and let my body settle itself or as I mostly always did when working outside, sit and rest a while. I had no problem with that. Over exertion was an easy thing to do in the garden, especially when mowing the lawn, although I hadn't on this occasion?

I sat down and took a few sips of my pre-arranged Gatorade to replenish my electrolytes. Gladly swallowing a few gulps, I accepted, without guilt; commercialism in refreshments influenced me like most, but it didn't matter; it tasted nice and anyway, for me; life was good. *Enjoy all, in every way it comes to you.* It was a simple motto, edict, that I embraced easily.

Our garden was a retreat, a joy I never tired of, loving to idly sit and gaze at all that surrounded me, to drink in its beauty, the color. The varieties of Crepe Myrtles were in full bloom as were the Honeysuckle Rose climbing higher and higher with deep dark orange bursts all over and the Azaleas, would they ever stop blooming? Flowers were a sight to behold. I loved them.

As I sat alone, looking, thinking, day-dreaming, a rather large red to orange-colored Cardinal perched on my bird feeder, immediately followed by another, his friend, his partner I wanted to believe. They fed on the seed in the bird house I kept filling for them; delighted, as always, that they would choose to grace our home, welcome as they were, summer, spring, winter or fall. Sarah Austen will love sitting here with me, to watch them I thought, just as she will the many absolutely gorgeous butterflies' that fly in to settle and play and feed in our garden. And what about the little red-black lady bugs? Oh how she will love them all; I know.

Recovered from my momentary light-headiness, I didn't want to get back to work anyway. I decided to stay put, more than happy to sit exactly where I was, to continue looking, and thinking. I had so much to be grateful for in my life and there could be no better place on the Good Lords planet called Earth than where I was – right now.

Loving my wife with a passion, with all my heart, Chelsea had become, more every day, the most inspirational of people to me. Not only, for her incredible love of life, but for her love of people, all people, and with a caring that I might never have once believed ever existed to such levels in a human being. Her calling, her dedication to, and in being a Doctor, was testimony to all, and who she was.

Without her, I was sure; Sarah Austen may never have lived. Without Sarah Austen, could we, would we have survived? They weren't answers I sought; they were mere thoughts I harbored. It seemed Chelsea was given to me, not in the literal sense, but in the sense, I had found in her a new lease of life, my life.

It further occurred to me, as I sat in the solitude of our garden and all it offered of Mother Nature's gifts, the love Chelsea has given me, the love I hoped I give her in return, could they all have been the very *reason* we were spared, what could have been, would have been, the pure heartbreak of losing our little girl? Had a higher being seen the unconditional love two people shared, and to make them fully complete, rewarded them, with the gift of life

I wanted to be the arbiter. I willed; *yes!* I wanted us to all to be spared sickness, disease, heartache, sadness. I wanted us to be forever happy, jubilant, carefree, and above all, healthy. I wanted us to live eternal. I so loved Chelsea and our little Sarah Austen.

I again gave thanks; I was truly, a grateful, very lucky man…and now, with a most wonderful family. My life, my world was full to the brim,

CHAPTER

SEVENTEEN

I'd shopped everywhere, it seemed, but still couldn't find what I was looking for. Specialty items were hard to come across, then; it was posed to me as if it were the natural, obvious thing to do, '...*have you looked in any of the stores, antique type stores on the Boulevard, that have an ever-changing range of things on the shelf that seem to appear out of nowhere. You might find it there*'. I had to admit; I hadn't, and yet; on my own back door-step, opportunity abounded no doubt, as well I should have known.

With the city of DeLand being an historic landmark, with a very active and well promoted downtown, maybe one of the stores would have my searched for treasure. Sarah Austen was turning one-year-old, Mommy, and Daddy wanted a really nice, lifetime keepsake. What we had in mind and dearly wanted to find for her had so far eluded us both.

First stop was the Rivertown Antique Mall, then BackHome Antiques where, sadly, of all the marvelous treasures available, for what I wanted, I came up empty, twice. A few doors along was the smaller Victorian Rose Anteaque store, a unique way to spell a word, I thought, looking at the signage on both the door and the overhead hanging plaque. No, the spelling wasn't a mistake, wrong; it was just different; I accepted. Maybe that was a sign to me that I'd find what I was searching for? In I went to the swift sound of *'Hello, welcome to Victorian Rose'*. It was a nice touch and friendly enough.

Surprisingly, in the front inner cabinet, under glass, was the closest yet, to what I was looking for. Either way, it would do. Overjoyed, not even the price would deter me; I hoped. A penny short of one-hundred dollars; I had found a bargain. The prize they were offering was mine for the keeping.

Someday, Sarah Austen Thompson will treasure her first birthday gift; velvet lined; it was a sterling silver ring box, that played 'Aura Lee'. We envisaged, one day, many, many years henceforth; she would take *my* gold wedding band *and* her Mother's rings, and keep them safe, forever, in this, the little ring box that played 'Aura Lee', and of course, someday, too, even hand them down to her children? Tokens of true love, *'down through the ages'*. To us, it was all very romantic.

Later, shopping over, I sat for a while, on an outside bench, out on Woodland Boulevard, happy to watch the world go by. It was a layback, almost lazy world, the people taking their time, enjoying the downtown surrounds. What was it about smaller towns I'd always wonder, be in awe of?

Reflecting back to New England, an understood region of typical British lifestyle in America's settlement days, and all very predictable, accepted as quaint, nice, and picturesque, by contrast, here in DeLand, almost daily, I'd learn there was something extra special in what was Southern Style; 'Great America Main Street'.

Now, here I was, at my time in life, well and truly living it. DeLand certainly *fits the bill* of the claims, having won awards even as the best in the country, and true to form, the town, the people, never failed to amaze me. I could see it; feel it and every day, reveled in it. Yep, I was really happy to be a resident of this, the glorious south!

I chose not to view myself as a 'turncoat'; *that* I could never really be. Connecticut, I loved, always would, but leaving all I had grown up with as a child, to marry and resettle in this extraordinary, likeable city, had not been hard at all. Chelsea had changed me and all who I once was. DeLand was changing my way of living.

I had absolutely nothing to complain about, and everything to be grateful for, however, call it pangs of guilt if you will, every now and then, I admit; I missed Hartford, after all; apart from once being my childhood home, prestigiously, it is the State's capital, its seat of Government and as a big city, made it good for business which I had certainly capitalized on, right up to now, this very moment. Through Jack Montgomery buying me out, it allowed me the freedoms I enjoyed in raising Sarah Austen.

Continuing, for no reason, shaded by a tree, leaning as I had been, on whimsical reflections, I thought of the humorous old man I'd met recently who had shared with Jack Montgomery and me, his philosophy of the south if the Civil War had turned out differently. Smiling, hoping I'd meet him again someday, with Chelsea, the same thoughts of boyhood memories in Hartford came to me.

Growing up in school I recalled, as if to claim him, we had learned that Mark Twain, a fringe Southerner by definition, actually wrote the impactive legendary Adventures of Tom Sawyer and Huckleberry Finn, in his later years, ironically in his adopted, but my hometown of Hartford, Connecticut. Pure Americana folk lore, I, like millions, read of Huck and Tom's adventures many times, and similarly, today; like the boys, I chose to see myself through them. I seemed to be living in *my* very own exciting adventure.

DeLand, indeed, this region of Central Florida, had so much to offer; including even, the kind of waterway's Mark Twain loved to write about, except here, it was the well-matched St John's River system, that oddly, flowed north. Huck and Tom, of course, had the mighty Mississippi. Oh well!

Mark Twain, to my way of thinking, was a fascinating character. His real name was Samuel Langhore Clemens; he took his writers nom de plume from the very simple *'two fathoms of depth'*. From his riverboat days, as a pilot, depth measurements were constantly read; when recording them, the call would be made; *'mark twain'* (mark two). From simple origins of fact – an author of note would emerge.

By sheer default *'of boyhood yesterdays'*, our connection today would be both Hartford and Florida; he once lived where I came from, and by name only, I live where Clemens/Twain was born; Florida, (but in Missouri). It was all quite irrelevant really, except; he was a Southerner, who went north. I was a Northerner, who came south.

From physical, geographical changes of magnitude, such as it had been for me, today, I could honestly say, unequivocally, *'I love the South'*, and of course, my Chelsea, who, in expression only, lured me here. Yes, I thought, choosing to daydream; it's amazing how we can twist facts and stories to suit the moment? Twain's memories, Huck and Tom, they linger within me still.

With my downtown visit done, while walking back to the car, I came across a doll store, a rather large one; impressive! It had never occurred to me before, but instantly I thought, and it wasn't buyer's remorse or a massive sudden change of heart of *'what were we thinking'*; it was more realistically, in suddenly seeing so many dolls, including a large doll house in a wonderfully displayed shop-front window; the mere sight of it all took me thinking down a totally different line. Maybe an Aura Lee ring box might be construed somewhat too sophisticated this early as a keepsake gift and that, alternatively, maybe, a small one-year old baby girl might really love her very own little baby doll instead.

I could only reason against both gifts, with my form of probable misplaced male logic, that she was far too young for either? Until she moved from the crawling stage to walking; *that's* when, I told myself, a doll might be more appropriate. I was, nevertheless, intrigued. Love as a Father took over, male logic was abandoned immediately.

I walked through the doors to be greeted, again, by a most welcoming *'Hello, let me know if I can help you at all'*. Was this what they call neighborly shopping Southern charm? I loved it, would never tire of it.

On volume alone, Dolls of DeLand was a most appropriate name. If one could not find a doll, they liked, or wanted, in *this* store, then it probably didn't exist, or customers were only browsing anyway. The place was huge, with a massive array of dolls from very old vintage, to modern day up to the minute, from very large ones, right down to the small or tiny, and all dolls in between, including many; I would be informed, from all over the world. *Why* I ever walked in, now; I really wasn't sure? I was completely overwhelmed by it all.

My doubts were quickly allayed, as the owner, introducing herself as Lynne-Kristi, obviously rightfully proud of her store, was soon by my side wanting to help. Well, I was here, why not be overwhelmed? I briefly shared with Ms. Kristi about Sarah Austen. My story clearly touched her, deeply.

Totally surprising me in her response, smiling, she told me *'you don't need a doll',* to then, by way of recommendation, qualified, *'you need a Teddy Bear'.* We spent the next half hour talking about babies and teddy bears. Ms. Kristi was not only right, but I wondered - *why didn't I think of that?*

I left Dolls of Deland with the cutest, most loveable little teddy bear in the whole wide world, beautifully wrapped for a birthday party, along with my promise; that I would return soon, with Chelsea and baby Sara Austen. We all had a date for the future. Deliriously happy with now, two gifts, I marveled again at Southern small-town charm and how persuasive it all can be.

Back out on the Boulevard, I realized; the day had begun to get away from me. It was already one-thirty. I took a deep breath. For some inexplicable reason, just like that, it seemed; I was tired. Again, as only days ago it seemed, I wondered why, thinking that it had to be nothing more than lack of nutrition. I'd fix it! My quick lunchtime filling snack came from right next door to the doll store, a Caribbean chicken Panini at Manzano's, after which; I was soon homeward bound.

Chelsea was due home at three, to be ready for five o'clock when, M & M as I liked to call them, Meghan and Mark would join us for the well arranged little birthday party, comprising of a single lighted candle in a cupcake; a happy birthday sing-a-long and a glass of wine for us 'oldies.' We'd celebrate a true wonder as a milestone – the first birthday of our miracle child who, every day, was closer and closer to her very first steps. What a joy to us all.

Three Days Later

An even bigger joy for me personally: hugging it close to her, never wanting to let it go, she fell in love with her little teddy bear.

~~~~~~~~~~

"Oh my, my, Tony" Chelsea cried 'She's done it, how precious!" Rushing to her side, she picked Sara Austen up, lifted her as if to the ceiling, before carefully swinging her around to balance her back firmly on her two very unsteady feet. Then, cautiously, she let her go to try for three steps maybe? Two steps were the best we'd get before the floor claimed her once more. We laughed, almost until we cried.

"We don't want her growing up too quickly" Chelsea said, retrieving her from the floor, before handing her to me as if, now, it was my turn.

Neither of us wanted little Sarah Austen to grow up too fast. She was such a joy to us, now that the worst of our fears were virtually over. All the tests and double checks revealed only, that she was a normal, healthy baby, with a projection to grow up to be a very, normal, healthy girl. We could never ask for more.

Later, with our little miracle fast asleep, that evening, sitting under a clear sky, full of many thousands of bright, twinkling stars, over a glass of wine, I posed a serious question to Chelsea. Through a faint smile, she queried in reply *'whatever made you ask that, under the circumstances that have prevailed.'* To me, it seemed just about the right time.

"Because I'd love a little baby brother for Sarah Austen, plus, I'd also love to have another baby with you. My life seems so complete, so wonderful, and another child would make it all so very perfect. Furthermore, important to *both* of those reasons, I love you Chelsea Thompson. You are my light, my beacon, and not a day goes by that I don't thank the Lord above for you. Are they all good enough reasons?"

I think I might have shocked her with such a loaded response. However, without a second thought to giving me a verbal answer; Chelsea put her glass down on the table, stood up from the chair, to start moving in a tantalizing way directly toward me. Sitting in my lap, she placed her hands around me and proceeded to kiss me firmly on the lips. I responded without hesitation.

One kiss led to another. Falling on to the soft grass beneath us, I moved my body over hers. Our kisses became more passionate, more intense. Slowly, one garment of clothing was shed, followed by another, and another, until we were both naked, entwined in each other's arms. As we became one, I heard a soft moan, Chelsea held me tighter and closer to her. If tonight, Mother Nature meant for us to be, as we came into this world, she was also responsible for taking us both, for just a short while, to another world, she probably knew plenty about too. Being in that world was pure ecstasy.

The love in our two hearts beat as if they were a unified orchestra, ready to play a passionate melody, with a rhythm to be enjoyed, savored, and shared. Oblivious to any fanfare, or pace, soon, the strings began to reach the full intensity of the moment. The instruments of two played furiously, in perfect harmony, unison, until they reached a growing, deafening crescendo, where they stayed, holding the final note…until exhaustion took over, until they could play no more. As the tempo fell, so the music softened. Finally, the players rested, their instruments, silenced. Satisfied, a deep breath was taken, and calmness returned; the joy of the command performance – amazing!

Lying back, I gazed on the naked beauty of my wife. More beautiful than ever, I could want for nothing more in life than to be with her, and our little family, that soon, hopefully, if we could agree, would turn from three to four. No sooner had the thought entered my mind; Chelsea surprised me a little…a lot!

"I'm of the opinion we can start counting down the days as of this very moment" she said as her opening statement, her way of agreeing, confirming that our mission had already started and having clearly demonstrated, in her almost wildest of abandonment, that she too would love to have another baby.

"And I couldn't think of a better way to have shown you; I was more than willing!" she added, lifting herself up, leaning over, to kiss me.

Three Days Later

"You are an *incredible* woman Mrs. Thompson, *simply incredible*...and, in the words of a once, very popular song, simply irresistible too. To think, one word about having a baby and I had my hands full" I told her laughingly. "*And...* might I add, I too, will willingly share many more command performances."

"You're on, tomorrow, the next night, whenever..." she said in a very playful tone coupled with a cheeky grin "...but then again..." she tipped her head while raising an eyebrow, "...I doubt right now again, huh?"

Was that a challenge? She knew the answer; I'm sure, but it was all in good fun. Having tempted, questioned, my male stamina, ego, I would love to have shocked her, but I chose not to try, just in case? It was time to turn in, officially, to our softer, warm and inviting bed. With that thought in mind, '*maybe I will shock her*' thoughts ran through my mind but...?

~~~~~~~~~~

Turning fifty was a milestone. Truth was; I *hated* it! Too many times, over and over in my mind, I wished I had met Chelsea fifteen years and more ago. Now in the absolute prime of our lives, sometimes, too often, I felt parts of it were slipping away. Middle age plus, to me, was a bummer! *Nothing* would make me feel any different, although Chelsea reminded me, time and time again; it's all a state of mind. It probably was, but my state of mind was telling me something different. I wanted my years back, and I wanted them all with her, in a time warp - with me. If it was a small consolation, *that thought alone*, at least, was one thing she could agree with me on, having confessed to me at times also, that yes, it was too bad we had both lost so many good years we might have had together, and yes, if only we had found each other sooner.

"Tony..." she had posed to me one day "...young as you still are, but being our Mr. Mom, important as that role is, do you ever feel the need to get back out there in the everyday work force? Being so much at home, maybe you're missing the camaraderie of people, of other men, who make you feel like some things are more every day normal. I'm not saying I *want* you to, and I'm not saying you *need* to. Heaven knows; with my job, you don't *need* to, but do you feel, or miss, the outside interaction?"

It was an excellent point, but no, mostly; I didn't, was my generalized response. Sarah Austen was the love of my life and I'd have my time with her no other way. I couldn't think of doing anything differently right now. Chelsea, meanwhile, as a woman and a wife, was my absolute solid Rock of Gibraltar. I couldn't wait for her to walk through the front door of our home and not want to hold her, hug her, kiss her and tell her how much I had missed her, and fortunately; Chelsea knew and felt that in me…she had no qualms at all in telling me so, often. Middle-age different, we never pursued the idea or conversation.

As it turned out, my fiftieth birthday was shared exclusively with *'my two girls'*. Chelsea asked me, but I was I was adamant; I didn't want any type of ceremony. No ceremony, of any kind! Friends, neighbors, associates…I'm sorry, all I wanted, was to be with my little family, alone. Assuming control before I might have been hijacked in some way, and I was sure I would be, I made my own bigger, personal wish come true. Chelsea agreed wholeheartedly.

1-95 south, direct to Miami, became our chosen route to get the freeway part of a supposed *'no plans made'* journey out of the way, where on completion, it was visually, clearer sailing.

Linking from Homestead and Florida City to the South Dixie, Highway 1, we were Key Largo bound. Then Islamorada on the Overseas Highway, to link on to the Seven Mile Bridge, which, in mileage facts were actually 6.765 to be exact. But who was counting? If one needed to be impressed, I most assuredly was. This section, indeed even, many others, turned out to be a lesson in remarkable engineering, a feat that stood alone; bridges, roadways, construction that was truly, quite amazing! The highest point of the slow rising elevated bridge reached 65 feet, the clearance made for ships on the waterway below.

The Seven Mile Bridge connects Knights Keys at Marathon in the Middle Keys and Duck Keys on the Lower Keys. Now – I had to confess, on a need to know basis, with so many 'Keys' on this journey, my curiosity actually got the better of me and somehow; I had to link it all together. Chelsea, meanwhile, couldn't understand why I'd take the time to know, asking *'what was the point?'* Recollecting, all I could say in a sort of justified reply was, *'I'm trying to be a knowledgeable Floridian, but you're right'*. I was ultimately only interested in one 'Key' – Key West!

I gave up worrying, although she didn't leave it there, getting the better of me with what she called *'a useless information question'* asking – *'Name one movie, featuring the Seven Mile Bridge and a big time feature too'*.

Quickly assessing, I had no idea, she gave out a clue.

'The lead actor was a Governor'.

I hesitated momentarily in reply. Too late - she'd got me!

(True Lies and Arnold Schwarzenegger).

'See...' I told her, turning the tables *'...we are having fun, aren't we?'*

The Keys, chains of islands, was nothing short of spectacular. Big Pine (Keys), Sugarloaf Sound, on to Big Coppitt (Keys), we finally arrived at our chosen destination - Key West. The spectacular trip was a drive of memories, a drive, never to be forgotten, one I'd gladly say to any and all – *'you've got to see this part of the USA.'*

We checked into a rather quaint little motel called The Deep South Inn, a name that made me smile, of course, remembering my one time history lesson from Chelsea. I didn't see this area as the South at all – it was more Caribbean, the Islands. It didn't matter! The Deep South Inn was an excellent choice. Built right at the water's edge, we proceeded to do nothing more than go walking in the sand, or strolling the beaches, to visiting the adopted home of pirates, poets and others, one, notably, the acclaimed writer Ernest Hemmingway, another; President Harry Truman. It was easy to understand why the former President was once quoted as saying, *'I've a notion to move the Capitol to Key West and just, stay'*. Eleven trips and over 175 days later throughout his tenure, the President lived up to his love of the Keys region of Florida. His 'Little White

House' made his point, and of course; he was accurate in his description of the absolute magnificence of the tropical paradise so full of shipwrecks, colorful flowers, music, Old Town, Mallory Square and much more.

These days, I determined first hand, King Parrot-head himself commands more of the modern-day attention, and I never tired hearing, as many times as I did, by many a performer, Jimmy Buffett's, Margaretville. Infectious, his way with words was most appropriate, as was his colorful everywhere presence.

Down in Key West, I couldn't have enjoyed a better birthday than the, relatively, quiet one I had, surrounded by love, and two of the most beautiful girls I could ever know, or would ever know, in my life – my darling Chelsea and my little Sarah Austen.

Our shared adventures did include one excursion; exploring Fort Jefferson on the Dry Tortugas National Park Island out in the Gulf of Mexico, enjoying first the long ride over, making sure Sarah Austen was safe and dry as the ferry made its water spraying way to the popular attraction full of history. She did, however; seem to love the open air, and the light spray of the water in her face as evidenced by her smiles of happiness that were so infectious, to not only Mom and Dad, but many of our fellow sight-seeing passengers.

Time together, sharing, I deemed, was such a precious, special commodity. Our Key West trip had it all. No grass grew under our feet.

Three days later, my birthday vacation over, we headed home to DeLand where, as anticipated, results were back, waiting for Chelsea to peruse. She was pregnant, confirmed. This time we agreed, no more riding the highways, no plane rides, no excessive activity, no over indulging in even the simplest of things and together, we would spend the next nine months as the typical family…a little work, a little play and a whole lotta lovin'! Praying for a boy, being positive in confirmation, we'd already chosen his intended name while down in the Keys – Nelson James Thompson. We crossed all our fingers.

Three Days Later

An irony in time, yet to me, totally expected, infrequent as our contact had been lately, out of the blue, Jack Montgomery called to say he and Robin were getting married; he wanted us to join them up in Connecticut, inviting us to stay. They hadn't set a date yet, he told me, allowing for flexibility, in the hope, we might be able to be there. He'd go with our decision of availability before locking down the actual date.

With huge regret, reluctantly, we had no alternative but to decline. Now five months into her pregnancy, Chelsea remained paranoid about traveling. I did too. Memories of our last trip north had never left us. Extremely personal, Déjà vu we didn't want, odd as it sounded. He understood!

CHAPTER

EIGHTEEN

It wasn't the first time, but a derivative, oft quoted phrase, or line, from a 17th century poem, *'Light Shining Out Of Darkness'*, composed by William Cowper, again entered my world of thoughts and began to haunt me, and for the longest while, I couldn't really understand why? *'God moves in a mysterious way (his wonders to perform)'.* It played over in my mind, mostly in times of solitude, not for the double meaning way it can often be espoused but, in the really deeper reasoning of *why?* He can and does; I believed, move in mysterious ways for the benefit. However, if it were for reasons of a challenge, then maybe that could be construed as, crueler. Given it began to dwell heavy within me, was that a premonition? *Why*, would soon surface?

Mid-way through her pregnancy, although scaled back, Chelsea continued to work at The Stone Street Clinic; Sarah Austen remained in my ever loving care. Often, I'd sit to just watch her, marvel at her, especially when she was sleeping, in awe of such innocence that brought so much joy to me, to us both. And as I would ponder the days ahead, the times, our future, her future, I could only hope that the life Chelsea and I had brought her into, including now our expected new addition would be filled with happiness, of peace, but particularly, one of safety.

I deplored, especially, the global headlines of any given day; terror, war, poverty, natural disasters, famine and so many other of the worlds, dastardly events. Where was the sanctity of peace, love and good will? The world could be, indeed was, is, a beautiful place, but it could also be mean, nasty, a disgrace unto itself, to humanity. Today's headlines suggested *too much* of the latter.

Patience being a virtue, finally, our wait was over. When Nelson James made his grand entry into the world Chelsea and I had crafted, together, two people and a little Sister could never have been happier or felt more blessed. A true delight, he made sure everyone knew he had arrived, certifying, at the top of his lungs; he was pleased to be around, come see me!

The staff at the DeLand Florida Hospital responded. Drawn like a magnet to one of their favorite Doctors, Chelsea's room quickly filled with flowers, stuffed animals and congratulatory cards. To me, *'my little man'* was all I could ever have hoped for, and I couldn't wait for our Daddy to boy days to begin. The next few months would fly by…sometimes though, way too fast.

~~~~~~~~~~

Lately, for no real, explainable reason, I had been more tired than I believed I should be. Coupled with a nagging lower-back pain and some other minor associated ailments I felt along the way, one's that I basically always fobbed off, Chelsea, ever the doctor, became more than concerned. Initially, in the privacy of our home, she decided to find out *why?*

Conversational questions she basically knew the answer to, filled in the ones always asked first. They were the traditional blank spots - eating, diet, sleep, and exercise; all basic routine, followed by a simple, personal examination. Other *'normal procedural tests'* as she called them, conducted at the clinic would cover the rest.

As if that wasn't enough, Chelsea continued, relentlessly, with whatever else she could dream up, covering everything she could to the point of, to me, '...*was this all really necessary*' I'd ask, reacting to her after I felt as though I had been interrogated by the military. *'Yes'* was her lovingly, rapidly snapped back answer – now that scared me just a little too, but in the end, I knew there was no use complaining.

Something was on her mind, and the first big clue came with her referencing BPH, which meant little to me, in fact, nothing. Benign Prostatic Hyperplasia, she would enlighten me in explanation, was not a clear or well understood problem, but, from the way she was speaking; in laymen's terms, it got my attention; an *'enlarged prostate gland'* changed my attitude dramatically. A slightly uncomfortable DRE examination and Ultrasound soon meant, a Urologist and PSA (prostate-specific antigen), was added to the list and swiftly undertaken: '...*a safe-guard, a precaution'* was all Chelsea had said initially. Frankly, none of it sounded good.

Three days later, I had every reason to be, *'scared',* just a little. Chelsea, on the other hand, was not happy, using the word, 'borderline'. Although my PSA came in low, at 3.5ng/ml edging toward 4, it placed me close to a 20 - 30% plus range for the possibility of prostate cancer.

As another safety precaution, I called it over-reaction; an immediate biopsy was called. When the tests came back from the urologist, she was right; it revealed an equal reason for added concern.

In the prime of my life, just fifty years old, the diagnosis was confirmed – mild prostate cancer. Not so bad, but when you love someone, definitely, not so good!

Doctors have options; prescribe drugs to relax the pressure, use radiation treatment, block the hormones responsible for enlargement; it depended on the severity. In tandem with counterpart experts, Chelsea took the avenue she was more comfortable with, opting initially, for drug combatants (Finasteride) that she said was more tolerable to relieve the symptom, the belief also; it would help shrink the prostate, halting any progression.

Three Days Later

In a discussion with a fellow doctor, not far from where I was sitting, I overheard her mention the word Lycopene. It was a foreign word to me, being scared; I filed it for now, thinking, she'll tell me when she decided if there was a need for me to know more, if at all? With all that was going on, frankly, I was actually more petrified to ask her about it anyway. That's why I chose to just quietly double-check it later, find out *what the word* really meant?

Apart from that small point, from here on in, I guessed, all I could do was hope, pray. I hated *all* of it! My mortality resonated.

Devastated at the mere mention of the word cancer, with no consideration to the level of degrees of the disease I may have, or what treatment options were available, that night, without the comfort of my wife, I doubt I could ever have overcome the sheer anger I felt, followed by the deep inner feelings of anguish I suffered. I admit; I cried too!

"Am I going to die?" I asked of her, as if seeking professional assurances…I mean, she was a Doctor, and it's not like I'd be the first to ask such a question.

"Of *course* not Tony, of *course* not…" she emphatically told me."…this is a very beatable disease, and we caught it early, an exceptionally good thing, but regardless, let me tell you, let me be very honest with you as I see it. There will be treatment, there will be side-effects and at times, you'll be annoyed at life but, we'll see it all through together, okay? Finally, and again, there is no way you are going to die, so *please*, rid yourself of those thoughts. It's not going to happen, and I will see to it. I love you, Sarah Austen and little Nelson James; we all need you, so be prepared my dear husband. You have another 50 good years in you, and yes, we'll grow old together when it's all done. Is that going to work for you pray tell me?"

To say Chelsea made me feel less scared, to say she tried to rid me of my inner fears, to say she had rid me of thoughts I should never have entertained, would be an gross understatement. Prostate cancer was very beatable she implored. I believed her, and in her.

As a Doctor, it was a powerful statement she had made. As my wife, my lover, my very best friend, she had given me every reason to be strong, to be positive, confident, confirming that, with her love, and the love of our children, I had every reason to rise to the occasion of adversity and fight – to overcome and in time, to be a survivor.

Holding me close, comforting me, Chelsea had seen it all before, through her patients, the big difference now, she had a very personal one, all her very own.

'Don't worry, we'll see it through together...' she repeated constantly '...I'm here for you. It'll be fine, just wait and see, however, listen to me, a couple of things to clearly understand, to be cognizant of. First and foremost, like immediately, we need to change your diet. That's a must, and I hope you like vegetables, all the colored ones because we'll be eating plenty of them and for now, as a precaution, we'll back off red meats too'.

She had given me, what I took as, an instant warning. As my wife, I could expect the shared support, her love, her many welcomed words of caring. As a Doctor, I knew she would move heaven and earth for me, in the sense of, medical well being. Her knowledge was vast, her support infrastructure, within reach. I could have no greater gift on my side for both reasons.

My only, many times, silently asked question was the same one penned by the singer-songwriter Kris Kristofferson, *'Why Me Lord?'* I *really* wanted to know - *Why Me Lord?* Besides, I was far too young to die. What then of my babies, my wife? *'No Lord'* I told him, loud and clear. *'This one, you lose'*. That very same day, I began, probably, the biggest battle of my life!

Precious, fragile and depending on me, Nelson James brightened up some of my darker days. If I ever had reasons to fight, he was certainly, without question or doubt, at, or one of, or indeed the top of my list reasons.

Sarah Austen delighted in seeing and sharing with her new baby brother; despite not fully understanding, he wasn't competition for attention; he was just a helpless little boy who needed feeding, bathing, changing and more, just as she once enjoyed.

Helping me immeasurably, Chelsea knew exactly what to say and do, explaining, the phase Sarah Austen would go through was natural, and we as parents had to be sure we showered as much love and attention on an older child as we did on a newborn, to take away the fear of them feeling they were being left alone, left out. This Daddy couldn't do that!

With love, I soon had her sharing in our joint caring for Nelson James, giving her little things to do, telling her I needed her to help, and cute as she could be, she stayed by my side, always ready.

Fearful of my own insecurities, as I often could become, our two little babies would never feel it. Chelsea took a *'leave of absence'* from the clinic, and we did everything we could to share the load, loving every minute of our new-found time together.

Sometimes, when both children were asleep during the day, we'd sit and watch a DVD, or maybe spend time working in the garden; prepare a special meal in the kitchen to be enjoyed later that night, even the next day. Life was simple enough, while still concerning.

In my own challenge, never once missing a beat, Chelsea remained my very personal Doctor. Every avenue was traversed in my treatment. Every word was spoken for encouragement. Not a stone was left unturned in her efforts, to ever allow, or make me ever doubt, I, she and we, would beat the odds. Prostate cancer, caught early, was not only curable, but at the very least, most manageable. Relentlessly, she drove that message home.

Appropriately, living with medical woes and apart from many long personal chats with Chelsea, I had also taken, these days, to the Internet, the well known, accepted avenue and ever growing instrument source of incredible knowledge. It surely was, and is! I studied every word, every phrase, and every single reference Chelsea had ever made to me about prostate cancer, mild or severe. I had an insatiable appetite to learn, to understand my predicament, I, we as a family, might be in.

I was staggered to learn, by my exact age of 50; in America, up to forty percent of men have cancer in the prostate, unlike Asian or Latin American counterparts.

I had not forgotten either, the word Lycopene, the one that had intrigued me earlier. Scaring me a little back then, now breathing a huge sigh of relief; I learned it was a good thing, nothing more than a bright-red pigment responsible for providing color in fruits and vegetables. Aah, that's what Chelsea had said *'eat plenty of colored vegetables'*, I got it! It was significant, specifically coupled with diet, as Lycopene, a member of the carotenoid family, is a powerful anti-oxidant found in, of all things, one of my very favorite vegetables – the tomato!

Naturally, and with wide-open arms, I heeded all recommendations about a plant-based diet, especially tomatoes, along with regular vegetables and fruit, and the best part of all the many warnings and advice Chelsea gave me along the rocky road to well-being – I actually, genuinely, loved them all. Coupled with steering away from many dairy products, I rapidly believed I'd be a winner, and would prevail. Well, I hoped.

~~~~~~~~~~

Accepting all we were going through, our personal trials, there was never one single doubt in my mind, Chelsea had become the epitome of the most demanding pledge in our wedding vows, repeated for all to hear on our Thanksgiving wedding day, the words too often, flippantly discarded, or possibly forgotten, as years go by, *'...in sickness and in health'*. Today, of huge comfort to me, in that one phrase alone, I had, in her, my beautiful wife, a troubadour, my found and truly treasured gift.

It would be, with that thought in mind and with glowing memories of that special, joyous occasion, when we vowed our love; I sought our saved, beautifully printed program and copy of our vows, our dedication of life and pledge to each other. I had a need to read them all again.

Three Days Later

I'd find them, safe, in our chest of memories. We'd saved everything, never wanting to lose the magnificence of the day, all with a fervored hope, someday maybe, the children; grandchildren too, might find comfort in them, even use them at their own wedding.

With my heart full of love, in my hands, I held the copy of our vows that meant everything to me. Too much water was flowing under my bridge to ever forget the magnificence of that incredible day, here outside, in this, our very own home.

While Chelsea was asleep, that afternoon, I chose to re-read the beautiful words we spoke to each other, marveling at their simplicity, their dedication to love.

'I (Anthony Robert Thompson), take you (Chelsea April Martin), to be my wife, my constant friend, my faithful partner and my love from this day forward. In the presence of God, our family and friends, I offer you my solemn vow, to be your partner, in sickness and in health, in good times and in bad, and in joy, as well as sorrow. I promise to love you, unconditionally, to support you in your goals, to honor and respect you, to laugh and cry with you, and to cherish you - for as long as we both shall live'.

In my heart, troubled though my mind was today, I had wanted to reflect all that I had promised, hoping, yet wondering, if I had lived up to my pledged words, my words to the woman I adored, who loved me in return. I began to sectionalize our vows; looking to be sure I had not failed her.

'To be my wife, my constant friend, and my faithful partner' didn't require a moment's thought. I could find no greater friend or partner than with Chelsea. Since the day we met, we had become almost inseparable. Our two different worlds collided back then; however, we were destined to be both friend and partner…and we were!

'…and my love from this day forward' - that, was already, clearly, unconditional.

'In sickness and health' – those four words alone were a one-hundred percent given. Chelsea, as a doctor, excelled in fighting sickness, but as a wife and partner, she excelled, for me, beyond the greatest of expectations. I could ask, neither expect, more.

As for *'good times and in bad'*, my life was filled with the good; I was surrounded by all things good, not only with my wife, but Sarah Austen and now, little Nelson James. So much good, so much happiness had entered my life since I had met Chelsea, I was more than grateful, while bad, it was merely a word to me, one I could never embrace - period!

In *'joy and sorrow'*, unquestionably, joy I had experienced in abundance, my cup over flowed, it runneth over. Any sorrow I felt had more to do with my current plight in health I was now strenuously trying to overcome. I did not like the word; I had no will to recognize it. However, truthfully as I was trying to be, I knew I had my moments, and I did wallow in sorrow sometimes no matter how hard I tried not to.

Okay, so far, so good. I was beginning to feel, analytically to my values, our vows spoken were more than holding up.

'I promise to love you unconditionally' would be the one phrase Chelsea would show in every way, this and every single day. Through the strain of life, we were currently experiencing (mine); she was caring, steadfast, unwavering, and never once allowed a moment of angst to show. Her love for me was her passion, truly, unconditional, and her battle for me, my much contested life; she single handed was winning.

'Support, honor, respect' – this was easy. I believed, quite adamantly, Chelsea and I had practiced these values to each other from the very first day we met, and very much doubted, not a single one of the three words, would, or could ever be, contested by either of us. Mutually, I doubted either of us could succumb to any in a negative way.

'To laugh and cry with you', - oh, we'd had our share of both that coupled both happy and sad, and in accepting that, I guessed we were as normal as the world at large in that arena of life and living.

'…and to cherish you' - Chelsea would remain my soul, my love, my inspiration. Cherish her, I surely did, every single day of my life…and yes – I would gladly say *'I do'* all over again.

'…for as long as we both shall live.' I wanted to live with Chelsea – forever!

Three Days Later

I turned my head, and with a smile of complete satisfaction, slowly, gently, placed our vows back in the trunk. What a blessed man I was, truly blessed. I think we were doing okay – so far.

Interestingly though, in my deeper reflection of our vows and our life, I quickly realized that it had been, for the most part, quite the opposite of my original intention. Initially, to be about *me,* and had *I* lived up to *my* vows to *Chelsea*, it was obvious; I had taken my circumstances, and viewed them more, the other way, Chelsea to me?

Yes, my wife not only lived up to her pledge to me; she had excelled in a gargantuan way, and I could only wonder, be amazed, what she meant to me and all she had given me.

Never needing to be reminded and without a moment of hesitation in the thought, I realized, I had unwittingly, with the best of intentions; suddenly opened my own eyes to the most incredible woman a man could ever hope to meet in his life. If, in her eyes, I had achieved merely, only one-half of what she had given and shared with me, I would accept it humbly, knowing, there was much more room for me to do so very much better for her. She deserved it.

I pledged, silently, to rally and rise to meet her very high standards. Every day, for the rest of my life, I needed Chelsea to know how much I loved her, and that I wanted our life, our lives, to never end. Whatever protests, large or small I might sometimes have in her quest for me, to fight the good fight, to never give up, I would endure them all, for her. I wanted, every morning, to wake up beside her, to see her face. I couldn't bear for her to be alone. We were a team. Sarah Austen and Nelson James needed a Daddy too.

I was not what you'd call 'religious', in the sense that I (we), went to church every Sunday, or indeed, had worshiped faithfully, either as a child growing up in Connecticut, or on into my later adult years. I did have faith, believed there was a higher being, and if it was my consolation of justification, I did happen to have a love of gospel music.

A fairly regular to the Gaither Gospel Homecoming Series on television, I loved many of the artists, Jake Hess, Linda Randle, Vestal Goodman, David Phelps, Guy Penrod, to name but a few, and the songs they sang; the show was a joy to sit and watch. I had, in the past, attended a couple of their live concerts that toured the country.

Qualification, justification, or not, I even had a favorite gospel playlist on my mp3 player, including a duplicate of them on my cell phone. I was; I am, a believer; I felt religion, but in fairness, truth, I'd always done it my way. I'd found my faith, not through preaching, sermons and the like, but; through music, my most favorite of gospel music as a song; The Old Rugged Cross.

With all of those harbored but very good intentions over my lifetime, and of at least having degrees of religion in my life, I expected, hoped; I would be granted clear passage to take it all up a notch - no questions asked!

Chelsea and I chose to attend the little white church with the big tall steeple we knew of, out on Grand Avenue, not more than a mile or so from our home on Glenwood Road. Both children would be christened in our newly found sacred spot, and I hoped, with our guidance; the church could serve as the embryo of their future in religious instruction and worship. With reverence, and welcome, it fast became our place to give thanks for the many things we both felt so blessed for in our lives and before too long; the church also became our safe haven each Sunday for worship that we looked forward to being a part of.

Not being able to walk the distance; it was too far; the drive there, on the quaint Avenue with well designed bike tracks and central nature strip, laden with trees and bushes separating the dual lanes would be a Sunday morning delight. Oak trees, resplendent visually with a plethora of thick deep hanging Spanish moss, to the many magnolias, magnificent Florida palms, pine and fir, even bright green leafy sycamore trees, Glenwood always had more to offer than typical suburbia.

Very much DeLand, within *'city limits'* proper, the area was also a bird sanctuary. My favorites, ones I loved to watch – the woodpecker and cardinals. Deemed *'a designated place, a community'* it could even boast its own little, almost ancient, but very well-established and run, Post Office. Suffice to say, the area in which we lived was...well, somewhat varied from and certainly, different, unique.

Our newly chosen church was a wonderful attribute to Glenwood, and the congregation, with open arms, quickly, willingly embraced us as a family. They loved the children, and Sunday school; it was abundantly clear, one day, a year or two maybe, would be in their future.

For no apparent reason, somewhat reticent initially, finally, I relented and soon began to join in the singing of the hymns, albeit more quietly than others. Most of the songs I knew by heart. Chelsea, meanwhile, who I'd never heard sing, *ever,* chose the more conventional route, happy to mouth the words, always looking, smiling, at the more robust me. Sunday's were nice, church; a nice place to be.

If it was my belated way of giving thanks for the relief, I was feeling in the fight against the dreaded, albeit mild Big C, then I had no qualms attending and participating in our Sunday ritual, admitting, it was two-fold true.

So far, I was winning the battle, and I readily accepted, along with faith, the prayers of others for me and the extra help of medicine, treatment and most importantly, the love of my dedicated wife, to say nothing of singing in the church, then I'd found my unknown true calling. Life was my greatest gift; my wife and children needed me. I needed them more.

CHAPTER

NINETEEN

Jack Montgomery, his new bride Robin, and her daughter Belinda, all came to visit. They told us it was a sort of belated honeymoon exploratory visit all in one. The premise he put forward, was primarily, to see and spend some time with old friends, to get away from the hustle and bustle of city life, and importantly, to consider vacating their one time stomping grounds of business and life for a change of scenery and better lifestyle.

The mere mention of leaving Connecticut, to me, was unthinkable, the last thing Jack Montgomery would *ever* do, or could *ever* have contemplated. I was floored! He was a dyed in the wool New Englander, or so I thought, but according to him, I was dead *wrong*! I was most happy to be wrong of course, as to see him, be with him; it would be like turning back the clock. Jack was, and always had been, my dearest friend. If he had *any* intentions of joining the outward bound, to come our way, and not as a 'snowbird' but to share our life and lifestyle permanently, then I was going to be his biggest champion in persuasion and give him every reason to *'head south'*.

Chelsea and I, and the children, met them from their direct flight to Daytona, ready to spend a few days in and around *'our neck of the woods'* and to make sure they not only had a good time, but actually like Florida too. I guessed it was the old salesman coming out in me again. Silently, my inner voice told me to pull out all stops, to encourage them to move. Their company, in our midst, would be an asset to our lives.

What a treat to see them walk from the plane to where we stood, anxiously waiting. Innocently, the first words out of Jack's mouth as we greeted one another after so long, unfortunately, couldn't have been more badly chosen, or under the circumstances, ill timed.

"What the hell's going on Tony? You've lost some weight; have you been sick or something?"

Chelsea looked immediately at me, angst clearly noticeable at the observation. Simultaneously, I wondered if my face showed the same. Had we both missed something, seeing and being with each other every day, that others, friends we knew, or strangers even who would have no idea, that they, one, could recognize my plight straight away? It was true; I hadn't shared my illness with Jack, and maybe I should have. Anyway, the answer, according to Jack's first reactions, was going to have to be a truthful one.

Totally unprepared as his question made me feel, but as jovial of sorts as he had been, expressing his visual reaction to me, it, nevertheless, had me thinking, *'how different do I really look? If an old friend who hasn't seen me in months reacts as Jack just did, how sick must I actually look to anyone? Can one really tell, simply by casually looking?'* It was a strange feeling, and in reality, almost, a stinging moment of truth!

"Fact is Jack; the answer is yes" I somewhat belatedly admitted, still giving him a big hug of welcome. "I *have* been a little sick, I'll explain it later, in the meantime, and more to the point right now, how are *you* all? You're the ones on vacation, let's all enjoy it and see where we might be able to help you huh?"

Introductions followed. Apart from being older, now, physically seeing her, I did remember Robin straight away, and she certainly still had the head-turning beauty about her that we, as younger men back then, never failed to notice. Speaking softly but with a tinge of humor, she shared her momentary reaction thought.

'I'd have liked it better if Jack had chosen me first, maybe I could have avoided the bad bit in between, except of course for…' as her words trailed off, she glanced immediately at her daughter. Sensitivity took over.

I got it straight away. Oops!

What was it about us, many of us, as we move from our teens to the twenties or older, I wondered. That we as adults, seem to have to make one mistake, or two, before we finally get it right? The thought of course applied to both men and women alike. I immediately shrugged it off, smiling at our gathered crowd, standing together, marveling at how we'd all been victims of the same result, except Jack maybe, who avoided the first marriage, but still lost the girl, fortunately, now to re-find her. But…that was life. We headed straight for DeLand.

Up early that first and next morning, after a quick breakfast, we all piled into my Ford Excursion and headed for the Wednesday DeLand Farmers Market at the Volusia County Fairgrounds. Enjoying the weekly trip as I did, it wasn't just the wonderful selections of the many and varied fresh fruits and vegetables that I had learned to take huge advantage of when I had long ago made it a ritual in going there, it was, in particular, the fun of finding the specials, the little treasures, the marvelous and many knick-knacks that were offered by the literal thousands…and most of them pretty cheap too!

For Sarah Austen and her new best friend Belinda, my two dollars each DVD prize of the day became the much-loved Scooby Doo, Tinkerbelle and Shrek movies that I was pleasantly, quickly assured, would keep their attention for more than just a little while. Different as an outing for our guests, the morning out was a winner, we all had fun.

And so the day by day choices of planning their itinerary in Florida, in and around the area of Deland began. One thing I loved was listening each evening, or every morning, as the choices were laid out, checking off in the *'things to do', 'places to see'* and whatever other categories, they could conjure up?

Three Days Later

Some things were made too easy. Apart from having Jack dutifully, as part of his daily entertainment chores, surf the Internet at DiscoverDeLand.org, - in anticipation of their visit, I'd also picked up from downtown, the attractive promotional printed card brochure that headlined *101 Things To Do in DeLand*. With everything at their fingertips, including Chelsea and me, I pumped out my chest looking like a complete know-all of all things local. Me – the transplanted one! Either way, it didn't matter. Everyone was enjoying themselves, and the weather remained picture perfect, confirming; in their eyes, Florida was indeed, the Sunshine State. So much so, eight days started to fly by for Jack and Robin pretty quick.

Accepting the schedules, in what activities we were able to share, Chelsea was quite stalwart, vigilant, in her policing of my personal shared activities with them, friend or no friend visiting. Disneyworld, Universal – they were out! The tourists could make the trek without us. Everyone understood, especially Jack, who had been fully briefed and brought up to date of my mild, but concerning bout with cancer, the need to be cognizant of activities and treatment, and to heed doctor's orders, particularly my personal doctor.

Later, chatting, "I feel so bad" he said with a hint of unnecessary remorse as we sat, mulling over my personal dilemma. "Who could have guessed, but you should have told me Tony, *long* before now" he added, more than disappointed by my earlier silence of not sharing my plight with him.

"I couldn't Jack. I just couldn't." I confessed honestly. "Not for any other reason than I wanted to get through it and not burden others. I didn't want sympathy votes no matter who it was. *My* biggest worry though is Chelsea, despite being a rock, and a true believer that we can get through it all, be cured even, but then again, she's a medic too, so she of all people, understands reality. Having said that though, she will *not* hear a word of defeat, negativity or any other form of downer conversation, so my friend, *always* watch how you phrase anything about it, or me, because she'll be all over you."

Throwing his head back, he laughed. I did too. It was all good therapy, however, for Jack Montgomery; other important things were on his mind. He wanted to talk, seriously.

"But Tony, what are the chances in *real* terms for you? Is there something you're hiding maybe, because you want to put on the brave face? As an old comrade of many years, your close comrade I might add, I'd rather know the truth you know, the absolute, no hold back, truth!"

There it was again, that old comrade word used only by him, I mused, but that was Jack! Forgetting his rather annoying trait, plus not having to hear the word so much these days, trait or no trait, only a true friend (comrade), could be so honestly blunt. It was a fair question he'd asked, and straight to the point.

"I appreciate that Jack, but no, seriously, so far so good and my treatments are pretty dang sophisticated. Believe me; I can handle them, although I do get a bit tired sometimes and more than I openly admit. Call me vane if you will, the big thing is, no hair loss, *and* I eat pretty well too so, it's all got to count for something, doesn't it?"

I trusted it to be no, but I did wonder if my explanation sounded at all like; I was looking more for hope, false hope even.

"*Yes and that's great,* really *great,* for sure…" Jack readily acknowledged "… but accepting that, has anyone, Chelsea, other doctors, has *anyone,* and I mean *anyone,* ever put odds on you like, well, years as a time frame for…oh damn it, you know what I'm trying to say Tony. It's kinda hard to put it but…?" I did. I could hear his angst, his caring. It suddenly occurred to me: no-one had asked *that* question before?

"Nope…" I told him with the same honesty as the questioned posed. "…Nothing! None of that, and in fact, nothing even remotely like that has *ever* been tabled. Not once. I've thought about it myself; I must admit, but I'm not sure I'd want a real answer, so I don't go there either. They all, the doctors, Cancer Society too, they all just tell me to follow the routine so to speak, to fight the good fight, be positive, and to never, *ever,* give in to bad or doubting thoughts, so I don't. Now, in acknowledging that entirely old friend, I have got to add, must add, given your questions, with a doctor in the house, on call twenty-four seven in Chelsea, do you *really* think I can't have every reason in the world to be confident? I'm here to tell you, living proof, there's not a chance, not one solitary chance in the whole wide world. Chelsea is my life, my one true biggest supporter and I thank the Lord a million times a day that our paths ever crossed. I mean, how incredibly fortunate am I? "

Jack asked a few more questions, soon exhausting what he thought was probably all he needed to personally know about my situation. He seemed genuinely happy – no, make that *ecstatic* - with the prognosis ahead for me, and I'd had no problem in answering him, to the best of my ability, or as I understood it, about absolutely anything, he wanted to ask. We'd been the same with Meghan and Mark, our faithful neighbor friends. Frankly, I couldn't be more cared for, or thought about, to the point that sometimes, in fact; my care could even be tantamount to overkill!

Being with Jack had actually been a family day off, for him, from trekking around as tourists. Robin had told him to go, she'd take care of the children, something that had been planned anyway, and as it turned out, the time had provided us the opportunity to spend an afternoon together, man to man, and friend to friend. It felt really good, kind of like Connecticut old times for me.

Strangely, though, as we sat there, I had a thought? I was reminded of, in part, the question Chelsea had asked of me not so long ago – '*...do you ever miss the camaraderie of people, of other men, who make you feel like some things are more everyday normal?*' Sitting with my friend, enjoying his company and conversation as I was, reminiscing a little even, I began to think that maybe the answer could have been a sure fire yes, but then again...? Sarah Austen and Nelson James sprung to mind. I dismissed the thought!

Lunch was extremely convivial, relaxing on the outside street seating at Dublin Station downtown, watching the busy townsfolk go about their business as we casually sat and talked. The simple Irish style meal ordered had been cooked to perfection and devoured quickly. And a light-hearted moment, for me - surprising Jack no end when I ordered a Yuengling beer to go with it.

'Are you sure you can drink alcohol' he asked, as if I was committing a cardinal sin.

'If I couldn't I wouldn't…' I took great delight in telling him, before adding '…relax Jack; you might have thought I'm dying, but I'm here to tell you; I'm *not,* okay already? A beer with my meal will be fine, believe it.'

It was a magnificent comeback and I knew it. Everyone hears the word cancer, and their first thought is death, dying, and mortality, fading away to a shadow; months left, weeks and the like. It wasn't true!

Modern medicine, care and treatment, works wonders these days, and although the words I wanted to hear, *'you're in remission'* had not been spoken as yet; they were certainly words I was working on, every day. *That* diagnosis, and I believed I'd get it someday, would be my first major, *major* boost, psychologically - after that, I'd fight hard, make that harder, to maintain the status quo, to then be told, I'd gone from remission to 'cancer free.'

Lunch and socializing over, Jack Montgomery moved on to the subject he really wanted to talk about, specifically from a business point of view. Factually, this was part of the added, known, real purpose for their visit. Intrigued, I was now going to give him my fullest and utmost attention.

"You know Tony." He started, finally "One of the things we, Robin and I, had on the agenda to talk about, long before I ever knew about your situation of course, was maybe coming down this way permanent, to Florida that is. That bit I've already shared with you."

I nodded in agreement; he'd been on and off quite vocal about it since arriving. He continued; however, there was a noticeable doubt in his voice, and it was obvious.

"To be brutally honest though, now, I'm not sure anymore whether to consider it or not, because, facts were, my greatest wish was that I wanted to team up again, with you. *That* was my original intention, but I'd have to gather, realistically maybe, that's probably a no-go now, and probably not where you're at anymore. Would I be right? Either way Tony, I just need to get it out of my head officially before I consider a whole different tack. So, my old partner and friend, my comrade, what are your thoughts in general, and of course, I *was* talking real estate, that was a given, it's what we both know?" I'd also taken that as a given.

My answer didn't need pondering pontification, or a time-out period, or lengthy dissertation of reason. Somewhat unprepared as I might have been at his interesting suggestion; lingering would be counter-productive when it came to giving him my honest answer.

"As to my thoughts Jack, none, absolutely none" I told him forthright. "I like them but hadn't really thought about *anything* until we started chatting, and that's the truth. I mean, what would have been the point? I liked the idea of y'all heading on down south here…"

I noticed the faint smile as I said it, knowing I had, without thinking, spoken my best southern drawl with their *'y'all'* and more. I guessed it was catching! I continued without missing a beat.

"… but other than that, all I can really do right now is to listen to your proposal, however, please, *please*, don't treat me as an invalid. I'm hardly that. I have a challenge *yes*, but we're meeting it, and as for Chelsea, whatever I might think, or ever wanna do, I'd *never* consider a thing without her input, in fact, anything I do would *have* to have her blessing, regardless. It's that simple. My top priorities are her, and now, the two children, and *that* I know you'll more than understand."

Jack Montgomery nodded his head in the affirmative before taking the cue, going immediately back to where he had left off a moment ago. If he had learned, or picked up on one thing in what I'd just said, as an answer, it would be, I had *not* said an outright *No!*

"Well, I do have to say, admit being probably a better word…" he followed up "…we like it here in Florida, and maybe a bit like you, or even a *whole lot* like you, Robin and I have had about enough of Connecticut, to say nothing of the cold that seems to get harder every year to handle. We think also, if for no other real reason, except, as we get older, we have to start thinking about Belinda as well. That said Tony, and important to what I am proposing, the business back there is still actually going fine, but ya know, it's never been the same without you man, and that's the God's honest truth. We're still in pretty good shape as a Company, despite the turndown and political strife out there, but you know; facts are; it won't be getting any better anytime soon. I know that, which is why I'd rather get out while I still can, while I have something still very tangible to sell. If I can make that transition out, sell up at a fair price, Florida looks pretty good to me and who knows, by then, the tide may have turned for you, and I hope so for sure. Maybe that's when we can talk with more substance of reality and conditions. Does that sound reasonable to you, y'all, to Chelsea I mean also of course?"

Mimicking the moment, it was a cute touch that brought a returning smile from me that he picked up on, something I was quite sure he had also intended to do. About to respond, I never got the chance.

"*No* commitments right now, *nothing* set in concrete, just an open door, and if Robin and I do what I think we will; we can always talk again then, maybe, but of course, that would be only if any of what I've said makes sense to you so, whada'ya think? Can we keep it as open ended for now, or should I shut it all down completely and believe me Tony; I *won't* be offended in your answer, if it's a straight out *No?* I'd rather you be honest with me right at the outset."

What a speech, admission even. All up, I had no problems at all with the general scenario, in fact; I actually liked it. I fully understood Jack needed reassurance, which was fair and taking everything he had said on board; I chose to embrace what I hated, leaving him with the old, *'yes-but'*…generally understood double speak that really meant, *'expression of interest.'* He got my drift. I knew.

"Done deal old friend, don't shut it down. I'll talk. I'll look, but importantly, I'll be around *'if the good Lord's willing, and the creeks don't rise'* as they say in these here parts. Regardless, it all sounds fine to me. Truthfully, I'd like to be in."

We shook hands on our chat, our shared thoughts. For all the right reasons, I felt comfortable about it all; our look ahead. I'd love to get out there, active again, especially with my old friend, and with the door left wide open, a chance to talk to Chelsea, and a time frame that accepted what might transpire ultimately with my prostate and the treatment, I had nothing to lose, actually, something to look forward to.

In the meantime, though, looking at the much bigger picture, it was really up to Jack, to take his own major personal leap of faith, about his life first. What he was planning to undertake, and proposing, were a couple of huge, really big challenges. There were risks.

Philosophically, as I saw it, how I was looking at it; life's a crap shoot, a gamble anyway, full of risks. If this all turns out to be his moment in the sun, his look at a new future, then all I could think was, *'shine on down!'*

Meanwhile, Robin didn't need any convincing at all that Florida was a place she could enjoy. In anticipation, exploring possibilities, looking at housing in and around the area of DeLand, eye-balling Lake Helen, Deltona, DeLeon Springs, DeBary, Orange City and the immediate surrounds of Glenwood where we lived, she, for different reasons, was convinced they could easily make the transition. Interestingly, Chelsea, who not only liked the two of them, and Belinda, she also thought Jack's presence could have a big impact on me and my well being; therefore, *she* became their biggest advocate in considering the possibility of sharing life with us in Florida, no matter where they might ultimately choose to settle.

The South was beginning to rise yet again, and I smiled, just as it had done more than quietly over many years as history had proven, particularly with the older generation who chased milder weather and greater benefits of lifestyle.

And now, the great state of Connecticut, a region almost two-thirds forest, that could boast The Fundamental Orders; the first written constitution in the Americas, was in danger of losing *another* family, lured away by a lifestyle so vastly different in the deeper South.

Back in Daytona, our airport farewell said it all.

"We're gonna miss y'all, so make sure you c'mon back to the sunshine huh? If there's one thing you can rely on in Florida, for the best part, brilliant one day, perfect the next."

They were true simple words of encouragement from Chelsea while hugging my friend Jack Montgomery, who she had adopted, over time, a very soft spot for.

"Like everything in life, we'll make it work and *that's* a promise we can surely keep." She added, turning from Jack to hug Robin, then Belinda who Sarah Austen was going to miss a lot.

Our farewells over, they headed off to check in and lengthening security line.

For no reason, except clinging to time, we waited, to watch their plane lift off. There was an element of sadness in us both as their plane soared through the puffy white clouds and Florida blue skies we know they had enjoyed while here with us. We'd miss them all – for sure.

Chelsea had already confirmed to me, the Montgomery's being with us, sharing a friendship and talking openly, were all good and positive signs, ones that could enrich everyone's lives, not the least me, but also the children.

Good friends in life are hard to come by, *'and you can count them all on one hand'* she reminded me, again. I'd remembered. And I had such a friend in Jack Montgomery. She saw it, loved it, and endorsed it, and if that meant helping them make the transition to Florida, we would be there, by their side, all the way, when the time came.

As always, I couldn't fault the wisdom and love in the heart of my wife. Being a doctor had already made her a pillar in the community, and nothing, ever, was too much trouble to, or for her. And when it came to friends she held near and dear, the effort magnified. I couldn't wait for Jack and Robin to return, and hopefully next time – permanently.

Deep within my soul and in my heart, the past week had inspired me immensely. Friendship, love and camaraderie were all I, any of us, could ever ask for, and given all I'd experienced personally; I knew I'd missed it too, but above all, unquestionably – I felt wonderful, on top of the world. The good Lord, I believed, was definitely smiling on me. Come Sunday, in His house, I must remember to thank Him.

CHAPTER

TWENTY

*I*t wasn't a relapse, but I did succumb to the cooler weather, picking up a bad cold. Chelsea didn't take any chances and kept me pretty much holed up in the bedroom to get over the coughing, sneezing and wheezing and most certainly, well away from both Sarah Austen and Nelson James. She became very protective, not wanting them coming down with anything, especially the dreaded flu. They were allowed to come to the door, wave and shout *'Hi, or bye Daddy'* but that was all. No entering the room was their strict order. They didn't!

Comfortably lying there, watching the big-screen television and some of my favorite older movies on DVD - The Patriot, 3:10 to Yuma, Dirty Rotten Scoundrels and of course, schooling up on the politics and news of the day, I couldn't help but think, if this is what the alternative of being in a hospital is all about, coupled with the care and attention one gets from a personal doctor, to say nothing of the food, particularly the kind Chelsea was bringing me, then there'll be no fussing from me versus the sometimes other horrifying stories often told? I had the best of *all worlds*. Meghan and Mark, meanwhile, could never be faulted.

Three Days Later

While Chelsea made extremely well planned periodic visits to the Clinic, in her absence, the children spent their time next door. It was tough...and I took my medicine, gladly.

~~~~~~~~~~

The house was silent. Everyone was gone. Amazed, why, I don't know, but I had the most negative of thoughts, and yet they were interestingly wonderful too. With no-one to talk to, I conjured up in my mind, some of the things I'd like to do if I was ever given a 'red-light' to my life, that my time was over. In the modern idiom of phrases, we'd all heard of *'the Bucket List'*, those things you'd like to do before you leave this world, if you had the time, inclination and money. The thought alone made me want to see the movie again, although I doubted Chelsea would ever let Messer's Nicholson and Freeman and that cinematic masterpiece grace our household?

My mind wandered; if I was given a choice of ten, no, that's too greedy I thought, make it five – what would my bucket list really look like and not necessarily why?

First – England; To wander all over London town again. I loved the history, the buildings, and the landmarks. I also wanted to see one more time, the White Cliffs of Dover (I considered that a bonus of being in London, not separate).

Second - Travel over the corkscrew road of the Andes Mountains - from Santiago, Chile, up and over to Mendoza in Argentina and from there, back down to Buenos Aeries.

Third - Visit Australia to see the magnificence of the Great Barrier Reef and from there, trek in the Outback maybe.

Fourth - Drive through Czechoslovakia and Poland. I wasn't sure why with that one?

Fifth - Witness and photograph the Aurora Borealis.

And for good measure, I snuck in an extra one...Egypt. See and touch the Pyramids and Sphinx.

With *'the list'* secure in my traipsing around the world mind, moments later, it wandered further, more toward reality. None of them were ever going to happen, what with two little children, a busy wife, and me. Suddenly, all I had felt that I had wanted to do, I realized, could be construed as selfish, shallow even. I suppose that's a personal thing, however, having actually thought it, there had to be some truth in it, because facts were, I had more to be grateful for already, from life itself. Surrounded by what I currently shared – all of it was without a doubt - a true blessing.

Dozing, maybe I was sound asleep, but anyway, the slight noise I heard caused me to open my eyes. My blessing appeared in front of me. Chelsea was standing at the door all smiles. A cold hard dose of life and the everyday returned. Without an ounce of hesitation, I immediately changed my mind. I'd forsake the bucket list I'd conjured up, if I could spend the next fifty years with the lady who just lit up the room where I lay with nothing more than her mere presence.

As always, she was beautiful. Right there and then, there could be no contest. Seeing her; I wanted my life back, my health; I wanted to be with her, Chelsea – always.

With reality back in place, I responded to her presence.

"Now, my dear sweet wife, that's one heck of a big smile you're wearing..." Buoyed at her vision, gazing into her eyes, I added "...can it be that you're glad to see me, and I hope it is, and by the way, something that should please you, as of this very moment, three days later, I have to tell you, I'm feeling a whole lot better."

She ignored everything I had said. About to repeat myself and get a reaction, she beat me to it with a simple question.

"Guess what?"

No hello, request, or endorsement of my better condition I wondered.

"I have no idea."

She was supposed to have been delighted with how I was feeling; so much better and ready to get out of my confined bed as I was sure she'd had enough, by now, of pandering to me and my confinement.

"Guess?" She asked me a second time.

Okay, I'll play along. I wasn't going to get in front of her news anyway. And I supposed, whatever she had to say to me, had to have merit. Dinner maybe; at a restaurant, if I was *that* well again?

"Well, whatever it is, it's got to be good" I replied; now really itching to know.

"It is" she teased.

I obviously have to guess *something* I realized. I'll play along.

"It is?" I threw back.

How I wished I'd had some better quip instead of giving her a return question by repeating her very words, but with a different inflection. It became a question with a question.

"Yes, everything we've been waiting for and more."

Aaah! Got it, I believed. No wonder she had a smile on her face. I decided to slightly hedge my bets on the answer.

"Don't tell me. Is it what I think it might be? I mean, is it?" Another question!

I genuinely thought I knew, and my excitement was now building. I so wanted to be right.

"Your latest tests are back, and in simple terms, Mr. Thompson, you are improving. More invasive treatment won't be necessary. Things are looking very good. It's a plus in every way, which tells me; you can get on with the rest of your life, and that means with me. Good news you'd agree?"

Another question, forget it! Game over, for me. What a thrill, a joy, a relief.

From leaning in the doorway, Chelsea bounded toward me, landing straight on the bed to lie down on the covers beside me, her arms engulfing me, looking me straight in the face as she did. Her smile had never left her. Moving to kiss her, she pulled away.

'You're too sick for that I believe' she threw out playfully before relenting, softly placing her lips on mine.

Who'd have thought, my wife had become a tease? We lingered in a loving embrace. Stunned, at our mutual responses to each other, minutes later, under the covers, slowly, gently, without expectations, we shared the thrill of nothing more than uncomplicated, unashamed togetherness. It all seemed so right.

"God I love you" I told her, wrapped in her arms. "You're my love, my life. You've worked miracles, and I could never thank you enough. Thank you Chelsea, for coming into my life."

"Never stop loving me" was her simple, heartfelt reply. A tear fell from her eye.

I'd loved Chelsea from the first day, first moment; I had ever laid eyes on her, had met her, and I knew; I would go to my grave loving her. I would say it, declare it, always; no greater gift in life could I have had, than that of my dear, sweet, loving wife. I brushed my lips over hers while moving my hands to touch the body that never failed to thrill me, or leave me with a glow and happiness, indescribable - all of that and more, despite my personal shortcomings. We lay together for what seemed like forever. If I'd been sick before, I was getting better by the minute. With the news Chelsea had delivered, I was immediately a new man, in so many ways.

Then it happened! Suddenly, she sat bolt upright. She actually gave me a minor fright.

"The children, I'd better get to Meghan's right now" she blurted out, almost panicking. Within seconds it seemed, presentable again, she was gone.

I lay my head back into the pillow, full of wonderful thoughts, reminiscing, our last; I guessed, half hour. Smiling, feeling happy, and dismissing totally all my bucket list dreams I'd now gladly discard to be forever with Chelsea, I too, moved from the bed, heading straight for the shower. The hot water felt so refreshing, like life itself.

The children were getting bigger every day, Sarah Austen, particularly. At last, our happy home was all we had ever wanted it to be, and especially with the patter of little feet. Could one ask for anymore? Don't get me wrong though, idyllic as our lifestyle might seem to be, with no really definitive seasons in Florida, except summer and winter, *both* had moments we could do without. The searing heat of summer, week after week of 90 degrees plus temperatures, would take its toll, especially on me as I was not used to it.

Winter of course was another story; mild as they were, compared to my old home town and State, overnight lows of close to 30 degrees, and sometimes less, seemed colder in a vastly different way. Sweaters, jeans and jackets helped ward off the chill of the winter time highs that might get up to a low 49 degrees or more, however, taking everything into consideration, the biggest, only complaint about the cold I could truthfully make, was the destruction of my prized plants, unless I covered them up or, the potted ones, put them inside the garage to protect them. Small worry really and frankly, who was seriously complaining? I never could.

Eyeing the news on TV, watching huge sections of the country dig itself out from mountains of snow, cars piling up on ice road freeways, and howling winds - Florida, *'the Sunshine State'*, the south in general, or especially, here in Deland, we had it mighty good. With an abundance of everyday sunshine and mostly, manageable temperatures, there really was little to complain about. And who'd listen anyway?

By the time Halloween, Thanksgiving and Christmas had come and gone, followed by the return to daylight saving, knowing spring was rapidly approaching, our souls were cheered early. In any New Year, we were refreshed and ready to do it all over again. And the children took it all in their stride!

Chelsea had long ago returned to full-time work, while I, again, assumed the most welcomed responsibility for Sarah Austen and Nelson James, ahead of anticipating the possibility of the arrival of Jack and Robin Montgomery from Hartford. We knew the Realty business had been sold, and their house was due to close within the month, and if no unforeseen glitches occurred, they planned the permanent journey south to Florida shortly thereafter.

Early in the New Year, Jack had flown down on a quick visit, to again grasp a better lay of the land as it applied to me, and so far, with my health stable, and Chelsea's blessing, it remained a clear green light situation to proceed in a joint venture, with the solid rock caveat, *'assuming no unexpected setbacks in my condition'*. According to the doctor, my personal doctor, with a hug and a smile, she took great delight in confirming to us both; all prognostications for me still remained positive, most favorable.

"Are you sure you want me to do this Chelsea?" I queried to my wife. I valued her opinion.

"I could never be surer" she lovingly, confidently confirmed. "You are, and will be, just fine!"

"Well, my dear sweet lady, with your words of endorsement, maybe it will be good to get back in the workforce and active." I had to admit, thinking more, as I had, of Jack Montgomery's plans for Florida; I now really wanted to do it.

The only small reservation I had about going back to work, and it bothered me somewhat, was who would look after the children? I loved being a Dad full time – Mr. Mom. As always though, Chelsea had an answer. She'd make a whole lot of sense that I'd find mighty hard to refute; I wouldn't try. It would have been pointless.

"It's what modern families do these days Tony, and it's not like we're Robinson Crusoe...," she professed, adding firmly, as if for a reason "...you *understand*, of course, I certainly can't leave the practice; however, in accepting that as a fact, thankfully, we do have Meghan, who has confirmed; she is more than willing to take up a part-time agreement with us, paid for services rendered we agree, plus we have select day-care facilities nearby that all come well recommended, if we need them. Those are the first points; now, next and important thing is; I believe this chance for you to be outside active will do wonders for you, no question. Taking all of that into consideration, and as far as the children go, we'll see how it goes; if it doesn't work, or work out, then we'll regroup and figure a different move. Frankly, it's all too simple, and let's face it my dear sweet husband; it's not like either of us will ever be far away. This is DeLand remember, not Orlando or Hartford."

It all made sense, it was all true and anyway; I was ready. Actually, really ready! I had confirmed it to myself again; I *wanted* to be out there, working. Chelsea had seen it in me, and had no reservations about it. To her way of thinking; I needed to re-enter the working world. That settled, together, all of us; we set the wheels in motion.

Three Days Later

Montgomery-Thompson Properties Inc. had a nice ring to it. Situated on New York Avenue, five blocks west of the Boulevard downtown, the building we bought, was a Spanish style, low set office complex, boasting six large partitioned offices, a designated board room for exchanging documents and a large reception foyer, perfect to meet and greet customers and most comfortable as a communal waiting area.

We contacted The DeLand Beacon newspaper, set up editorial coverage based on our grand opening press release, an advertising package, then, patiently waited for the phone to ring, and of course, for customers to *'come visit and talk'*.

From opening our door, sourcing new business, to securing some very key clients, time, from a business point of view, flew by. We must have been doing something right, as even in harder economic times, initial business was brisk, calls were plentiful, new listings were above our expectation and sales, while slow in their execution, were, by and large, mostly, all making their way to closure.

They were all positive signs of hopefully, making our presence felt in DeLand and the surrounding areas of Volusia County.

Feeling much more secure, and confident, as Jack Montgomery and I now were, on a whim, any excuse, to celebrate our first seven weeks of activity, we planned to shut the doors earlier on a Friday evening and take Chelsea and Robin to dinner. We'd all earned it.

Picking a convenient spot, Jack and I agreed, BBQ ribs and more at The Pitmaster out on the highway toward Deleon Springs made it really easy. Chelsea had immediately proffered The Shuttered Firefly when I had called her, but to me, firstly, it was much further out of town than any of us might want to venture, and anyway, importantly, when it came to The Shuttered Firefly, I preferred to keep it and its memory, always, for the two of us, alone. *'Maybe our anniversary'* I suggested, adding *'...that's when we'll include Jack and Robin'* by way of concession.

'Agreed, and I'll hold you to it' was her simple reply.

Close to home, The Pitmaster turned out to be more than perfect; it suited our needs and was a convivial enough place for us all to be together. And one thing didn't escape us; true to the reputation held widely of the restaurant's popularity; the place was packed!

As a foursome, the way we pre-thought it, (an excuse really), we were all happy, business was picking up, and in general, for all the changes made in our lives, overall, life was kind. Jack and Robin didn't stray too far from us in Glenwood.

Searching for, and then buying a property, they quickly settled on a picturesque, all white color, two storey home on Mercer's Fernery, complete with two acres of lush green grass, resplendent also with many trees. Idly chatting about everything and nothing in particular, Jack Montgomery was, given the deal they secured, metaphorically speaking, *'blown away.'*

"In a million years I couldn't have bought this style of a house in Connecticut for the price I paid here in Florida? It's a chalk and cheese situation, and I know what I'd prefer and where…" he was openly confessing, adding "…what we've got is incredible, unbelievable, almost a dream."

"It all comes down to life-style and way of life, period…" Chelsea put forward, while reminding them both at the same time "…DeLand is Main Street USA, and you'd go a long way to do better, no matter how far and wide you traveled. Smaller communities, throughout our nation, have always been the very lifeblood and strength of America."

Jack quickly picked up on her drift, her message.

"You're right Chelsea, so right, and I agree. Who'd had ever thought? With wide-open spaces, sunshine, all the basic freedoms we crave for, and of course, as you say, small-town living, it's relevant, different, preferable and especially for children. You'll get no argument from me, and let me add, I'm joining y'all, and DeLand is my town now…"

Glancing at Robin, remiss in his comment, he added on a rephrase, "…*our* town now that is, and we're mighty proud to be here, aren't we Robin?"

His wife glanced at him with an approving nod.

"Proximity to anything we might ever want is here, but it's the camaraderie, the closeness, the niceness of the people I like most.

Three Days Later

Where else can you get that and call it natural, the way it is, the way it should be?"

Jack Montgomery had told himself, and me, over and over lately, he had not only made the right decision to change his life, marrying Robin, and moving to Florida, he also made it adamantly clear; he had never been happier, more satisfied in life, suggesting, had it not been for me and Chelsea, in the way it all played out, he and I both, probably, would still be sitting up in Connecticut, conducting our lives in the basic mundane way we were back then, never knowing, believing, there was a world outside waiting to embrace us all. They were *his* words, and he couldn't have been more forceful in tone stating them. He gave me credit for the motivation, glad he had supported all of my original suggestions in a sabbatical in Florida and especially, the way it all turned out. I kind of agreed. Naaah...I agreed wholeheartedly. Every word spoken was true.

"Well here's to all we've worked for and for much more ahead too" he toasted.

Drink glasses were raised high. Heading out for the evening had been a great idea.

But wait, Jack wasn't finished yet.

"And thank you Chelsea, I don't know how Robin and I could ever have made it to where we're at today without your encouragement, to say nothing of the support, the love, the care and more you've given my old comrade here. You're an angel, and I hope you don't mind, but I love you for it all."

I was personally touched. Again, my old partner and pal, (comrade...and yes, Chelsea hated it too!), had shown a side of him that had taken much too long in life to surface. He was, unquestionably, a different guy from the one I grew up with in Hartford, and a whole lot better as well. I really liked it.

"I can only tell you this Jack...' Chelsea began "...this man, your comrade" – What! She smiled as she turned to me, knowing my thought "...devoid of your eloquent words, has been a real inspiration to me, believe it or not..."

I was about to get somewhat embarrassed, I could feel it. She was way too serious.

"…this man…" she glanced at me "…he has taught me more than I might ever have admitted to anyone, *especially* about myself, but equally, about love, and I mean *true* love. I actually thought I was in love once; I even married for love, as I thought I knew it, but the fact was; I was pretty much deluding myself. The *real* love I have seen and shared from this man…"

She glanced at me again with a look that never failed to melt my heart before continuing.

"…this man has taken me to places I didn't know existed. He has shown me life and love, *far greater* than I could ever have found alone. If what you say, in calling me an angel, and I appreciate it, believe me, but for whatever I've done in your eyes to be an angel, I can only say, admit, it pales ten-fold by comparison to what Tony has given me, shown me, and continues to show me. I can surely tell you, both of you…"

Chelsea turned to look straight at Robin.

"…I love this man with all my heart, and no matter what; I'll love him forever. I want him always with me, and I want all of us together too."

She paused. Her moist filled eyes moved swiftly to look directly at each one of us. We were all, without question, somewhat mesmerized.

"But enough, my speech, my declaration, from this point on - it's over."

An unexpected silence followed. Jack, Robin, me – were rendered totally speechless.

"Thank you darling, you flatter me, but don't stop now" I jokingly chipped in, attempting to break the silence.

Happiness abounded, joy filled our immediate space.

"You give me more credit than I deserve, but I love you for it."

I leaned across to kiss her on the cheek only to hear Robin's query, as she turned toward Jack.

"Why don't you show me that kind of affection when we're out in public? It's nice and they do it, why not you?"

Without a single moment's hesitation, Jack leaned toward Robin to mimic my actions of affection, pecking his wife lightly on the cheek.

"There, was that so hard?" she challenged him, in jest.

With an initial smirk, a frown, he looked directly across at me.

"Trouble maker," we all heard him mumble before changing his expression to a big, broad smile that beamed clear across his face.

"Kidding" he added

Unquestionably, my friend was slowly changing, and it was nice to see.

Next day I woke up not feeling the best. Chelsea immediately ran her instant tests. Not tempting fate, she took my pulse, as well as my temperature and blood pressure.

"Did this start last night or this morning?" she asked, double checking a time frame as to yesterday's activities and my agenda as far as the day went.

My retrace in answer gave her no clues she could readily link. Her best advice for me, take the day off, rest and let her keep a watchful eye out for any changes that might occur. Fact was; she was fearful of a set-back in my overall health given things generally, were so far, going so well. It was Saturday, sometimes a busy day for us at the Realtor Agency; however, Chelsea was having none of my mild protesting.

'I'm the doctor here. You're the patient, so Mr. Thompson; we'll follow my orders, okay?'

I called Jack Montgomery, who also showed instant concern, reiterating my wife's advice, insisting I stay home, adamant, that he'd handle the office.

With everyone against me, I took the mild pain I felt in my stomach and general lethargic approach to my stamina, off to bed, content to watch, of all things, on DVD, Gone with the Wind. Five hours later, Chelsea woke me, holding a small bowl of vegetable pasta with chicken bits, telling me; it was time to eat, but more importantly, asking me how I felt? I knew I'd seen virtually nothing of the movie, conceding it to be the best way to fall asleep if you're going to, but, for five hours? I was not sure that was a good or bad thing. Chelsea assured me; it was okay, depending on how I felt now?

I sat up, shrugged my shoulders, twisted my neck around, moved my arms up, down, and out, before returning a verdict of *'absolutely fine doctor, absolutely fine'*.

"Then eat this…" she ordered,"… and when you're done eating, you should get up, out of bed, take a walk around the house, the garden, after which you can take a shower. When that's all done, I'll listen more intently to how you feel."

"No problem" I gladly told her. "My pleasure Doctor, and thank you."

~~~~~~~~~~

CHAPTER

TWENTY-ONE

The pre-arranged phone meeting, lasting upwards of fifteen minutes, went exceptionally well. The to and fro of questions had flowed smoothly.

"If he'll sign to your finally agreed to price, a full ten-percent under the original listing, with no further changes than what has already been accepted, then it's agreed; I'll be there. We'll consider the contract a final firm *'locked down done deal'*." I knew the owner would.

The long wait was almost over. Jack Montgomery had been nervous, his mouth and eyes wide open as he listened. I was about to close, in principle, with guaranteed verbal commitment, for the biggest sale yet since we opened doors in Deland to Montgomery-Thompson Properties Inc. A second part property management rights deal had also been offered our Company. We glanced at each other, almost unable to contain our smiles.

"Thank you Sir, I'll get back with you shortly to confirm the time and place, then we'll put this all to bed, okay?" my head nodding up and down in the affirmative as I spoke.

Placing my cell phone down on the desk rather heavily; I stood up; my right hand palm fully opened, ready to 'hi-five' the palm of my partner, who had been forced to listen to a one-sided conversation only. Confirming plans for our next meeting, Jack was relieved; finally satisfied he could rest easy. We had been successful - nailed a big one! Old school type in salutation recognition, he couldn't contain himself. Stretching his arm out instead, he avoided a 'hi-five', moving instead to clasp his hand in mine to shake it vigorously, a genuine Montgomery compliment in itself. 'High fives' weren't quite his style, yet!

"Well done Tony, well done. This is a winner, a real winner, and timely too."

His smile spoke volumes, his words, more than gratifying.

"Man, he started out as being one hard nut to crack but that said, a few meetings later, he mellowed and things got easier right up to this point…" I sat back down "…but to be fair; it's a buyers' market, so more power to him. He got a deal and a damn good one at that."

"Yeah I know, but if you have the money and he obviously did, or has, then it's amazing what you can get, and *that* building, *that* complex, it was a prize, a really honest-to-goodness prize. He'll never regret it I'll bet!"

"You're right, but the added good part; he does want to extend the agreement about the follow through rights we spoke about, and told him we'd take on. Words to the effect, he basically confirmed his confidence in us as a Company telling me; *'we've come this far and I'm feeling pretty comfortable with you all, so, you've got it. When we meet, we'll sign that agreement too".*

Jack Montgomery couldn't believe our good luck. The way it all came down, and so fast after opening our doors in Volusia County.

"Fantastic! Love it, but it'll also mean some changes to accommodate it all and talk about timing; it's perfect. What a *major* breakthrough and well done again Tony. Man, you really hit it out of the park. I'm proud of you, great stuff!"

Having met earlier, and then working with the local developers to the complex, I had secured the rights for Montgomery-Thompson to sell an extremely attractive apartment block on the north-side of

Three Days Later

Highway 17-92 on South Woodland Boulevard, a location considered choice, given its proximity to a strip mall, anchored by Sears and Publix Supermarket, major draw cards for the rest of the fast renting, many small businesses. With all twenty-four, of the one, two and three-bedroom units now complete and available for occupation, the complex, named for simplicity as 'The Boulevard Towers,' was picturesque, with exquisite landscaping, featuring a host of Florida native trees, and especially, magnificent palms.

The buyer, located in Tallahassee, who wished to remain anonymous, had initially seen the property on a driving trip he had made to Cape Canaveral to witness one of the few remaining launchings of the soon to be ended Space Shuttle program.

As a diversion to his normal method of transportation, it just so happened, this latest time, he had driven through the city heart of DeLand, via the Boulevard. Impressed with the building and its landscaped environs that clearly caught his attention, he followed up his interest in possible acquisition, initially, only as a matter of interest; that was until he realized the property was an absolute bargain waiting to be *'snapped up!*' He saw it as a top notch, good investment; he doubted would last very long on the open market. He proved himself right on both accounts; we had launched the marketing campaign less than five weeks earlier.

Comfortable with the negotiations, and the back and forth repartee with me as the agent whom he had dealt with exclusively, in finally securing the sale and purchase, we arranged the signing and settlement up in his hometown. I would have to go to him in Tallahassee; he did not have a free schedule.

Given the magnitude of the transaction, his request was never going to be a problem from our company point of view.

The unexpected bonus followed. Not originally sought by us, but as the Realtor, the buyer, on his own volition, offered the property management rights to us, if we agreed to appoint a resident manager and handle general maintenance and rents. In a slow economy, we accepted; under the premise, all business is good business, and if it meant wider diversification, then, as relative newcomers, time wise in real estate to DeLand, Montgomery-Thompson would take the property under our wing, set up a separate rental division and expand our company accordingly.

Time was of the essence. Both Jack and I knew, from painful experience – *strike while the iron is hot*. Too many real estate deals fall through if not secured quickly or if any degree of hesitation is felt, it has the ability to spell *'problem.'* We did the deal.

Driving to Tallahassee would be easy enough, the trip could be done, up and down all in one day, but I didn't like the thought of it, expressing my thoughts to Jack who instantly offered to make the trip for me.

Taking in personal circumstances, we both knew it could be quite taxing; I also knew what Chelsea would have to say about me traveling alone, and such a distance.

"Thanks old friend, I appreciate it, but I don't think so. The buyer is comfortable with me. We've had a great rapport and frankly; he's expecting me, and I mean *me*, not a stand in. If I reneged now and sent someone else, no offence, of course, to you, he might…I dunno, it just doesn't seem right, that's all. I've been his get-go, one and only, go-between, from day one. Plus, he likes me a lot too!"

"I know, but I had to offer. It was a just thought, a way to help, contribute." Jack counter-acted, knowing what I meant.

"It won't take long really, I guess…" I added, almost as if I had to qualify my actions, my independence, thinking nothing in the bigger picture of the undertaking "…it's only what, about two-hundred plus mile's driving, which is about three hours or so up there and back, seven max, including the meeting and I'd guess maybe, a quick lunch if he wants. All up, probably it'll be a ten or eleven hour day which is not so bad, looking at it that way."

Fast as I had calculated it, I knew, on saying it out loud, a bigger problem was looming. That was a lot of hours straight, company would be a better proposition.

"And what is Chelsea going to a have to say about *that*? Jack asked prophetically. "You know she's not gonna be too happy, and I don't want to say, *'because of your condition'* you know that, but it *is* something she'll be protective about, the stress, the driving, getting tired, whatever, and the rest. There's a problem out there on your horizon comrade. Be prepared."

Montgomery was exactly right of course. Chelsea would be, not only more than concerned; she'd also be super furious! Frankly, it really bothered *me* a little more than I might admit. However, this was the big one, the one that makes the difference in business and a bold statement from a company's image point of view. It was a major deal.

Accepting all the obvious, I had an immediate thought: maybe Chelsea could join me. I'd canvass it tonight.

"You know Tony..." Jack motioned, with a suggestion "...you could fly you know. There's an airport right here in Deland with plenty of smaller planes available. We could negotiate a quick flight to Tallahassee for you that'll probably get the job done in maybe less than five hours all up, but having said that, there are some regular commercial flights out of Daytona as well. Why don't we check all the air possibilities that are available to us first?"

It was an excellent proposal, a really viable means of saving time, and although a more expensive alternative to driving; it never became an issue. Without hesitation, I made the calls; unfortunately, they all came up bad news.

Major carriers went through hubs well removed from Tallahassee, which really meant going through either Atlanta or Charlotte to get to there, only to have to reverse the journey to get back. That idea was immediately out!

Light, local, private aircraft was the only way. I decided to check out, what was now, the final and only other option...or drive of course?

One phone call later, locally, I had secured a tentative deal, subject to confirmation. Unfortunately, without having had a chance to discuss the alternative action ahead of the negotiation, as predicted, Chelsea was not happy at all.

"I understand business, and I more than understand clients, but this is a call that makes me mighty uneasy Tony. Sadly, as always, I can *never* just drop what I'm doing and wander away on a whim. I am far too heavily committed; so no, I *can't* come with you. Much as I'd like to, there are the children, we have to think about them as well. Accepting *that*, you're on your own, but flying, I *hate* small planes; furthermore, and I have to say it, I *hate* the whole idea of what you're doing as well. I'd rather you drive, you and Jack together preferably. That scenario would have me rest easier about the journey."

I wasn't happy about small planes either, dreaded them. However, versus driving, considering the time factor; a light plane was totally worth it, cutting the traveling time by more than half.

Reluctantly, I got back to the charter company and confirmed the booking, but not before Jack Montgomery repeated his offer; that I take his appointments, he'll make the trip for me and get the signatures needed on paper. He doubted there would be a problem.

Again, unfaltering, it was a nice gesture, and although I hesitated for second, he knew the valid reasons why I felt I had to say 'No'.

Next morning, after kissing little Sarah Austen and Nelson James goodbye, I turned to Chelsea, who, despite begging me, almost pleading with me, to call Tallahassee, to see if there was another way to close the deal that was timely and didn't involve traveling to the city, I told her; it either happens now as planned, or we run the risk of it falling through, plus; the meeting is confirmed; my client is expecting me. Finally, she caved in to the need to do business, understanding, but nevertheless, remained unhappy with the choice.

Taking her in my arms, holding her tightly, I gave her the reassurance I know she needed. In a form of loving reply, her arms around me tight gave me the confidence to get the job done and to get back home to her and the children as fast as possible.

Truth was; I hated having to leave my little family. This would be a first. I vowed, struggling hard with the way I felt about it all – never again! I'd wished a million times over; I had not put myself in this position.

"It'll be fine darling, believe me, it'll all work out. I'll be home in a few hours, in plenty of time for dinner, and then the whole thing will be behind us, trust me. That's when we'll also be able to put aside for good our idiosyncrasies of traveling. Some things just have to be done and this one, as it turns out, more expeditiously, and of course, at the end of the day, there's a lot of money at stake."

"I know you're right Tony, but as always, I worry for you. I can't bear the thought of you away. I'll get over it though, after all, I was the one who suggested you get back to work again, remember? Heaven knows; we could have lived fine based on me and my line of work because there's never any shortage of people needing medical attention, or doctors. Looks like we'll have to re-think this whole working idea over again someday huh, even soon maybe?"

Food for thought as it might have been with our needs vastly different now; it didn't change our immediate situation. The road ahead was set in concrete. Also, being extremely happy about the lucrative real estate deal I'd brokered, I was pretty upbeat about the next few hours ahead knowing how fast the time would fly.

"Too late…" I told her, blurting my reply as if it were a game show question. "…I'm back working already. All is good. Jack and I are going well, especially after this deal so, like it or not Miss Chelsea, you and I, we're now a full on professional family again, or at least until the children start school, Sarah Austen that is. Maybe then we'll reshuffle our activities, but until then, we keep going. Love ya darling. I'll miss ya too."

I pulled back from our hug, looked directly at her, into her face, kissed her on the lips lingering longer than I intended to before withdrawing, reluctantly, ready to leave. I then kissed both of my children who, in return, hugged my neck, hard. At about now, things got tougher; I really didn't want to leave. As the kids retreated, I was about to turn for the car when unexpectedly, Chelsea pulled me back to her for one last kiss.

"I love you Tony, more than ever. Stay safe and travel well won't you. Call me when you get there and also when you're done at the meeting okay? I have to hear your voice, call me, anytime. I'll keep my cell on vibrate so as not to interfere with my patients so, no excuses."

She squeezed me one more time before letting go. I gently kissed her again.

"Love you sweetheart and yeah, I'll miss you too."

I had an instant thought and aired it.

"Do you realize; this is the first time we've *ever* been apart when it comes to traveling anywhere? It's always been the two of us, together. I wonder what made me think of that. Oh well, bye, love ya again Chelsea, love you too kids, be good for Mommy. Soon, sweetheart."

I stepped toward the car, opened the door, climbed in, sat behind the wheel, looked at them all through the windshield, closed the door, kicked over the motor, moved the window down, put the car in gear, partially put my head out the window and then, slowly, began to edge out of the driveway calling back loudly as I did.

"Love you all, bye Sarah, bye Nelson, bye Mommy, love you all lots. See you tonight."

Moving down the dirt driveway, in my rearview mirror, I could see my little family, still waving me goodbye. It was a poignant moment. The love I felt in my heart was overwhelming. Everything I loved most in the world was now all crammed into that tiny mirrored reflection.

At Glenwood Road, I turned my head for one last look back at them all still standing in the same position, still waving to me. With the road all clear, I turned right, pressed the car horn and headed for the DeLand Municipal airport.

Driving in, a place that caught my eye that I hadn't paid attention to before, which was strange given I'd tried to learn all I could about DeLand and its environs, was the DeLand Naval Air Station Museum, touted to be a *'must place to visit'* to learn about the role West Volusia played in World War II. Straining my neck at the F-14 Tomcat aircraft, carefully positioned in the museum grounds along with, a bigger than I ever realized, PT boat well in to restoration; I knew it was a place I had to come back to. How it had ever slipped by me over the past many months was an absolute fault of mine. A re-visit was a must, sooner than later.

Three Days Later

Ready to get on with the task ahead and get it behind me, walking with airport staff toward what was described to me as a single-engine four-seater Birraus SB20; I suddenly remembered *why* I was not a fan of light aircraft. It was an extremely nice-looking plane, and if it wasn't; it sure looked new, but in reality, to my eyes, it was also tiny. However, I was comparing it to regular, conventional commercial aircraft.

Right about now, I was glad Chelsea had not driven me to the airport; she might have had other ideas about me, anyone, getting into such a small plane.

Officialdom of client and pilot introductions over, minutes later we were airborne.

High in the sky, I had to confess; the views below were quite spectacular, especially DeLand. How idyllic as a setting, I thought. Downtown, the streets, the buildings: I could see them all so clearly, picturing even, people I now knew and shared my daily life with.

Slowly, it all changed. The topography of the ground vista below was stunning. And then, for some very strange reason, the Tim McGraw song, 'Southern Voice' started running around my head, '...from Memphis on down to Apalachicola...' Typical of many great country songs, this one reeked of everything to do with, not only *the South* and all things related, but also, what I envisaged as, my hometown turf, and especially our emphasized honeymoon area that Chelsea and I had always agreed on; to revisit, someday; the Florida locale known as Apalachicola. Everything about the glorious scenery below me, coupled with Tim, and his 'Southern Voice', made me feel very much a part of all I knew about the South I had learned to love.

"Tony, where are you? Is everything all right? Are you back here in DeLand already?"

Chelsea was all questions. I hadn't even had a chance to say hello. She had seen my name come up on the cell phone screen and was immediately into wanting to know everything.

"Whoa!" I interjected. "Slow down darlin' a little bit huh?"

I more than understood her concerns. I was supposed to call her on landing in Tallahassee, but I hadn't. Unexpectedly, being met personally by my client/buyer; a financial planner and tax preparer/consultant, instead of a limo driver, we were straight into business conversation. He had many questions wasting no time in asking them, especially while driving to his downtown office.

All that transpired, happened so fast! At his office, after enjoying coffee brought to us by his secretary, he closed not only the door, but also on the paperwork for buying The Boulevard Towers, and the management rights of the units to Montgomery-Thompson Properties Inc. It had all been achieved within the space of a solid work period of just ninety-minutes.

With a firm shaking of hands, he then invited me for a quick lunch, choosing a spot that I admit, impressed me; a clear visual look at the State Capitol Building that was actually quite stunning.

'So this is where all our hard-earned money goes?' I thought, now as a new Floridian.

"All is complete Chelsea…" I had great delight in telling her "…It's a done deal, but no in answer to your question. I should be out of here in the next forty minutes or so…"

She came over the top of me, again, first with a huge sigh before beginning to express what her *real* concerns were. Her voice told me she had been clearly worried.

"Thank goodness, you've no idea how glad I am we've managed to connect, finally. I was actually a little frantic when you hadn't called, but thank goodness…" she repeated "…*now* I can breathe easy, well almost anyway. What time did you say again that you were leaving Tallahassee?"

Apart from confirming my estimated time of departure, explaining as best I was able, the circumstances of all that had transpired, it was a wonderful feeling to hear such glowing words of congratulations and encouragement from my wife. She was also very relieved to hear that it was a closed done deal, all over, and that now we could get on with our lives.

Without a single glitch, the biggest transaction so far in our growing, fledgling, real estate venture was indeed finalized. We, as new realtors, Montgomery-Thompson were in the money, finally, at last, in the color of ink that came up black.

"Call me the moment you land Tony" Chelsea asked, before once again telling me "I'm so proud of you sweetheart, well done and darling; I love you. Celebrations tonight, it's a promise. Stay safe, love you again."

"I love you too Chelsea, and always know; you are my inspiration in life, thank you. And don't worry, I'll be home soon. Bye for now and I promise to call. I'll see you, okay? Love you sweetheart."

Slipping the cell phone in my pocket, I really couldn't wait to get back home; Chelsea had that effect on me. God; how I loved that woman. And to see my two babies also.

I couldn't wait to be airborne again – homeward bound to DeLand.

CHAPTER

TWENTY-TWO

I'm sorry Mrs. Thompson, there really is nothing more I can tell you right now, that's all the information we have? When there's more, believe me, I'll get straight back to you."

Chelsea, almost in shock, slumped into the couch in her office at the medical clinic.

State Trooper Dwight Logan had made a special trip over to The Stone Street Clinic to find a Doctor Chelsea Thompson, to impart the news that a light plane had crashed landed somewhere south of Tallahassee, and confirmed to be on board was her husband and the pilot, a fifteen-year veteran of flying, David Johansson Roberts.

Devastated, shocked; Chelsea had managed to maintain her authority, asking as many relevant questions as she was able, in trying to ascertain any single piece of positive information she could from the State Trooper, all to no avail. Every shred of detail law enforcement had shared, except names, was also rapidly breaking as major news across Main Street and Cable News Media.

Sympathizing, against usual practice, but as one public care giver to another, police officer to doctor, he gave her a direct line phone number to one of his counterparts in Tallahassee where she could get

Three Days Later

access to information faster than waiting for him to relay whatever news he could, whenever he received it. She was grateful for his caring and kindness.

Reports aired indicated, a light aircraft, a Birraus SB22 had come down, out from the Tallahassee Regional Airport. The known flight path logged, had the plane heading directly out toward the Apalachicola National Forest, before expecting to change direction, south-east toward Ocala, on to DeLand. The primary concern to the first responders was to pinpoint exactly where, in the 565,000 acre mostly pine flatwood forest, the plane came down. Furthermore, to be considered was the 2,700 acres of water, which would make the search even more difficult if it had crashed in any of the rivers, lakes or swamp area, which was highly possible. If a lake is determined, the depth factor alone could hinder a search dramatically. Helicopters were already in the air, and park officials were on full alert to hike the many trails, once they knew an exact or better location.

Immediately, after the State Trooper left, Chelsea phoned Jack Montgomery to give him the bad news. In utter disbelief of all he'd been told, he rushed quickly over to her offices to share in the grief of the accident, as well as to support and console Chelsea in every way, as best he could, while they began the wait together for more details, but also to plan their next move when they had been given updates. They were both ready to drive straight up to Tallahassee to be near the crash site area, to help in any way they could, realizing; time was of the essence, and time would be against them given the distance.

"Oh God Jack, what now? What if, if..." Chelsea, distraught with anguish, began to think the worst. "I can't lose him now Jack. I can't. We need him, the children; we all need him. He's the backbone of our family, and I love him. He's just got to be all right. I mean..."

"Chelsea, let's be positive here. There's a great chance all will be fine. We have to believe it, the pilot, and the plane. He was in the hands of experience; let's believe they'll be safe, please."

Jack Montgomery had no choice but to put forward positive vibes, positive words, even a positive prognostication of an outcome. Upset as Chelsea was, he knew he had to be stronger. Doctor or no doctor, times of personal stress affect everyone in different ways and skilled as Chelsea was, had shown too often, this time, it was all too close to home. She never wanted her husband flying in the first place and now, all she could do was sit and wait for more information. Jack Montgomery took the lead.

"Chelsea, here's what I believe. If Meghan can take the children, let's get on the road now, let's not wait. Every *second*, every *minute* is valuable. We should head for Tallahassee *immediately* and cut the odds of time waiting for any sort of news. We'll be closer to the scene, ready to move, hike in if need be, and who knows even, you're a Doctor; you may be able to get on one of the search helicopters, and if you can, you'll be ready – wife and Doctor. C'mon, grab your bag. We have cell phones; they can call us anytime on the road. What do you think?" Instantly, a spark of determination registered on Chelsea's face.

"That's a *great* idea Jack, a *great* idea." She didn't need convincing.

Within twenty minutes, they were both bound for Tallahassee, via SR40 to Interstate 75 linking I-10. The estimated arrival time at the airport, as a base start, best-case scenario, was put at four hours give or take, but unfortunately, by then it would be dark or probably getting dark. It didn't matter, there were no real choices. The wheels went in motion.

Chelsea's cell phone rang. "Oh no, much as I want it, I dread this…" were her first words as she glanced at the screen, not recognizing the number. "…I pray it's good news, God; I hope it's…hello, this is Chelsea Thompson."

Jack Montgomery eased the speed a little, straining to get an idea of the call, hoping for the best. The first few seconds seemed an eternity as Chelsea sat in silence, listening, the phone glued to her ear. Slowly, her head began to move from one side to the other. Her face grimaced with obvious anxiety. It didn't look good.

"Uh-huh. I see. So what happens *now*, what does that *really* mean?"

Three Days Later

Immediately, nothing sounded good.

"*Tomorrow. Too dark! Are you serious?*"

A momentary silence prevailed.

"Are you telling me that helicopters *can't* fly at night?"

More silence.

"First light, no way *please, please,* you have to keep looking."

Her head continued to nod back and forth, sideways. She looked across at Jack Montgomery. Angry, moving the phone away from her ear, in a one handed simple move, it looked like it was about to be thrown straight out the window. Her finger pressed hard down on the cover, ending the call, such as it had been?

"*Crap, what crap! That's ridiculous, it's inhuman!*"

Chelsea, in breaking the news to Jack, was furious at the update she had just been given.

"With darkness coming, unless something dramatically changes in the next fifteen minutes, or even less, the search will be called off until morning as they can't put pilots, rescue crews or helicopters at risk. According to the guy who just called, he said, they have no options. I mean; no options. That's exactly what he told me, no options" she repeated, exasperated.

Jack Montgomery was speechless as he kept a firm hand on the steering wheel, moving the car back up to 70mph on the freeway. What *could* he say to make her feel better? Within seconds, unexpected but understandable, Chelsea burst into tears. The news so far was all bad. Her emotions were stretched. Her fear had risen for a successful end, and as she thought of Sarah Austen and Nelson James, her tears flowed almost uncontrollably.

Taking the next exit, they headed straight for the nearest rest-stop gas station. A new plan was needed, as well as to gas up. While Chelsea headed inside the well lit complex, Jack Montgomery took the opportunity to place a call to Meghan and Mark back in DeLand to give them the latest updates, as best they now understood them. Shocked; their only supportive response, *'stay in touch, the children are safe.'*

Last night, pulling into Tallahassee, finding search headquarters, being briefed with complete details of efforts and events so far in the rescue, to finding a nearby motel and managing to partake of needed sustenance, the transition from dark to light, night to morning, had been both nerve racking and stressful. The only thing Chelsea could think was; Tony, her beloved husband, out in the forest, lying helpless, if alive, or alone if dead. Brave as she was, on and off, in her private moments, her tears never stopped falling, it was heart wrenching.

Impatiently waiting, at 5.30 next morning, at the first sign of light, Jack Montgomery and Doctor Chelsea Thompson were at search headquarters at the Tallahassee Regional Airport as instructed. It had been a rough, sleepless night.

"C'mon Doctor…" the pilot finally said, as he and two other uniformed men headed for the helicopter "…let's pray for a miracle, let's go find your husband."

His words were thoughtful, positive and confident. Chelsea followed instructions, her medical bag in hand despite full medic facilities to cover emergencies already on board. The only real reason for her carrying the bag was that it helped her feel involved, personally equipped; it provided a form of comfort, to know she had help in it, no matter how minimal.

Jack Montgomery was not included in the rescue mission, or invited on the flight, not for any reason other than, room on the helicopter and protocol. Chelsea was a Doctor, her presence on board could be well justified, if it was to be required or challenged anytime later.

As she strapped herself in, the first thought she had was not fear, or dreading the journey and mission, aware of what an outcome may well bring, it was her recollected thought of urging her husband not to fly in the first place, her voiced concerns for small planes, and now, here she was, on a helicopter, flying to find him.

While waiting for instrument checks, Chelsea silently prayed, willing her prayers to be answered. Cognizant she had called on a higher being once before for a miracle, Sarah Austen, here she was again, in desperate need of another one. Could that be asking too much? Was that fair? How many other people needed miracles, help?

In life, she too had come to believe that *'God moves in mysterious ways'* and this time, she hoped, again willed herself to still believe, He would give her another chance, that He would perform another miracle. She prayed that He might understand just how wonderful it was, had been, that she had found, late in life, the real true meaning of love, now complete with two little children who needed their Father, and that she, desperately needed the man she loved back by her side. *'Please bring him home to me, please let him be safe, please let him not be hurt and tell him, I'm coming to get him, that I will find him and Lord; I love him dearly, so I ask of you, I beg of you, give me one more miracle in life, please, and I promise; I won't ever ask again.'*

To the sound of loud whirling blades, the helicopter, in tandem with two others, lifted off the ground moving quickly away from the Tallahassee airport, toward, and then deep over the thick, lush, green trees of the outer Apalachicola National Forest. The on-board radio blared with rescue crews' interaction of different directions and inner locations. The morning sun was already well up into the sky. A clear, bright new day had dawned.

One of the first and obvious areas searched, based on the known logged flight path of the aircraft, were toward Lake Munson, the Wakulla State Forest and River on down through Crawfordville Road and the Leon-Wakulla County line regions. State Park Rangers, many who stayed out overnight, were still on high alert; they spearheaded and would continue the ground search covering all the walkways, trails and camping sites, especially all that were readily accessible by vehicles.

In the absence of Chelsea's cell phone being answered, Meghan, back in DeLand called Jack Montgomery, anxiously looking for the morning updates, on-site base news, anything to ease her mind. Assuring him first, the children were fine and happy, no problems at all, and that they knew nothing of the crisis at hand about their father, she added, with consternation '…we've seen it all and heard a lot on TV here, but what's happening up there, in Tallahassee?" she frantically asked, anxiously needing, desperate to know, more.

"Chelsea's phone is turned off on direct orders…" he replied while confirming to call him in the short term if anything arose of importance back home, "…meanwhile…' he continued "…Chelsea's up in a helicopter with one of the rescue teams and has been gone for almost three hours or more now. There's nothing firm that I can share with you except, unofficially, it doesn't look good. One guy told me that if they had managed to get the plane down safely and were okay themselves, the first thing anyone, and especially an experienced pilot would have done is get a little fire going and get some smoke up into the atmosphere given the skies are clear, but so far, there's been no smoke sighted, either yesterday or this morning. The temperatures, by the way, they say, are just mild enough for at least comfort in survival mode and also, and pretty important I know they believe, there are any number of little cabins and such that one could make their way to, all plus factors of course. Apparently, the forest is a haven for hikers and campers and the like, but Meghan, much else I don't know. It's a real concern. I wish I knew more to tell you, and of course; I will, as soon as I know, that's for sure, count on it please."

Most of what Jack had gleaned had been from radio interactions of ground operators to air surveillance choppers back to headquarters.

"What are they telling you about the odds, if any?" Meghan asked, fearing the answer.

It was a problematic question in reality, as not a soul could put odds on any plane crash, large or small. Jack knew it, but realized; he would have asked the same question, in fact, had, last night!

"The odds can only be our prayers Meghan. That's it, but you know; I feel so guilty about it. We could have stalled the reason for Tony going there in the first place if we really thought about it, and if I'd been more persistent. I offered to drive up to Tallahassee with him; I should have straight out canceled my appointments and stayed with it. We could have been up and back in a car the same day with both of us driving, and now I feel physically *sick*. I feel for Chelsea. She's heartbroken, strong in her own way, but she has such a burden now, and we could have avoided it all. I'm so crushed, my friend, my…"

"Jack, listen to me…" Meghan told him firmly, hearing his anguish, "…it's *not* your fault, *anyone's* fault! It was a business decision that's gone astray for now; let's not blame anyone, especially not you. He'll be fine, let's pray for it okay?"

Understanding, she accepted the remorse of the comments just listened to. Friends they were, yes, but when tragedy strikes, the first thing that's absolutely necessary is for everyone to pull together and not play a blame game. For now, it was a waiting game, the only problem was; it was already playing out far too long. Plus, the lost plane was all over the local news channels and none of what they were reporting could be considered favorable to a successful outcome.

"Jack, call me as soon as you know anything and please, get Chelsea to call me, no matter what, when she gets back in. Will you do that for me?" He promised her yes.

Re-pocketing his phone, he couldn't help but think about an earlier remark, overheard from one of the rescue crews as he walked by on his way to a waiting helicopter. The very thought of bears, alligators, muddy swamps and the like was too much to literally comprehend and yet; that kind of wildlife was out there, in the Apalachicola Forest region, along with many other creatures, some nice, many gruesome. He shuddered at the very thought, especially if one was helpless, or lifeless. He kept his thoughts, and their comments, to himself; it would have been the last thing Meghan would have wanted to hear and from her line of conversation, the thought had obviously, thankfully, not even entered her mind at all.

Suddenly, a deafening noise took over the silence of the area as one of the search helicopters came into view, slowly making its way back to the base pad. It was more likely to be a routine return as any news, of the location of the downed plane, would have been immediately radioed back to get ground rescue crews to the spot, but so far – still nothing! The chopper set down. The rotors were turned off. One by one, the crew alighted. Chelsea was not on board.

Minutes later, a screaming red alert siren sounded. Pinpointing the location, reported as somewhat remote, approximated at 50 miles from Tallahassee, south of the Sopchoppy Highway near Alligator Lake, there appeared to be plane wreckage sited in a very small open area, close to the water's edge of a swamp type lake in the St Marks National Wildlife Refuge. No sign yet of survivors or any activity. It was suggested the pilot might have been trying to make it to the Wakulla County Airport that had a north-south 2,600ft turf runway. He was well short!

~~~~~~~~~~

CHAPTER

TWENTY-THREE

Her heart thumping, as if it might jump out of her body, Chelsea Thompson was poised to be out of the helicopter and over to the twisted metal as fast as her legs would carry her. Accustomed to accident and injury, she was prepared for anything; all she wanted was to find her husband. Somewhat more realistically, the helicopter medics on board, who clearly understood their practitioner counterpart, braced themselves for the worst considering both the wreckage scene below and the time factor in locating it. Unfortunately, they had another problem to contend with first!

With very little room to maneuver, the pilot wasn't sure if he could get the helicopter down at all and after two attempts, he began to vocalize openly about abandoning the landing all together, regretfully suggesting, they might have to radio in the exact position and let ground crews make the journey in on foot. Chelsea was frantic, imploring the pilot not to give up. It wasn't to be.

Try as he might, he couldn't find the exact right spot to land. If the helicopter blades hit the trees, he explained, it would cause a whole different set of circumstances he was not prepared to deal with. The answer was no! She reminded him of the two words she dreaded to say in the hope of changing his mind. 'Alligator Lake' scared her, fearing what it could mean. The pilot, while sympathetic, stood firm, indicating his intention to lift higher and retreat.

Sensitive to Chelsea and her predicament and sensing defeat, divine intervention stepped in. Immediately, one of the rescue medics on board spoke up to ease her plight, offering a do-able landing alternative to the pilot. Accepting that it might be a little difficult, given the terrain, he offered to be the candidate, if he agreed to attempt it.

From the slightly higher than regulated altitude, as a normal procedure, by dropping one of the rescue winch ropes, the suggesting medic would go down first, then, coordinating from the ground to the helicopter; a joint effort could be made to guide Chelsea down using the two-rope human strapped method. Successfully achieving the drop, their presence on the ground, he added, would get the desperately needed medical service to the site faster, then, through radio alerts; a foot rescue crew could more accurately be directed to join them.

Dangerous, and somewhat more than mildly so, it was, at the least, feasible. Chelsea, willing to chance it, willing to do anything, again pleaded to the pilot, urging, any protracted wait could be crucial to the life or death of her husband.

Highly questionable, not usually permitted, against conventional wisdom, precarious, unwise even, the pilot certainly had compassion, more than he had originally displayed. The look on Chelsea's face gave him his answer. With the hint of a smile, albeit with reluctance, he gave thumbs up before moving to reposition and steady the helicopter over the larger of the two small open areas below.

The helicopter door was immediately retracted. Clearly explaining, with Chelsea taking in every word, after the trained rescue medic had scaled his way down first, she had to fully understand, with one rope from the helicopter attached to another on the ground, she would be strapped onto a specially designed board, then slowly, horizontally lowered, guided by the rescue crew from both top and bottom. They didn't have to wait for her reply or agreement. Confirming to the plan with confidence, she accepted her acknowledgement, loudly shouting; *'affirmative',* that she understood, they could get her down safely, despite the risk. To her, it was a slam dunk! She would have already slid down the rope by herself, unaided, if they had let her or suggested it. Seconds later, the team went to work.

In exactly, seven minutes and fourteen seconds, both medical practitioners were on terra firma. Standing in the wind tunnel below, glancing up as the helicopter pulled away, Doctor Chelsea Thompson and the helicopter rescue medic began their frantic search for two people. They ran immediately, straight toward the wreckage.

Ten minutes later, neither of them had located anyone at all. It was as if the two people on board had disappeared into the thin air. Full of despair at not finding her husband immediately on hitting the ground, Chelsea's moment of bewilderment turned instantly to a more positive sign as she deduced, if no-one was at the wreckage; it could only mean they had survived, and together, maybe, began a trek away from the plane to find help? She looked at her equally surprised companion who said openly, exactly what he thought - *'not quite what I expected, but hey, that's got to be the good news. Now, where is the better or bad?'* The word bad sent chills down her spine.

If the miracle Chelsea had asked for on setting out to find her husband was granted, it might be solely in the fact, looking at the incredibly twisted, mangled metal of the light aircraft; that the occupants of the plane extracted themselves to walk away at all, simultaneously wondering, if they did; in what condition? Assuming now they had, the remaining question was, where to start to find them?

Splitting up, they scoured the immediate inner area, then the river bed edges, the nearby tall trees that would have provided shelter, the bushes and the thick underbrush. Ten minutes later, nothing! One moment of consternation that bothered them both was the fact that, there weren't any clear signs of anyone dragging oneself away from the wreckage; a mystery unto itself?

Back together at the plane, blankly looking at each other with an air of bewilderment, they stood and tried to second guess any moves that might have been made? Unexpected, disturbing the momentary silence of the forest wilderness, a loud crackle came over the helicopter medic's walkie-talkie firmly strapped to his side. Unclipping it, he pushed the on button for a response, looking at the dial at the same time, double checking the live open active frequency. Nothing! Muffled static prevailed. It was obvious; the whole process frustrated him. The unit went straight to his mouth as he looked for someone, anyone, to respond.

"Ground Division One, come in."

More static.

"Ground Division One, come in."

Broken static remained his only response.

"Damn modern equipment. It never works just when you need it to. Now what?" he stammered, frustrated at the failure. "Why now, at this crucial time of all things?"

In the still of the moment, silence again all around them, devoid of wishful thinking; Chelsea thought she heard a noise. It sounded like a groan. A groan a human would make. Could it have been? It might have been an animal maybe? Certainly not a bird! Thoughts of an animal, any animal, horrified her.

"Listen…" she whispered confidently, holding her pointed finger high. "…listen. I definitely heard something, there's a noise coming from over that way, coming from over there, that way" she professed, motioning repeatedly more toward the river, away from the wreckage, the forest, the trees.

Silence prevailed; the air was still. Seconds later, she believed she heard it again, another soft, very faint sound, like a groan; an alert maybe from someone, a person, trying to be heard, knowing others were nearby, close, yet so far away. Definitely not birds; the thought had crossed her mind again. Troubled, she was hopeful, and now sure it was not an animal nearby in the underbrush.

Her heart began to pound as she headed frantically toward where she believed the distant sound originated. It was near the water. She was sure. Moving closer, balancing precariously at the river's edge, her eyes began darting everywhere, looking, searching, for anything that resembled not only the sound, but hopefully, a person, hopefully, her Tony.

Three Days Later

She pushed slowly forward, brushing away tall grass and shrubbery as she did. Moments later, she froze! Her feet felt like they had taken instant root, right where she stood. Horrified, but morbidly thrilled, in the short distance ahead she saw an undistinguishable person who was obviously covered in a lot of blood.

She shrieked *'Tony, Tony. Is that you? I'm coming.'*

Willing it to be who she dearly hoped it was, her husband, seconds henceforth; she would be by the person's side. Finding new spirit, hope and strength, nothing stood in her way, or could deter her as she clumsily clambered toward a small sandy clay section of the river bank to find the man's battered body, half propped up against an old dead tree stump. Without fear or trepidation, on a closer look, her prayers were answered. Tony. Cautiously, frightened, she reached down to touch his badly, blood-stained body, then hand. He groaned a light guttural sound; eerily, the same as the one she'd heard before.

~~~~~~~~~~

Chelsea had found me. I could hardly see her, but I knew her voice. Her soft hands touched me again, as if for the very first time. I was safe. Heaven had performed my begged for miracle that I knew, believed; she would have asked of Him, the same. My dear sweet Chelsea was here to take me home. Now I could relax, rest easier, in the knowledge I was in the best hands ever given to me, ever shared with me.

I heard her say, *"Oh my dear sweet Tony, we have to get you out of here darling. You're so battered and bruised, beat up and hurt, but don't worry; I'm here. I found you and oh, oh, oh, how you scared me. I love you Tony. Trust me, I'll get you out of here, believe me. I will. You'll be safe, soon."*

Her voice was like one of an angel, so comforting to hear. I felt her hands on me again as she touched my forehead, brushing back my hair before gently lifting my arm, both arms, only to carefully place them down by my side. I remembered, that had been done to me once before. Next, she touched my leg before gently trying to raise it. It wouldn't move. Her attention went to my other leg. Same; it didn't move either. I'd been through all that before too. I didn't want to be there, in *that* place again. Her hand went back to my face, my cheek. It felt so good; my Chelsea's touch was ever so gentle, so caring.

"Oh darling" I heard her whisper. "What have you done?"

I heard another voice. I couldn't turn my head. It was somewhere over there. I didn't know where over there was. I knew it was somewhere. I heard the voice again. It was a man. Everything going on around me was vividly déjà vu. I remembered too well!

"Don't try to move him huh" the medic (the voice) suggested to Chelsea.

As a Doctor, she knew better. Many vital signs were not encouraging, expert help was needed, not only for evaluation but specifically, to help move him.

"I won't" she told her partner who, throughout the ordeal, had been remarkably sensitive, accommodating, and incredibly reassuring in every way.

In his presence, consoling and caring for her husband, she knew, if it weren't for him, she never could have been in the position she was; at the crash site, taking care of the greatest love of her life. Devastated, scared, a nightmare; containing her deep, silent thoughts, Chelsea would be forever grateful to her partner in rescue. However, it was time to be a Doctor again, to continue looking for hopeful signs.

"Tony, can you hear me. This is Chelsea. I'm here with you. Can you hear me?"

I could hear her; clear as a bell, and her voice was music to my ears. However, I couldn't tell her that I could hear her. In my mind, I was strong; I was ready to release myself from this position I had been in for what seemed like – forever. I wanted to jump up and shout, hold her close to me, to feel her body close to me, to hug her, to kiss her, to never let her go. But I couldn't move.

"Tony, if you can hear me, if you know it's me, please, squeeze my hand."

I felt her hand gently lift mine; she held it in both of hers. I felt myself grimace with great pain; I attempted to squeeze her hand,

Three Days Later

just as she had told me to. I heard her voice again. What? I begged to no-one. I had done as she had asked, had done what she wanted; surely, something must have registered in return? I forced myself to let out a soft groan. Oh how that hurt!

"I felt his hand squeeze mine" Chelsea shared with her co-medic now down by her side, wanting to help, all the time knowing he'd be powerless under the circumstances. He willingly gave in to any active interaction, choosing instead, for just a few minutes, to be her supportive by-stander. Keenly aware of Chelsea's credentials, he did not want to interfere with her actions, or her need to believe, understanding; this was her moment. Silently, within, he knew too well; it could also be her last. She had to be given the time.

"He knows it's me, oh God how wonderful. There's hope. There's plenty of hope, now we've just got to get him out of here. What can we do, what do you suggest?" she asked in a form of pleading, desperation, helplessness.

Given there was no magic formula for instant extraction to get her husband out of the awful place, position he was in, the medic could only suggest the obvious; comfort him, talk to him, keep him alert and awake until more help arrived. Let him feel your love, your strength. Let him hear your voice.

Amid the heartbreak of the situation, she found herself in; Chelsea's heart was filled with just enough joy to remain forever the optimist. All the advice given was as accurate as could be. She knew she had to have hope. She'd found her love, the man she adored, in a wilderness of nothingness, a broken body, forlorn, covered in blood, helpless, almost empty...of life. With all her heart, she needed to get what was left of that life out of where they were, to safety...and soon.

A walkie-talkie burst into life. From a clearer location, with audible radio contact finally made, the ground position of the one located party could be relayed as accurate; help was confirmed as *on its way*. With the success of renewed outside contact, reluctantly, Chelsea was alerted she was on her own.

There were still no hard clues as to what had happened to the other man, the pilot. And someone will need to know where a David Johansson Roberts was? Her emergency partner advised her; he would temporarily leave her to continue his search in and around the area for the other man; that she'd be left to tend to her husband and his immediate needs, which in of itself was crucial, as well she knew. It was the right option. Chelsea wholeheartedly agreed.

Awaiting the incoming ground help and rescue would give her just enough time to comfort her patient, and be sure he was given all the emergency treatment she could administer without either moving him, or overly prodding and probing. There was far too much unknown, of not only his outward visible condition, but of equal, even greater concern, what was his internal situation? Her early diagnosis information would help speed up what other medical actions had to be taken, on, or during the air-lift, and at the hospital, on arrival. Miraculous for survivors at all, looking at the aircraft, its mangled condition, it had obviously been a most horrific crash!

~~~~~~~~~~

I cried from the inside. My voice was screaming, but no-one seemed to hear. With somewhat clearer vision due to Chelsea's loving care, I could see her face, her eyes, her lips, and her mouth. She was beautiful. I wanted to tell her *'I love you Chelsea. I love you, don't leave me here will you?'* Silently, I continued to cry inside.

As she carefully washed my arms with cool water from the river, I was absolutely sure that I could feel the damp cloth on me, but could I? Gently, she took care of my many outer needs, my body, but I wanted her to hear me from within. My eyes darted back and forth. She knew that! I could see when she gazed ever so close to me, into my eyes. She even lifted my eye lids, I knew that too. I couldn't smile. I tried to make her see me smile, but my mouth wouldn't move. I heard her whisper *'I love you Tony'* over and over. I remained still, only she could move me, my arms, and my legs. I wanted to do it myself. I couldn't!

Three Days Later

Looking at Chelsea, seeing her, vivid memories flashed before me. I longed to see our little baby's faces, Sarah Austen, Nelson James. I wanted to ask Chelsea; bring them to me, but words failed me. The anguish from within me was growing. I could feel it; I was scared, really frightened; I also wanted to cry, to cry real wet tears. However, tears would not form. I could only cry inside. Tears were there; I thought, but none fell. I so wanted Chelsea to know I was really okay, just a little banged up, and that soon I'd be back by her side, just as I always and only ever wanted to be. She was my love my life.

Strangely, I thought, what if something happens to me, and I could never say out loud to her, *'Chelsea, I love you my darling. I love you'*. What if...but then, this *is what if*, I'm living it - something *has* happened to me! For just a moment, I felt my heart was dying; my hurt was deep; the pain was too much to bear, excruciating. All I could do was look at her. My most wonderful, dearest, darling wife, if only I could speak out loud, talk to you...

Unexpectedly, without control, I let out a groan, another gurgle that came directly from my throat. Was that my cry to let her know I was all right, and everything would be all right, and that I really understood everything? I hoped she thought so.

Estimated at almost forty-five minutes, a rescue team finally made its way to the crash site. Complete with vehicles and medical equipment to secure safe passage of the so far one survivor of the crash, Chelsea supervised the immediate ground treatment and uplifting of her patient, personally near and dear to her. Watching over the evacuation, tears streamed down her face. The doctor in her had checked out. The loved one had surfaced, and she feared for the outcome of the ordeal.

Joining the exit medical vehicle team, she silently prayed for the safe return of the unaccounted for missing pilot, comforted in the knowledge, there were many people now in the area, not only to locate him, but hopefully, bring him safely out of the dense forest.

By mid-afternoon they would find him. It was determined; David Johansson Roberts was thrown from the smashed front end of the small plane. Concussed from the impact with little more than a broken arm and broken collar-bone, he had made his way from the wreckage, wandering afar, aimlessly, to nowhere in particular. Documented, official reports qualified; he ended up trapped, almost waist deep, at the edge of a huge swamp. His injuries prevented him from extricating himself from the thick mud patch; he died, upright, leaning against a tree. Sadly, added to the report; had he stayed with the plane; miraculously, he would have survived.

~~~~~~~~~~

Chelsea called Jack Montgomery from nearby Crawfordville, named ironically after the town's doctor, to tell him that not only was her husband alive, but she had him with her, and from there; they would transfer by road, direct to Tallahassee and on to a medical plane standing by for a mercy flight to the DeLand Florida Hospital where Tony would be attended to, operated on, in her care. She gave no further detail except request that he contact Meghan, Mark and the children and have them prepare for her to arrive back home within about three hours.

Jack Montgomery himself prepared to drive home to DeLand immediately. It would be a long day ahead - alone. What haunted him most were Chelsea's parting words *"I'm scared for the brightest light in my life; I fear it might be dimming."* Jack too, feared for his lifelong friend.

~~~~~~~~~~

CHAPTER

TWENTY-FOUR

*M*ere mortals, sometimes, we're left asking why? Why Lord? I was brought to the Florida Hospital in Deland to recover…I never did!

Three days later, the bright light that engulfed me, surrounded me, was quite magnificent. Was *this* the surrealism of transition I'd heard about so often, of the moment life actually leaves a body? It had to be; too many have said it, believing it as fact, just as I had always believed it. Now I know…it was true. My heaven on earth had moved to a different sphere. However, memories prevail, and where I lay, peacefully, incredibly so, as a vision, I could see all and everything before me. A body may depart, but does a spirit really live on?

In life, to speak with so called authority of the great beyond would always be a personal belief, in fact, to many – it's a stretch! It seems, realistically, you have to go there, to really believe it, to understand it, to then be able to share it - but then, with whom?

Deep within my heart and well traveled soul, I now knew differently. I watched and shared a joy unimaginable; I wanted to shout from the highest rafters *'I'm here. I'm here'* - my words though, could never translate to sound. But I *was* there that day, still and silent, as close as I could ever be.

I may not have been able to share my presence before my children or my beautiful wife again, to physically hold them, to tell them I loved them, or share in any of the daily routines we loved so much to do together, but I did see them all, standing – side by side. Chelsea, Sarah Austen and little Nelson James, they were all looking at me. I could see them clearly; it was the most glorious of sights to this soul that had moved on. I never wanted them to leave. But it hurt me too, that they were so incredibly sad.

Chelsea was wearing the dress I bought her, back now, what seemed not so long ago. An impulse buy, she knew I loved it. A dark cream in color, adorned with a soft flower pattern, I'd gushed at the look of it on her immediately. *'You have to have it'* I told her that day. I was never quite sure that she liked it as much as me, however, as was always her loving way, with a radiant smile, she gladly gave in, watching, as it was wrapped in a special box, then tied with a bow, before being handed to her. Today, that dress, seeing her in it, meant more to me than ever.

Unknowingly, admiring her as I was, looking directly at me, she kissed my cheek. At that very instant, longingly, I willed her, please, to kiss my cheek again. She did, as if she knew my thoughts. I believed I could feel it. I hoped she knew of the love I gave in return.

Sarah Austen was carrying the teddy bear I bought for her on her first birthday. What a special gift it was, and to think, like her Mommy's dress, I bought her the teddy bear on impulse too. She had to have it I believed that day I so casually walked into Dolls of DeLand downtown on a whim. It was really meant to be I now understood, and I hoped she would cherish 'Teddy' for the rest of her natural life, and always remember that her Daddy picked it out as special, because he loved her. Looking at me, somewhat sad, but with the faint hint of a child's smile, she was hugging it, what seemed like, hard, and very close to her. Was that my little Sarah Austen's way of telling me that she cherished Teddy, and that she loved her Daddy too?

Nelson James was my little man, but my time was too short to really get to know him. And now, I'd leave him all alone, to go on without me. If my heart could ever be broken, then it had probably shattered in a million different pieces. How I so much wanted to hold him…one last time. All I was left to believe was that, someday, he'd understand, all the while hoping as I gazed at him, small and precious as he is, that he would grow up big and strong, and would always look after his Mother, just as his Daddy surely would have, if time had allowed. Then, another thought, soon, he'd have to step up too…he was also the man of the house now.

Looking back toward their Mother, again, to see her standing, rigid, all alone with the children – my emotional heart, if it were possible, would break all over again. I had loved my Chelsea like no other person on earth. She had been, as I'd always wanted her to know, my greatest gift, my greatest love, my very best friend in the world and…and, emotion within me began to take over. I almost couldn't take it. I lingered for a moment…full of memories of our time together, short as it was, had become.

My thoughts returned…and as I gazed on her lonely, solemn, sad face, my most fervored wish as always, then, now forever lost, was that we might have, in life, somehow, someway - lived together, forever. What a most beautiful lady. But I'd let her down.

'*Why did you have to take me away from all I ever loved Lord? Why? There was no reason to - was there Lord?*'

There could be no answer, but if it can be - I will always be there, beside her, for the rest of her days. I'd find the way if it exists.

Thankfully, a redeeming consolation of magnitude, the children were in the very best of hands. The warm, loving heart that beats inside Doctor Chelsea April Thompson, was the biggest one ever known - I already knew that. The short life we lived, the huge love we shared, and the many memories we created, if they can last for… say…another one hundred years, then we will have gotten the best out of the so few we had time to share.

For this moment though, all I had was my one-sided vision.

Then…all too soon, it was time to go…someone was calling? I begged for just a little more time…but, it wasn't to be. The light was beginning to dim, darker…and darker.

~~~~~~~~~~

In life, there are two known journeys. The first is the one forward. It will take you into the complete unknown – it's the daunting journey of life itself. And there are no guarantees.

Then, someday, we're confronted with a second – this one is the journey home. It's never planned. Mine wasn't! But it's an equally daunting task, and by the time we're ready to take it, maybe we've learned just enough, maybe we'll better understand, maybe we are better prepared - what to expect. Maybe, that is?

I'd completed my first journey; now - my calling was to embark on the second, and sadly, to all we love and leave behind - the second and final journey has no return. It's the last farewell.

Chelsea couldn't hear me, but I was calling out to her from the inside; I wanted her to know, before I left her; that for as long as it took, I would wait for her. Watching my little family standing firmly together, hands joined, thinking of and praying for me, I promised her, that on my journey home, I would walk slowly, ever so slowly, waiting for that glorious someday when she would be able to catch up to me. Then - in the bright light of the unknown yonder - once again, we'd walk side by side, hand in hand, to make that journey's end – together.

It was a stunningly, beautiful, marvelous last vision…and I so wanted to reach out to her, to hold her, for what could and would be, my last time. Again; I begged the Lord, please Lord…but, it could never be.

Three Days Later

Oh the hurt, the pain, to watch them walk away, to take those heart wrenching final steps…one step, two steps, three steps, more…slowly, slowly…they began fading into the distance. And too soon – my Chelsea, Sarah Austen and little Nelson James - they were gone from my presence. My time was given. My race had been run.

But I'll always be watching over them - with love.

CHAPTER

TWENTY-FIVE

God *does* work in mysterious ways. Of that, I'd be a true believer. In life, miracles are performed every day, and everyone has their more than fair share. Mostly never realized, we are surrounded by them. They are a given. I had mine. Specifically, I knew, I had actually asked for two…they were granted.

My dear sweet little Sarah Austen was given life against the odds. She was a true miracle. And to think, I was able to spend so much time with her - a true blessing in my life.

Cancer is a cruel word, and the mere mention of it sends chills through the very body of everyone to whom it is used, when attributed to them. The fight begins that very day, to overcome; the plea is for a miracle, to be cured. In life, I was dealt the hand for the potentially deadly disease, however, in the diagnosis - *'mild'*, I had no difficulty believing, I had received a second miracle – it included, remission. I know I would have beaten it.

Reality; unwittingly – with miracles everywhere, too many are taken for granted. Our very first miracle is in life itself, a chance to live. If I was to count my blessings, throughout the life now passed from me, I'd had countless *'given'* miracles. To list them specifically would be folly...however; I'll share a few, but know, they are not mine exclusively. You; everyone is afforded them.

To be born, to live - from a small child to a grown man.
To love, truly love - man to woman. I so my loved Chelsea, dearly.
My small garden, well lived in – Our loving family home.
My large garden - The world (and all I was able to see/experience/share).
Exploring the gardens – To know the cultures, people, our vast and many ways of life.
Finding one person (family) - through them, the extension of life and living – evolution.
Children, and all the animals of the world – part of life's most beautiful blessing, who bestow their (innocent) gifts of comfort to enjoy.
Happiness – given and shared freely, sought and taught. To love, laugh and cry.

Acknowledging but a few of those *'given'* miracles in life, I could loudly claim, boast; I had participated in them all, each and every single one. And I had to be grateful for the time afforded me, despite it being *'cut-short.'* With no guarantees in life, my miracles were lived as best as I was able to experience them. I had been blessed.

A mere mortal - along the way I had also wished for many things in life. Wishes, though, are more for dreamers; wishing *never* made something happen. I had learned; you had to work at all you dream for. When, and if you did – they really could come true.

My miracles and all of my wishes were now all wrapped up in my little family, left behind. Gone as I was, leaving all I loved prematurely, became one of life's accidents for which there is no warning, no pre-destined calculation – for anyone. I had suffered such a fate.

If everyday life is called 'living', at least I knew, I had lived mine to its fullest. Sad as I'd be to leave, in life, I could never have been happier.

With love abounding, I'd experienced my heaven on earth - Chelsea and the children. I would watch over them all, as I promised. And I'd wait, as I promised. My last known accomplishment; I prayed for their happiness for a long and lasting life. Legacies, in life, will prevail.

A believer - forever safe, beyond the sunset - this is what I was able to share.

EPILOGUE

A POSTSCRIPT TO THE LIFE OF ANTHONY 'TONY' THOMPSON

Chelsea would not remarry. After the grief and mourning of my untimely passing, she threw herself into both raising the children and work. As a Doctor, she would stay five more years with The Stone Street Clinic before extending her accomplishments to move to a greater pressure and challenging position; Trauma Surgeon. Highly specialized, she was offered many lucrative positions all over the country.

Content in, and wanting no more than what she had, as a family and lifestyle, she chose to stay and live her life out in DeLand. Her dedication was to her hometown where she served on various community boards, and to Florida Hospitals in Volusia County.

When called on, Chelsea continued to give pro bono, to not only local causes, but all over the globe as tragedy struck and people suffered. As Mother Nature inflicted her wrath on human kind, when and where she could, she willingly gave of her time and skills in the effort to save lives – always her lifelong mission. I was so proud of Chelsea. My soul and spirit were always with her, wherever she went; Indonesia, Europe, the Caribbean, South America.

I shared with her, all the love she gave, unconditionally, and especially to our children who, under her loving guidance, found their rightful passage to life.

Passing peacefully, at age 82 years, work aside, the joy and love our children had given her was immeasurable. Sarah Austen and Nelson James were with her that day she left them…to come looking for me. I heard her softly whisper to them, *'I need to go find Daddy now. It's time'*. They understood.

And I was still waiting; I'd walked ever so slowly, just as I had promised. But oh my, what a wonderful sight, when I finally saw her – I stalled for a moment - to let her catch up, then, with hands outstretched, with all the love I remembered; I felt her soft hand - her fingers touched mine. The final stop of both our journeys was now within reach.

Three days later, Chelsea was brought to lie next to me. From touching fingers, finally, I took both her hands to clasp them, fully, into mine, and once again; we were as one. *'Welcome home Chelsea, and oh darling, how I have missed you'*. Gently, she rested…close beside me.

~~~~~~~~~~

Sarah Austen made it safely through DeLand High school, graduating with honors. She grew to be a beautiful girl with a heart of gold. Choosing to stay close to home, and to her Mom, she enrolled in Stetson University, majoring in Integrative Health Science.

Very quickly, she took up a position at the Florida Hospital, Daytona Beach where locally, three years later; she met and married Francis 'Frank' John McDonald, who literally swept her off her feet.

When they met, he was a local Councilman, who seemed to know exactly what he wanted in life and where he was going. Progressing politically, his appointment to City Manager spurred him on to even greater heights; Mayor of Daytona, home to *'the world's most famous beach.'* (Should I have smiled? I wondered, reflecting clearly my introduction to Florida from Connecticut and my first visuals of what became my most wonderful life-changing experience). But smile, I did; with reverence.

My dearest Sarah, and her Frank, became quite the couple. Professed openly, with larger sights set for his future, looming, in the distance, would be either, Senator Francis J. McDonald, or maybe, Governor to the great state of Florida.

More important than any vocation or aspirations of stature or position – they remained, always, that happy two who met by chance, and they loved each other dearly. Chelsea and me, we could ask for no more. They too were blessed.

When we both last checked in on them, their two boys, Anthony Robert, named after his grandfather (they called him Tony) and Mark Shaun - both had chosen higher education; Tony with FSU (Florida State University) in Orlando, while Mark, he stayed close by, choosing Daytona College. Sarah Austen, a humanitarian, following in similar footsteps to her mother, anxious to give back, willingly participated in many community needs.

Chelsea and I were both convinced, Mayor Frank and Sarah Austen McDonald, and their boys, would live long and prosperous lives. It made us both gloriously happy to see the love they all shared as a family, but then again - we did wish it on them - every day!

~~~~~~~~~~

Nelson James would have a wonderful childhood, and be doted on by his Mother. He missed not having a Dad to play ball with, to fish or hike with, or teach him how to drive a car and many other boy to man things, but he managed without me. And I must say, I was really pleased when his Mother said *'yes'* to have a dog that ultimately became his best friend throughout his youth and beyond. He named him Deefer, which threw me initially, until I realized his growing sense of humor was coming into play. Simply put, it was 'D fer dog' - Deefer. That was the little boy in him.

Along the way, he was about twelve; he asked his Mother, *'...what was Dad like, and who was he? Did he know me at all?'* It was a tough question, and I knew Chelsea would have to dig deep, to find the right words. I gulped!

"*I loved your Father…*" she told him in her usual soft, caring voice. '*He was everything to me, and I must say, there is not a day goes by, still, that I don't miss him, or think of him and yes Nelson; your Father certainly knew you, and he loved you. He was so proud of you, to have a Son, and young as you were when he died, I know, just know, you too would have loved him as I do, but life you know, sometimes, has a way of testing us all. However, you rose to the occasion, and I am so very proud of you, just as he would be. Always know Nelson, he loved you dearly. He loved us all.*'

To hear her words, watch her expressions; see the look on the face of Nelson James, listening intently, seemingly, so full of pride; she never once failed me, even in death. Love and inspiration spread right through my departed soul, however, still very much with them in spirit. What a marvelous woman I so tragically left behind. Together, we lost so much. And oh how I still missed her, my sweet, dearest, darling Chelsea.

And then, innocent as only it ever could have been, Nelson James asked another question, this one though, had the power to tear right through me, as he lovingly suggested to his Mother '*…shouldn't you, maybe, someday, find someone else to share your life with Mom*'. As always, Chelsea again seemed to find the right answer in reply. '*Not just yet Nelson, maybe someday, but not right now, but thank you for your caring thoughts*'.

I smiled. I would have understood, but then again, had she; I would have had a small dilemma. If that happened, I would not have been quite sure what course I might have had to take while waiting for her; she would, rightfully, be torn in her two different directions. I'd deal with it, I told myself. I never had to, so I kept slowly walking, and waiting, for the most beautiful lady ever, to grace God's green earth.

Nelson James, the teenager, liked school but couldn't seem to find himself, or a direction, beyond DeLand High. He graduated successfully, and despite being taken under his wing and mentored for what seemed the longest time by his football coach, 'Smiling' Kevin

Williams, he remained torn, twixt and between, *what* really to do with his life? 'Coach Kev' kept him motivated, while his Mom encouraged him always to follow his heart; no matter how long it took.

Finally, he decided he'd like to fly planes, become an airline pilot even. He had *no* idea how *that* scared his Mother, but she never denied his ambition, indeed, unselfishly, she helped him achieve his goal. At least he was flying the bigger commercial jets.

Expectedly, a wonderful delight entered his life to help change it in the very best of ways. Over time, he became quite attached to a rather beautiful flight attendant and within six-months of their meeting, like his Father when he first met his Mother; Nelson James quickly fell in love. Four months later, they were married.

'I want a big family' he told his new wife, the most striking Mrs. Danielle Nicole Thompson. Five years hence, they began to reach their family goal. If only they knew how much we both loved to look in on the children, Chelsea April, named for her grandmother (and yes, we were very happy for tradition), and of course, her sister too, LuLana Leigh, (they called her Lulu), who together, paid great attention to their effervescent little 'baby' brother Max, who had all the traits of being just like his Father.

~~~~~~~~~~

Mortal life, it turned out, was kind to our little family, now well extended. Chelsea, me…we beamed ear to ear every single day. From far, far away, in our children, and at last count, five grand-children, we could see, feel and hear life's evolution hard at work. And from our world - we saw only the good. Adversity, hardships, pain, or hurt, for any of them, didn't exist, they never translated. It was the way we wanted it to be.

Heaven on earth abounded on the slow spinning planet we knew well, and just as the sun, moon and stars made their welcoming daily appearance, another world traversed in step, beyond the realms, but in a much different way. The minds, the souls, the spirits…they are never far from the so-called real world. And we watched it all with love.

Gone, but not forgotten... ever in our family's thoughts and memories...Chelsea remained by my side, never to leave me again. Together forever, we never grew any older. And there are no days. Reveling in the rewards that had awaited us, for what we hoped, He, thought was *'a job well done'*; we rested high on that mountain, amidst strikingly glorious sunsets.

A redeeming lesson learned, expressed – while you can, treasure the gift of life.

A Note from the Author

Sometimes, fiction imitates life (and vice-versa) – Reality.

When I first started writing this book, I was motivated to write a simple love story. Finding the theme came relatively easy, crafting the words and storyline was, as is normal, not as easy as it may appear, but my thoughts and words did flow, and I completed the book in what would be, compared to my previous book The Sleeping President, in under half the time.

The premise, idea, started while driving across Florida to the Gulf. Three simple words kept revolving in my head – and from them, quickly, my storyline emanated. Immediately, I knew; the same three words would be the title of the book – *Three Days Later*. That said and accepted, I hope you enjoyed the book for what it is…a simple love story, but with questions maybe?

Forgive me – but let me share something with you, as oddly, I had no sooner completed the manuscript, when an irony in my writing presented itself. I'll explain.

I prefaced in the Prologue as to why I chose the location of Deland, never thinking, or believing, at the time, a small part of the story, as I had written it, would, in a totally unrelated and indirect way, become part of my real life. Cancer is an awful word…one we all dread! And yet, I had no sooner closed the lid of my laptop, my basic story written, to then begin preparing to proof read, edit, format and spell check it, when, not integral to, but as you have read, a relative part of the very script in the pages (Tony Thompson/Cancer) became the irony.

Days later, my wife would be diagnosed with breast cancer. All the fears surfaced as we embraced what the road ahead would look like, and how our lives would change – and they surely did. While worry, pain and hurt emerge, love surges. Her initial operation, the healing, the chemotherapy that would follow, plus radiation, it all became part of a routine of normalcy that we, together, a long 10 month journey of intensive treatment, learned to live with.

My wife, Lynne, to whom I dedicate this love story, is an incredible woman. Not only is she very talented in her own right, but importantly, as she would need to be, is also, extremely upbeat, confident, positive, personable and engagingly out-going - and it shows in her every day, her very life. But then, that's who she always was, in my eyes, long before cancer and her battle to beat it, to survive, like so many before her. I am also quite sure, all the qualities I have bestowed on her, actually played an important part as to *why* she has fared so well, so far; in finding a life again that is as normal as it once was and can be.

Cured, or remission, are words we embrace in every way offered; we never let a day go by, not to give thanks, for life. (And yes, in case you wondered – she is one and the same person in the story; Ms. Lynne-Kristi, Dolls of DeLand).

My heartfelt point - in accepting our joint challenge, and while preparing for the release of Three Days Later - we certainly found, that living in a small town (DeLand) and having the camaraderie of so many around us, of so many who care, and with their outpouring of love that surrounds our everyday, it was an unexpected but most gratifying benefit. It qualified ten-fold; my initial reasoning for choosing Deland as the base city for this story, is and was, for a very good reason. Somehow, folks in smaller towns really *'get it'*...people are important.

Believe me; DeLand rises above being just a notable, rewarded Main Street USA *'place'*. It is a City, a close-knit community that I can fully and truthfully endorse, for so many more reasons than we could have originally anticipated or expected. And yes, cognizant of the battle my wife, and many others have, or do endure; we wish with passion, fervor, hope; that cancer will someday become a disease relegated to a forgotten past, and with added anticipation that soon, *real soon*, a cure will be found for all cancers, so no-one has to suffer - ever again.

Thank you for allowing me my indulgence here, and please, love one another with all your heart. Family and friends are the greatest gift one can ever be given. Share every single moment in life to its absolute fullest, and take every one of them as being truly magic and so very precious. No matter life's adversities, never despair. Love, can and will, conquer all. To my brothers, Robert and Malcolm, to my children, Justin and Lisa, to my grandchildren, Lulu and Max – also to David and Kerry…I love you all. My life is so full and complete with you in it…thank you sincerely. And of course, to Lynne, my wife – I love you girl…thanks for the journey so far.

To repeat the closing words of this, my prose - Three Days Later – *treasure the gift of life.*

ALSO AVAILABLE

At www.amazon.com - Kindle, iPad, iPhone, or Barnes & Noble (www. bn.com) - on Nook and eBooks – also, as a paperback/hard copy, ordered at good book stores everywhere.

THE SLEEPING PRESIDENT by Peter L. Harding.

When Mustafa Rahman wed Shereen Taraki in the small village of Khaimaad in Afghanistan, they dreamed of a life together. War, a Russian invasion, quickly shattered that dream. Offered a chance to escape, terrified, they accepted, and then fled over the infamous Khyber Pass into Pakistan on what they deemed, their 'flight to freedom', to a final, unknown, well planned destiny. What they didn't know initially, the offer accepted, carried with it, huge personal cost.

Securing refugee status, on arrival in America, the penniless immigrants are befriended by New York based Afghans. Grateful to be liberated, the guidance and friendly mentoring willingly given, soon see them amass a personal wealth unimagined. Shawn, their first born, will achieve enviable popularity in media broadcasting from where he will capitalize on his fame and popularity to enter public office seeking his ultimate pinnacle of political success. Chagrined, at his life in tatters, against his Father's wishes, younger brother George joins the U.S. Military only to be sent to Afghanistan, his Father's grave concern, to fight the ongoing war on terror. His talented multi-linguist twin sister Kristen gravitates to a lucrative career in Washington DC.

Three Days Later

With the children gone, and with the advantage of money and connections, Mustafa Rahman decides to follow a fragmented mail trail in his efforts to honor a life-long and once, heartfelt and honest, youthful promise. Unwittingly, in undertaking the search for left behind family in his war-ravaged homeland, the help he freely accepts will soon expose the unknown and meticulously well planned evil plot, formulated all those years ago, linking him inextricably to the two words he dreads for the connotation connection he unquestionably understood – Mission Accomplished. A powerful beneficiary, without options, the ultimate high price for his freedom would be finally, shockingly, claimed!

Spanning almost one hundred years, this epic story with factual historical events and people, woven through news headlines of the day, is as much about love and survival, business and high-stakes politics, as it is about patience and intrepid masterful forethought that will conclude in both amazement and the terrifying question – **Could it actually happen?**

CPSIA information can be obtained at www.ICGtesting.com
Printed in the USA
LVOW05s0726160713

342993LV00001B/3/P